W9-BTL-218

INDIAN RIVER CO. MAIN LIBRARY

3 2901 00594 3908

Indian River County Main Library
1600 21st Street
Vero Beach, FL 32960

# UNCLE JANICE

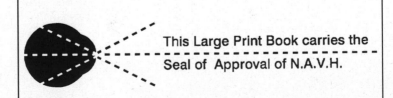

This Large Print Book carries the
Seal of Approval of N.A.V.H.

# UNCLE JANICE

## MATT BURGESS

**THORNDIKE PRESS**

*A part of Gale, Cengage Learning*

GALE
CENGAGE Learning·

Farmington Hills, Mich • San Francisco • New York • Waterville, Maine
Meriden, Conn • Mason, Ohio • Chicago

GALE
CENGAGE Learning·

Copyright © 2015 by Matthew Burgess.
Thorndike Press, a part of Gale, Cengage Learning.

**ALL RIGHTS RESERVED**
This book is a work of fiction. Names, characters, businesses, organizations, places, events, and incidents either are the product of the author's imagination or are used fictitiously. Any resemblance to actual persons, living or dead, events or locales is entirely coincidental.
Thorndike Press® Large Print Core.
The text of this Large Print edition is unabridged.
Other aspects of the book may vary from the original edition.
Set in 16 pt. Plantin.

LIBRARY OF CONGRESS CATALOGING-IN-PUBLICATION DATA

Burgess, Matt, 1982–
    Uncle Janice / by Matt Burgess. — Large print edition.
      pages cm. — (Thorndike Press large print core)
    ISBN 978-1-4104-7819-1 (hardcover) — ISBN 1-4104-7819-X (hardcover)
    1. Policewomen—Fiction. 2. Undercover operations—Fiction. 3. Drug dealers—Fiction. 4. Drug traffic—Investigation—Fiction. 5. Large type books.
    I. Title.
PS3602.U746U53 2015
813'.6—dc23                                                      2014047073

Published in 2015 by arrangement with Doubleday, an imprint of Knopf Doubleday Publishing Group, a division of Random House, Inc.

3 2901 00594 3908

Printed in Mexico
1 2 3 4 5 6 7 19 18 17 16 15

*For the real-life J.I.,*
*whose courageous dishonesty*
*made this book possible*

Only the knife knows what's
in a pumpkin's belly.

— GUYANESE PROVERB

# CHAPTER ONE

Two dirt-gray pigeons perched close together for warmth. They were fifty-some feet above Roosevelt Avenue, in a tangle of steel girders beneath the elevated train tracks. The night before, a late-season storm, the worst so far of 2008, had whitened the sidewalks and packed the el's eaves tight with snow. For the birds it was still too cold to coo. They hugged their wings tight to their bodies, their chests swollen with a stubborn civic pride, because unlike the upstate robins, wrens, hawks, and white-throated sparrows, the city's pigeons felt far too urban to even consider migrating south for the winter. Where would they go? Myrtle Beach? West Virginia? Yeah right. Good luck finding a decent discarded bagel on the sidewalks of Morgantown.

Fifty-some feet below them on Roosevelt's slushy street, an overweight Korean leaned against an el pillar. Zippers crisscrossed his white leather jacket along the shoulders, at the elbows and cuffs, and across his wide chest. Greasy strands of hair, in a bowl cut so terrible it could only have been ironic, hung down to his eyebrows. He played some sort of game on his cell phone. Or maybe was just typing an extra-long text message. In the midwinter, late-day, rush-hour light, the phone's blue screen cast his face in a ghoulish glow.

The pigeons felt a tingle beneath their splayed feet. Time to go. They took off toward the nearest rooftop, where the stubby arms of satellite dishes thrust their round fists into the air. Time to go for the Korean as well. Seeing the pigeons fly away, he heaved himself off the pillar and retreated a few steps onto the sidewalk. A minute later, maybe less: the rumble. A little black kid bouncing a freshly purchased handball paused to plug up his ears. In the nearby, too-close apartment buildings, old women set teacups back onto saucers and young women recapped their eyeliners. The avenue's flyer-hander-outters rested their vocal cords. All the cell phone walkers/talkers put their callers on hold and at last a Flushing-bound 7 local train went screaming overhead. Knocked loose, a heavy clump of snow — a real nasty neck-shiverer — fell from the eaves and landed plop in the spot where the Korean had been standing only moments earlier. Once the train safely passed, both he and the pigeons returned to their posts.

Janice Itwaru went up to him and said, "Hey, yo."

He did not bother to look up from his phone.

Did she feel extra hopeful he'd have drugs on him for sale because he was a person of color? And if she did, did that make her a racist? Well, yes, sorta, and yes, sorta, although probably less racist than most, plus she herself was a person of color, Guyanese, with a mother from the capital, Georgetown, and her fuckface father born and bred in a much smaller place literally called Paradise, but whatever, listen, racism aside, the real reason she approached the guy hopefully was because when an ordinary citizen gets tired he goes home or sits on a bus bench, but an on-the-clock drug dealer with no other place to go leans his expensive white jacket against a dirty-ass pillar. Unfortunately this alleged on-the-clock dealer seemed more interested in his phone than the twenty-dollar bill crumpled up in her back pocket. Hey: no judging. Maybe his mother told him to never talk to strang-

11

ers. Maybe the last person he'd trusted was a barber at Supercuts, and lookit how that had turned out. Maybe — and this was perhaps most likely — maybe, not recognizing her, he worried she might be an undercover cop. Fine. Understood. Trapdoors abounded for these dealers. On today's walk down Roosevelt, starting in the Queens neighborhood of Woodside, then Jackson Heights, and now into Corona, the guys who *had* recognized her suggested she go fuck herself, go rape herself. Compared to those creepazoids, this Korean came off like a prince. Skittishness she could handle. When she needed to make a buy, she liked to step up to every potential dealer, close enough to smell the fast food on their breath, but she also knew how to take half a step back and let the particularly paranoid shuffle over to her.

"Has the guy come through yet?" she asked. She tilted her chin toward a red-and-yellow bodega across the street. "The guy who's always out there?"

His eyes flicked up at her before returning to his phone. *"No hablo inglés."*

A Spanish-speaking Korean? Sure, why not? On this stretch of sidewalk, one of the most ethnically diverse in the world, with sari shops smushed up against momo carts smushed up against stores that sold both Communion dresses and Mexican wrestling masks, Janice was willing to believe any sort of miscegenation mash-up was possible. Again: understood. Addicted, along with the rest of her work colleagues, to the cheesecake telenovela *Rubí,* which was running in chronological syndication on channel 47, Janice said, "You *know.* The *guy. El hombre siempre de la tienda.*" The man who's always out there.

"No speaky a Spanish," the Korean said.

Disgusted, or rather pretending to be disgusted, she hiked her purse strap over her shoulder and dashed into the street without looking. Somebody nearby screamed. A dark blue gypsy cab skidded through the slush to a stop, inches from Janice's hip. She meant to cut it close, but not this close. Her fingertips brushed the warm hood, as if petting a giant, purring, predatory cat. Inside the car, a dashboard Virgin Mary trembled with whiplash. The cabbie seemed too stunned to honk, but on his behalf all the other drivers behind him leaned into their horns. Surely the Korean had to be looking at her now.

She kept moving through stalled traffic toward the bodega's bright lights. Out in front, flanking the front, was a pair of relics

13

from an earlier New York, when people walked around with loose change instead of cell phones: a coin-operated, music-making, up-and-down, carousel-for-one machine that kept kids quiet and off their feet for about half a minute, not a fantasy unicorn in this case or a flying elephant but a grounded-in-reality yellow taxi, albeit one missing a backseat; and next to that, a pay phone, still functional, its receiver slickened with germs. Both waited to be used. The bodega's window signs advertised — as they had ten, twenty, thirty years earlier — LOTTO TICKETS and COLD BEER, with a more recent handwritten placard promising HAVE CURE FOR BEDBUGS.

Inside, the store's closed-circuit television footage — assuming the security camera was even on — showed a grainy, black-and-white Janice wandering up and down the aisles. She scanned the newspaper headlines. "High Noon," said the *Post*. "Hill & Obama in Shootout," beneath a picture of the presidential candidates wearing Photoshopped cowboy hats. Janice thought they both looked like assholes. She read the nutritional information on a box of Hamburger Helper. (Poor.) She compared Red Bull to Sugar-Free Red Bull. Because her feet hurt, because she was cold and thirsty and needed at least fifty cents in change anyway, because technically she was allowed two alcoholic beverages while working, she bought a tallboy of Modelo Especial, paying not with the twenty-dollar bill in her back pocket but with her own money instead, and drank the whole thing standing up at the counter while the nervous Pakistani bodega man made shoo-shoo gestures with his hands.

Out on the sidewalk she burped. Excuse her! Across the street the Korean was still leaning against the pillar, but now it was she who wouldn't look at him, not directly at least. The musical taxi, meanwhile, had found a driver: a little boy who drove with both hands on the wheel, as if afraid he might crash. His father, or at least the man Janice assumed was his father — a twenty-something Latino with the gray polyester suit and cheap pleather shoes of a doorman or security guard — stood nearby and jabbered into a cell phone. He was not the guy Janice had been talking about, *el hombre de la tienda*, because the guy Janice had been talking about did not actually exist.

"Hey, where's Corona?" she asked the doorman.

"What?" he said. He cupped a hand over his cell phone to muffle an angry woman's

15

voice wah-wahing out of the receiver. He said, "You're *in* Corona."

"No kidding?" Janice said. "Hey, you know where Manhattan is?"

When he pointed east, she stepped off to the side to give the Korean across the street a better view. He saw, she hoped, a fiending addict asking some random dude where her dealer was at. You know. The guy.

The Korean watched her — she assumed — pick up the pay phone's receiver with only her fingertips. After depositing her quarters, she called what she imagined he imagined was her dealer, or maybe somebody who could get ahold of her dealer. Or maybe some other dealer she knew in front of some other bodega. Her mother answered on the second ring.

"It's me," Janice said.

"Where are you? Are you okay?"

"I'm fine, but I think I might be getting some overtime tonight." Intensely superstitious, but without any wood to rap her knuckles against, she used her forehead, *knock knock.* "I probably won't be home until pretty late," she said. "Okay? Will you write that down on the whiteboard?"

"What is that noise I'm hearing?"

"A musical taxicab," Janice said. "Will you write down on the whiteboard that I won't

16

be home until late, please?"

Janice had recently commandeered a label maker at work to post little reminders for her mother. LOCK ME UP, GOOD LOOKIN' for the back door's dead bolt. HEY HOT STUFF, TURN ME OFF above the stovetop's burner knobs. The whiteboard, hammered to the kitchen wall, was for the more temporary items, like *buy flaxseed, make dr appt, don't panic: jan called and is working late.* Savita Itwaru — Vita for short, objectively speaking the world's most beautiful woman, whose hands always smelled like the lavender lotion Janice's sister gave her every Christmas — had been diagnosed sixteen months ago with early-onset dementia.

"I don't need to write it down," she said.

"Okay, but it'd be a lot easier if —"

"What?" Vita said. "I can hardly hear you!"

"I'm saying if you just wrote it —"

"What?!"

Janice rested her forehead against the pay phone shell, its icy metal biting clean through her wool dockworker cap. Her eyes ached. Her feet throbbed. A sticker inside the phone shell offered nontraditional psychic services at what it promised were reasonable rates. DON'T GIVE UP HOPE, it said. SEE MADAM SANDRA. Some previous caller, possibly Janice without even realizing it, had picked away at the sticker's four corners. "Listen, Ma," she said. "I gotta get going, okay?"

"Be good," Vita said, her standard good-bye.

Janice waited until her mother hung up before slamming the phone into its cradle. She stuck her finger into the coin-return slot, just in case, but the metal flapper thingy wouldn't go all the way up, its chute probably jammed full of cotton balls, an old hustle her father had taught her many, many years ago. You come back later with a wire hanger to empty out a week's worth of free laundry. Her father's lesson, as always: there is a world beyond this one, a world made more glamorous by its cigar-scented sleaziness, with ports of entry as diverse as an usher's open palm or a pay phone's dark chute. She picked up the germy receiver and slammed it again. With a last glance at the boy in his taxicab, she headed toward the other side of the avenue, more carefully this time, looking both ways before crossing the street.

As she walked past the Korean, he said, "Hey, mama, what you need?"

He banged on the apartment door with the side of his fist. Weirdly chatty on the walk over here, he'd told her to call him Marty and had promised his boy would hook her up with two top-of-the-line crack vials for only ten dollars apiece. Family discount, he'd said. She had the money in her palm, ready to go, hopeful that she could get out of the apartment in under a minute with both Marty *and* the drugs. She needed him outside so the Narcotics investigators could grab him for intentionally aiding the criminal sale of a controlled substance, a felony. He knocked on the door again, for some reason softer this time, as if communicating a secret message. Two tiny golden screws affixed a mezuzah to the frame. Before Marty could knock again, a fair-skinned white guy opened the door. Short and squat, as wide as Marty but a good six inches shorter, he was much older than she'd expected, in his early to mid forties. Skin tags hung off his eyelids. He dressed young, though, in baggy shorts that went past his knees and an Anchor Steam bicycle jersey too tight for his body. Some semblance of a blond mustache grew only at the corners of his mouth. With a glance he seemed to register her presence in the hallway, but after that he looked only at Marty, without apparent recognition or interest, his face emptied of expression, as if

19

he were posing for a passport photo. She thought maybe they'd knocked on the wrong door, but no: a sudden head jerk waved them into the apartment, which felt feverishly hot. All the radiators were clanking. Dirty cast-iron frying pans crowded the kitchen's stove range, and when she saw them she knew for sure she was in a crack dealer's apartment. WELCOME, said a welcome mat. It was kept inside the apartment, not out in the hall, probably to prevent it from getting stolen. PLEASE WIPE OFF YOUR PAWS. Behind her, Marty turned over the door's dead bolt, her least favorite sound.

No one had spoken yet. The dealer did not offer to take her coat or even bother to introduce himself, nor did he say anything to Marty, who wandered off alone toward the back of the apartment. A little bowlegged, as if the bicycle jersey were not merely an affectation, the dealer led her into the living room, where an enraged pit bull rose up in its little doggie bed and started barking at her. All the muscles along its sleek back were tensed. The roof of its snapping mouth appeared ridged like a dried creek. And yet, instead of blitzing across the hardwood toward Janice's throat, the dog stayed, for now, in its fuzzy bed, as if unwilling to leave it. A massively pregnant belly with distended pink nipples hung low to the ground. The room reeked of cigarettes. The windows were all closed, the dusty blinds all pulled down. There was some other shit, too — a futon, a wicker chair, amateur paintings of city skylines hanging on the walls — but she struggled to focus on anything beyond the dog's barking. Her fist still clutched the twenty-dollar bill. Concerned primarily with keeping that dog in its doggie bed, she acquiesced to its owner and allowed him to lead her farther into the room. She didn't know what else to do. She hoped the less she resisted, the faster she'd be allowed to leave. Told to sit down — the first words he'd spoken to her — she fell backward into the huge round Papasan wicker chair. A baby Glock 9mm pistol lay at the bottom of her purse. A small strip of body adhesive kept a nonfunctioning kelmic taped between her breasts. Every time she went out onto the streets as an undercover she thought she might die, but — despite the investigators in a Chevy Impala a couple of blocks away, despite her partner and ghost, Chester Tevis, probably right across the street under the Peruvian restaurant awning — never before had she felt so alone. In this flytrap of a chair, her feet couldn't reach the floor.

21

"Geronimo!" said the dealer, and the pit bull stopped barking. Exhausted, breathless, it dropped down on its side in the doggie bed. A dark tongue unspooled from its mouth.

"Good girl," said the dealer, looking at Janice.

He left the room, but the tiny men in all the radiator pipes kept swinging their tiny hammers. She wondered if she could outrun a pregnant dog to the door, get out before the dealer came back, but here he was now, with his bowlegged walk and a tall can of air freshener. Pure Citrus Lemon. He pointed it at the ceiling and kept his finger too long on the nozzle, as if to drain the entire can. She started coughing into her armpit. A cloying lemony wetness misted her face.

"Sorry," he said, sounding delighted. He sat down on the end of the futon nearest his dog. "It's a lot, I know, but it's better than the cigarette smoke, yeah?"

"I guess."

"No, it is," he said. "For sure."

Her hands clutched the purse in her lap. "So Marty told me you could maybe like hook me up with some vials or whatever?"

"Marty told me, Marty told me," he said, his voice retaining all its good cheer. He

22

looked up at the ceiling through an invisible grove of artificial lemons. "Yo, Marty! What the fuck you doing?"

From the back of the apartment, Marty said, "Where'd Cerebral Pauly put the kung fu dummy?"

"You know Marty's not even his real name," the dealer told her. His hand dropped over the futon's edge to scratch the dog behind its ears. "What am I talking about? Of course you know that. You guys are old friends. It's my name that's Marty. His name's some ching-chong Korean shit you can't hardly pronounce, so he takes my name like I'm supposed to be flattered. Meanwhile, I am sorta flattered. Hey, so what do you think of my paintings?"

"You did all these? Wow. That's amazing."

"You didn't even look. What's that one over there? Right there."

"Chicago?" she said.

"That was an easy one," he said. "The Sears Tower, it *gives* it away. Tallest sky-scraper in North America. Also known as Willis Tower. What about that one over there? What's that one?"

"I don't know," she said. "Listen, I'm really just trying to —"

"Take a guess."

Still wearing her cap and coat, in the hope

23

they might communicate her eagerness for a speedy transaction, she felt beads of sweat rolling down her chest. "I really don't know," she told him.

"I know you don't know," he said. "Take a guess."

"Los Angeles?"

"You kidding?" he said. "Los Angeles?" The pleasure he took from her wrong answer scooted him forward on the futon, his hands bunching the bottoms of his shorts. "Try Abu Dhabi. Capital of the United Arab Emirates, the most balling country in the world. Took me three months to get the details correct on that bad boy. No joke. And it lights up, too."

The dog lifted its head to watch Marty, White Marty, hoist himself off the futon and cross the room toward the painting. A small green cord hung off the bottom of the canvas. When he got down on his knees to fiddle with plugs along the baseboard, she undid tooth by tooth the golden zipper of her purse. She looked first to Marty, then ridiculously to the dog, to see if either of them had noticed.

"There," he said, sliding the plug into the outlet, and the lights came on in Abu Dhabi. Scores of embedded teeny bulbs lit up behind the buildings' painted windows.

He gave Janice a falsely modest little shrug. "It looks better at night," he explained. "I did some of the detailing with this special kind of paint. You should see it. Get a black light going, smoke a bowl, it looks crazy cool. The paint's very expensive, though, so you can't really use too much."

He unplugged the canvas before sitting back down. One at a time, to show her his tattoos now, he rolled up the bicycle jersey sleeves. "This one here, that's North and South America obviously. It's a little faded. I'm going to have to get it touched up." He pointed to the other arm. "And over here, that's Europe, Asia, and Africa. Because we're all citizens of the same world, know what I mean?"

"Totally," she said. "Listen, I really don't mean to be rude, but I sorta have to bounce pretty quick here. Marty, the other Marty, I guess, was talking about like two vials for twenty? Does that sound all right?"

Once again he looked up at the ceiling. "Hey, Marty? Can you come here real quick?"

He was already on his way. Without his white leather jacket but sweating even more heavily than Janice, he tottered into the living room carrying what she assumed was the kung fu dummy he'd been looking for.

The one Cerebral Pauly — whoever the hell that was — had tried hiding on him. An enormous wooden beam, it must have weighed more than two hundred pounds, with a single wooden leg, bent at what was supposed to be its knee, and a pair of arms, also wooden, sticking straight out, as if, truly a dummy, it expected a hug. Dry blood crusted its chest. Made out of what appeared to be high-quality oak, designed to absorb punishment without splintering or complaint, it hit the ground hard when Korean Marty set it down, startling the dog.

"In the closet?" he said. "Like I'm not gonna find it there?" He wiped the sweat off his face with the hem of his T-shirt. "Jesus H., man, it's like a million fucking degrees in here."

White Marty said to him, "Hey, before we start punching and kicking here, I just wanna know: where'd you meet this Miss Thing? You know her a long time? This nice lady you bring up into my home?"

"Ah man, what's the matter with this one?"

She dropped the twenty into her purse, without of course zipping it back up. "Listen —"

"You're on time-out right now," White Marty told her. "It's quiet time for you,

26

okay? You understand?"

She was worried they thought she was a cop and they'd try to blow her cover. She was worried they thought she wasn't a cop and so they felt they could . . . forget it. Don't even go there. Awkwardly lurching, she wiggled herself out of the chair, both of the Martys watching her with what seemed like amusement. She draped the purse's cross-body strap around her neck and positioned the bag so she could reach into it easily. The dog was watching her, too, although with less amusement than impatience. A yawn snapped its jaws open. Sweat pooled along the backs of Janice's knees, in her armpits and elbow crooks, and all across her chest. The tape came loose. The kel-mic plummeted, but she caught it, trapped it against her stomach with a hand outside her coat. Her shoulders were hunched. If she moved her hand away, the small black gherkin of the mic would drop out into the open between her knees.

"What's the matter?" Korean Marty said. "You gotta take a shit or something?"

"You scared her," White Marty said. Still rolled all the way up, the jersey sleeves seemed to bunch uncomfortably around his shoulders. When she started to walk away, he said, "Hey, hold on! Where you going? I haven't even told you my dog's name."

Korean Marty reached out and grabbed her arm. "Don't be rude," he said.

"Yeah," White Marty said. "Don't be rude."

"Geronimo," she said, and the dog pricked its ears. "Great name. Thanks. See you guys later."

"Oh, you stupid fucking cunt," White Marty said. "The dog? The dog's name is Marty. Come *on.* You kidding? Geronimo, please, that's just like her chill word. You understand? She's got like a chill word and an attack word. You wanna hear the attack word?"

"No."

He quickly nodded his agreement. "That is correct. No you do not. So guess what?"

These two men, especially the bigger Korean Marty, worried her more than the pit bull did. Rolled over on its side, it seemed minutes away from labor contractions. Matter of fact, a normal dog would've already slunk off into some quieter, calmer, cooler corner of the apartment. Back when Janice worked as a patrol officer in the Housing Division, she had met some truly cop-hating pit bulls, trained either to come right up on her and bark or come right up on her and bite, but never before had she

28

deep-enough breaths. On the corner, next to a stop sign, two teenage Latinas in puffy jackets tossed an egg back and forth, higher and higher with each throw. Janice was chewing on cuticles when her ghost, Chester Tevis, materialized behind her to take her arm. As always, a bushy and magnificent soupsoaker of a beard obscured his round and black face. His eyes swam in yellow. Wiry gray hair burst from his ears. She leaned into his soft body, his long brown coat smelling of cocoa butter and Salvation Army bins, its rough wool scratching her cheek. Tasked with the responsibility of her safety — supposed to follow close behind her while remaining invisible, supposed to report via a Nextel walkie-talkie all her drug buys to the four investigators in their unmarked white Impala — Tevis felt most helpless whenever she went into buildings, with nothing for him to do except stand across the street and try to guess the window and scratch at his beard with both hands. The next time they go out, they'll switch. He'll be the uncle and she'll be the ghost and it'll be her job to worry. But for now, he had his arm around her shoulders. Together they turned the corner toward Roosevelt Avenue, which seventeen months ago he had told her to pronounce *Ruse-uh-*

*velt,* not *Rose-ah-velt,* so that she'd sound like one of the locals.

"You okay?" he asked her.

"I'm fine," she said.

Meanwhile, at around this same time, New York governor Eliot Spitzer was in a hotel room banging call girls. The CIA announced that waterboarding didn't qualify as torture. China blamed the ongoing unrest in Tibet on the Dalai Lama. Barbers, bartenders, prosecutors, defense attorneys, street-corner lawyers, and tabloid op-ed writers insisted that the Sean Bell shooting — in which an unarmed black man, intoxicated on the morning of his wedding, rammed his car into police officers before they fired back with fifty bullets — was obviously an open-and-shut case of insert your biases here. Despite obvious rage issues and a fat face getting exponentially fatter over time, the baseball player Roger Clemens told a congressional committee that he had never self-injected steroids. Just as preposterously, presidential candidate Barack Obama vowed to end the divisive tone of D.C. politics. In sports fibs, the back page of the *Post* read, "Attention Knicks Fans: There's Hope." Three out of four economists claimed that the best way to solve the subprime mortgage crisis was to give more money to three out of four economists. The Academy of Motion Picture Arts and Sciences awarded the Best Picture Oscar to *No Country for Old Men,* the very title of which was a lie, see above re: the economic solution to the subprime mortgage crisis.

And over at the original House of Lies, One Police Plaza in downtown Manhattan, the NYPD's Big Bosses told young, ambitious minority cops like Janice that if they lasted eighteen months in undercover narcotics work, then they'd receive an automatic promotion to detective. See their silver shield turn gold . . . but that's not all! Act now, last another eighteen months without getting killed, and you can switch over into Narcotics *Investigations,* not only a safer job but a jump in the queue toward the upper balconies of Major Case, Special Victims, Homicide, and Counterterrorism, the kinds of squads with the kinds of stories that get turned into movies.

Janice couldn't remember where or when she'd first heard about the narco guarantee — it seemed to be something every young cop knew, and had always known — but she could remember the first time she saw an uncle on the job.

She was straight out of the Academy, a

sore-footed soldier in Operation IMPACT, Commissioner Ray Kelly's plan to deluge the city's most dangerous neighborhoods with the department's most inexperienced cops. She worked Housing at the Queensbridge projects, where she spent her days and nights telling residents to extinguish their blunts, turn down their music, steer their bikes off sidewalks, and stop swinging baseball bats inside the bodegas. The worst, though, was verticals, schlepping up and down every step of every building to make sure nobody was hunched over a bottle of brandy in the stairwell or taking a leak off the roof. Within months her calves had hardened into bocce balls. Once, while resting in a lobby, she watched a middle-aged black man and an older black woman come into the lobby together, chatting about the things people chat about: the weather, the neighborhood, the way things used to be. They looked right through her, not even nodding, a uniform in their lobby as unremarkable as the Chinese takeout menus wedged under the front door. The woman carried her grocery bags into the elevator and asked the guy if he was coming up.

"Nah, Ma. Go ahead. I gotta check my mail." As soon as the elevator door shuddered closed, he turned to Janice and said,

"Listen, I'm on the job."

He told her he was an undercover narc, sent in by the gang squad to clear out the lobby so they could execute a search warrant. An envoy from the secret world beyond this one, he talked quickly, quietly, his lips thin and chapped behind his overgrown beard.

"And your mom lives here?" she asked.

"My what?"

"Never mind," she said. "I thought the lady in the elevator . . . it just seemed like you really knew each other, but I guess that's the whole —"

"You wanna act like you belong," Tevis said, his first-ever lesson for her.

"Right." If she was going to hang around undercovers, she would need to think faster. She hiked the heavy patrol officer belt up over her hips, tried to make herself appear taller. "So," she said. "Executing a warrant, great. What can I do to help?"

"Go away," he said pleasantly. "You're making everyone nervous."

The other narco cops outside? The potential dealers upstairs? Both? She didn't ask. He'd slammed the secret world's door on her, but she could still see the light bleeding around the edges. When her shift ended, she drove down to One Police Plaza to fill

35

out an application with Narcotics. Young, brown, from the city, no college, desperate to move up, single and childless, without anyone to collect her pension if she got killed in the line of duty, she looked on paper like the perfect uncle, a narco lieutenant's dream. But because nothing ever moved quickly through the department's lymphatic bureaucracy, it took months for the Big Bosses to call her out for an interview at Rodman's Neck, a little hamlet in the Bronx where the NYPD trained dogs for the K-9 unit, blew up suspicious if-you-see-something-say-something packages, and vetted all their potential undercovers.

An Asian woman with a clipboard gave her forty dollars and told her to go into the role-play room to buy some drugs. Five chaotic minutes later, the pretend dealers were shoving real shotguns, presumably unloaded, into her face. They went through her pockets. They ordered her to snort a line of powder off the desk, and when she bent her head to it, the exercise ended. She'd failed. But that was okay. Everyone failed, although she didn't know that at the time. The Big Bosses were impressed that she'd lasted a full five minutes, that before going into the room she had stashed half the buy money in her sock. That sort of commitment to the department's precious bottom line earned her a follow-up interview, also on Rodman's Neck, with the clipboard-toting Asian woman and an old white bald man. The wizard who'd come out from behind his green curtain to meet her. Every time the bomb squad blew up another package outside the window, they flinched, all three of them, and the dogs for a moment barked a little bit louder.

She did not get a call. Or an email. No one came to find her in person or sent her a letter saying, *After a careful review of a number of highly talented applicants, we are pleased to offer you . . .*

Nope, she found out in the regular way, on the daily sheet, with the news of all the latest transfers and memoranda: ITWARU, J, TO REPORT TO NARCOTICS, 0900, 10/1/06. She snuck away into the nearest stairwell and called her mother. *Guess what, Mom,* she whisper-shouted into the phone. *Guess what, guess what, guess what.*

On her first day as an uncle she gave twenty dollars to a crack fiend, who told her to wait out on the sidewalk while he ran up to his apartment real quick for some primo-quality rocks. He of course never returned. The investigators all whooped, crowing, happy to root against the new girl.

"Fooled by the fools," they said, and so she followed the next potential scam artist into his apartment building and made sure to come back out with both him and an eighth of weed. Tevis radioed Sergeant Hart and the investigators, who showed up a minute later to head-steer the dealer into a prisoner-transport van. A perfect buy, her very first.

And there were plenty more. Because female undercovers were a relative rarity, and because most dealers start dealing to impress girls, Janice's early buys came quickly, in bunches. It helped that she hadn't been in law enforcement very long. Her posture had not yet hardened into the policeman's stance: hands on hips, feet spread apart as if expecting someone to knock you over. She could still speak to people, especially young men, without the automatic assumption of their deference. Half black and half Indian, assigned to the Babel of blocks in Jackson Heights, she bought weed, crack, coke, heroin, opium tar, and baking soda beneath the el, at the Manuel de Dios Unanue Triangle, in alleyways, liquor stores, apartment buildings, and on practically every corner of Roosevelt Avenue from Sixty-First Street to Ninety-Third.

But every time the investigators head-

steered those dealers into a p-van, the U.S. Constitution compelled Sergeant Hart to inform them that they were being arrested for the criminal sale of a controlled substance to an undercover cop.

And the dealers would say, "The chick?!"

And Sergeant Hart would say something along the lines of "Shut the fuck up and take a seat toward the back."

Now, seventeen months into her Narcotics career, with scorched sidewalks behind her, she had to travel far beyond the Jackson Heights border, all the way into Corona, to find willing dealers who didn't yet know her face. Dealers like the Martys. And even then she still hadn't made the buy!

That same night, when she and Tevis got back to the rumpus — aka the Queens Narcotics Division, a bland three-story office building hiding out on the edge of the borough — Richie the Receptionist asked them if they'd heard. Actually, to be technical about it, Detective First Grade Richard Szoke asked them if they'd heard.

"Heard what?"

He smiled with a mouth full of shredded cabbage. Outside of janitorial services, the narco Big Bosses refused to hire civilians, not even in an administrative capacity, and so as far back as anyone could remember the rumpus's uncles and investigators all rotated two-hour shifts up at the front desk, where they frittered away the time reading the *Post* and playing *Snood.* But then one day last November, Richie sat down and the seat became permanently his own. The Big Bosses didn't dare complain. With the exception of that miserable prick Raymond Gonz, *no* one complained, for ever since Richie had taken over he made sure that the kitchenette's water cooler kept glugging, that photocopier jams were quickly fixed and toilet clogs discreetly handled. Invitations to the holiday racket went out on time for once. He kept the vending machines — don't tell Mayor Bloomberg — consistently well stocked with sugary candy bars and high-fructose sodas. And most important, best of all, rumpus gossip was efficiently disseminated from the lightning-rod top of Richie's bald head. All this in addition to his crime-fighting responsibilities as an undercover cop. An expert multitasker, he ate an egg roll while transferring a phone call while watching both Tevis and Janice sign themselves into the logbook.

"The bosses put up a buy board," he told them. "A cheap shit piece of Taiwanese plastic. Completely gauche, not that anyone even bothered to ask me."

"What's a buy board?" Janice asked. "Like a board with all our buys on it?"

"See?" Richie asked Tevis. "It's those kinds of instincts that'll serve her well when she makes detective."

"Har har," she said, but with only twenty-seven days until her eighteen-month promotion, she knocked her knuckles against his desk.

They were on the second floor, the Queens narco squad, with phones ringing everywhere. Thick sheets of construction paper covered the windows. At scattered desks, confidential informants described apartment layouts to investigators taking notes. The uncles all sat together in the corner, far from the Big Bosses' private offices but close to the rumpus lounge, where from three to four every afternoon they watched their girl Rubí on TV. *¡Sacrificarás todo por ella!* No kidding, Janice thought. She'd missed today's episode and had hoped to hear a recap, but she could forget about that now. With the exception of Grimes, who was asleep in the rumpus's cot room, and that miserable prick Gonz, who was antisocially reading a *Planet Fitness* magazine, the uncles converged around Tevis the instant he sat down, before he could even begin his

41

post-street ritual of rubbing cocoa butter onto his face and elbows to keep his skin from getting ashy.

"You seen this buy board?" Morris asked him.

"How's he gonna seen the buy board already?" Klondike said. "Come on, man, you just *saw* him walk in."

Morris, the rumpus's unofficial psychotherapist, told Klondike, "You need to think about where this aggression of yours is coming from and whether or not it deserves to be directed at me, okay?"

"Fair enough," Klondike said.

They parked their bubble-butts on opposite ends of Tevis's desk. Fiorella, a single mother and chronically fatigued, had wheeled herself over in a rolly chair. The full-namers — Eddie Murphy, Pablo Rivera, and James Chan — all stood together, hovering, James Chan at near military attention. Puffy, who'd thrown his back out a week earlier, lay himself down across Janice's desk, atop her manila folders stuffed full of blank pages, which were carefully arranged into a tableau of busyness. He'd chosen Janice's desk either because it was next to Tevis's or because — another knuckle-knock here — he wanted to get as close to her as possible. The same reason he came over every morning to pluck the crossword puzzle out of her copy of the *Post*. Two words, eleven letters, starts with *off,* ends with *ush* — "work desire or crowd." He smiled at her. A little embarrassed, a little nervous, she tried focusing on the uncles' bitchfest by waiting for the inevitable *It is what it is.*

Offensive, Eddie Murphy said. Immoral. Almost criminal. Morris considered it the latest example of this corporate police department's CompStat-crazed disregard for the people risking their lives on the street. Klondike, who was always threatening to quit, threatened to quit. James Chan never spoke, but even he looked sort of agitated. Pablo Rivera asked that no one get him wrong, he hated this buy board as much as the next uncle, but he worried it might distract them from the previous crisis: their suspicion, Pablo Rivera's certainty, that Internal Affairs was keeping them all under surveillance. Tevis thought the two might be linked. He had a story about buy boards and IA, but because his stories tended to last forty minutes minimum, the uncles asked him to please table it for another time. Still lying on his back, Puffy wanted to know how the department could afford fancy new buy boards but not functioning kel-mics.

"Fancy?!" said Richie the Receptionist over speakerphone.

"Did y'all ever consider that you're just a bunch of pussies?"

"Who was that?" Richie asked. "Was that Gonz?"

Of course! Who else could've been such a miserable prick. He went past them on his way to the bathroom, with his *Planet Fitness* tucked under his hypertrophied arm. "A bunch of pussies," he repeated, "afraid of a little competish."

"Thanks for the pep talk!" Puffy said.

Morris attributed Gonz's latest burst of antisocial behavior to a deep-rooted identity crisis, for Gonz was pretty much born to be one of the other guys, an investigator, somebody who came out of the womb with one of those grip-strengthening doodads, but because of the color of his skin the NYPD and hence the rest of the world refused to accept him as anything but an uncle, and so the hatred he directed toward the group was really a sublimated reaction to —

"You know over two hundred people work in the rumpus?" Klondike said.

"I'm sorry, but I thought I was talking," Morris said.

44

"Two hundred people, but it's only *our* names that go up on the buy board," Klondike said. "*We're* the only ones that get slid under the microscope?"

"Yeah, well," Fiorella said. "It is what it is."

That was Janice's cue to leave, to go check out the blight for herself. For the walk over she took an important-looking folder, a real thick one, in case she ran into any of the Big Bosses. Although quite a bit bigger, in a frame made out of aluminum instead of plastic, the rumpus's buy board looked not unlike the dry-erase board she had at home, except instead of *take pills* and *buy flaxseed,* this one had all the uncles' initials in a column. The next three months were written across the top. Under that, nothing but empty white space. She didn't yet know if she considered the buy board offensive, as the others had, or immoral, practically criminal — part of Narcotics' appeal was the opportunity to be judged objectively on performance instead of connections — but she did think it unfair that the uncles' previous buys weren't included. So as to acknowledge and better contextualize their hard work throughout the year. She found her initials toward the bottom, a less than encouraging sign. She knew that if she

45

touched the ink, it would come off on her fingers.

By the time she got back to her desk, all the other uncles had scattered, probably chased away by the macho presence of Vincent Hart sitting in her chair. A sergeant in Narcotics Investigations, where Janice hoped to land in nineteen months, he wore what he always seemed to wear: a tight-fitting Polo tucked into a pair of nylon exercise pants that swished when he walked. The spare-tire cover on his Hummer said, THE VIN-MAN!

"It's called the vending-machine challenge," he was telling Tevis. "Pretty self-explanatory. You gotta eat one of everything in the machine. Obviously. But with like the Starbursts? You can't eat just the one thing of it. You gotta do the whole package. Obviously."

Tevis tilted his head back, unsure if Hart was fucking with him about his weight. He said, "What about the breath mints? I'd have to eat all the different brands of those, too?"

Hart tilted his head back, unsure if Tevis was fucking with him about his terribly rancid, protein-shake breath, about which Hart was so self-conscious that he went everywhere with an Altoids tin clattering in the pocket of his swishy pants, the man as quiet as a rattlesnake. "Itwaru!" he said when he saw her standing there. "I ever tell you about the time I'm lovemaking my wife and she asks me to get awesome?"

"Lieutenant Prondzinski was just here looking for you," Tevis told her.

"For me?"

"Ask us what she wanted," Hart told her.

Janice caught herself biting the cuticle around her thumb. "What'd she want?"

"How should we know?" Hart said. "She did seem pretty mad though that you weren't at your desk, but don't worry. We told her you were late for your shift and hadn't come into work yet."

"No we didn't," Tevis said. "We told her you got here on time but then left to run a personal errand."

Janice tilted her head back, unsure of everything. These guys, all of them, they lied recreationally, professionally, to stay sharp, to stay alive. Habituated to misdirection and subterfuge, they kept mistresses and backup mistresses, until it got to the point where Janice couldn't expect an honest answer if she asked about the weather.

For instance. On her first day in Narcotics, as Tevis led her around the rumpus on her introductory tour, he pointed out a handsome, expensively dressed, somber-looking black man reading *Variety* and said, "And that guy over there? That's Eddie Murphy."

"No kidding," Janice said. "Wow, he looks just like him. Seriously. He could be like his body double."

"No," Tevis said. "That's him. That's Eddie Murphy."

She rolled her eyes. "The movie star."

"Well, yeah, movie star, comedian. He's like an amazing musician, too. And an undercover, obviously. Full-time and everything. Here, you wanna meet him? He's really down-to-earth . . ."

A genuine gentleman, the guy who looked like Eddie Murphy stood up from his desk to shake her hand. He even made sure he was pronouncing her name correctly — It-*wah*-roo? — before offering his own: "Eddie Murphy, nice to meet ya." She looked back at Tevis, who gave her what appeared to be an encouraging nod.

"Okay," she said, playing along. "What are you doing here? Researching a role?"

"He *was*," Tevis said. "But then what happened, Eddie? The financing fell through or something?"

"Well, it's never one thing, of course. The producer, I don't even want to say his name, but there was that big kerfuffle when he made some . . . indelicate comments? On a certain radio program? Anyway, so then he's gone, poof, see you later, so they approach me, ask if *I* could finance the whole thing on my own, and it really was a neat little picture, but —"

"He was gonna play a guy from Brooklyn," Tevis said. "Which is where Eddie's actually from. Originally."

"Good memory!"

"Thanks, Eddie."

"The story took place in the sixties," he said, "with the whole Black Panther thing? And my character had grown up in Brooklyn, like Tevis was saying, under the tutelage of this kind of Huey Newton–type figure, who gets *my* character to enlist in the police department as a way of spying on cops. But at the same time — and here's the interesting bit — at the same time the cops have someone infiltrating the *Panthers.*"

"Like *The Departed,*" Janice said.

"Well, yeah. Yeah. Except this one was first. And I'd be playing both characters, the guy who infiltrates the cops and the guy in the Panthers. But yeah. Like *The Departed.* That was the other problem. We hear Scorsese's developing a similar project, and it's like, well, how many undercover-cop

49

stories can the market sustain, right? And if one's going to Shelf City, it's gonna be the one with a little less mass-market appeal, if you know what I mean."

"It was going to be Eddie's Oscar role," Tevis said. "Roles, I should say. Then we all thought he'd finally win it last year with *Dreamgirls,* but of course he gets frickin' robbed again."

"Alan Arkin was excellent in *Little Miss Sunshine,*" he said humbly, but behind his eyes all the houselights had dimmed. "Anyhoo, long story short, I was researching one of the roles, shadowing Tevis here — stick with him, you'll learn a lot —"

"Oh, come on." Tevis beamed.

"And after the movie fell through, I just sorta stuck around, I guess." He laughed a sad little laugh, slow and deep and no louder than a murmur. "The department needs undercovers pretty bad right now, and it truly is a kind of guerrilla theater out there, the purest form of acting in my opinion —"

"Let me see your driver's license," she said.

"Itwaru," Tevis scolded.

"No, that's fine," he said. "I get it." He flipped open a gator-skin wallet to show her an authentic-looking New York State driver's

50

license that said *Edward Regan Murphy,* and then a homemade-looking — although how would she really know? — Screen Actors Guild card. He said, "Sometimes I wake up in the morning before work and I can hardly believe it myself."

"You guys are good," she told them. "Seriously. Very good. This is . . . thorough, that is for sure. But what exactly am I supposed to be buying here? That the reason Eddie Murphy hasn't made a movie in forever is because he's —"

"What do you mean, haven't made a movie in forever?" he asked.

"I haven't shown you the copy room!" Tevis told her. "We should probably go check that out. You can scan, you can check email —"

"*Shrek*?" Eddie Murphy said. "Is that not a movie? I'm pretty sure it is, because it made four hundred and eighty-four million dollars in worldwide grosses. And it's my understanding they only track those numbers for actual movies. *Shrek 2*? *Dr. Doolittle 2*? *Shrek the Third*? Do these ring a bell? How about *Norbit*? You heard of *Norbit*? Hundred fifty million dollars right there, in domestic tickets alone."

"You know what I mean," she said, unable to ever resist an argument, no matter how

51

absurd. "I'm talking about like old Eddie Murphy movies. You know. Like . . . you know . . ."

"Like funny?" he said. "Like funny Eddie Murphy movies? Because over a billion dollars in worldwide grosses these last couple of years, that sounds pretty hilarious to me," he said, and as if to prove it he laughed his quiet little laugh.

"See," she said, pointing at him. "That's not the Eddie Murphy laugh. Heh heh heh heh, *that's* the Eddie Murphy laugh. You really wanted to get me, *that's* the laugh you shoulda done."

He shrugged. "I don't really laugh like that anymore," he said. He gestured to the rumpus all around them, the wrinkled clothes and hovering bosses, the purple bags under everyone's eyes, the shocks of gray hair, the mildewy smell coming out of the cot room, the pukey coffee, and the beer guts. "The job," he said. "It takes a lot out of you."


After leaving Tevis and Sergeant Hart, Janice went looking for Lieutenant Prondzinski, but she wasn't in her office. She had, though, hung a picture of a clock on the doorknob. WILL RETURN, it promised, its movable hands pointed to three minutes from now. Janice could either wait here with nothing to do except tap her foot and roll her folder into a telescope, or she could try to look busy. She scanned the rumpus for the silvered top of Prondzinski's head. Nothing. She wasn't next door in Inspector Nielsen's office, either. No one was. It was empty, or at least it appeared empty, but Janice couldn't be certain because the department's rumormongers — which is to say everyone — claimed the inspector's vicious migraines forced him to sleep all day under his desk. His office lights were off, his windows papered over. She peeked into the kitchenette, where dirty mugs filled a sink under a sign that said DO NOT LEAVE DIRTY MUGS IN THE SINK. She rescanned the rumpus. Preposterously — preposterous because the overcaffeinated Prondzinski seemed incapable of sleep — Janice opened the door to the cot room, but the only one inside was of course Grimes, snoring, a long white nightcap snug around his head. She thought maybe three minutes had passed. Hustling back to the lieutenant's office, she at last found Prondzinski by almost tripping over her.

The lieutenant lay facedown on the floor, half in and half out of the copy room. Long, jagged runs split her dark stockings. Usually there'd be a line of investigators waiting to Xerox the serial numbers on their buy money, but not now, not with Prondzinski flat on the ground, one ear pressed against the carpet as if she were snooping on the first-floor office workers. Her arm snaked under the copy machine, her tongue poking out between her teeth.

"Uh?" Janice said.

One of Prondzinski's giant blue eyeballs rolled in its socket to consider her. "Itwaru," she said. "How long are your arms?"

Janice held them out in front of her. "I don't know. Average, I guess?"

"Gotchya, you little bastard," Prondzinski said, and her hand came out from under the copier holding an untwisted wire hanger, at the end of which she'd just speared a paper clip. Immediately Janice began mentally rehearsing the story for the other uncles: a paper clip, and not even the fancy kind with the plastic coating, either, but a regular old metal one, three hundred to a box. "Waste not," the lieutenant said as she got to her feet.

They stood facing each other, Janice and this intimidating white lady whom Janice wanted to become in fifteen years, hopefully sooner, although Janice would probably dye her hair and come to work in stockings without runs in them and let her paper clips die a natural death behind photocopiers. The rumormongers put Prondzinski's age somewhere between forty-four and sixty-four, but they also claimed she suffered from vaginal dentitis and used to topple skyscrapers in Tokyo.

"You got a minute?" she asked, always a bit of a trap question coming from one of the Big Bosses, who considered an unoccupied moment tantamount to truancy.

"A minute?" Janice said. She let her eyes linger on the folder of empty pages in her hands. "Yeah, okay. I can probably do a minute."

Prondzinski swiped the WILL RETURN sign off her doorknob as she led Janice into her office. A gigantic map of Queens, color-coded by precinct, hung on the wall. The 115 — encompassing East Elmhurst, Corona, and Jackson Heights, where Janice, Tevis, Sergeant Hart, his investigators, and occasionally Gonz all worked — was shaded a light purple. Tall mounds of paperwork buckled plastic in-box trays. In the entire rumpus only Janice kept a messier desk, and that shouldn't even count since all her folders functioned as props. Not her fault. When stuck in the rumpus between buy days,

Janice, like every other uncle, had nothing to do.

She sat across from Prondzinski in a hardback wooden chair that kept sliding her butt forward, a chair that was impossible to get comfortable in, its two front legs probably sawed off a quarter inch just for this purpose.

"So," she said, resisting the urge to ask if she was in trouble. "What can I do for you?"

"Do you like it here in Narcotics?" Prondzinski asked.

Afraid of another trap, but hopeful that Prondzinski was asking her to consider a potential transfer to the NYPD's counter-terrorism bureau, a legit possibility considering Janice's vaguely Arab-looking face, she said, "I'm happy wherever the department thinks I'd be most useful."

The answer, which she had considered perfectly diplomatic, seemed to disappoint the lieutenant. "And if the department thinks you'd be most useful back in patrol?" she asked. "In that polyester bag of a uniform? With all those guys you left behind patting you on the head, saying, 'Hey, kid, don't sweat it, not everyone's cut out for Narcotics.' You'd be happy? Really? At the bottom there?"

Janice scooted herself back up into the

chair. "No," she said. "Not at all."

"Then I need you to make *buys,*" Prondzinski said. "You seen this board they put up? There are new expectations around here. From on high, you understand?" The usual justification for a browbeating: *Hey, it's not me, it's my boss.* Shit might roll downhill in the department, but responsibility always got deferred the other way, up the chain of command, from lieutenants through captains to Commissioner Kelly on to God and beyond, until the buck settled where bucks always seem to settle, around His Honorable Mayor Mike Bloomberg. New expectations. From up high. It never ended. To be fair to Prondzinski, though, she was the first woman Janice had worked for in the department who did not make a special effort to torture her female subordinates under the pretense of tough love. She stretched her hands out across the desk blotter, the better to make her appeal. "With this Sean Bell trial going on," Prondzinski said, "I've got people all over me in full-on panic mode, okay? Telling me we *need* to make more buys. We *need* to come in under budget something awful or I don't even know what. And Internal Affairs? Are you kidding? Internal Affairs is actively looking to cut someone's nuts off, Itwaru, so if you see *anything,* anything remotely shady or questionable, I'm going to need you to bring it straight to me so we can sort it out in the, you know, most efficient way possible. And that's assuming you'll even still be here next month. Because can I tell you something? I've got people over my shoulder looking at the downward slope of your buys, all right? And they want to know what's going on. They're asking me, 'Does she not care anymore? Is she getting worse?' "

Imagine that: overexpose an uncle in a neighborhood, tell every dealer she gets arrested that they've just sold drugs to a narc, and all of a sudden she starts to make less buys over time. Again, Janice scooted herself back into her seat. "It's an improving neighborhood," she said lamely. "Less street crime, more gentrified. I heard there's even supposed to be a Starbucks going up on Thirty-Seventh Avenue."

"A Starbucks." This answer, too, seemed to disappoint. "I'm not singling you out here, Itwaru. I know you're a hard worker. I *know* you're ambitious, and believe me, I admire it, it's admirable. Honest to God. But what I'm not going to do? I'm not going to go into Inspector Nielsen's office and tell him to take it easy because guess what, there's a Starbucks about to open on Thirty-

Seventh Avenue. No, but what I *am* going to tell him? I'm going to tell him that this Officer Itwaru, who he wants so badly to toss back to patrol? So he doesn't have to promote you in two months. So he doesn't have to find room on this shrinking budget of ours for your new detective-grade salary —"

"One month," Janice said.

"One month, what?"

"You said two months, but it's actually one. I'm seventeen in already." Seventeen and four days, but who's counting? "I'll make detective on April first."

"I hope so," Prondzinski said. "And I'm going to do what I can, all right? I'm going to go into Nielsen's office and I'm going to tell him that you are a hardworking, ambitious young cop whose rocket is soaring. Who's going to do great things for this department one day. And you want to know why? Because you are willing to take on accountability. I'm going to tell Nielsen you have a message for *him.* That when I met with you just now in my office you guaranteed four buys." She held up an equivalent number of fingers. "Four buys before the end of next month. And if you don't? See you later. He'll send you back to patrol, which is what he wants to do anyway. You got it? He is rooting *against* you, Itwaru. Own that. Embrace that. You're going to make these four buys and you're going to make them fast and you're going to shove them in our faces. You want to know why? Because you understand that we're not in business here to give away detective shields for free. Right? Right. Now, what questions do you have?"

As soon as she returned to her desk, she told the other uncles almost the whole story, omitting only the part when Prondzinski asked her to report anything shady or questionable. The last thing she wanted to seem like was a potential informant, a narc among narcs. Without IA anxieties to distract them, the uncles' reactions to her story were the expected ones. Fiorella reassured her that four buys in a month was difficult although not impossible, but then Gonz reminded her that when you subtract weekends, days when they had to stay in the rumpus, and ghosting assignments, Janice actually had far fewer opportunities to make buys than you'd think. Prick. Klondike and Morris, talking over each other, agreeing without realizing it, complained about quotas, which they said wouldn't have been so offensive if the department would just admit they kept quotas. Under interrogation, Puffy — who, like Janice, was nearing his eighteen months — admitted that he had not received a similar ultimatum, but maybe that was only because he worked for a different lieutenant with a more hands-off management style. Or maybe, Gonz suggested, Puffy wasn't even worth warning and the Big Bosses planned to boot him back to patrol any day now because, correct Gonz if he was wrong, but didn't Puffy make far fewer buys than Itwaru? Once again on his back across Janice's desk, Puffy gave Gonz the standard rebuttal: thanks for the pep talk. Tevis warned that internal pressures like these only ended one way, with people getting hurt, just like in the story he wanted to tell them.

"Not now," the uncles said.

Worried as always about appearing idle, she wandered away toward one of the rumpus's open computers. To any Big Bosses passing by, she looked — she hoped — as if she were typing up an important buy report, even though she didn't have any buy reports to type up, important or otherwise. With her mouse pointer ready to maximize a departmental database, she signed into her Amazon account to check the delivery status on a book order, which was at least a work-related book order: *Sway: The Art of Gentle Persuasion,* by Wanda R. Rearsman, PhD. Apparently, according to Amazon, UPS had delivered the book to her back porch last Friday. And either her neighbor, Mr. Hua, had stolen it or her mother had brought it into the house and then forgotten to say anything. Probably the latter. Janice planned to go straight home after work, find her package somewhere in the towers of unopened mail on the kitchen table, and read a couple of chapters before bed, to be good, she really wanted to be good, but at the end of her shift the sergeants told all the uncles they had to report back to the rumpus in five hours. The Big Bosses wanted everyone out on the street, fishing, when the early-morning methadone clinics opened for business. The uncles who lived farthest away, out on Long Island, retreated to the cot room to sleep alongside Grimes. The rest, Janice included, took their muttering complaints over to A.R.'s Tavern.

She sat at a booth in the back with Puffy, Fiorella, Tevis, and James Chan, who used to jump out of airplanes in Afghanistan and now went everywhere with little white iPod buds in his ears. Other uncles sat at other tables. Because many still pitied Janice her four-buy ultimatum, they sent over shots, soft stuff like Liberaces and Lemon Drops that she foolishly underestimated. An hour into the night, after slamming back something ridiculously yellow, she stood up to go home and the ceiling swung down to knock her back into the booth. All around her, on A.R.'s dozens of televisions, a New York Knick tomahawk-dunked a basketball in slow motion. The bartender asked her to please stop shredding the coasters; like her nail-biting, she didn't even know she'd been doing it. When a Coors Light appeared in front of her, she reached for it carefully, with just her fingertips, as if a sudden movement might cause either her or the bottle to shatter. Without anyone noticing, James Chan fell asleep. The next time she stood up, to take a cab home to Richmond Hill, Puffy pulled her into the booth. They all had a kickback round coming. Then they had to wait for Fiorella's jukebox songs to come on. The Knicks won by four. James Chan eventually woke up. At exactly 2:31 in the morning, Tevis announced that they had crossed the Rubicon, the point in the evening when it made more sense to stay out drinking than it did to go home. With a captive audience, too drunk to resist him, he started his story.

# CHAPTER TWO

He said, "I haven't been here forever, you know. I started in Narcotics in 1995 with even less experience in the job than you have now. They were more desperate back then for guys with my coloring, right? So I started in 1995, but I haven't actually been here all that time. I left and then came back in 2003. That's what? Five years? That still makes me the most senior guy here in terms of uninterrupted tenure, because Gonz came over in 2004, I think. After me, anyway.

"But like I'm saying, I haven't been here straight through since '95. I left in July of '01 to go to the Firearms Unit, which is probably one of maybe three departments here that doesn't go by its own initials.

"That was a joke.

"But it actually really doesn't go by its initials.

"Now, I know some of you have like

doubts about what we're doing here. In Narcotics, I mean. That it's kind of messed up or whatever. And there's actually a whole other story I can tell you about that . . .

"Okay, okay, okay. But point being, any doubts we might have about *this* job, well, you wouldn't worry about that if you were in Firearms because the job there is completely straightforward. Buy guns. Get them off the streets. You went home, you weren't like, 'Did I take advantage of that kid who sold me that nine-millimeter fully automatic handgun where you squeeze the trigger, it empties the clip?' You didn't spend a lot of time worrying about the ethics on that one. We worked all over the city and we were very passionate and very obsessed. Because every gun you don't buy, a bad guy does. And so you naturally felt very driven. And the department by then had gone completely over to statistics, so you felt compelled to get these guns off the street because, you know, they're *guns,* but also you really wanted to get your numbers up, too. Because as a cop of a certain color, you're thinking the stats are great. You can demonstrate now that you're outperforming some of your peers who might, like, be better connected. You can say, 'Look at the numbers.'

"So what was this very natural, internal competitiveness became a kind of external competition *between* guys. Which is exactly what the NYPD wants. Or thinks that it wants. What you saw in places like Firearms were these buy boards just like the one that went up today. It had our names, it had our numbers, and it even had Polaroids up there. Pictures of the guys holding these big-mama machine guns they'd gotten off the street.

"But now this is obviously a very stressful job. You arrest stockbrokers for solicitation or whatever, and they tell you how stressful their days are, the big deals they gotta make. You wanna laugh. Because nobody dies, right? But with Firearms you're bringing massive amounts of money to these parking lots to meet some real scumbags and you're not worried that they'll think you're a cop. You're worried they're going to rob you. With Narcotics, and I don't mean to suggest Narcotics isn't scary, but in Narcotics your big fear is does this guy have a gun on him. In Firearms, I mean that's the whole point, right? You're hoping.

"So you take ambitious cops, you put them in a stressful job, and then you hang boards on the wall. Listen, I don't mean to put my mistakes on anybody else. I'm responsible for the errors I've made. I don't mean to suggest otherwise. You hear the politicians on TV: 'Mistakes were made.' As if, like, mistakes happen without people. Listen, you have to take responsibility. And so for a couple of years there in Firearms I was self-medicating my anxieties with alcohol. While working. While at work. And you know there are other people's lives at stake there with a thing like that.

"Anyway. One day, me and my partner, Isaac Caspars, you know the name, we split a bottle of . . . what's the one, tastes like cough syrup? Jägermeister. We split a bottle of that, and normally that'd be fine, we were drinking so much back then, but sometimes it's your day and sometimes it isn't, and I got really, really wasted. But we both have three hours before our shift ends, so he hustles me through the office toward the cot room in the back so I can sleep it off. This is over at the Manhattan rumpus. Our captain is a guy named Landry who's this teetotaling Born Again, and while there's not a captain in the universe who likes his cops getting drunk on the job, this guy is going to be particularly hostile to the idea. So I'm having to go hide out in the cot room.

"I don't even know how many hours later

I wake up with my feet in Caspars's hands. Maybe you all don't know this about me, but I'm a little weird about my feet. Like I wear flip-flops in the shower, my *own* shower. And socks to bed and all that. I'm surprised I'd even taken my shoes off in the cot room, but there they are across the room, still knotted, like I must've kicked them off in my sleep. So that's a surprise. And Caspars, who knows about my foot thing, he's kneading my arches.

" 'Get the f off me,' I tell him, except I don't say *f,* I use the actual cuss word, which as you know is not something I like to do.

"And then Hart sticks his head into the room. The very same. Sergeant Hart, except he wasn't a sergeant back then, he was just starting out as an investigator with Firearms. We've known each now, oh my goodness, like forever. He came out of Queens Narcotics like I had, and transferred back when I did, too. Nothing intentional like he was following me or something, but sometimes you'll just go your whole career linked up to somebody. He's my shadow, and I'm his, and it could be a lot worse, let me tell you. Anyway, he sticks his head into the room and he says, 'Did you tell him yet?'

"And Caspars looks at me and he says,

'Guess who called?'

"Actually, what he said, he tells Hart that I'm grouchy. Then he asks me who called.

"I guess 'Nene Singleton,' who was this kid at the Ravenswood projects in Queens, this guppy we'd been trying to hook for *months*. And Caspars goes, 'See, you don't *have* to be a detective to figure that sort of stuff out, but it helps,' which was a favorite line of his. He goes, 'And guess what Nene's got?'

"It's around midnight now. Something like that. And I *am* grouchy. I've just been woken up by a man touching my feet and I'm in that headache zone between drunk and hungover. I don't really feel like playing, so I go, 'Why don't you just tell me?'

"And he says, 'Our boy Nene just called because he's got an AK-47 he wants to sell.'

"From the doorway, Hart says, 'An AK-47,' like that's all he needs to say, because really that is all he needs to say.

"You guys ever see one of those things? You ever *hear* one of those things? We're talking about a gas-operated, rotating-belt, Kevlar-piercing, fully *and* semiautomatic assault rifle that fires six hundred rounds per minute with a maximum range of four football fields. On top of that? It's moron-proof. Ridiculously reliable, almost no

70

maintenance required. And what am *I* thinking about? I'm thinking about holding up that big bad mama for a Polaroid that'll go on the board.

"Nene, though, he wants to make the sale that night, and our captain won't approve it. We're in his office, you've never seen such a clean office, Bible quotes on the walls, me and Hart and Caspars giving the pitch. I've got a cup of coffee to help sober me up, but of course I spill it on the floor.

" 'What's the matter with him?' Landry asks, and Caspars tells him I've got the flu, but I'm getting better every second.

"So after we give Landry the pitch, he tells us there's not enough time to set up all the stuff we have to set up: put together an op plan, order the cameras, put together all the scenarios, scout the location, set up surveillance, look for countersurveillance, note all the one-way and dead-end streets in the neighborhood, *distribute* the op plan, hold the TAC meeting, all of it. He wants us to stall Nene until tomorrow, but Caspars tells him that Nene insisted it's tonight or never. He's got alternative options otherwise, Nene's exact words according to Caspars. Alternative options.

"We let that hang in the air a bit.

"Landry shakes his head and says sorry.

71

'There's not enough time. It's just too dangerous.'

"And I go, 'It's dangerous not to make this buy.'

"My breath must've still smelled like Jäger, because he points to me and says, 'What is this drunk fool doing in my office? Whose buy is this anyway?'

"Caspars tells him it's his buy, but he wanted me along because Nene usually rolls deep and if he brings a friend, I'd be there to like even out the numbers.

"But that's just more ammo for Landry. He rattles off all the problems: not enough time, the possibility Nene will bring a friend, Nene's youth, by which he means his stupidity. 'It's too many variables,' he tells us.

"Hart can't say anything because all of Landry's objections are safety-related and it's the undercovers with their necks in the noose, not him. So I take it upon myself to say, 'Listen. What if we can get the op plan put together in time?' And what if we let Landry pick the location? And what if — because clearly he's not sending a drunk onto the set as an uncle — what if I run surveillance and Caspars partners up with this new undercover we had named Debbie Barnes, who was great, just a pro's pro. She

72

could pose as Caspars's girlfriend and hopefully soften the mood a bit, make it a little less testosteroney. And what if we don't buy this AK and somebody else does?

"Now, Landry, to his credit, before he was Born Again, he was an AA twelve-stepper, and before that an atheist, and before that an agnostic, and before that a Catholic. So in other words, the guy is willing to change his mind. He goes out onto the rumpus to see if Barnes is even still around, and when he comes back into his office he's visibly relieved because she'd signed out half an hour ago.

"But I've already called her on her cell. And I've got her turning around, making the next available U-turn by promising her that *she'll* get to be the primary. And what does that mean? That means the buy will go up on the buy board, directly under her name.

"For the next couple of hours we've got investigators mapping routes to the nearest hospital just in case. Hart and I, we're putting together the op plan. I'm writing the scenarios, all the ways it can go. Well, of course, not *all* the ways it can go. Really just three ways, because that's all the space I have on the form. Just a drop in the bucket, really, in terms of possible futures.

Hart is putting together a Nene packet with photos of all his known pals, plus anyone we have in the computer who lives in Ravenswood, more photos than we could possibly go through in the time allotted. Barnes is getting mic'd. Caspars is in Landry's office, talking on the phone with Nene, setting up the buy for tonight. It's going to go off outside Nene's apartment building in Ravenswood, just a simple hand-to-hand on the street. Caspars wants him to bring the gun in a duffel bag of some sort, so it'll be concealed, of course, but also so the AK will be harder for Nene to pull out in case something goes wrong. Nene says, 'I'm not trying to give away bags for free here.' Tacks on another thirty dollars for the duffel, which puts us at seven hundred and eighty dollars. Does that not sound like a lot? For an AK-frickin'-47? Well, it's not, right? But *that's* how many guns are on the street. That's open-market competition driving down prices on an *assault* weapon. Anyway, so now we gotta get the money, copy it, get the cars, get the cameras, and race over to the set, eating red lights the whole way.

"And then it's that old story. The life of a cop? Hurry up and wait. We're all just sitting around. Waiting on Caspars and Barnes to decide to show up. It's four o'clock in

74

the morning and me and Hart are slouched down in a Toyota Camry with tinted windows. Parked outside Nene's Ravenswood residence. Nene's up in his apartment, waiting on Caspars and Barnes himself. Across the street there are two more detectives in a yellow taxi. Around the corner, within kel frequency range, not that it matters since we couldn't find a single working mic, are Landry and two more detectives in the command car. My phone keeps vibrating. It's my wife — I was married at the time — wanting to know if I'm still alive, but I can't answer because I don't want the glow of the cell phone lighting up the car. Of course I could've called her before I left for the set, but that's only about one of maybe four million reasons why I got divorced.

"At the time, though, all I'm thinking is at least I don't have to pee. Then I have to pee. Then I'm wondering if I have enough time to run to Dunkin' Donuts and use their bathroom, not that I ever would, not that it was even open probably, but I just wanted to torture myself with the possibility. Hart, meanwhile, is blowing his nose into this disgusting handkerchief because he gets sick when he's nervous. I don't know if you knew that. The whole car reeks of the cough drops and Altoids he keeps popping.

He's blaming me for giving him the flu, and I'm apologizing, even though we both know I never really had the flu, but that's what happens on surveillance. You start to lose your mind.

"Finally we see Caspars and Barnes drive past us in a gray Pathfinder. The ghost car's right behind them. Caspars parks the Pathfinder in front of a hydrant about thirty yards away from the Ravenswood entrance, exactly as he was supposed to. So far, so good. All three of my op-plan scenarios started just like this, with the uncles putting some distance between themselves and the entrance. It's like I always tell you: make the fishies swim to you.

"Caspars gets out of the car with the engine still running and he comes over to Barnes's side, the street side, so the detectives in the cab can get some good pictures of him on his cell phone. He's calling Nene and the idea here is that he gets Nene to come down with the AK in his bag or whatever, walk the thirty yards to the car, complete the sale out in the open, that's scenario one, or in the car, that's scenario two, and when Nene's walking the thirty yards back, we all grab him before he reaches his building.

"After Caspars gets off the phone, he

reaches into the open passenger window and comes out with a cig, Barnes's, I guess. He takes a drag, something I've never seen him do in my life. Different partners, different vices, I guess. Barnes's hand is dangling outside the window and she's wearing what looks like an enormous purple cocktail ring, big as a plum. Before he slides the cigarette back between her fingers, he bends over and gives the ring a big kiss. I don't know. I'm glad they're relaxed and having fun, but my hands are shaking like they straight got banged with a hammer. I show them to Hart. I go, 'Look at this,' and he says, 'Tell me about it,' then blows his nose into the hankie.

"Nene comes out a little later with a buddy, just as we knew he would. They're both dressed all in white. White sneakers, white denim shorts. This is February, mind you. White T-shirts. White do-rags under white Yankees caps. In the dark, from a parked car, they looked identical, except Nene's got his tube socks pulled all the way up like he's worried Caspars is going to kick him one in the shins. And the friend's a little bit taller, too. Me and Hart, we're flipping through photos fast as possible so we can radio a name to Landry, but we don't recognize the kid. The good news? Nene and the kid don't recognize us, either. Don't even look for us, like they've got nothing to worry about, no reason at all to keep an eye out for police, because, the bad news, they've come out of the building empty-handed.

"Nene pats his chest, like, 'My bad, my bad.' We don't need to hear him to know what he's saying. We've heard it literally a thousand times before. 'My bad, the AK was supposed to be here like hours ago, but we just gotta go pick it up, take a quick drive, no problem, my bad, my bad.'

"Listen. If black-market gun-sellers were organized and responsible, they wouldn't be black-market gun-sellers.

"The problem, though, is that only scenario three had anticipated Nene showing up without the gun. If that happened, the uncle was advised to cancel the buy and pursue it another time. Nothing wrong with punting. But of course, as always, all real-time decisions remain at the uncle's discretion.

"While Caspars's thinking about what he's going to do, Nene moves past him to see who's sitting in the Pathfinder's front seat. He leans his head in through the window, like maybe he's kissing Barnes on the cheek, even though they've never met before, and

then he pulls his head out laughing, cracking up at something she said. She was pretty
charming. Caspars meanwhile is giving
Nene's friend one of those macho upward
chin tilts. That was a little unusual because
normally when Caspars met somebody new
on a buy he'd step forward and give whoever
it was like this big double-handed hand-
shake. It was his shtick to act super corny.
He wanted people to think, No police
department in the world would hire a guy
this fake to work undercover. He'd act like
he was running for office, slapping backs
and cracking jokes and talking crazy loud,
horsing around, but in a real buddy-buddy
way, like with the ring, kissing Barnes's ring,
but he gave Nene's friend just the chin tilt,
without smiling, like he was in the mood to
intimidate. That pleased me, but my hands
were still shaking. I kept telling myself,
'Take it easy, take it easy. If these kids had
violence on the brain, they wouldn't have
dressed all in white.'

"Do you know what that is right there?
Itwaru, it's like your big Korean in the
leather jacket. You see him leaning up
against that pole or whatever and you're
thinking, Boom, that's a dealer. A lot of time
you'll hear people say they felt something in
their gut or whatever, but one of the things

I very much admire about you is that it's always facts, proofs. You articulate very well. 'I think this because of that.' Ninety-nine out of a hundred people, they don't see the world closely like we do. We're paying attention in a way almost no one else is. And we're also building little stories, right? This happened because of this. One thing leads to another. We're seeing the world very closely and with the stakes being what they are for us, being this sort of life-and-death kind of thing, we need to assess that world accurately, immediately, and so we tell ourselves these stories. Like because he's a drug dealer, he's tired of standing, and so that's why he's leaning against the pole in his nice jacket. Because Nene and his boy are wearing white clothes, they're not going to do anything that might risk them getting bloody.

"But see, your Korean guy *wasn't* a dealer. He *knew* a dealer, sure. But he himself? He was just a guy on a pole. Maybe he *works* for a dealer, as a steerer or whatever, but we don't know, right? Saying this guy is probably holding down drugs for this reason or that reason, that's just a story we tell ourselves. And it does what stories are supposed to do. It makes us feel better. Where we get into trouble is when we forget it's just a story.

"Barnes opens up her passenger's-side door. See if Caspars was going to take this much time to decide what to do, then she was going to get out and stand next to him. That way, if Caspars does decide to play chauffeur, she can easily offer Nene her seat up front. 'Your legs are longer. You can give directions. We're in a fight and I don't wanna sit next to him. I barely met your friend yet. You boys can haggle over prices up there.' Whatever it takes to avoid the tactical disaster of two possibly armed men sitting behind you in the backseat of a car. I'm sitting in *our* car, smelling Hart's cough drops, and I'm powerless, but when I see Barnes's door swing open . . . my goodness. I'm telling you, she was simply a pro.

"But Nene, the Casanova, he pushes the door closed for her, won't let her give up her seat. He's pointing west as he goes around to the back. His buddy gets in next to him, neither one of them asking permission as far as I can tell. Caspars heads to the front. He's walking stiffly with the cement legs he gets when he comes to work straight from the gym. The door slams and the Pathfinder pulls out into the street.

"Not one of the scenarios provided the backup teams with further instructions if the uncles left the set, but we didn't need further instructions. If the uncles leave, everybody follows. While Hart's radioing Landry, the ghost car turns onto Thirty-Sixth Avenue in slow-speed pursuit. The cab goes next. Because me and Hart are faced the wrong way on Twenty-First, we go in the opposite direction and will just have to catch up. Landry gets on the radio and says he wants to run leapfrog, with the ghost car trailing the Pathfinder then heading back to the end of the line and letting the cab pick up the Pathfinder then heading back to the end of the line and letting us pick up the Pathfinder, around and around, for as long as it takes. Almost right away, though, for whatever reason Caspars pulls up in front of this twenty-four-hour Laundromat on the avenue. The ghost and the cab have to coast right on by so they won't get burned. Me and Hart, we're not even there yet. By the time the ghost circles the block, the Pathfinder's gone and there's all this broken glass in the street, but the ghost team can't remember if the glass had been there before or not.

"Landry's on the radio asking who's got the eyeball, who's got the eyeball, but no one has an answer for him.

"Hart's choking the steering wheel by

now, lipping the curb, and I'm on my cell dialing Caspars's number but it keeps going straight to voice mail. 'You know what to do,' it says. I'm on the radio now with Landry telling him I can't get through and he tells me to keep trying. His voice is like weirdly calm. He tells me he's calling Barnes but can't get through, either. Maybe they were in a cellular dead spot, but I've since walked all around that neighborhood and never lost reception. Maybe all the other guys were calling Caspars and Barnes at the same time. Maybe that's why none of our calls got through. At one point, this sanitation truck backs out of an alleyway and Hart has to swerve out of its way and ends up sideswiping a parked car. He's driving sixty miles per hour down these little streets. I think about telling him to buckle his seat belt, but I don't because that would be like a defeat somehow, like an acknowledgment that something bad might actually happen. At last Caspars's phone starts ringing, but nobody answers.

"We make a hard left onto this little narrow one-way, squeezed in by row houses on one side and an elementary school on the other. As soon as we're on it, Hart has to hit the brakes hard to keep from running them over. I don't remember bouncing off

83

the dash, but I must've. I'm out of the car now and there's no Pathfinder anywhere, but a couple yards away from each other Caspars and Barnes are lying in the street. The air had this really thick burnt smell, from the gunshots or Hart's braking, I don't know.

"Caspars was the one closer to me, but I leapt right over him to get to Barnes. That's another thing I don't know. Why I did that. I think maybe because he was so, like, irretrievably dead. He lay on his side with his legs bent at the knees and his face was gone, but Barnes was on her back, like maybe just asleep. Except not really, of course. She already had some slight burning across her forehead, all the way up to her hairline. The real damage, though, went down the right side of her face. It looked all dark and sort of charred. Her eye on that side was filled with blood and she had blood all over her chin. Her eyebrow, too, was like super long there, with the inflammation maybe. Like Caspars, she'd been shot through the back of the head, but the bullet had come out at a weird angle, through her cheek. The exit wound looked like this little perfect Valentine's heart, tipped over on its side. When I was breathing into her mouth, the air came puffing out of that hole.

"Hart was working on Caspars. He can't find a pulse, he tells me, and there was no mouth for him to breath into, so I tell him to come help me with Barnes. He puts his hand on the hole in her cheek and the entire time he's chewing the heck out of a pen, a cheap little Bic, I don't know where he got it. Her lungs won't inflate, so I start chest compressions. Hart is still holding on to her cheek for the compressions, even though he doesn't have to. I start with the breaths again and it's like screaming down a well. I'm back on chest compressions when Landry pulls me off her. 'It's over,' he tells me. They're all here, all the guys, para-medics on the way. I see now that the ring on her hand is not a real ring, but one of those lollipop candy rings.

"By the time the paramedics arrive, I'm sitting on a stoop outside one of the houses. I'm sitting there and I'm watching them go through the same CPR rigmarole. But it's hopeless, right? After they gave up, when they were loading Caspars and Barnes onto the bus, one of the paramedics puts the sheets on their faces, but the other medic pulls them off. He won't pronounce them dead in front of all of us. The bus takes them away with the sirens going all crazy, and after they're gone I hear Hart saying

85

that was very respectful, the way the guy took the sheets off their faces, and I can't tell if he's being sarcastic or not because to me it's such a pointless gesture. And maybe even a little cowardly to let the hospital doctor declare them DOA. But that's probably unfair of me to say. I take that back. Those medics work hard, I know. And what a spot they were in. What a difficult spot with all of us staring at them.

"A little later Landry finds me on my stoop to tell me they found the Pathfinder eight blocks away. Abandoned. It'd take another two days before we found Nene hiding in the woods in Pennsylvania and his buddy at a relative's in Towson, Maryland. At the time, though, out on that stoop, Landry is telling me IA will be here soon to investigate the shooting. He reminds me that I can delay the interview for up to seventy-two hours. Then he says he's gotta ask me something. Do I remember if the kel-mics were working when we left the rumpus?

" 'No,' I tell him.

" 'No you don't remember, or no they weren't working?'

"When I say, 'No they weren't working,' he tells me to take a second to think about it. What you have to understand, guys, is that this is a good man. A decent, moral human being who's lost two decent, moral human beings, and he wants to protect as many people as possible now, people above and below him. And that's natural, in my opinion. That's why we go into this job, to protect as many people as possible. And really, when it comes right down to it, if I can keep a brother away from the wolves in Internal Affairs, then that's what I'm going to do, ten times out of ten.

"I ask Landry what does he want me to tell them, and he says, 'If you don't remember, I want you to say you don't remember. There's nothing wrong with that.'

"He didn't have to say, 'No one will trust the testimony of a cop who was blotto drunk on the job.' But he didn't say, either, that by protecting our butts today we might be jeopardizing the lives of future uncles, who at the very least should expect to have working kel-mics. But that's all theoretical, you know? And this is a real person standing over me on the stoop, saying, 'If you don't remember, you don't remember,' and I dropped my head between my knees, which I guess he interpreted as a nod of acceptance, which I guess it sort of was.

"He asks if he can get me anything and I tell him a bottle of water. Ten minutes later this pretty blond patrol brings me a warm can of Diet Pepsi that's probably been sitting in her squad car all day. I popped the tab so she wouldn't feel offended, but I didn't drink any of it. I wasn't even thirsty. The whole reason I wanted the water was to wash off my face. I had this crazy thought that my wife was going to show up and I didn't want her to see me with Barnes's blood all over my mouth.

"Later, back at the rumpus, Landry pulls the buy board off the wall. He dismantles it in front of us, gets rid of the Polaroids and everything. Okay, well, that's a nice gesture, but now what? Because we are properly traumatized, let me tell you. Dudes are bugging out, so a couple days later Commissioner Kelly gives every undercover in the department — Firearms, Narcotics, whatever — he gives every uncle an opportunity to flip over to investigator, no questions asked. Now, I don't think the Big Bosses really thought that one through. Because what happens is pretty much every uncle abandons ship. Almost all these guys, they had become undercovers in the first place so they could get to investigator one day. And even if you wanted to stick around, your wife was going to make you switch, or, like me, you got divorced. So now the department's all out of uncles, and the only people buying drugs are the drug addicts. Unacceptable, right?

"So the department reaches out to you guys. The replacements — and I don't mean that in a bad way. You're just the next wave is all. And now here we are, déjà vu all over again. Five years pass and none of you have *heard* these stories, so the Big Bosses figure, 'Hey, let's get some buy boards back on the walls, what's the worst that can happen?'

"I'm just telling you, God forbid, if I get killed from all this crazy numbers-chasing? The one-upmanship? Not a single Big Boss is allowed to come to my funeral. No one above sergeant. Not Prondzinski, not Nielsen, not Captain Morse, *none* of them. I'm serious. If any of those snakes gets within three hundred feet of my casket, I will hold each of you responsible and haunt you all for the rest of your lives. Remember that. It's gonna be some idiot drug dealer that pulls the trigger, but it's the department pushing us in front of the gun. Just saying. God forbid."

# CHAPTER THREE

Unable to see clearly, unable to breathe deeply, Janice woke up on a white leather couch. Her nose was congested, her eyes inflamed and leaking water. A rancid fuzz coated her tongue. Mister Maplewood — an obese orange tabby cat — sat atop her chest, crushing her, pawing at her blouse as if kneading dough. The good news: he belonged to Fiorella, which meant Janice hadn't accidentally fucked a stranger last night, and, even more important, her gun would be locked up inside the apartment's safe. The bad: she was allergic to cats. She sat up on the couch, to try to get some air into her lungs, but the inertiaprone Mister Maplewood clung to her by his claws, disengaging himself only when she let loose a fantastic, head-clearing sneeze.

"God bless you," said a tiny voice.

With her vision still bleary, she rubbed at her eyes — the very worst thing she could've done — until she could see the outline of Fiorella's nine-year-old son, Hector the Magnificent, magician/superhero. He stood in the living room's entryway wearing his beloved Superman costume, the cape more orange than red, hand-sewn by Vita as a replacement for the original, which he'd lost on what Fiorella called a disastrous horse-drawn-carriage ride through Central Park. His head turned to watch the cat gallop past him toward the back of the apartment.

"What are you doing up so early?" Janice asked him.

"Couldn't sleep." Like so many children of police officers, he had the haywire hair and shiny eye baggage of the apprentice insomniac. "Bad dreams."

"I get those, too," she said.

"I tried to tell Mama, but she wouldn't wake up."

"Oh, honey, I'm sorry," she said. She swung her sweaty legs off the sticky couch. Normally someone who slept in the nude with an eye mask and earplugs, she had — thank God — kept her shirt on, matted now with dander, and her underwear, but her wool-felted pencil skirt lay crumpled on the carpet. Her purse strap curled out from under the coffee table. She pulled it toward her to check the time, but apparently her phone battery had gone dead. Of course it had. She squeezed her saddlebags, hating herself. She hated everything, everywhere, except for these eye-rubs, which felt amazingly good and for which she'd suffer all day. "Mama and Aunt Janice had a rough night catching bad guys," she told him. "But we'll get her up real soon, okay?"

"She was all cold," he said.

"What do you mean?"

"Her mouth was full of upchuck."

Janice ran past him. Still in her underwear, she burst without knocking into Fiorella's room, where the bedsheets were crumpled but empty. Thick curtains on the windows made it difficult to see. The room might've smelled like upchuck, just as he'd said, but she couldn't tell with her nose stuffed. A humidifier puffed steam into the room. She stepped closer, hunched over, for some reason afraid to make a sound. She worried Fiorella had rolled off the bed at some point in the night and got herself trapped on the floor, wedged between the box spring and the wall. A clown jumped out from behind the door. It wheeled toward her, quickly through the darkness, with its pasty skin and green hair and bloodied lips, and it rose up into Janice's face and said, "Boo."

She staggered away, screaming, until she

hit the edge of the mattress and fell backward onto the bed. Hector's cape trailed behind him as he vaulted into the room. He, too, was screaming, but with laughter, like the clown, whose face was softening into a thick rubber Joker mask. The body beneath it belonged to Fiorella. Already dressed for a day of meth clinics, she wore a white Mets jersey, number 13, yellow under the pits, and acid-washed jeans with a pair of guns — her own and Janice's — holstered to the waist.

"Yes!" she cried. "Oh man, Itwaru — you shoulda seen your *face.*"

"I could've attacked you!"

"Oh yeah," Fiorella said, gesturing to Janice collapsed across the sheets. "You was all ready to bust out your jujitsu moves."

"Did I do good?" Hector asked.

"Jesus Christ," Janice said.

"Hey, no cussing!" Fiorella told her. "I don't want you teaching my baby boy no bad habits." She tried poking Janice in the ribs but kept getting her hand slapped away. "Hey, but I bet you're not hungover anymore, am I right? Huh? Huh, huh, huh? Am I right? Man oh man, Itwaru, your face is like covered in hives. You want some Benadryl?"

One question at a time: did she still feel

hungover? Yes, as a matter of fact, she did, maybe worse than before. And no, she did not want a Benadryl. Well, actually, yes, she did want a Benadryl, but with her four-buy ultimatum she couldn't risk its drowsy-making side effects. A lint roller, though, would've been great. And maybe an EKG machine. A couple of Advils. Before leaving the room, Fiorella tossed the Joker mask into Janice's lap, and Hector, who surely sensed time running short, followed his mama out into the hall. She'd have to call a cab soon, to take her and Janice to the rumpus, or rather eight blocks away from the rumpus, outside A.R.'s Tavern, where they'd both left their cars, but in the meantime Fiorella was telling him to get dressed for school. He'd be waiting for the bus downstairs at Mrs. Bakkemo's, she said, to which he responded that he'd spent all night at Mrs. Bakkemo's. No fair. Nothing ever was. Janice lay back down across the bed and put on the mask. The only oxygen she could breathe in there was her own. Out in the hall, but sounding much farther away, Hector was asking if he could at least keep his Superman costume on under his school clothes. The humidifier's puffing became harder to hear. Strangely peaceful inside this mask, Janice pretended she was dead, her go-to method for falling asleep. Down at her ankles, unseen, Mister Maplewood, who hated to be ignored, tensed his jaw, ready to chomp.

The Flushing Hospital Methadone Maintenance Outpatient Clinic opened its doors at seven thirty in the morning for the usual motley of men and women in dress shoes, tennis shoes, flats, pumps, clogs, Uggs, stilettos, galoshes, wellies, high-tops, Timberlands, and Timberland knockoffs. A skinny young white guy had a jump rope tied around his raggedy loafer, to keep the sole from flopping away. Every time he took a step he had to pull up on the other end of the rope, as if he were both puppet and puppeteer. Surely a rubber band or some tape would've worked better, but maybe he liked the attention. Or maybe the shoe had fallen apart only moments earlier, on the cold walk over here, and he'd found the jump rope in a sidewalk garbage can. Hey. Whatever works.

Heroin addicts, these men and women filed into the clinic every weekday morning for a prescription bottle half full — they might argue half empty — with enough liquid methadone to curb their daily cravings. Better a patch than a carton of cigarettes, the thinking went. Better a shot of opiates than a plunging needle. Back in the day, addicts were instead given a small white oblong pill. A nurse behind glass in a little prison of the clinic's construction would ask for ID, fumble the card, look up names in the system, potentially order a urine test, pass back the ID card, collect the ten to fifteen dollars, root around in the register for change, pour out a little cup of water, slide the water and pill over to the patient, make the patient swallow it all right there, then ask the patient to open their mouth and say ahhhh. Needless to say, all that nonsense gunked up the cogs. Patients who braved the long lines went to work late, got fired, and returned to the streets with even more incentive to get high. But in a rare case of bureaucratic pruning, New York's meth clinics adopted a grab-it-and-get-lost policy. Keep it moving, no more mouth checks. As a compromise to law and order, however, the clinics converted their meth into liquid form, which was theoretically harder to resell, especially since patients needed to present their empty prescription bottle the following day to re-up. A few old-timers with cast-iron stomachs downed their shots then and there, top o' the morning to yis, but most brought it back home, where they could chase it with soda to wash out the medicinal cherry taste. Or they took it to work, to their cubicles and corner offices. But unfortunately there were some, because there are always some, who sold their doses outside the clinic to meth addicts unable or unwilling to put their name in the system. All liquid? No problem. Patients poured their doses into empty coffee cups. They doubled the ten dollars they'd just given the nurse and used the twenty to buy heroin from one of the many for-profit dealers stalking the sidewalk.

With all that activity, the department's Big Bosses assumed making buys here would be as easy as fishing with dynamite. Just show up and collect bodies. But meth clinics were a closed-circuit ecosystem, with hand-to-hand-to-hand-to-hands, from the nurses to the heroin addicts to the meth addicts to the heroin dealers. They all knew each other. Of course they all knew each other: like coworkers, they came to the same spot at the same time, every morning, Monday through Friday. Occasionally the uncles might get lucky and find someone who didn't know any better — St. Michael, the patron saint of police officers, supplied them with a lemming-like stream of stupid crimi-nals, fuck-ups guaranteed to fuck up — but even then they had only about five minutes before the word hit the wire and they got burnt.

At the Flushing Hospital Methadone Maintenance Outpatient Clinic, it took less than thirty seconds. All the uncles had to do was step out of the car.

"Hey," said the guy with the jump rope around his shoe, "who called the cops?"

They got back in the car. With that miserable prick Gonz riding shotgun, and Puffy sitting bitch between Janice and Richie the Receptionist, Tevis drove toward the next set, the Narco Freedom Clinic in Long Island City. The rest of the uncles — Fiorella, Eddie Murphy, et al. — were on their own respective meth tours, bouncing around Queens in unmarked Impalas that Janice imagined smelled exactly like this one, like a small and toxic distillery. Her stuffy nose provided only so much interference. Her stomach grumbled without hunger. At the rumpus she had pounded down two cups of coffee, but now in her hands she was holding an empty Dunkin' Donuts cup, her prop for today's role. Tevis and Gonz kept their own empty cups in the plastic holder beneath the radio, which had been turned off so the uncles could more effectively argue. Not about — are you kidding? — the efficacy of the methadone clinic system, or rehabilitation versus incarceration, or Clinton versus Obama, but whether Puffy should be allowed to piss into a plastic bag.

"I'm telling you," said Gonz in the interest of mayhem, "it's not good to hold it. Really. That's how people end up on dialysis."

"Dialysis!" Puffy pleaded.

"Forget it," Richie said with a cell phone against his ear, on hold with an office-supplies wholesaler so he could replace the buy board with a better buy board, a magnetic one in a more tasteful wooden frame. "It's unacceptable," he told Puffy. "Seriously, I'm dead ass here. Just . . . just think of something else."

Puffy, who misunderstood the suggestion, said, "I could go in the Dunkin' Donuts cup, but I'm not sure it'd be big enough."

Claustrophobic, per usual, she powered down her window, but Tevis powered it back up from the front. No cool air allowed. They needed to look as sweaty as smack addicts when they reached LIC's Narco Freedom.

"Cup or bag," she said, "either way, I'm a definite no."

Tevis also claimed to be a definite no, but

then why'd he keep driving past all the gas stations? There wasn't any time to stop, he said. The clinics shuttered around noon, but by nine o'clock most of the for-profit heroin dealers would have moved on to their second shift outside NA meetings. Tevis pushed the odometer's needle past forty, as far as traffic would allow. After Narco Freedom, they would have to drive to the meth clinic at Elmhurst Hospital in the 115 Precinct, to appease Sergeant Hart and his investigators, who were all still annoyed she'd left the Martys' apartment empty-handed. Usually urgency didn't start building until closer to the end of the month, but with that nonmagnetic, aluminum-framed board hanging on the rumpus's wall, everyone felt added pressure to clock out the day with a buy. After Elmhurst, they'd go to the Psychiatric and Addiction Recovery Services center in Rego Park. Then a storefront meth clinic on Archer Avenue. But hold up, one thing at a time: they needed to argue about the fastest way to get to Narco Freedom. Jump on the Grand Central Parkway, the most direct route? Or stay on Northern Boulevard, so as to bypass JFK traffic?

It sounded like water spraying the shower curtain, Puffy pissing into that plastic bag.

"Unacceptable!" Richie said.

"Shh," Puffy said. "You're gonna make me spill."

It seemed silly not to at least take a peek. And there it was: circumcised, thin and long, without any stage fright. She was unimpressed by all this, but a part of her, a pinkie-size part of her, appreciated his willingness to treat her as an equal. Was that insane? Probably, but she grew up with a sister, no brother, spent half her life in a house with three women. She imagined that if she weren't here in the car, there'd be four dicks in one bag, with Gonz potentially shitting into a Pringles can.

"A satin finish?" Richie cooed into the phone. "Now is that on the whiteboard itself or just the frame?"

Gonz also had his phone out, not to talk to anyone, but to take a picture with the camera. She turned away from them all to stare out the window. Go ahead and crop her out of this photo. Unseen, but close by behind Northern Boulevard's billboards and gas stations, her father was probably standing on the artificial putting green in his auto-repair shop, practicing his stroke, a busy Big Boss himself. Up ahead, under a broken traffic light, an Indian patrolman blew softly on a whistle. He windmilled his arm with the listless energy of a cop out in the cold for too long. She thought she recognized him, or at least that big nose of his, from the Academy, or maybe the department's Desi Society for South Asian American police officers, or maybe she just wanted to recognize him, or rather she wanted him to recognize her so she could give him a little flutter wave as they drove by. Make him wonder: Hey, what's Itwaru doing in that unmarked Impala? How'd she get out of the uniform already? Because even with the stench of urine filling up this already cramped backseat, she still felt happier to be here and not there, her and not him, Patrol Officer Nobody who had nothing to look forward to all day except the possibility of catching a car without its tags, or a passenger littering out the window, as Puffy was asking her to do now.

"What?" she said. "No, are you crazy? Get that out of my face."

"It's heavy!" he said. "Just lean back and *I'll* throw it out the window."

"Why's it so brown?" Gonz asked.

"I'm like super dehydrated, okay?"

Looking back at Puffy through the rearview, Tevis said, "No one's dumping a bag of piss out into the street."

"What, he should keep it in here?" Gonz said.

Up at the intersection, the traffic cop blew his whistle at them to pull over. He must've noticed that besides Tevis none of them was wearing a seat belt, a summonsable offense. At last! the guy must've thought. A little action, but Tevis pressed his detective shield to the window and drove right on past him. When Janice turned around smiling to see the patrol officer's reaction, she made accidental eye contact with Puffy, who somehow interpreted her happy expression as tacit permission to toss his pee bag out her window.

"Come on," he said. Holding the bag by its handles, he leaned across her and tried to hit the window button with his elbow. "Tevis," he said, "take the window off lock."

"Don't take it off lock," Gonz said.

She said, "Throw it out the other window!"

"Guys!" Richie said. "I'm on the phone!"

Later, in an attempt to assign responsibility, these professional finger-pointers blamed the cold air that gusted into the car when Tevis finally unlocked her window. They blamed Puffy's hangover. His shaky hands. They said there might've been a rip in the plastic, but that made little sense because the bag would've sprung its leak earlier. Unless the bag had *just* ripped,

103

which they couldn't verify because it lay behind them in the street and they didn't have the time to turn around. In Puffy's own defense — frantic, genuine-seeming, close to actual tears — he claimed Tevis must've hit a pothole, or maybe Gonz intentionally jerked his seat back, but both accusations were denied. She wasn't really listening anyway. A bladder's worth of urine seeped through her pencil skirt.

A young lion, whose name would turn out to be Brandon Hughes, aka Bam-Bam, and who had a warrant open for his arrest after skipping a domestic-assault court date, watched what must've been the surliest-looking bitch in all of Queens marching toward him. Man, something about him just seemed to attract these sourpusses. She was small, how he liked them, a spinner, half black and half Indian, and once upon a time, before she'd dropped down the pipe or into the bottle, he might've asked for her number. Now? Forget it. Her nose oozed mucus. Purple hives splotched her face. He couldn't see much of her hair beneath her wool cap, but he imagined at best it was greasy, at worst infested with lice. Honest to God, someone oughtta put her out of her misery. As she came toward him, she broke stride only twice, once to blast a sneeze into her armpit and again to pick a penny off the sidewalk. Both times he was surprised she didn't spill coffee out of her Dunkin' Donuts cup. Probably because there wasn't any in there. Probably because she used the cup only for begging. Her eyes were blood-shot and cloudy and getting closer. He rolled his shoulders back to make himself bigger than he already was, worried she might charge right through him and leave a body-shaped hole in his chest, cartoon-style, morning light shining clean through him.

"You got twenty?" she asked.

He peeked into her cup and it was empty, boom, just like he'd called it. Now that he was this close to her, though, he had to put a hand up over his nose. "Girl, you need to go on home and change."

"Motherfucker," she said, "I am not in the mood."

They never were. It is what it is. If Bam-Bam wanted a classier clientele, he should've sold shoes. To get this stinky skank out of his face and on her way, he swapped her some heroin tar in wax paper for her crumpled twenty-dollar bill. She of course did not thank him. As she walked away, she pulled off her dockworker's cap and a dark ponytail spilled down her back, the hair not as greasy as he'd imagined, but then again he couldn't be right about every goddamn thing, could he?

Twenty-six days until the end of the month, and her shift here just starting. One buy down. Three more to go.

The uncles parked in a legal spot outside a 99-cent store, around the corner from the Archer Avenue meth clinic. It was their last stop of the day. Technically, according to the TAC plan, she should've been ghosting, but everything got fucked up when Tevis had been unable to find the Elmhurst Hospital meth clinic. They'd tried, though. They had walked around the perimeter of the entire hospital, even asked an oncologist on a smoke break for directions, but they eventually gave up and returned to the Impala. Janice was supposed to ghost in Elmhurst and make buys in Rego Park, but now she had to ghost in Rego Park and make buys with Tevis on Archer Avenue. Or at least attempt to make buys. When she got out of the car, she rapped her knuckles against a tree trunk.

It was late. It must've been late. With her phone battery drained, she didn't know the exact time, but it had to be close to ten o'clock, or even later, because only a few people were left outside the clinic. Most of them, especially the younger ones who'd already copped, stood far apart from one another, balanced on their flamingo legs with one foot propped up against a stone wall or streetlamp. They smoked cigarettes just to have something to do, to delay the return home to their mothers and mothers' couches. A trio of older black men, the more social of these asocial addicts, huddled close together for company. They talked about al-Qaeda, the Sean Bell trial, yesterday's Knicks win, the lesbian stripper who won an Oscar the other night, the malignant snow clouds darkening the sky farther east. Janice was just guessing here. She couldn't actually hear what these old men were talking about, because Tevis had reached them first. Forced to work the other side of the street, she counted — let's see — only six people outside the corner post office, five of them with care packages to send back home to Bangladesh, El Salvador, East Africa, wherever. The sixth, a bearded black man, sat smoking on the hood of an idle Volvo.

"You got twenty?" she asked him.

"What?"

She narrowed her stance so she'd look less like a cop. "I said, 'You got twenty?' "

107

"I don't know." He took a drag off his menthol, white smoke pouring from both his mouth and the Volvo's exhaust. "Twenty of what?"

She didn't really know. Or, more accurately, she didn't really care — a buy was a buy — but she couldn't ask for heroin then change her mind if he was holding down only methadone. You bought one or the other, not whatever was in stock, unless of course you were an undercover narc. So the question then became: was this guy an addict or a dealer, more likely to have methadone or heroin? His pupils were normal size, or at least not constricted, but his poorly groomed beard crept all the way down his neck. And he smoked 100s, the better value. And without a hat or a scarf or a particularly heavy coat, he looked ill prepared for an extended stay in the cold, so she guessed addict, not dealer, and hoped he still had his shot on him.

"You know," she said. "Your dose. I can give you twenty for it."

"My *dose*?" he asked. "You think I got drugs on me? Bitch, I oughtta smack you upside your face."

"Sorry," she said. "I didn't realize you was such an upstanding citizen."

"You seriously need to back up off me

right now."

She backed up off him and walked slowly down the block, past Puffy, who was ordering breakfast from a bagel cart. Except for Elmhurst, where they hadn't had any time, he'd bought her an apology gift at every stop: a roll of paper towels from a bodega in Long Island City; a can of V8, her special hangover cure, in Rego Park; and now, it seemed, a bialy that she'd have to eat on the drive back to the rumpus. Under a red awning that advertised AFRICAN WIGS AND HUMAN HAIR, Richie Nextel'd a car full of investigators around the corner. Across the street, Gonz window-browsed an adult bookstore.

She looked for a working pay phone, but the closest one was too far away, down at the end of the block outside a greasy Crown Fried Chicken joint she used to make secret trips to with her father. She did, though, find a second penny on the sidewalk. One more and when she got home she'd be able to toss the *I Ching*, forecasting her future, yet another daddy/daughter ritual. She had three ghosts malingering around her, but it was Brother Itwaru, her father, who did the real haunting. She spun around, back toward Tevis. She had an ultimatum to reach. With its extra-wide street and two-story buildings and sunken-eyed men, Archer Avenue resembled a Wild West gold town, primed for a shootout, but surely this stretch of sidewalk outside the meth clinic was big enough for both her and Tevis. He seemed to have whiffed with the trio of old men — he was walking away from them with his hands empty and coat unbuttoned, his positive signal unsignaled — but she thought for sure she'd have better luck. Old people pretty much loved her.

"Can you guys help me out?" she asked them, a poor choice of words, for Tevis had long ago taught her to appeal always to self-interest, never mercy or gratitude. "I got money," she quickly added.

"Boy, they out tonight," said one old man to the others. Small and soft looking, he cupped his chin in his hand to make a show out of scrutinizing her. An ebony stone sat in a gold ring on his pointer finger. "We was just telling your partner there," he said, gesturing to Tevis, who was working on one of the solitary smokers propped up against the wall, "that if he wanted that methadone high, all he had to do was get himself on the list. But he didn't seem too interested."

"Partner?" she said. "That guy over there? Are you kidding? That's my dad."

"You serious?"

"Not at all," she said. "You think he's what — a cop?"

"More and more every second," he said. He put his arm around her waist, as if to pull her close and point out all Tevis's policeman giveaways, as if to check the small of her back for a pistol or kel wire, but as soon as he'd grabbed her he let her go. "Good golly, Miss Molly! What'd you do, wet yourself?"

One of his buddies started laughing, but the third old-timer, a gentle-seeming man with a pink scarf around his neck, told his friend to be nice. A lifetime of either too much coffee or too much nicotine had browned his front teeth. He was the grayest of the three men and clearly the sweetest, and if the investigators were going to head-steer one of them into the back of a p-van it was going to be him. Assuming he still had his dose. Assuming she did her job. She called out to Tevis: *Hey, yo!* Got him to turn away from his smoker and look over at her, annoyed, his lips so chapped that she wanted to peel them.

"You a cop or something?" she asked him.

"No," he said. "Are you?"

She gave the old-timers her cockiest shrug. "Well, there you go," she said proudly. "They got to identify themselves if

111

you ask them. Even the undercovers. It's against the law for cops to lie."

"That's a myth," the third man told her.

"You sure?"

"Oh yeah, I'm sure. Police? All they do is lie."

"Well, let me ask you this," she said. She leaned slightly away from him, to make him lean slightly toward her. "You think maybe you could pour like half your dose in this cup? I can't go twenty on a half, but I could probably do ten."

He appeared to be thinking about it, tugging on the fringed ends of his scarf. "Why don't you just put your name on the list?" he asked her. "It's cheaper than the alternative, believe me."

"I'm trying, I'm trying. I still gotta get all that paperwork together, but right now I'm just worried about today, you know? I'm trying not to get sick out here and —"

"Janice?!"

She turned toward this strangely enthusiastic, strangely familiar voice, and saw a young black man, her age, coming out of the meth clinic with a big smile and even bigger aviator sunglasses. My God, she thought. Jimmy Gellar. Recognized him right away, as quickly as he had recognized her. Beneath a thrift-store blazer he wore a thin T-shirt, not the old green one with the lamp, or the old red one with the lightning bolt, but a plain white generic, a promising blue ink spot staining its collar. He was probably Jim now. Or maybe even James. With the addicts, dealers, and narcs looking on, James or Jim or Jimmy Gellar — whoever he might be — spread his twiggy arms out for a hug.

# CHAPTER FOUR

Nine years earlier he had asked her if she wanted to be a superhero or supervillain. This was around midnight, back when her parents were still together. She had a test early the next morning in Mrs. O'Regan's Ancient and Medieval History class, on the pharaohs or something, but she'd smuggled Jimmy into the house anyway, the first rule she'd ever broken without her father's assistance. Both he and her mother were sleeping. She hoped. The living-room sofa, the Bollywood magazines flipped open on the coffee table, her grandfather's grandfather clock, the family photos along the mantel, the crystal dolphins in the glass cabinet, they all watched Janice, a famously good girl, take her new friend by the hand and lead him up the stairs, the two of them hugging the wall to avoid creaking any steps. She brought him into her bedroom, where he took a seat at her desk and began softly tapping his graphite pencil against a blank sheet of drafting paper. The joint he'd smoked on the walk over had reddened his eyes, but he smelled of lemons more than weed, from the Citrashine he rubbed into his natty hair by the palmful. He was fifteen years old, a colossal nerd who smiled easily and danced with his eyes closed, and Janice was in love with him.

"Superhero," she said.

Hunched over at the desk, he got to work. He drew her, or rather he drew the comic-book version of her: older, with basketball breasts that strained the stretchy fabric of her unitard. He gave her a domino mask, which would allow him to render facial expressions, and a long rectangular cape modeled on the Guyanese flag. While adding shadows and cheekbones, he barely looked over at her — sitting Indian-style on the bed, in a pair of gray cotton gym shorts that cut off above her knees — and she realized, with a honeyed warmth filling her throat, that he was working from memory.

"We need a name," he said.

Neighborhood-proud, they called her Captain Richmond Hill. Why not? As Jimmy too loudly explained, Forest Hills had Spider-Man, Hell's Kitchen had Daredevil, Westchester had the X-Men, and now

115

Richmond Hill would have its own hero, a West Indian crime fighter trained in ancient martial arts and blessed/cursed with the supernatural power of the ghetto touch, which was based on Jimmy's own unfortunate propensity to fuck up — without entirely breaking — pretty much anything he laid his hands on, e.g., the inky nibholder that now required duct tape, e.g., the plastic lettering guide that had cracked in half but still remained functional.

He said, "We'll need to —"

"Shh!" she said.

"Sorry," he whispered. "We'll need to explain how she got her powers. Like the origin or whatever."

Like everyone before who's ever been stuck for ideas, she looked out the window. An ancient wooden tree spread its branches between the Itwarus' alleyway and a gas station on the corner, the branches studded with a year-round fruit, genus unknown, as large and heavy looking as mangoes, but not mangoes, not exactly. When they fell, they fell hard. No one, or at least no one Janice knew, had ever dared eat one, but the neighborhood's younger children sometimes used the fruit as ammo in their bruise-inducing games of War. Seedy purple stains blemished the pavement.

She said, "What if she has an alien tree growing magical fruit in her alley? And she gets her powers from, like, its juice?"

Perfect!

They gave her alter ego an appropriately alliterative name, Gabby Guyana, and made her a hardworking homicide detective in the NYPD. Frustrated with the bureaucratic limitations of the job, she made sure in her off-hours to dole out vigilante justice from behind the mask. Obviously the police backstory idea came from Janice, but Jimmy got behind it right away. He told her Barry Allen, one of the Flash's many alter egos, had been a cop. And Nightwing, too, and the Specter and the Guardian and Martian Manhunter and —

"*Please* lower your voice," she said.

"Sorry!"

They completed only one page that first night, but at least it was the cover. CAPTAIN RICHMOND HILL #1, it said across the top. A PLEASE ACCEPT ME COMICS PRODUCTION. The issue was supposed to be his scholarship application to Cooper Union, the prestigious art school in Manhattan. The cover image showed Janice — the comic-book version of Janice — with her fist cocked, ready to deliver a haymaker to the admission board's fat jaws. Her cape un-

117

furled in black and white, but Jimmy promised to add the coloring later. It was one thirty when his ghetto-touched pencil snapped in half. He massaged his wrist. He looked over at Janice, let out a giant breath that he seemed to be holding for hours, and headed out through the front door. The next day she bombed her pharaoh test and fell asleep in sixth period, but she was awake at midnight to once again sneak him into the house. They touched only on the walk up the stairs, holding hands through a darkness that either one of them could have easily navigated on their own. Once safely inside the bedroom, he sat at her desk until his wrist cramped up again and it was time for him to go. He came back the next night, and every night after that until the disaster.

While he boxed the panels and drew the pictures, she stood close enough behind him to whisper plot points and inhale the lemony smell of his hair. Because a lone superhero cannot sustain a story on her own, Janice gave Captain Richmond Hill a nemesis: a cockroach of a man named Ned Shu, based on her real-life classmate Ed Shu, who had disseminated through the entirety of Richmond Hill High School a rumor that Janice liked to masturbate with carrots. A fictitious rumor, by the way. Ned Shu, who like Ed had a pimpled forehead and long, disgusting fingernails, was running for Queens borough president with a tough-on-crime, let's-clean-up-the-streets platform. But unsurprisingly given the inspiration for his character, he turned out not to be the idealistic politician his supporters had imagined, but was in fact a criminal kingpin who'd orchestrated a number of high-profile muggings and robberies in an attempt to discredit his opponent, the incumbent, name to be determined. By the time Captain Richmond Hill figures all this out, though, she's squirming inside a seemingly impossible-to-escape death trap of Shu's sinister design.

"What kind of death trap?" Jimmy asked.

"You have *got* to start whispering," she whispered.

"Sorry!" He asked her again what kind of death trap, softly this time, and when she couldn't think of anything, he said, "Well, what's she most afraid of?" He rolled a pencil between his palms as if trying to kindle a spark. "You see what I'm saying? We need to figure out her biggest fear first, then we'll put her in some sort of thing that's like that. Like if she was afraid of water, we'd put her in a shark tank, except not that because it's been done a million times and would be sort of hard to draw."

Biggest fear, biggest fear, biggest fear. Right at that moment? Losing her virginity, not losing her virginity, doing it wrong, crying halfway through or otherwise embarrassing herself, getting pregnant, catching one of the cauliflower-like STDs from the school nurse's slide-show presentation, the dreadful possibility that Jimmy Gellar might once again leave this room without even attempting to kiss her. But in addition to her obvious reluctance to voice any of these biggest fears, she also felt they'd make for poor death traps. She looked out the window again. She looked around her room, at the tired green carpet, the wooden dresser in the corner. Okay, how about this? She was afraid of not living up to one of the handwritten quotations thumbtacked to her wall: MAKE NO SMALL PLANS; THE CREDIT BELONGS TO THE MAN WHO IS ACTUALLY IN THE ARENA, WHOSE FACE IS MARRED BY DUST AND SWEAT AND BLOOD. She was afraid that something — a failed physical, a botched lie-detector test — might prevent her from one day becoming a police officer. She was afraid she'd grow up to live a spectator's life. What else? Ghosts. She was afraid of ghosts. What else? Spiders and cramped spaces. Cramped spaces with spiders.

"Okay, what if she's claustrophobic?" Janice said. "And we put her in like a coffin or something? Or like a room that keeps getting smaller?"

He groaned at the triteness of it, a groan potentially misinterpreted by her father, who charged into the room wearing only his boxer shorts and holding a bottle of Pathmark-brand seltzer water. He had, apparently, woken up thirsty. The bottle put a crater in the wall above Jimmy's head. Without thinking, Jimmy tried to scramble under the desk, as if a portal to safety lay waiting for him there, but her father's thick, hairy fingers caught him by the shoulder. *Nigger this, nigger that,* her father said as he dragged Jimmy down the stairs. *If I ever see your face round here again, blah bitty blah blah.* She was picking bits of plaster from the wall when her father — already crying, his shoulders trembling — came back into the room to have a conversation about her future.

Her future: she was grounded into perpetuity, a sentence Vita quietly reduced to eleven days. The front door, though, would remain forever locked on the assumption that it would be significantly harder for

121

Janice or her sister to sneak boys in through the back door, which opened and closed beneath the master bedroom. *Thanks a lot,* Judith said. The following fall Janice enrolled at the Townshend Harris magnet school for gifted kids whereas Jimmy stayed on at Richmond Hill High. They never finished Captain Richmond Hill #1, he never applied to Cooper Union, and the last she'd heard he was a junkie who had spent a few long hours locked up in the trunk of some drug dealer's car.

And here *she* was: covered in cat hair and urine.

"Oh my God," he said, releasing her from the hug. "How long has it been? Like years, right? I can't even believe it. You look . . . good." He took his sunglasses off and clipped them to his shirt collar, a relief for Janice, who when staring at him had seen only her own ridiculous rictus grin reflected and doubled in the wide silver lenses. "So what's going on?" he asked. "How have you been?"

"How have I been," she said.

"Hey!" he said. "You're a cop now! Marwan Mehta told me. Just the other day. Right here, matter of fact. Congratulations! What you always wanted, yeah? Officer

Itwaru? Man, that's crazy. Well, not *crazy*. Hey, listen, are you doing anything now? I got my brother's car here if you need a ride or whatever." He turned his head toward her, as if about to confide something, or as if volunteering his ear for secrets of her own. "Your father's not gonna kick my ass, is he?" he said. "Ha-ha, just kidding. You need a ride, though? Seriously. My brother's car is right there."

The smoker Tevis had been working on slunk away down an alley that separated the clinic from a computer repair shop, but nobody followed him. Two separate skinny white kids lit up brand-new menthol cigarettes. A leashed poodle tried dragging its owner, a buff-looking Chinese guy who had stopped to look around as if he sensed the sudden good mood all around him. Except for him and his dog and Tevis and the third old man, everyone was smiling at her.

"I think maybe what you heard got a little twisted," she told Jimmy. Not like this was her biggest problem right now, but because she had brushed her teeth with her finger that morning, she tried speaking without really moving her lips. "I was *gonna* join the police," she said. "I tried, but I got flunked on the drug test, so . . ."

The second old-timer, the one who'd

laughed at her earlier, laughed again, a caustic bark that seemed to jolt Jimmy. At least widen his eyes. Yank him away from the recovering drug addict's natural habitat — the Garden of Nostalgia — and plop him down into his gray-and-white sneakers, on this cold panel of sidewalk outside the clinic. For the first time he seemed to notice all the happy staring faces.

"Oh," he said.

"You know, I really wish we could catch up," she said, speaking into her cupped palm. "But I got an appointment. My mom. I gotta take her to the doctor."

"I'm so sorry," he said. "You know what? I think Marwan? Yeah, I think Marwan told me you, like, applied. Years ago. And I guess I just assumed. I'm sorry. About your test."

"I'll see you around, okay?"

She felt fairly certain that of her two parents he had met only her father, and only that one disastrous time, but as a way of saying good-bye he asked Janice to say hello to her mother for him. He hoped the appointment wasn't anything too serious. And again, he was sorry. Super sorry. He jay-walked across the street and got into the idling Volvo with the bearded black man who apparently was his brother. Janice put her head down. While the Gellars drove east, toward the darkly malignant snow clouds, she went the other way, headed for the Impala around the corner on Jamaica Avenue, leaving her meth clinic spectators without a word of farewell. The second old-timer, the laughing man, had already snapped her picture with his cell phone camera.

"I wouldn't worry about it," Puffy said on the drive back to the rumpus. He was eating her bialy because she didn't have the appetite. "These sorts of things happen."

"It's not your fault," Richie told her. "You shouldn't be sent out to make buys in your own neighborhood."

"Totally," Puffy said.

"They'll probably post your picture on the Internet," Gonz told her. "On some cop-killing site. That'd be my guess, at least."

"Not funny," Tevis said.

"Oh, I'm not trying to be funny."

Later that afternoon, when she came home from work — from two days of work — her mother attacked her. Janice had just walked through the back door into the kitchen, where the microwave was heating up what smelled like leftover goat pepper pot. Power-drained, the ceiling's fluorescents burned at half strength. Tap water

125

rushed into an electric kettle. The radio blasted the day's news: Hillary Clinton had won the Texas presidential primary, surprising the pundits. And with an open palm Vita hit Janice in the mouth. Then caught her again, flush on the ear, the blows surprising Janice more than they hurt her. Vita fought too spastically, with flailing noodle arms, to inflict any actual damage, but still something seemed to come loose in Janice's chest. Nothing like this had ever happened to them before. When Janice grabbed her by the wrists, Vita stopped fighting and started crying and Janice did, too. They pressed their fingertips beneath each other's eyes, an old ritual, to trap the tears between the lashes, but it didn't work. It never worked. Dark reddish brown henna stained Vita's hairline. Her hands, of course, smelled like the lavender lotion she reapplied as often as her lipstick, which was bright red even though she probably hadn't left the house in days. Janice worried that her mother — who started everything early: marriage, pregnancy, dementia, dinner prep — had deteriorated to the point where she had mistaken her for an intruder.

"You didn't call," Vita said. "You always call. Always. Two *days,* Janny. I thought you were dead."

"Oh my God, I'm so, so sorry," Janice said, painfully relieved. "We had to work a double. My phone died. I didn't even . . . I got distracted. I'm so sorry."

"You always call."

"I'm sorry, Mama."

"Ding," said the microwave, and the kitchen lights brightened.

As if embarrassed by the slapping, the crying, the sincerity of her daughter's apology, Vita went to go turn off the tap, while an equally embarrassed Janice locked the back door just to have something to do. And of course to keep out the ghosts. They couldn't enter a house through a closed door, not even through a keyhole or under a crack. For a little extra insurance, Vita permanently kept on the back porch a pair of Brother Itwaru's old boots, their laces triple-knotted and slimy with rainwater, their soles, like Brother's own, completely corroded. She knew that ghosts — by design, naturally peripatetic — couldn't resist a pair of broken-in shoes. She also knew they'd spend all night trying to put the boots on, in vain, never quite able to do so because ghosts, or at least stupid West Indian ghosts, didn't have any feet. Janice wasn't sure how much of this her mother actually believed. Janice wasn't sure how much of this she believed herself. It was a game. Like calling Eddie Murphy Eddie Murphy. Like answering the phone when she was seven with "Analytic Systems, how can I direct your call," because her father had told her he'd started a fake company so he could declare bankruptcy on it and collect relief money from the government. Was he serious? Was Eddie Murphy? Perhaps alone among cops, Janice and her fellow uncles felt comfortable not knowing. The man on the radio reported that after Texas some of the experts who'd doubted Hillary thought she now had a chance.

"I'm sorry I hit you," Vita said without turning around from the sink. "That's unacceptable. It's insane. I'm going insane."

"You're not insane," said Janice, who had no place to sit because there were stacks of mail on all the chairs, and no place to set her purse because lipstick-stained water glasses covered the countertops. "I should've called."

"Yeah, but now I'm worried maybe you did call." For what might've been the thousandth time in the last two days, she looked at the whiteboard on the wall, which said, *pick up detergent* and *think positive*, both in Janice's hand. "And maybe I forgot to write it down. And now you're telling me you didn't call because you're trying to be nice, blowing smoke, and I can't tell *which* way is up."

"Since when have I been nice?"

After showering, Janice came back downstairs to eat an early dinner with her mother. They moved mail stacks off chairs so the two of them could sit at the kitchen table. They talked about pepper pot always tasting better the next day. They talked about the basil Vita wanted to grow in the front yard. That their neighbor Mr. Hua hadn't done anything crazy in a while. That this movie star was now dating that movie star. Eventually, inevitably, they got to the weather. Their spoons clanged their bowls. All their rhythms seemed off. Usually Vita had gone to bed by the time Janice came home and Janice would eat a toasted waffle over the sink, unplug the teakettle, put away as many lipstick-stained water glasses as she could find, write an *I'm alive!* note on the whiteboard, turn off the porch and kitchen lights that were always left on for her, and walk past her mother's door loud enough for Vita to say *Janny?* and Janice to say *Ma?* and that was their night. Now they had hours to kill. After dinner, Janice threw her clothes in the washing machine. Vita —

who'd spent last night with the cordless next to her bed, and this morning calling hospitals and listening to 1010/WINS for news of a dead undercover — took a nap on the couch.

But she woke up in plenty of time for *Wheel of Fortune.* Janice sat next to her on the couch with their shoulders touching while Pat Sajak did his heroic best to conceal his boredom. Like Bananagrams, oily fish, pumpkin seeds, and folic acid, television game shows were supposed to fortify Vita's brain, and so Janice was forbidden to solve any of the puzzles out loud or make sarcastic comments about Vanna's plunge line or really say anything at all until the commercials, when Vita muted the television with the remote, which lately she'd been calling the picture-stick. At the first commercial break they debated whether the middle contestant came across as cocky. (He totally did.) At the second break, Janice asked her if she wanted to go to the Salvation Army that weekend to pick out crackhead clothes.

"By the way," Vita said. "I talked to your sister earlier. Supposedly" — because anything Judith-related needed to be spoken of conditionally — "she's coming to visit tomorrow."

"Tomorrow?"

"That's what she said."

"Seriously? And you're just telling me this now?"

Her red shining lipstick cracked when she smiled. "Oh, I'm sorry," she said. "I guess I got . . . what's the word? *Distracted.* I guess I got distracted."

Janice knew that Judith's cell phone would ring the instant she walked through the back door. Her ex-boyfriends and ex-girlfriends, her former coworkers at White Castle, the friends she used to tag lampposts with, the overpierced sixty-year-old she'd met at the Shambhala Meditation Center, they would call her one after the other, as if they could smell her organic perfume — was there such a thing? — floating in the air above Queens. And then she'd be gone. Carved into skinny wedges and doled out. K.I.T. See you next Christmas.

"How long is she staying?" Janice asked.

Less sad than bewildered, Vita explained that supposedly Judith could get enough time off only for the weekend — she sold soap at an alternative supermarket in Scranton, Pennsylvania — and supposedly she intended to split her visit between the parents. Vita's phrasing, which must've been Judith's phrasing: *the parents.* From when she'd get in late Thursday night to mid-morning on Saturday, she'd stay in Richmond Hill. After that — and this was unprecedented — she'd take the LIRR out to her father's house, where he was supposedly throwing himself a fiftieth-birthday bash, even though everyone in his first life knew he was really turning fifty-one. *Wheel of Fortune* came back on before Janice could ask how Judith had even heard about the party. It was possible, she guessed, that they sometimes talked on the phone. Or were maybe Facebook friends. The cocky middle contestant, who'd reached the bonus round, received gratis five consonants and one vowel, but they didn't help him any because of course the game was rigged. Against protocol, Janice announced that she'd solved the puzzle, even though she hadn't yet figured out the final word. Add it to her list of lies. Her mother told her to shush.

Later, unable to sleep, Janice looked through the stacks of mail in the kitchen for an invitation to her father's birthday. She didn't find it — she would've torn it up anyway — but she did find a slim Amazon package with *Sway: The Art of Gentle Persuasion.* She also found February's mortgage bill. And the Con Ed and Time Warner bills. AmEx, Visa, and neurologist bills. The

March of Dimes sent her an actual dime, which they asked her to send back to them along with a donation. It was effectively guilt-making, but not so guilt-making that it made her reach for her checkbook. Instead she took the dime — and the two pennies the universe had gifted her earlier — up to her bedroom to toss the *I Ching.* Forget about Nostradamus. Forget about Miss Cleo, Mayan calendars, tarot cards, palm-readers, and psychics who advertise their services on pay phone stickers. From the recesses of Janice's closet she pulled out her only patrimony, her father's beat-up copy of the *I Ching,* its pages fattened by long-ago drained bathwater. Duct tape kept the spine intact. With its cover missing, the first page was a blank page, stained the color of tea. Unable to provide a generalized vision of her future, the book instead needed her to ask a particular question, the more specific the better. Will I make three more buys before the end of the month? She tossed the coins onto her bedspread six times in a row. The ratio of heads to tails corresponded to either a broken Yin line (— —) or an unbroken Yang (————). Theoretically she should've used only pennies, the humblest of all coins, but whatever, nobody was watching. Her coin tosses made a hexagram that looked like this:

☷☲

Which the *I Ching* said meant this:

Here the sun has sunk under the earth and is therefore darkened. The name of the hexagram means literally "wounding of the bright"; hence the individual lines contain frequent references to wounding. The situation is the exact opposite of that in the foregoing hexagram. In the latter a wise man at the head of affairs has able helpers, and in company with them makes progress; here a man of dark nature is in a position of authority and brings harm to the wise and able man.

**THE JUDGMENT**
DARKENING OF THE LIGHT. In adversity, it furthers one to be persevering.

Which made Janice wish she had asked a Magic 8 Ball. *Reply hazy, try again,* she at least could've understood. In its defense, the *I Ching* always rolled ambiguous, with a DIY-approach to fortune-telling, but this wounding of the bright business seemed particularly coy. She didn't know if she was the man of dark nature or the wise and able man or both or neither. And she didn't know if persevere meant she should sit around doing nothing, waiting for the three buys to come to her. Yeah right. Fat chance. She tossed the book onto the floor, swept the coins off her bedspread.

The next day at work Janice sat around and did nothing. Not her fault. She couldn't make any buys because her team didn't go out to make buys. It was a rumpus day. So she could read at her desk without the Big Bosses knowing, she photocopied chapters out of *Sway: The Art of Gentle Persuasion.* From the back of the lounge, she watched the *Rubí* finale, a humdinger of an episode in which the recently scarred heroine mentors her niece in the wicked ways of seduction. Afterward, Richie the Receptionist, who hadn't even seen the show, but perhaps looking for a mentor of his own, solicited the uncles' advice on how to finagle a threesome between himself, his girlfriend who worked in Payroll, and his girlfriend's lesbian roommate. Janice's sarcastic suggestion: alcohol. Richie thanked her without apparent irony, but again: you can never tell with these guys. At shift's end, Sergeant Hart told the team to report back to the rumpus in a whopping eleven hours. Tevis muttered on over to A.R.'s Tavern for the Thursday Amstel Light Special, but Janice sped home, giddy to see her sister despite Judith's historical tendency to bruise her feelings. Janice parked in the garage. As she hurried down the alleyway, she looked for Judith's size-six footprints in the pavement's alien-fruit splatters. She didn't find any tracks, but it was sort of hard to see anything. For the first time since Janice had become a cop, Vita had neglected to leave the porch and kitchen lights burning for her after a late shift. Darkness pressed its sad face against all the windows. Everyone was asleep. Of course everyone was asleep. It was almost one thirty in the morning. Janice wanted to accidentally ring the doorbell — whoops! — and accidentally wake up the house, but when she came into the kitchen she heard Indian music already thundering out of the living room. Sitars and drums, outrageously loud. And correction: there was one light still burning, the refrigerator's, its motor groaning with disbelief, its door

136

left open for God knows how long. She closed it, quietly moving through her own kitchen like a burglar. She wanted to make a grand entrance into the living room and see her sister's surprised face at the instant of recognition, before they both armed themselves with how's work, how was the bus ride, so nice to see you, you look great. Although Janice could have probably banged some pots together out here and still not be heard. Actually, maybe she should make some noise, just in case a strange man or woman or both had their icy hands on Judith's big boobs.

"Hello?" Janice said.

The music stopped, and their mother, who should've been asleep, said, "Uh-oh."

Alone, just the two of them, they sat next to each other on the couch, Vita in an unfamiliar gray T-shirt that said DUNDER-MIFFLIN across the chest, a reference to a Scranton-based television show that she had most likely never seen before. Tonight it was *their* shoulders touching. Lazy, relaxed, neither one of them standing up to greet her, they had their legs propped up on a coffee table that was even more cluttered than usual, with Vita's lipstick-stained water glasses, of course, but also a pair of St. John's alumni mugs, a perfect apple core tipped over onto its side, and a laptop, presumably Judith's, presumably the source of all that sitar-and-drums Indian music. The computer cast enough of a glow for Janice to see their faces, but she flicked on the overhead light anyway. She expected them to squint against the glare, or raise their arms across their eyes like creatures from the lagoon, but they giggled instead.

Even though Judith was nineteen months older than Janice, people frequently mistook them for twins, especially when they were kids and sharing a secret language. Until she was three years old — and this seemed almost impossible to imagine now — Janice refused to speak except in babbling asides to her sister, who then translated on her behalf. What had happened to them? Now Janice left her ace voice mails that went unreturned. They still looked alike, though, still had the same gray eyes that turned brown at night, the same plump mouth that reposed itself most comfortably in a smirk. But despite her employee discount on organic beauty products, Judith had much worse skin, with pimples pitting her jawline from the constant friction of a cell phone. And having always had the bigger boobs and butt, she seemed to have lost all the weight that Janice had gained since joining Narcotics. Plus some. Judith looked skinny as a bird, with bones apparently just as hollow, because when she at last stood up for a proper greeting she crumpled to the floor.

"Oh my God," she said, laughing. "My fucking legs fell asleep."

Janice rushed to help her. Judith kept protesting, kept saying, *I'm fine, really, I'm fine,* but even after she'd been seated back on the couch she kept a grip on Janice's hand. The nails were an abomination, her annual New Year's resolution unresolved so Judith gave her a mini-manicure, pushing down all the cuticles. It stung terribly, even drew small trembles of blood, but Janice let her big sister go through every finger.

"Am I hurting you?" Judith said.

"No," Janice lied.

For her own secret reasons, Vita started laughing. She scooted down the couch, up against the armrest, to watch both her girls at once.

"You should get a proper one of these," Judith said. "From a real-life Asian lady."

"We can go tomorrow morning," Janice said.

Judith reached for the other hand. "A friend of mine wears a hair tie around her wrist," she said. "Like a rubber band? And she snaps it whenever she feels like biting her nails."

"I usually don't even know when I'm doing it."

That Janice stood over them, still wearing her heavy coat, made her seem, she knew, like a fresh-off-the-boat immigrant in the insular land of Good Times. So had flicking on the overhead. So did reaching now for an alumni mug to sniff its contents. Given Vita's alcohol prejudices — forged in the coal-black smithy of an eighteen-year marriage to an abusive drunk — Janice felt sure they weren't actually drinking, but she wanted some way to acknowledge their cozy late-night goofiness in the hopes that they'd order her to change into pajamas and come join them on the couch's middle cushion. Unfortunately, as she quickly realized, her mug-sniffing came across as schoolmarmish and disapproving, the exact opposite of her intentions. With all the cuticles pushed back into the skin, Judith let go of Janice's hand. On the laptop screen a shirtless Indian man on pause looked ready to take a bite out of a fluorescent light tube.

"What are you guys watching?"

"Only the craziest video ever," Judith told her.

"It's apparently a religious thing," Vita said, and this time they both giggled.

Janice closed her eyes now that she understood. She should've sniffed the air above their heads, not the tea and honey in their mugs. "Really?" she asked Judith. "In the house?"

"What?" Judith said.

"I can *smell* it, okay?" Not true: the living room smelled only of living room, but that didn't mean anything. Pot smoke would've dissipated quickly. "In the fucking house, Judith? With *Mom*?"

"First of all?" Judith said. "Hypothetically? I'm pretty sure Mom's a grown-up who can do whatever she wants."

"Girls," Vita said.

"It's really great for your memory," Janice told her.

"Second of all," Judith said, "it's not like it's in your face or anything."

"You understand what I do for a living, right? That I lock people up for smoking weed?"

"That's totally fascist," Judith said.

"What's totally fascist? Having a real job?"

From walking through the back door to now: two minutes, maybe three. It wasn't even a new record. Still sitting, Judith tried to kick her, but Janice, too fast and too sober, caught her pins-and-needled foot and — in hindsight this was where she might have done things differently — yanked her off the couch. That newly bony ass of Judith's struck the ground hard. Her head snapped back. She kicked out again, missing Janice but hitting the coffee table. The apple core — oh duh, the apple core, their improvised pipe — rolled to the edge without falling.

"Girls!" Vita said.

"Where's *my* Dunder-Mifflin shirt?" Janice asked, standing over her sister.

"I got you a mouse pad!" Judith shouted. "For your fascist desk at your fascist job!"

Janice's fingers curled on their own, smearing the bloody trembles across her palms. On her way up the stairs to her bedroom, where she intended to slam the door behind her and stick her head under every one of her pillows, she said, "It's a stupid-ass show anyway," by which she meant: I'm sorry, I'm a bitch, I miss you, but *come on.*

"You're a stupid-ass show!" Judith said.

*"Girls!!"*

# CHAPTER FIVE

From behind his desk at the rumpus, Tevis said, "Sure, I've been called a fascist. You kidding? I mean, you do this job long enough, you'll be called everything under the sun. What you gotta do? You gotta *acknowledge* their arguments. You have to. Should we be *treating* addiction? Well, yeah, of course, someone should be, not us specifically, but someone, yeah. Are we doing more harm than good? Are we busting Colombian cartels so they can be replaced by Mexican cartels so they can be replaced by U.S. cartels once all this kerfuffle goes legal? These are important questions, Itwaru. But they're also very abstract, you know what I mean? And what we do on a day-to-day basis, that's the opposite of abstract. So someone calls me a fascist, okay, fine, I'm going to acknowledge that argument, I'm going to take it all in, but when it's my turn on the high horse I'm go-

143

ing to tell them about George Scheu. That name familiar to you at all? Have I told you this story already?

"He was a cop. One day — this is back in 1987 — he gets up at six thirty in the morning to go to a Naval Reserves meeting out in Nassau. It's his day off, mind you. Think about that. It's six thirty in the morning and this guy leaves his wife and kids at home to go to a *meeting.* That's who he was. Vietnam War vet. Medal of Honor recipient. Fourteen commendations with the department. He worked the One Fifteen in Jackson Heights, where they still got his picture up on the wall. You probably seen it. White guy? Super skinny? Anyway, he's walking to his car in his pressed navy uniform when he sees some bottom-feeder trying to break into a Mercedes. Guy's not even trying to steal it. He just wants the radio. Now, Scheu is unarmed. I don't know why. He's off duty. It was a different time, I guess. I don't know. Maybe he didn't like wearing the gun with his navy clothes, but he sees the guy breaking into the Mercedes and he decides to intervene.

"A neighbor ends up finding him. A woman out walking her dog. She sees Scheu on the sidewalk — this happened right around here, by the way. Flushing. This neighbor lady sees Scheu on the sidewalk, bleeding out of his eye, and she flags down an ambulance that happens to be passing by. That's the only break he gets, that ambulance, and it's not even really a break because he ends up dying anyway. On the ground, near the body, there's a thirty-eight-caliber pen gun, which is exactly what it sounds like. Looks like a pen, bullet comes out the top. You get one shot, and this bottom-feeder hits him dead in the eye. You give him that shot a thousand times and he couldn't do that again. But that's how it is. The guy drops the weapon, goes through Scheu's pockets — we find the wallet, empty, in the street — and just like that he disappears.

"The guy we like for it is this lowlife named Henry Vega. I keep saying we. I'm not even with the police yet. It's 1987? Summer? I'm in Ceylon with the Merchant Marines, but that's a whole other story.

"So they bring in Vega and they know he did it, but they can't get enough on him to bring him to trial. Twelve years later. *Twelve years*. George Scheu's three kids that he left behind? Twelve years older. His widow, twelve years older. And Henry Vega's still walking around. Now, what we're talking about is the second-longest quote-end-

145

quote unsolved cop killing in New York City history. But see, we never stop. I never even met George Scheu. Like I said, I wasn't with the police then, but to this day I'm still praying for his soul. One of many. And what are you thinking? You're thinking we got Vega after all these years on DNA. But it doesn't happen like that. What you gotta understand, a guy like Vega, he's a fish. And how does a fish get caught? He opens his mouth.

"We pick up somebody for drugs. The investigators say, 'You're going away for a million years. What have you got to barter with?' He says, 'I know who killed that cop out in Flushing. The one who got shot in the eye.' He tells them he was living out there at the time, right on the block where it happened. He says his friend was visiting him that day and ended up killing the cop. And this friend of his is a guy named Henry Vega.

"Now what do you do? Put this guy, this lowlife drug addict, in a witness box, have him tell a jury that he's pretty sure his friend murdered a cop twelve years ago? Course not. What you want, you want Vega saying it. 'I, Henry Vega, shot the man George Scheu, and this is how I did it.' But what, he's just going to tell us that? Yeah. Exactly.

146

That's exactly what he's going to do.

"I complain about the kel-mics never working. I complain because I know what this department is capable of. I understand we've got to pursue cop-killers with one hundred percent of our resources, absolutely, because George Scheu? His unavenged ghost? That should haunt the One Fifteen. That should haunt all of us. But a hundred percent of our resources should also go into keeping us as safe as humanly possible, to avoid these kinds of catastrophes in the future. So let's get some working kelmics, know what I mean? That's another story maybe, but it's also very much this story, too.

"We go to this two room storefront on Booth Memorial Avenue and we tell the owner we want to rent the place out now and again for like a day at a time. I don't know who found the place, but it's perfect. It's so far from where Vega's living at the time that he'd have to take two trains and a bus just to get there on his own. And he can't drive himself because he's an f-up with a suspended license.

"We put up a sign out front that says 'Charlie's Barbershop.' I don't know who thought of that, either, but it's such a nice touch because no one's gonna pass a place

147

like that and be like, 'Oh, I think I maybe need a haircut.' Because you got your usual barber and if you go anywhere else it's like cheating, you know? And we didn't even have any barber chairs anyway. So it was a lie that this place was a barbershop, but it was supposed to be a lie and Vega was supposed to know it was a lie so he'd think he was in on the joke when in reality the big lie, the real lie, was getting ready to gobble him up.

"We bring in card tables and chairs. We bring in *boxes* of liquor. Snack mix. We got those nice red candles you see at Italian restaurants. The candles aren't red, but the glass shell is. You know the kind I'm talking about? A candle on every table — and beneath every candle, a listening device. We got the camera buttons. And we fill the place with every Italian-looking undercover in the city. There were more Caucasians back then before . . . well, there were just more. But we don't have enough, so we have to throw some Puerto Ricans in there, too, but that's okay because they've already got the crosses and the gel in their hair, it's not a problem. We fill the place up with these guys and turn the place into a frickin' Scorsese movie. Charlie's Barbershop: wiseguy social club.

"And Vega's friend? Who we've got on the hook now? He goes to Vega and he says, 'I'm swooping by to pick you up. There's this place I wanna show you, you're gonna love it.'

"And what happens? He loves it. What you have to understand about guys like Vega is that he's watching *Goodfellas,* too. He's watching *The Godfather,* he's watching *The Sopranos,* like how we're all in the lounge watching *The French Connection,* or at least we used to before *Rubí* got started. And this guy, this lowlife radio-booster, what's his ambition? The nice suits. Okay? The free spaghetti dinners. His ambition is to get his foot into the clubhouse, and now here he is. The glass out front of Charlie's Barbershop is the smoky kind you can't really see through and the door is locked from the inside, but now it's opening for him and his friend, and Vega's looking around, he's balder than he was in '87, and he's got the beard bald guys have to make up for it, and he's thinking, 'My goodness, this place is like a *movie.*'

"That's because it is a movie, Henry. Me and this other black uncle are under the floor, under a trapdoor in this little room that's used for storage. And we're watching all this on the CCTVs we got set up down there, making sure everything's coming in okay, and there's just sweat pouring off us. We see Vega pressing his hands flat against the card table, like he isn't certain the place is real. He's looking around trying not to look around. He's buzzing, man.

"Eventually, after a nice long while, Charlie comes over with drinks. Charlie of Charlie's Barbershop. Not his real name. Now, let me tell you something: this is the greatest uncle in the history of the department. The best ever. And I know what I'm saying when I tell you that. Not to toot my own horn. And not to blow up your head, but if you continue to work hard and if you cool it on the unnecessary risks, then you have an opportunity to be right up at his level.

"So Charlie comes over with the drinks for introductions. 'Who's your friend?' 'This is that guy Henry I was telling you about.' And Vega goes, 'Call me Mr. Clean.'

"Now, that's not any of the known aliases we got on this guy. Dollars to donuts? It's a nickname he made up on the spot. Me and the brother under the trapdoor, we look at each other and now we *know* we got him. Mr. Clean? You kidding?

"Still, though, it takes five months, January to May. The friend will call us, tell us

Vega wants to come by the set, we tell him Tuesday, then go down there and set everything up. Every time he's there he's getting a little more comfortable. He's not testing the tables anymore to see if they disappear. The other guys? They're starting to pay attention to him, busting his balls a little and he's busting them back. When he leaves it's understood he can only come back with his buddy. But he doesn't want to have to come with his buddy anymore. He wants the door to open for Mr. Clean and Mr. Clean alone. So now he's gotta show these mafia guys that he's down, right? He's one of them, a good guy to have around. He tells Charlie he's got a cousin with the Bronx District Attorney's office. He can get his hands on the NYPD's secret radio frequencies for undercover operations. 'That way,' Vega says, 'you'd be able to tell if anyone in your club is a rat.' We look into it and find out he doesn't have any cousin working with the DA, but the next time Vega comes around he's got a list of random-frequency numbers that had nothing to do with anything. We loved that. But we're like: is he such a moron, he's not worried Charlie might test the numbers? Because then what, right? What's Vega gonna do? Just shrug his shoulders and say the numbers must've gotten changed or something?

"Who the heck knows? Guys like Vega, they're so f-ing stupid, you'd drive yourself crazy trying to rationalize the crap that comes out of their mouth. Charlie, meanwhile, he gets these frequency numbers and says, 'Okay, Mr. Clean. What else you got?' Vega comes back with some coke, sells it to Charlie. 'Okay, Mr. Clean. What else you got? Drugs? I can go down to I.S. Two Fifty, get coke off an eighth-grader. What else, what else?' So Vega's looking around at all these smiling wiseguys and he knows they're thinking he's small-time, he's nobody, but see what they don't know is that he's secretly the baddest of the bad. What else has he got? He's got a story.

"Now, this is why Charlie was the best ever. The department has since betrayed him, but that's something else for another time and it doesn't change the fact that he was the very best I've ever seen. He starts a fight with one of the other uncles in the room. It gets physical pretty quick, and Charlie ends up tossing the guy out of there. Then he sits back down at Vega's table, breathing heavy, annoyed, and he says if he could get rid of that guy he would, the implication being that if the guy wasn't a made man he'd take him out in a second.

" 'I'll do it for you,' Vega says. 'You ever need a piece of work done just ask for Mr. Clean. I'll take care of it.'

"Now, I'm watching all this down on the closed-circuit TVs. I can't see Charlie's reaction. I don't know if he's making like a skeptical face or if Vega just can't stop talking now that he's opened his mouth, but he turns to his friend and says, 'In the summer of '87, what happened on your block?'

"You never know what you're gonna get with these CIs. They're professional hustlers. They hustle their friends, their family. They think they're hustling us. They're addicts, everything that comes out of their mouth is either smoke or a lie. But that doesn't mean they're going to be good at *this,* right? We can coach them up, but what's coaching? I know you get mad that I don't give you more direction, but seriously, how do you teach this? You see new uncles come in here, they've got their month of Narco training, and they're completely clueless once they hit the street. You've got actors, professionals . . . and don't get me wrong, I'm not talking about Eddie here, he's a genius . . . but you see some of these doofs on TV and they're terrible, right? *Completely* unconvincing. Professional actors. With do-overs. Multiple takes and blanks in the guns. And that's with someone telling them what to *say*.

"But sometimes? Sometimes you find a CI who just gets it and it's like a gift from God. 'What happened on your block?' Vega asked the guy, and the guy says, 'A cop got killed.'

" 'Who does that belong to?' Vega says. 'That everyone pointed a finger to?'

" 'Scheu?' the CI says, and the brother under the trapdoor with me is, like, tapping my arm with his fist because that's exactly what the CI needed to say. It's five months we've been doing this. And the CI is talking to Vega now but everything he says also needs to be directed toward an eventual grand jury, too. And he's magic, he's flying, and it's because he's a gift from God, I really believe that, but it's also because Charlie made him better by being so very exceptional himself, by setting the bar so high like how Jordan did with Pippen. 'Scheu?' our guy says, and Vega says, 'Yeah. Who's everyone point to on that?' And the CI says, 'You.'

" 'You want a body?' Vega says.

"He starts telling Charlie how all he wanted was the radio, but this cop Scheu intervenes and the problem is they know each other from around the neighborhood.

154

What's Vega supposed to do? He can't run away. He's been recognized. As he's telling the story, he starts laughing, excited because the whole place is smiling at him now. And if he thinks they're hanging on to his every word, he's right. He stands up from the table and raises his arm like his finger is a pistol. 'Poof,' he says. 'Poof.' Then he gets down on the floor. Seriously. The guy's acting out all the roles because he needs to show everybody how he left Scheu bleeding out on that sidewalk. Then he stands up and hails himself an imaginary cab, and that's when we find out how he got away. A cab just happened to be passing by, just like that ambulance minutes later. Did the cabbie say anything to Vega? I don't know. We never found him. But Vega did say he paid the fare with money out of Scheu's wallet.

"Charlie stands up and he puts his arms around Vega and gives him a big Italian kiss on the cheek. Down under the ground we can see Vega picture-perfect on the television screen. His face, man. His face is electric with delight.

" 'I'm a natural,' he says. 'I know I did good.'

"Two years later, almost to the day, a Queens jury finds him not guilty. Even with the videotaped confession. Even with another confession at the precinct, after he'd been arrested and *knew* he was being recorded. His attorney argued that he was just bragging, making stuff up to impress his new friends. And the jury buys it, I guess. Reasonable doubt. A reporter overheard the judge, as he's leaving the bench, say, 'I'm very surprised.' No kidding, the judge is very surprised.

"I don't know where the ghost of George Scheu is with all this, but I do know where Henry Vega's at. He's serving a ninety-seven-year sentence for selling that coke to the uncles in the barbershop. You seen *The Untouchables*? Remember how they busted Capone at the end? Tax evasion? Failure to report? And maybe if I was good at math I'd be working for the IRS and then the only people calling me fascist would be the libertarians, but I ain't good at math. For me it's this and only this."

Saturday morning, on the drive out to their father's house in Great Neck, Judith expressed her doubts. How did the cops know Vega wouldn't make an unexpected trip to the barbershop on his own? Sure, he had a suspended license, but lots of people drove with a suspended license, especially guys like Vega. (As if Judith was an expert on guys like Vega; actually, on second thought, maybe she was.) And okay, a bus ride from his place to Flushing took over an hour, requiring more than a couple of transfers, but if he was soooo into this wiseguy social club, then surely he might make the time one day to schlep out there, just to look through the windows — and then what happens? He'd see it was just a regular storefront, without any red candles on the tables.

"Arc you saying it's not a true story?" Janice asked.

"No, no, no, no," Judith said, because that was exactly what she'd been saying. "I just mean, it was sort of a risky plan, that's all."

"Well, it's sort of a risky job."

The sun, after making only cameo appearances throughout the week, had at last asserted itself and forced Janice to drive with her visor down. To the east an enormous glass office building quivered with light. It stood tall over the Jackie Robinson Parkway, which would take them to the Grand Central Parkway, which would take them to Long Island, or so claimed Janice's GPS, its sense of direction much stronger than her own, especially beyond the city limits. When she'd agreed to drive Judith to Great Neck, Janice made it clear that she'd just be dropping her off in their father's pebbled cul-de-sac. But since when did Judith give a shit about what Janice wanted? Before the trip had even started, before she had even buckled her seat belt, Judith began pestering her to pop into the house for at least a second when they got there, if only to wish him a happy birthday. Foolishly, in an attempt to change the subject, Janice had told her a work story.

"Not to mention," Judith said, "all the people who aren't cop-killers, right? Who get thrown in prison just for smoking a joint."

*Jail,* Janice could've corrected. Not prison. And usually, depending on the neighborhood, joint-tokers just got a desk ticket, nothing worse. But so that Judith could score an easy point and luxuriate in her feelings of superiority, Janice told her, "Well, with weed, they only spend the one night in lockup. And with the backlog, most of the time the charges will just get thrown out, so . . ."

And on cue, Judith said, "Then why arrest them in the first place?"

Janice arranged her face into its most chastened expression. She'd spent these last twenty-four hours intentionally stepping on rakes, trying to make amends after boss-hogging Judith off the couch, and at last puncturing any illusion that the two of them operated according to the normal big/little sister hierarchy. And they never really had, or at least not since grammar school. As teenagers it was Janice who had the complicated highlighter system to study for tests, Janice who had flabber-gasted the family the one time she'd been truly bad, sneaking Jimmy Gellar into the house, and now as grown-ups it was Janice who paid her own cell phone bill, invested in a 401(k), and stayed home to take care of their mother. The flipped scripts — and their official exposure the other night — embarrassed the both of them. In the shower, lying in bed, waiting for the single-cup coffeemaker at the rumpus, in the car at this very moment, Janice caught shame shivers as she imagined looking up at herself from her big sister's body, sprawled across the carpet. And so ever since then she'd been aggressively playing the little-sister role, which is to say she tried to seem as if she idolized Judith while simultaneously taking her for granted. She asked to borrow clothes, bangles, shoes, and a legitimately gorgeous studded black purse that looked like a Victorian doctor's medical bag. She took her advice about wearing a hair tie around her wrist. She took her side in an argument with Vita about hip-hop. When the three of them went out to breakfast this morning, she ate half of one of Judith's pancakes without asking. She let Judith bully her into this car ride. And after the George Scheu story, with a younger sibling's limitless capacity for deference, she ate a bucket load of shit all the way to Long Island, listening to a series of lectures on corporate prisons, Rockefeller laws, New York's fundamentally racist police department, the misappropriation of taxpayer funds, a right-wing conspiracy to reframe the debate by nonsensically coupling words like *war* with words like *drugs,* and a few other rants Judith had most likely lifted out of *Mother Jones.*

Janice's tires kicked up pebbles pulling into the cul-de-sac outside their father's house. It was a three-story colonial with two separate chimneys and more than a dozen windows with expensive wooden siding. A Christmas wreath hung on the front door, months past the expiration date. Above it an American flag, bigger than the one outside the Archer Avenue post office, snapped with the wind. When she'd first got her license, she would drive out here sometimes, just to look at the place, but hadn't been back in many years. The attached garage looked wider than she remembered, the upper-floor additions more tumorous.

"You coming in?" Judith asked. "Just for a minute?"

Janice, who hadn't even put the car in park, said, "I gotta get to work."

"Come on. You wouldn't have come all the way out here unless you secretly sorta wanted to see him."

She saw him now, scurrying out of the house with such eagerness that when he'd flung open the door he knocked off its Christmas wreath. He was an Afro-Guyanese to Vita's Indo, a source of great disappointment to Janice's maternal grandmother, who had famously objected to their wedding on the grounds that he was as black as a frying pan. Which should've been the least of Ajee's worries. Janice hadn't seen him in, oh wow, nine years, but he was wearing almost exactly what he would've been wearing back then: a white tracksuit with red piping, penny loafers without socks. He even had all his hair, although its uniformly brown coloring most likely came out of a box now. From cowlick to loafers he looked heartbreakingly the same, except around his waist, where contentment had settled like a tire. He had exchanged Vita for a white woman who surely couldn't cook, Richmond Hill for Long Island — and according to Judith, alcohol for marathon running — and still he'd managed to somehow gain weight.

"Girls!" he said.

Judith stepped out of the car to be absorbed. He machine-gun kissed her cheeks, touched her hair, framed her face in hands calloused from untwisting millions of radiator caps. *My girls, my girls,* he kept saying. He came around to Janice's side and pulled open the door. When he reached into the car she thought he might try to unbuckle her seat belt for her, but really he just wanted to squeeze her shoulder. Her chin turned to cottage cheese. Back at the house, the white woman, Barbara, stood in the open doorway twisting a dish towel, as if to imply that she was more than happy to suspend some super-important kitchen business, the baking of a tasteless soufflé perhaps, in order to witness this Very Special Family Reunion.

"Let me look at you," he said. Always an easy crier, he wept openly without bothering to wipe away the tears. "Oh, honey. My God. You're beautiful, beautiful."

"Hi." She felt she had a kel-mic taped to her chest, tuned to her mother's secret frequency back at home. "Are you having a nice birthday?"

His hand moved up from her shoulder to lightly touch the rubbery flesh of her ear-lobe. "Look at you," he said. "Can you stay?"

Over the roof of the car, Judith said, "She has to go to work."

"Tomorrow, then," he told Janice. "For the party."

"I have to work tomorrow, too," she lied.

His tongue filled the lower fold of his lip, a habit of his when he was thinking especially hard. "I'll call all the criminals," he said. "Tell them to take the day off."

He probably knew enough of them, too, from his auto-body repair shop in Willets Point, one of the shadiest spots in all of Queens. Need an inspection sticker? A new license plate? Go see Brother Itwaru, but make sure you bring cash. He'd done well over the years, but not so well that he could have afforded this Long Island monstrosity, or at least not on his own. The real money — the money that trimmed the hedges and whitewashed the walls — belonged to Barbara, who was coming down the walkway with that dirty dish towel slung over her shoulder. She worked in cruise lines or something. Around her neck she wore — who cares? Who cares what she wore? She gave Judith a kiss and a surprisingly long

163

hug before opening the passenger's-side door to say hello to Janice.

"Hello," Janice said, snapping the rubber band around her wrist.

"She can't stay," he told Barbara. "She has to work. Today *and* tomorrow. Can you believe that? On the weekend?"

"You can come in for lunch at least," Barbara said. "Right? A quick lunch? I made more tuna macaroni than I know what to do with."

"I have to work," Janice said again as Judith reached into the backseat for Brother's birthday gift: another full-zip tracksuit, this one blue with orange piping, wrapped up in Vita's Christmas paper.

He said, "You guys know you didn't have to get me anything!"

"It's from Judith," Janice told him.

"What about for just a second?" Barbara asked her. "You have to have a second, right? Just so I can take a picture of you guys?" She dropped her voice to a dramatic whisper, as if the two of them were in some sort of conspiracy together. "I haven't bought your father a present yet," she said, "so you'd be doing me a big favor here."

Later, when telling the story to her mother over mugs of Sleepytime tea, Janice described the living room's high ceilings, the gaudy orchids in porcelain vases, the birthday streamers already taped to the walls, the weird harpoon-looking thing propped up against a fireplace that had probably never been used. Janice saved for last the framed eight-by-ten picture of her on the mantel. A relatively recent portrait, taken only two years earlier by the NYPD — *Don't smile!* the photographer had shouted — it showed her frowning, looking spooked, dressed in the dark blues of her old uniform. It was the picture newspapers would run if she ever got killed, the picture on her own mantel at home.

"How'd he get ahold of that?" Vita said.

"That's what I was going to ask you."

Janice first noticed the photo as Barbara was positioning the three of them in front of the fireplace. Brother stood in the middle with his arms across their shoulders, smelling like he'd always smelled, like sweat, popcorn, metal screws, and motor oil. When Janice was a kid, they used to watch *Columbo* and *Masterpiece Mystery* together, her head in his lap, and when he got up for another beer, or, later, when he got up for another Johnnie Red, she'd stick her face in his couch cushion. *Daddy, I think the killer left his teeth marks in that cheese. Daddy, I bet you* everybody *on the train is the murderer.* A camera flash split atoms of light across her vision. She lurched forward to get away, but Barbara apparently needed to snap another one because Brother had his eyes closed. Big smiles! Say cheese! The second flash re-dazed her. She tried to get away again, but now Barbara needed a real quick shot of the three of them jumping.

"All of a sudden she loves these jumping photos," Brother said.

"On three, okay?" Barbara said.

"I gotta get to work."

"I know, I know," Barbara said as she pulled the camera over her face. "It'll just take a sec."

On Barbara's two, Judith and Brother flexed their knees. On three, they floated up into the air away from Janice.

"Jan," Barbara said.

"I don't want to."

"Why not?" Judith said. The elastic waistband of her blouse had hiked up on her when she'd jumped; she pulled it down now, tucked it over her newly narrow hips and flat stomach. "You just refuse?" she said. "It's beneath you?"

Brother stood between them with his hands held up in front of his chest, as if to

166

show the living room his pale palms and absolve himself of any responsibility going forward or backward. His wife's camera, his daughters' dispute. Don't look at me. So Janice didn't. Instead she looked down at the ground and told the perfectly straight fringes on Barbara's Oriental carpet that she just really didn't feel like jumping.

"Then you don't have to," Brother said.

"Yes, she does," Judith said. "Yes, she does. You think she's just acting like a baby, but what she's really doing? She's bullying you. She picks on people's vulnerabilities because she can. If she sees them, she attacks them."

"Why're you looking at him?" Janice said. "You want to say these things, look at me when you say them."

"Okay, girls," Brother said.

"I hope you learn something from this," Judith told her. "Seriously. I hope you think about this and learn something."

"What should I learn, Judith?" she asked, smiling. "Tell me what I should learn from this."

"I don't know, Jan. That's something you got to figure out. I don't know. I can't tell you that." Then she told her. "I hope you, like, understand someday that this is no way to live. That the whole world, it's not all about you, you know?"

"Amen," Barbara said, and her eyes bulged when everyone turned to look at her, as if she realized only then that she'd actually said aloud what she'd been thinking.

"Barbara," Brother said.

"I am so sorry," she said. Because she kept her head down as she adjusted the camera strap, it was impossible to tell if she was apologizing to her husband, or to Janice, or most likely to her husband through Janice. The camera's proboscis retreated in segments back into its body. "It's not my place to get involved," she mumbled, re-capping the lens. "That was completely inappropriate and I am honestly sorry."

"Do you worry he's gonna cheat on you?" Janice asked.

Judith screamed. She wanted Janice to see. She wanted Janice to listen to herself, but Janice had heard herself just fine. She heard everything. She heard the old grandfather clock ticking somewhere deep in the house, heard her father back in their Richmond Hill living room telling her that the clock had belonged to his father, her grandfather, her grandfather's grandfather clock, but it seemed impossible that Brother would've shipped all those pulleys and boards from Guyana to Queens. A faucet was dripping.

Good. Out in the road, beyond the pebbled cul-de-sac, expensive car engines thrummed. She heard her father retreat cowardly into silence. She heard Barbara clear her throat before speaking, which was meant to indicate that Janice's question, however inappropriate, would not rile her.

"I'm sorry you're still hurting from all this," she said.

"Somewhere at the back of your brain," Janice said, "you gotta be thinking about it. You gotta worry he's gonna do it to you."

"Sweetie," Brother interjected. "I admire, I really honor your loyalty to your mother. I think that's a really great —"

"Your father and I are very happy," Barbara said. To her credit, she did not look to Brother for a small nod of permission, nor did she turn to Judith with some thin-lipped acknowledgment of their confederacy. "*Very* happy," she said. "And not that it's any of your business, but we trust each other completely."

Janice said, "Oh, sure, I know what that's like, but you're not worried he's gonna start beating the shit out of you, or has that started already?"

"Listen to yourself," Judith said.

"I'm a different person now," Brother said quietly.

169

"Yeah, a year younger," Janice said. She snatched the picture of her off the mantel. "We understand this, right? Not fifty. Fifty-*one*. He turns fifty-*one* tomorrow. We all know this, correct?"

The other pictures above the fireplace — the wedding photos, the cruise photos, the white kid (Barbara's nephew?) in a graduation robe and mortarboard, the photo of a grown-up Judith looking gorgeous with her legs dangling over a dock Janice didn't recognize — she left all those alone. But this one right here? This one belonged to her. She removed the felt backing, slid the picture out from behind the glass, and handed him the empty frame. The digital camera around Barbara's neck surely had plenty of other photos to take its place. Janice explained that now that she worked undercover, every picture of her in uniform needed to be destroyed, an obvious lie she regretted as soon as she said it, not only because of its obviousness but because it suggested she owed them any sort of explanation at all when really she could do whatever she wanted. A picture of her, it was her picture. Judith seemed about to challenge that, but Janice turned to her with such an icy look that it froze her mouth shut. Their father said something, though.

As Janice was leaving the living room, he called out an apology, but it was one of those fake apologies, like Barbara's: I'm sorry you feel this way, not I'm sorry I boozed to excess, battered your mother, cheated with a white woman, hired a better lawyer, and left you with multiple mortgages on one tiny house.

Janice hurried down the hallway toward the door, toward the sunlight and pebbles. Already her keys were in her fist. Behind her, Judith shouted something unintelligible, but Janice kept going. She had no reason to stop. She'd left her coat in the car and so now she didn't have to stand around while somebody fetched it out of the closet; in violation of Vita's standards of etiquette, she'd kept her shoes on and so now she didn't have to waste any time awkwardly wedging her feet into pumps. The drama of her dramatic exit was spoiled only on her way out the door when she caught her foot in the open O of her father's Christmas wreath. She fell down but picked herself up quickly.

A few hours later she watched Tevis reach under the driver's-side seat of the uncle car for their stashed bottle of Admiral Nelson Coconut Rum. They were parked at a broken meter with a red canvas bag wrapped around its face, on the corner of Broadway and Roosevelt, the neighborhood borderland between Woodside and Jackson Heights. Because ladies first, he passed her the bottle. This was no pity party — she'd told him nothing about Great Neck — but was instead a long-standing ritual whenever Tevis went out to make buys and she ghosted. They allowed themselves one swig apiece. She tipped her head back for a real neck-bobber, but as always Tevis took only a dainty mouthful, and even that was just for gargling. His bushy beard absorbed the dribbles; the rest he spat out the window.

"Let me see that bottle again real quick?" she said.

"See with your eyes," he said, and slid the Lord Admiral back under his seat.

A navy-blue Impala drove past them going thirty. It had been floating in her side-view mirror for miles, trailing them since Flushing, but no worries: it was just Sergeant Hart and three of his investigators from the 115 Precinct: the inseparable, indistinguishable Irishers, McCarthy and Duckenfield; and the Big Redheaded Boy, Federico Cataroni, who'd started in Narcotics on the same day as Janice. The Impala made a U-turn after passing them and parked across the street, in front of a Tibetan restaurant specializing in Himalayan yak. The car's suspension sagged under the investigators' collective weight, and because Janice was actively trying to torture herself, she thought, Oh, suspensions, my dad fixes those.

"I'm probably going to go with the limp today," Tevis was saying. "You know what I mean? That way, some homeboy wants me to go around the corner with him, rob me, maybe shoot me in the face, I can be like, 'Nah, sorry, can't really walk. Got this limp.' "

"Uh-huh," she said, thinking, He'd get that Impala up on the car lift and install some Chinese load-adjusting shocks that'd disintegrate in a hundred miles.

"Hello?" Tevis said.

"Sorry, sorry." Because eye contact and follow-up questions suggested engagement better than staring out the window, she shifted in her seat to look at him. "Which leg were you thinking?"

"What do you mean?"

"For the limp. Which leg?"

"Which leg?" he said. "What kind of stupid dang question is that? What difference does it make, which leg?"

"Seriously, let me see that bottle," she told

173

him. "I promise I'm just gonna break it over your head."

When the prisoner transport van finally arrived — it had taken the Van Wyck here, to avoid coasting down Roosevelt and tipping off dealers — Janice and Tevis stepped out of the car. An oncoming 7 train spooked all the pigeons. The sun, so bright on Long Island, fragmented in Queens as it passed through the el tracks. Once the train had gone by, Tevis spoke a few do-you-copies into his chest, as if he were asking the Looney Tunes characters on his lucky T-shirt — Bugs and Taz posed like early-nineties gangstas with backward ball caps and turned-around jeans — but they didn't answer him. Nor did the investigators in the presumably toasty Impala across the street. Federico Cataroni tried rattling the kel-mic receiver near his ear.

"Hello?" Tevis said. "Do you copy?" The lip-reading investigators shook their heads, which in turn caused him to shake his. "It's criminal," he told her. Another 7 was coming, an express chasing the local, and he had to holler into her face. "Make sure you stay close!"

Quick as a bear, he took gentle hold of her wrist and eased the thumbnail from her mouth. It shocked her, literally, a burst of static electricity forking from his fingertips into her body. For whatever reason, it seemed to embarrass him. He turned quickly away from her and limped into Jackson Heights; after a half-block head start, she followed.

"Uncle is proceeding west on Ruse-ah-velt Avenue," she told the Nextel.

"What's he walking like that for?" Hart asked. "You give him blue balls or something?"

She pulled the rubber band from her ponytail and wrapped it around her wrist.

It was a Saturday, but Manhattan's shoe stores still needed salesmen; its restaurants, waitresses; its paintings, protection. Double-parked gypsy cabs waited on Roosevelt for the returning workers too shift-hobbled to walk home. The arepa lady baked bread for the hungry, their grim faces hardened by the ascent from the subway, the descent from the el. And then there were the white-collars who went past them going the other way, headed into the City to buy shoes and eat out and torture their feet across museums. A block away from the train station, on the periphery of the commuter crush, a young Puerto Rican leaned against the plateglass window of a pet store. He looked promising, a possible dealer, and when Tevis limped up to him Janice raised the Nextel to her mouth. *Uncle is approaching a Hispanic male, early twenties, in a Mets cap, with what looks like a cardboard poster tube under his arm.* She leaned against an el pillar, too far away to hear the particularities of Tevis's pitch. Not that it mattered: the kid wasn't biting. He left before the pitch could even begin, abandoning Tevis outside the pet store talking to the turtles behind the glass.

"Location!" said Sergeant Hart.

"Never mind," she whispered. "The kid bounced."

"What?"

"Never mind!"

She stuffed the Nextel into her purse as the boy walked toward her, his ears pink beneath the Mets cap. Still needing three of her four buys, she wanted to ask him if he had any drugs concealed in that poster tube of his, but ghosts can't ask questions like that — they can't ask anything — and besides, maybe he was a nice kid from a nice family, a Queens College architecture student who simply didn't like the rummy smell of Tevis's breath.

The limp — on the right leg, by the way — made it hard for her to keep a surveillance-approved half block of space between them. Again and again she had to abandon all her better New York instincts and amble like a bumpkin. She lingered outside an electronics shop. She watched a video demonstration on eyebrow threading in the window of a salon. To the exasperation of all the commuters behind her, she slowed to take every flyer offered, then slowed again to throw them all away in a trash can. The languid pace of ghosting allowed her mind to wander toward unfortunate associations. When she passed a sporting-goods store, she thought of her father's birthday tracksuit. A travel agency that everyone knew laundered money for the Mexican cartel reminded her of her father's own shady dealings. A strip club . . . gross men . . . her father. The Scorpion Bar, her father. And when she passed a bank, a supermarket, a chicken joint, the Ping-Pong palace, and the neighborhood's one legal massage parlor, all without thinking of her father, she congratulated herself for not thinking of her father, and the loop started anew. Her thumbnail oozed blood. She snapped at the rubber band around her wrist. She felt ridiculous, but to be fair she always felt ridiculous when ghosting, certain the whole neighborhood had already made her as a narc. How could they not have?

Every time Tevis stopped, she did, too, and narrated into her Nextel.

Uncle is approaching two Indian women on the south side of Roosevelt between Eightieth and Eighty-First. One of the women wears a blue jacket that says SWEETIE in glittered cursive across the back. The other woman is, oh, never mind. Uncle is walking away. Uncle is approaching a kid pulling a shopping cart full of laundry. Never mind. Uncle is approaching an adult black male, never mind. Uncle is approaching an old Latino who's missing an arm. Scratch that: who's got his arm in a sling. The guy is reaching into his pocket, dropping something into uncle's hand. We got a possible oop, never mind. It was just some loose change. Sorry about that. Uncle is approaching a kid on a bike, an old white lady, a red Toyota Camry with its hazards blinking, a pretty Latina mama pushing a baby stroller built for two.

"Location," said Sergeant Hart.

"Never mind," Janice said, disappointed the woman didn't have any crack vials in her diaper bag. "Uncle just went into a bodega."

To avoid seeming even more obviously obvious — "The art of ghosting," Fiorella had once told her, "is doing jack shit con-

178

vincingly" — she drifted into a nearby taco cart line. It stretched far enough down the sidewalk that she could feign impatience and jump out whenever Tevis reappeared. And if she did reach the front, where the ground beef was sizzling on the grill, she could get a water or guava juice to ease her overstrained vocal cords. She shuffled forward, closer to the cart's garlicky steam puffs. Maybe she should get a taco, too, for authenticity purposes. Maybe — since this was her favorite food cart, one of the few never to have liquefied her bowels — she should get herself a couple of tacos, which were so much better than the ones her mother used to make, the Ortega kind out of the box with the little white packet of not enough red sauce. Her father always complained the shells broke as soon as he picked them up. And there he was! Back in her dome, making himself comfortable, twisting the anxiety dials. Her stomach was grumbling, her brain was on auto-flagellate. She looked in her purse to see if she could even afford a taco.

"Can we get an update?" the sergeant asked. The Nextel's obligatory beep-beep bookended his transmission. "Itwaru? Do you copy? Can we get an update?"

Up near the front of the line, a curly-haired Latino turned around. Atypically for her, she struggled to determine his age. He had the oddly angled face of a teenager whose features had not yet snapped into focus, but any potential boyishness was offset by a flaming eyeball tattoo on his neck and a goatee so finely groomed it looked like stage makeup. His chin jutted out to the left as if someone had long ago broken his jaw for him. With small white teeth — nubbins really — he smiled at her, and she smiled right back.

"Itwaru," the sergeant said.

"Oh, will you shut up already," she said into the Nextel. "I'm getting us tacos. I'll be home in a minute."

Tevis limped out of the bodega across the street. Unable to make any buys so far, he'd bought himself a pack of cigarettes, which he kept slapping against his palm. Her face must've betrayed some sort of recognition when she spotted him. She must've squinted or arched her eyebrows. She must've done something, because the Latino turned his head to follow her line of sight across the street. They both watched Tevis pat his coat and pants pockets, as if looking for matches. When the Latino, still grinning, turned back to her, she stepped out of the line and slunk away.

The Impala crept down the avenue no more than two blocks behind her. Maybe. Probably. Standard operating procedure dictated that backup teams stay within the kel's frequency range, but since the kel didn't work the investigators might still be parked all the way back at the Tibetan restaurant, or possibly in one of Woodside's Irish pubs with their white faces hovering over Guinness pints. She walked with her head down. The ghost watches the uncle, but who watches the ghost? She wanted to ask the investigators for their location, but she didn't know how without sounding like the chicken-shit little sister who needed her big brothers close by in case she got jumped.

At the intersection she braved a look over her shoulder. She didn't see the Impala or, thank God, the goateed Latino, but she did see Tevis, a hard man to miss when he wasn't ghosting. He had found a Smoker's Samaritan, a young black kid willing to offer his lighter. They were talking to each other — the kid, at least, was nodding — and Janice once again looked around for the goateed Latino before putting the kid's scrip over the radio. With his back to her, she didn't have much to say: *Uncle has approached a young black male, around six feet, puffy jacket and reversed Knicks cap, hard to tell his build.*

"Is it a buy?" the sergeant asked.

"Hold on," she said.

She stood as still as the traffic pole while street-crossers streamed past her. The kid had his hands in his pockets. A 7 train rumbled far away down the tracks, a local or express, she couldn't tell which. Her eyes were leaking wind-tears. She waited for Tevis to button his coat, his positive signal to indicate he'd made a buy, but instead he reached into his pocket for a cap of his own, a rusted orange Kangol that belonged to the early nineties as much as the thuggish Looney Tunes on his T-shirt. When he put the cap on, the kid began to look around, clearly nervous. He stepped off the curb and into a puddle, something going on here but she didn't know what. Still unbuttoned, Tevis's coat fluttered behind him with the wind.

"I don't think it's a buy," she said into the Nextel.

"It's not a buy, or you don't think it's a buy?"

The kid cut across Roosevelt into Elmhurst, a bordering neighborhood where the streets left the grid to zigzag without reason or logic. She told Hart it wasn't a buy, but with the 7 train now directly overhead she couldn't hear his response. She couldn't see the kid anymore, either, or the goateed Latino, who'd apparently vanished. But she could still see Tevis. That was her job, to always keep him in sight. He was laughing on the sunny side of the street, pleased with both himself and the world. As if to share the joke with someone else, he took out his own Nextel, which uncles kept on silent for obvious reasons. A slug of gray ash lengthened off his cigarette. When the train had slid far enough down the tracks to no longer be thundering, she heard both Sergeant Hart demanding an update and her cell phone ringing inside her purse. Tevis was waiting for her to answer. He stared blankly ahead, as if he couldn't see her, even though she was only fifty feet away at the intersection, the crazy lady with a phone pressed to each ear.

"I love that kid," Tevis told her, his lips lagging behind his words. "Hart, oh man, Hart is *really* going to love that kid."

"You made a buy?" she asked.

"Are you serious?" Now he turned to look at her because he always, *always,* knew exactly where she was — ghosting or buying, it didn't matter. He said, "I gave you my positive!"

"Your coat's not buttoned!"

He tugged on the Kangol. "My cap," he said. "I put on my cap."

"That's *my* positive!" Actually, in the winter, her positive was taking the dockworker cap *off,* but either way: she was hats, he was buttons, no need to confuse it, that's how it had been since they'd started working together.

"In the car," he said. "I told you. I wanted to switch. Because I've been in a slump. I *told* you."

"I'm sorry," she said. "I don't remember that."

"Because you weren't paying attention. The kid saw it. Do you realize that? He was like, 'That's your positive signal, isn't it?' Exact words, Itwaru. You understand what I'm saying? The frickin' *kid* knew."

"I'm sorry, okay? I've been sorta distracted, my father —"

"You're my ghost," he said. "You're not allowed to be distracted."

He hung up in her ear, but in the other ear Sergeant Hart kept chirping for an update. Without admitting blame — it seemed irrelevant — she told him that the uncle had in fact made a successful buy after all. She repeated from memory what little description she had: six feet tall, adult black male with a puffy jacket and at least

184

one soggy sneaker. And a Knicks cap, too, although he'd probably already stashed it behind the wheel of a parked car, along with all his drugs and the buy money. When she explained that he'd run into Elmhurst's jumbled streets over a minute ago, the line went dead. She pushed down the Nextel's antenna with her teeth. Not only had she allowed a drug dealer to evade capture, but she'd also cost Tevis a buy on the rumpus's whiteboard. Not only that, she'd robbed the investigators of an opportunity to fill out two to three hours of OT-approved paperwork at time-and-a-half. Not only that — it never ends! — now the investigators would have to fill out two to three hours of *non*-OT-approved paperwork explaining why the uncle had brought back without a perp. Oops, never mind. To save them all from that particular hassle, Tevis was crouched over the curb across the street, slipping his buy into the sewer, where one of New York City's mutated alligators would swallow it whole and spend the rest of this night happily swimming on his scaly back. The Nextel chirped back on with a series of miniature honks, most likely Sergeant Hart banging his head against the steering wheel. He told her his investigators had no interest in chasing a poorly described knucklehead they'd never catch. He also asked that in the future she try not to be a complete and utter fuck-up, which she thought was an entirely unfair criticism, which was itself a Big Boss specialty. She'd been alternating ghosting assignments between Tevis and Gonz for seventeen months now and had never before missed a positive signal. She hadn't even really made a mistake since her first day as an uncle when she let that huckster disappear into an apartment lobby with the department's twenty bucks. But the Narco Big Bosses, like Big Bosses everywhere, tended to fixate only on fumbles. Over the Nextel she heard either McCarthy or Duckenfield in the background asking if she had at least gotten the tacos.

Good news or bad news? Bad news: Tevis went buyless for the rest of the day.

The good news: it was March 8, and the end of Puffy's shift marked the end of his first eighteen months in Narcotics. He'd officially just made detective. Back at the rumpus, where Richie had strung up a congratulations banner, uncles and investigators came by to slap his back and shake his hand. Klondike and Morris argued over whether he should invest his new pay raise into property or a money market. Eddie Murphy wrote down the number of a good accountant. James Chan beamed but said nothing. A sleepy, yawning, nightcap-wearing Grimes was the first to call him Detective Okazaki, the name a surprise to half the rumpus who only ever knew him as Puffy. Pablo Rivera, now the rumpus's second-most-junior detective, bequeathed the ceremonial Sherlock Holmes deerstalker cap and pipe, with an added warning to watch out for Internal Affairs. Despite his strong chin and clear eyes, even Puffy couldn't make that cap look unridiculous. Fiorella pinned to his shirt a plastic badge from the toy department at Rite Aid, something Janice wished she'd thought of herself. He'd get his real detective shield later in the month, at a private ceremony at One Police Plaza, but in the meantime all the uncles except Gonz took him out for celebratory drinks at A.R.'s Tavern, which had a danger-ous Saturday-night special on three-dollar Cosmos.

She floundered down her alleyway at around two o'clock in the morning. Before going inside the house, she wiped her feet on the back door's welcome mat and saw little green needles stuck in its synthetic fibers. No wonder she'd fucked up Tevis's buy! She'd been hexed, walking around all day with bits of her father's Christmas wreath stuck to her shoe bottoms. His own stinking shoes sat near the door, as they had every day of her life, these boots as much as part of the world behind her house as the alien-fruit tree. She picked them up. Unwilling to pluck every pine needle out of the welcome mat, she instead carried her father's boots down the alley and threw them away in Mr. and Mrs. Hua's fishy-smelling garbage can. Immediately feeling lighter, feeling winged, she bounded back up the porch steps. She knew her mother had wanted to protect the family from ghosts, but what you have to understand, Mama, is that those boots were haunted all on their own. They *had* to go. Plus, Janice had drunkenly, definitively decided that she wasn't going to believe in ghosts anymore.

But since when has that ever stopped them?

# CHAPTER SIX

A couple of nights later, she and Fiorella dolled up for the triple T: Techno Techno Tuesday at the Pure Magic Dance Hall and Lounge. They wore shredded fishnets, shimmering shirts, a racoonish amount of eyeliner, and two spritzes apiece of Fiorella's Truly Pink perfume, which got immediately absorbed by the burnt dust smell of the club's fog machines. An actual disco ball splintered green strobe lights. Up in a crow's nest, a DJ spun bass-heavy *oonstoonst* records for a surprisingly dense crowd of dancers, most of them underage, almost all of them simultaneously grinding their teeth and the person in front of them. Janice's shoes stuck to the floor. Because coincidentally she and Fiorella were each expecting their periods, and because nightclub bathroom dispensers sold only cheapy brands at outrageous prices, they'd brought their own emergency tampons, just as they'd brought along their own ghosts: Tevis, like a proper specter, melted into the fog, but that miserable prick Gonz headed straight to the bar to pay no attention to them whatsoever and sip on nine-dollar Budweisers.

Janice pushed herself into the crowd, confused as to how ordinary citizens could party like this on a weeknight. Didn't they have algebra tests to take? Jobs to show up for? Unconcerned with what would surely be a miserable hump-day morning, they appeared high on weed, coke, Ecstasy, or some combination of all three. They tipped their mouths back to swallow the music. Their flowing hands fashioned invisible pottery from invisible kilns. Some of these children sucked on actual pacifiers, but not a one of them would be getting arrested. At least not for selling or using. At least not tonight. The arrests, when they came, were still a few months away. The Big Bosses had sent Janice and Fiorella here to make one buy apiece and then leave, so as not to stoke suspicion, so as to lay the foundation for an eventual case against the nightclub itself. Because Sergeant Hart preferred these two buys to come directly from Pure Magic's impure employees, Fiorella went looking for a bar-back with dilated eyes or a sniffy nose.

Armed with techno song names from a Google search before leaving the rumpus, Janice climbed a spiral staircase toward the DJ's crow's nest. There was no one to stop her. All the bouncers were outside pretending to check fake IDs. When she reached the DJ booth, a white DJ — a sticker on his purposefully dorky button-down said HELLO, MY NAME IS WHITE DJ — looked up from his turntables, annoyed, as if he expected her to request the latest Beyoncé song.

This little booth fly? With her tights tattered to shit? She came buzzing up to him to ask, "Yo, you got 'Dam Dadi Doo'?"

"IImm," he said, surprised.

One of them anime girls, then. Probably went to Comic-Cons wearing the plaid schoolgirl skirts with her hair twisted into fuck-me braids. Sure, he had "Dam Dadi Doo," had it right here, matter a fact, bought it like — what? Like two weeks ago, from Breakdown in Bayside. He planned to quick mix it in later, during primetime, with some of his other party-rocking tracks, but yeah, okay, if she couldn't wait — and the way she leaned over his table, hands held behind her back, she didn't seem the type who liked to wait for anything — he'd play it for her now, no problem, milk it for her, too. But first? To show her a little turn-tablism? He adjusted one of the muffs on his headphones, dropped the record, cut it twice with the cross-fader, dropped it again and gave it a reverse teardrop before drop-ping it for real this time, how do you like that? *When the morning come come, I'm dancing like you're dumb dumb.* She closed her eyes to move with it a little, just her hips and shoulders going.

"Me and my girlfriend?" she said with her eyes still closed and her voice real quiet like she didn't care if he heard her. "We lost our virginity to this song."

He pulled off his headphones.

When she opened her eyes again, she looked so happy, but a little out of it, too, a little heavy-lidded, like maybe she was drunk or tripping balls. "Your nose is run-ning," she told him.

Of course it was. He wiped it real quick with the back of his hand, then tried to distract her by baby-scratching "Dam Dadi Doo" over the beat on table one's record, which was, of all things, a remix of KC and the Sunshine Band's "Please Don't Go." Of course it was. *Please don't go,* he acciden-tally asked her without asking her, and she leaned even farther over his table.

"How much more of that coke you got on you?" she asked. "I'm not trying to score anything off you for free. Don't worry, I got money. But me and my girlfriend?" She tilted her head toward the dance floor beneath them, where he was making all those young bodies move. "We'll save half for you when you get a break."

"I don't get a break," he said. "I'm stuck up here until closing."

"But you got that coke on you?"

"A little."

"Well, that's perfect because I got a little money," she said. "You should probably take my number, too. When's closing at? Like five? I can't promise me and my girl will still have a whole half for you left, but I guarantee we'll both be up."

Dam dadi doo dam dam didoodi dam
Dam dadi doo dam dam didoodi dam
Dam dadi doo dam dam didoodi dam
Dam dadi doo dam dam didoodi dam

Two buys down, two more to go.

Cigarettes. Chewing gum. Breath mints. Dental floss. Mouthwash strips. Paper towels, a big stack of them, ready for Rose to disperse one at a time. Knockoff per-

193

fumes from the former love of her life, that dirty-dicked motherfucker Ricky Sprinkle. Lotion. Band-Aids. Hairpins and safety pins. A needle and thread, although Rose had never seen anyone reach for them. Condoms ribbed for her ladies' pleasure. Kleenex, aspirin, Tums, and Pepto-Bismol. A comb and two brushes. A lint roller. Some static-cling spray. Some antiwrinkle spray, which she twice had to explain was for fabric not faces. Midol. Tampons. Maxi pads. Shout Wipe & Go Instant Stain Remover. Windex for the windows when the nastier of these nasty-ass bitches popped their pimples onto the glass. Jasmine-lily hand soap to pump into the palms of women who too frequently avoided eye contact. A wicker basket loaded with one- and five-dollar bills, most of it money brought from home to remind these misers that tipping was always appreciated, that none of these goodies were free — except for the perfumes, which technically counted as gifts but had cost her all sorts of emotionally crippling capital — and it wasn't any fun to sit in a ladies' room all night on an ass-deadening stool and smell other people's shit, piss, farts, and vomit.

"Excuse me, ma'am?" a young lady said. She was half black and half Hindu, probably from one of those Caribbean islands near Jamaica. Her skirt was high enough for the wind to whistle through her you-know-what, but she'd spoken to Rose with more politeness than anyone in months. Ma'am? Please, Rose was just happy to have someone look into her face. "Can I ask you a question?" the girl asked.

"Anything you want."

"I'm not looking to buy one, but how much do you charge for tampons? I'm just curious."

"Everything here is pay-what-you-will, like the Natural History Museum, but if you're in trouble just take one and don't worry about it. You want some Midol? How bad is it? You want some OxyContin?"

She laughed. "You got Oxy?"

"Honey, if you can think it, I got it."

Behind them a toilet flushed. A chubby redhead, with eyes spread too wide apart on her face, stepped out of the middle stall. Head down, she hurried over to the sink, not to wash her hands like a civilized human being, but to drink water straight from the tap. Rose tried to give her a paper towel, but the girl walked away without taking it. Now that her cotton mouth was a little less cottony, nothing else mattered. Once the door swung shut behind her, the other girl, the nice Hindu girl, handed Rose a twenty.

"The Oxy," the girl said. "Is that pay-what-you-will, too?"

"It's more of a suggested donation." She gave the girl two fives from the tip basket and a small white pill from her purse. "That should do you for now, honey. It's a little-bitty dose, just the ten millis, but you come right back if you think you're gonna need anything else."

"Thank you, ma'am," the girl said, her manners exquisite, her mama having done at least a little something right. "You're a lifesaver."

"Well, I don't know about all that." Rose shrugged. "But I do aim to please."

With more buys on the night than she could use, Janice left the bathroom and went looking for Tevis. It was a quick search. She found him right there in the corridor between the ladies' room and the gents'. He stood on a line six dudes deep, whereas the women's had no wait at all, a disparity Janice had only ever seen at Mets games. Under the club's silly black lights, his cocoa butter glowed like impetigo. She wondered if he knew, if that's why he was waiting on line, to wash his face, but probably not. Probably, a conscientious ghost, he'd only been waiting for her. She slipped the DJ's coke into his palm. It filled half of a miniature manila envelope, the kind used in Clue to conceal murderers, weapons, and crime scenes.

"What's this?" he said.

"The one I owe you!"

"What?"

"The one I owe you!" Close to a cluster of speakers, they took turns shouting into each other's ears, certain none of the other guys waiting for the bathroom could hear them. "For missing your positive last week," she said. "Now we're even!"

He untied the golden string on the manila envelope and peered inside. "Are you crazy?" he said. "I can't take this!"

He meant — she assumed — that as the ghost he wasn't allowed to make buys. But what if he'd only been doing his job? What if he'd gone up into the crow's nest for its better vantage point, to keep an eye on both uncles at once, and the envelope got forced on him, pushed into his palm, which was with a few minor differences essentially the truth? What if the coke was so cheap he couldn't give it back without arousing suspicion? Seriously — who did it hurt? Over at the bar on the other side of the club, Gonz was in no position to contradict

197

anything. Nor was Fiorella. And the DJ wasn't even going to get arrested. So why shouldn't Tevis score a little boost on the buy board, especially since he unfairly got screwed the last time he went out? As far as Janice was concerned, this was merely the universe leveling itself out, *I Ching*-style. Plus, even better, now she could stop feeling guilty.

"But they know I didn't come out here with any buy money," he said.

"Who's they?" she hollered into his ear. "All this gets buried in paperwork. Just say you used your own money."

"I would never use my own money."

"I just used my own money to buy Oxy off the bathroom attendant."

"A bathroom attendant?"

Fiorella snuck up behind them to bump their heads together. It was, apparently, the most hilarious thing she'd ever done. She couldn't stop laughing, her grin glittering in the black light as if floating in a photo negative. Because it was impossible to get mad at her, because Janice and Tevis were both happy to have found another familiar face in this overcrowded nightclub, they rubbed at their foreheads without complaints. The music cross-faded into a novelty song, a remix of "Cotton-Eyed Joe," something

198

Janice actually recognized from long-ago quinceañeras and bat mitzvahs.

"Tevis accidentally made a buy off the DJ," she told Fiorella.

"No shit?"

"You want it?" he asked her.

"Nah, I copped molly off the bartender like twenty minutes ago. Where you guys been? I've already taken three tequila shots on Gonz's bar tab."

"He's buying?" Tevis said.

"Yeah right. He left it open and then got distracted talking to this chick, some poor chubby white girl who wandered into his talons."

"Redhead?" Janice asked. "Eyes super wide apart on her face?"

"You know her?"

"I saw her."

"So we're done, then?" Tevis said. "Back to the rumpus?"

"What's wrong with your face?" Fiorella asked him.

"What's wrong with my face?"

Fiorella looked around at all the dudes, nine deep now, outside the bathroom. "Why's there such a long-ass line for the men's?"

"I think someone's getting a blowjob," Janice told her.

"What's wrong with my face?" Tevis said again.

"Your lotion," Fiorella said as she pulled Janice away by her elbow. "Go wash up, then meet us at the bar. I'm thinking Gonz is gonna be buying rounds all night."

"My lotion?" he said, confused, touching his cheeks, the manila envelope still in his hand. "What's the matter with my lotion?"

"You're glowing," Janice said.

"I'm what?"

"You're glowing!" she shouted into the music, but Fiorella had already dragged her too far away.

Hours later the uncles staggered out of the club. The bouncers told them to take it easy. The sidewalks, wet with rain, reflected light from brontosaural streetlamps. Gonz insisted on driving back to the rumpus, and because he'd paid his tab without bitching — or more likely without looking at it — they indulged him. He got as far as the first traffic light before a tall and beautiful Latina transvestite lay down on the hood of their car. Five months late, or seven months early, she wore a slutty Halloween costume: a police-girl uniform with blue short-shorts, a plastic billy club, reflective sunglasses, and a neon squirt gun holstered to her hip, everything but the detective badge from the Rite Aid toy aisle. Her dark curly hair spread like algae across the windshield. Gonz honked and cursed, but she just laughed, sprawled out on the hood through an entire traffic-light cycle, from red to green and back to red. Then, as delicately as she'd hopped on, she hopped off and strutted away toward a parked van on the opposite side of the street. QUEENS #1 CARPET CLEANERS said the side paneling. Its back doors swung silently open for her.

"What just happened?" Fiorella said.

"I'm gonna tell you something," Gonz said. "If patrols actually looked like that, I'd *volunteer* to get demoted."

Janice said, "You know that was a tranny hooker, right?"

"Amazing observation," he deadpanned. "You know, it's a shame you won't last the full eighteen and get to put those incredible detective skills of yours to use."

If Puffy were there, he would've thanked Gonz for the pep talk, but instead Tevis asked him, "No, but seriously, you do know that was a tranny hooker, right?"

When another beautiful transvestite hooker, this one dressed as a slutty nurse, climbed up into the same van, Fiorella said, "What is going *on*?"

201

Janice thought it might have had a bizarro connection to the big news of the day, that a federal wiretap had caught the New York governor paying for sex. "Ho No!" said the *Post*. "Gov in Romp with Hooker 'Kristen.' " But that didn't really explain these particular streetwalkers or their getups, not that Janice even wanted them explained. She felt happier not knowing. She wouldn't have changed any of this. While Vita and Judith and Barbara and Brother and all the high school friends she didn't have time for, while all those people were at home, in bed, asleep, Janice was getting paid to be here, in the backseat of an unmarked car, drunk on free booze, awake and somehow simultaneously inside the rubric of dreams. Before another ass could plop itself onto the hood, Gonz sped through the intersection without waiting for the light to turn green. Nobody honked. Except for the party in that carpet-cleaning van, they had the entire road to themselves.

The *Post*'s headline the next day, day two of the Spitzer scandal, read: "Hooked: Sex Addict Gov Spent $80,000 on Call Girls." The uncles were inspired. Stuck in the rumpus all afternoon without any buys to look forward to, they whittled away their shifts trading stories about the worst things they'd ever done. Fiorella confessed to stealing twenty dollars out of her son's sock drawer. Tevis said he probably didn't remember the worst thing he'd ever done, but the last bad thing happened just this weekend when he went to drop off his daughters at the ex-wife's house. Because he seemed ready to slip into his epic mode, the uncles told him it sounded like a very interesting story but could he please maybe table it for another time. As if troubled by the overly serious tone of the conversation, Puffy said the worst thing he'd ever done was spill wee-wee on Janice's lap. Gonz refused to play along, so they answered for him: being born. Pablo Rivera, paranoid as always, citing the wolflike ears of Internal Affairs, also refused to participate, but Grimes admitted to burning down his own house. On purpose? On purpose. The uncles didn't seem to know what to do with that. They turned to Eddie Murphy, who said he had two worst things: wearing a leather beanie in *The Golden Child* and that long wig in *Vampire in Brooklyn*. A total lame-azoid, Janice told them that her sister had once dared her to steal something from a gas station and so she snuck out a can of Sunkist under her sweatshirt, but afterward she felt so guilty and so eager to get rid of the evidence that she puked halfway through guzzling it, and to this day couldn't drink orange soda without throwing up.

"Are you serious?" Klondike said.

"I know, it's pathetic, but I can't really think of —"

"No, no, no," Morris said. "It's amazing."

They sent James Chan to go buy a Sunkist from the reception area's vending machine. Well, not exactly to buy a Sunkist, but to use his weird button-mashing trick to get one for free. Because the uncles had nothing better to do, and because *Rubí* had gone off the air and its replacement — the Mexican telenovela *Amigas y Rivales* — had yet to gain traction for them, they gathered in the lounge to circle around Janice and watch her drink orange soda over a garbage can. She slipped the rubber band off her wrist to tie back her hair. She didn't want to do this.

"I don't want to do this," she told them.

"We appreciate that," Fiorella said, "but this is really about the greater needs of the group as a whole."

To encourage her, the uncles got a chug-a-lug chant going. Their fists bobbed in unison. The soda can's metal tab, after Janice had bent it back and forth a few times, broke off on D, the first and/or last initial of her future husband. Matt Damon? Danny DeVito? She started chugging. She knew if she didn't puke, she'd disappoint everyone, so she bolted the soda in painful gulps until its orange fizz sprang tears into her eyes. Without her quite noticing, the chanting had stopped. When she paused to take a breath, she saw Sergeant Hart looming over her.

"Sorry to interrupt," he said, "but you do realize I got a deck to get fixed, right?"

"I'm sorry," she said, not yet understanding.

"Don't be sorry. You didn't build it. McCarthy and Duckenfield, *they* built it, that's the problem. Irene's worried it slopes too much, it's slipping into the foundation there, and the grandkids are gonna hurt themselves. Okay? Now I gotta get a contractor to level it all out. That's parts, labor, work permits, the whole thing. Hold on. Then I got Thomasina starting Haverford next fall. Can't go to SUNY like a normal human being — she needs a liberal-arts education. If I told you what that costs, Itwaru, you'd call me a liar straight to my face. But what about Irene? Can't forget about her. What do you think? You think she doesn't need money? She says she's worried about empty-nest syndrome. She says she's gotta get certified for a yoga instructor license. What that costs, you don't want to know. It's an investment for our future, she tells me. That's fine, Irene, that's great, but you gotta have *money* before you can invest, am I right? You gotta have *money* to send Thomasina to Haverford. You gotta have *money* to fix the deck so the grandkids don't fall off and crack their heads open. Meanwhile, Itwaru, we don't even have any grandkids yet. You see what I'm saying?"

"Not really, sir, no."

"Oh wow," said Puffy, God bless him. "I thought it was just me."

"Oh wow, where's my fucking overtime?" Hart asked. He booted the garbage can across the lounge, the circled-up uncles finally scrambling out of the way. Shredded papers spilled across the carpet for someone else to clean up. "You ain't making buys, Itwaru, we ain't making overtime. What does that mean? That means I'm home an extra ten hours a week. No one wants that. You think Irene wants that? Irene doesn't want that. Where I'm sitting out in the backyard staring at a sloping deck? Fantasizing about the fancy juicer I can't afford, three hundred bucks, practically cleans itself, not that anybody cares what I want, right? Right?"

"I'm trying to make buys," she said.

"Oh, obviously!" he said, looking around the room. "Obviously you are working very, very hard here." He took the Sunkist from her and smelled it before handing it back. "Can I give you some advice?" he asked. "Stop trying and start doing your job, yeah? I don't care if you've suddenly gone incompetent, if you can't remember how to make buys anymore. I do not care. Figure it out. Because right now? Right now you are fucking with my money and my money is not to be fucked with."

To be fair, she'd made three buys in the last week, two of which went up on the board next to her name, but none of them had led to an arrest for the 115 investigators. As far as Sergeant Hart and his team were concerned, she was the girl who missed Tevis's positive, left drugs up in the Martys' apartment, and hadn't been able to find the Elmhurst Hospital meth clinic. Of course none of the uncles had been able to find the Elmhurst Hospital meth clinic, but why not blame only her? Why not! Hart's pants swished and his Altoids tin rattled as he strode away from her, past the uncles who'd all hung around to witness her humiliation, past Lieutenant Prondzinski who stood in the lounge's entryway to stare at her over the top of a mug that said STOP, THINK, GO GREEN. A grainy tadpole of vomit swam up into Janice's mouth, but she forced it back down.

Two days later she vomited for real, no Sunkist required, in an apartment building stairwell. This was over in LeFrak City, municipally speaking not an actual city but a twenty-tower cluster of affordable housing at the southern edge of Corona, within the 115's jurisdiction. The original developer, Monsieur LeFrak — like Janice, prudently superstitious — had designed the buildings without thirteenth floors, and so it was somewhere in that negative zone between twelve and fourteen that she threw up her dinner. But hold on. A little backtracking: the day before, she'd spent her entire shift sort of ghosting Gonz. Unlike Janice and Tevis, who worked almost exclusively with the 115 investigators, Gonz got passed around from team to team, always on temporary assignment, as if he were the gun in Russian roulette. Yesterday it had been Janice's turn to ghost him, but — without any of the investigators knowing — he'd decided to play hooky with his chubby redhead, the poor Pure Magic girl who apparently lived nearby in a Jackson Heights co-op. Lucky for Gonz, awful for Janice. Awful for the redhead probably, too. To cover for him, Janice had sat in a bar across from the co-op, sipping on Dos Equis and telling stories into the Nextel. Uncle is approaching a homeless black guy. Uncle is approaching an Asian bag lady. When their shift ended without any positive signals, the investigators all blamed her. Reasonably, of course, because what wasn't her fault? So she couldn't fuck up two consecutive fishing trips, Sergeant Hart paired her with Narco's best confidential informant, a guy named Kevin Loquaio, but please call him K-Lo. A civilian snitch in the department's employ, he stood upwind from Janice in the LeFrak stairwell, two steps above her, his fingers overdramatically pinching his nose. Vomit had splattered her sneakers.

"Yuck," he said. With skin the color of whiskey, he was of an indeterminate race, even more so than Janice. He wore glasses covered in scratches. A deep dimple collapsed his chin. Normally he worked cases with Puffy in Astoria, but he'd told the investigators about an apartment in LeFrak that'd sell crack to anybody, no problem, something Hart assured her even she couldn't botch. "You pregnant?" K-Lo asked her. "Because Mrs. Lo? When she's carrying, God bless her? She's liable to get sick all times of day, don't have to be morning exclusive."

"I'm not pregnant, you jackass."

He grinned, thrilled to have goaded that out of her. He trafficked in information; spent his nights collecting data, secrets, confessions, and accidental admissions; his days splicing it together until all the angles revealed themselves. "You think it was maybe them carnitas you scarfed?" he asked. "Can I tell you something? Street carts, restaurants, I don't trust any of them. You hear they gonna start putting sanitation grades in the windows? Now, why they wanna do that unless there be something nasty going on behind doors?"

"Can you please stop talking?" she said, hunched over, her hands on her knees.

"What's the matter? You nervous? Because my tummy, it'll get upset when I'm nervous. Puffy says it's okay to be a little nervous. You'd be weird if you weren't, he says. Hey, how come you all call him Puffy? You ask me, he don't look like a Puffy." He touched the skin on his face, as if testing his own puffiness. "Mrs. Lo, she met him. She thinks he's sort of a handsome devil. I can see that, I guess. How long you known him for? He's a pretty nice guy, yeah? How come —"

"I'm not nervous," she said.

"You don't got the flu, do you?" he asked, backing up another two steps.

Truth be told, she was sort of nervous — she hadn't stepped inside an apartment to make a buy since the Marty incident — but that had nothing to do with the vomit between her shoes. Blame that on physical exhaustion. She had insisted they skip the coffin-like closeness of the elevator and instead walk up the stairs. Fourteen stories? Shouldn't have been a problem. On vertical patrols as a Housing cop, she had climbed project stairwells all day every day, but now, seventeen months later, she felt as if she'd swallowed a box of needles. Blame it on all those hours of rumpus inactivity. Blame it on A.R.'s Tavern, their cheap drink specials, the six pounds she'd gained since the holidays, the Planet Fitness membership card that perpetually languished in her wallet, and yeah, sure, blame it on the two carnitas she'd gobbled down and the spicy aji verde sauce that tasted like flames as they came up. She wiped her mouth with the back of her coat sleeve.

"You know," K-Lo said, "there's no shame in taking the elevator the rest of the way."

"What's the matter? You're tired?"

■ ■ ■ ■

Two flights of stairs later, they were walking down a poorly lit hallway toward apartment 16–. Toys covered the floor: Smurf dolls, a wooden elephant, plastic fruits and plastic veggies, a Baby's First laptop lying open as if some child had been called in to dinner in the middle of data entry. The closer she and K-Lo got to the apartment, the more shit they had to step around. No rush, though: a cock diesel black guy stood in front of 16–'s open door. Another customer, she thought. Ahead of them on line. Just as the stereotypes would have indicated, cocaine seemed to attract a far nattier dresser than the weed- and crack-buyers she was accustomed to seeing. The guy wore a dark suit with black shoes most likely made in a non-Asian country and a bright-red Fruit of Islam bowtie. He spoke to the tired-looking Latina inside the apartment with the aggressive patience — which is to say no patience at all — of a man who, wherever he went, was almost always bigger than everyone else.

"Yeah, okay, but I'm her *father,*" he was saying. "I've got custody rights."

"Yes, but your name's not on the pickup

list," the woman said.

"You keep telling me about this list. This list? I don't *need* to be on your list. That's what I'm trying to explain to you. I'm her *father.* I'm on the legal custody rights list. *That's* the list I'm on."

"I'm going to have to ask you to please keep your voice down out of consideration for my neighbors," the woman told him, as if it were a well-rehearsed line.

"Excuuuse us," K-Lo said and squirted himself through the doorway with weaselly ease.

On behalf of the New York City Police Department, Sergeant Hart would pay him a flat fee for his CI services, and the faster K-Lo got in, the faster he got out, the faster he got his palm laid with cash, the faster he got to move onto his next up-the-block hustle. Impressed with how easily he'd insinuated himself into the apartment, Janice decided that when they finished here she'd let him take the elevator down without her. But first, apologizing, squeezing past both the black guy and the Latina, she followed him inside, where more toys, hundreds of them, overstuffed the living room. A little black girl sat still and quiet on the carpet with her back to the door. Plastic beads covered the tips of her cornrows. She drew purple weblike lines on her arm with a Magic Marker, presumably nontoxic, for the whole apartment had been marshaled to protect her. Duct tape covered the electrical sockets. A waist-high plastic gate kept her out of the kitchen; another gate prevented her from reaching a glass door that opened onto a balcony. Somehow, even with all these precautions, a flesh-colored patch — flesh-colored for white people — covered one eye.

"Hiya, sweetie," Janice said as she crouched down in front of her. The girl didn't look up, wouldn't look up, but Janice pressed on: "What happened to your eye?"

"Who the hell are you?" asked the man in the entryway.

The Latina, her own voice rising now, hollered out for somebody named Rose Marie. It must've been her sister. The woman who came out of the kitchen — unlatching the safety gate, holding a wooden spoon coated in red sauce — looked exactly like her, a little younger and thinner maybe, but with the same burst-capillary expression more commonly found on the faces of new parents and combat soldiers. Her slumped shoulders asked the world what impossible weight it expected her to burden now; as if in response, K-Lo held up eight of his fingers. She waved him toward the balcony with her spoon. Red sauce dripped onto the carpet, which seemed to bother her less than it did Janice. Everything about this place, but perhaps especially its disorder, Janice found frightening.

"What the hell?" said the black guy.

Puffed up now, he filled the entryway in its entirety, his hand braced against the door to keep Rose Marie's sister from slamming it in his face. He wanted to know what list *those* people was on. They continued to argue, he and the Latina, until a neighbor lady came into the hall to complain. Pots and pans, or at least what sounded like pots and pans, clattered across the kitchen floor, followed by Rose Marie crying out for Jesus, Joseph, and Mary, the whole gang. The little girl, though, continued to quietly tattoo her arm. Without any hope of getting her to look up, Janice followed K-Lo onto the balcony, but she left the sliding-glass door open a bit just in case.

Fifteen stories above the ground, she thought the moon seemed almost snatchable. A whirling wind stung her face. Typically for her, whenever she found herself at these great heights, she imagined leaping over the edge. She didn't want to — leap or imagine it — but there it was, an image of her tumbling off the balcony with her arms outstretched and the dark ground rising to swallow her. Down in the street, cars as small as armored insects made a slow circuit of the block, the investigators' Impala somewhere among them. Her hands gripped the icy railing.

"You recognize that little girl in there?" K-Lo asked. To try to keep warm, he was stomping his feet on what she hoped was an exceedingly stable balcony floor. "Remember a couple years ago?" he asked. "The kid that shot her cousin by accident? Just playing around?"

To see inside the apartment, past the yellow glare of the city's lights, Janice had to press her face to the glass. The girl was up now, following Rose Marie around the living room. She'd ditched the wooden spoon for a cell phone, which she cradled against her shoulder. When she stopped at an end table to search through its drawers, the girl stopped, too, and tenderly rubbed the back of Rose Marie's knee through her sweatpants. Behind them in the apartment's entryway, the sister and the black guy and the neighbor lady all continued to argue, their features eventually dissolving behind the white mist of Janice's breath.

"What's she doing here?" she asked.

"The little girl?" K-Lo said. "I don't know. I guess she goes to day care here."

Janice slowly turned around to look at him. In the TAC meeting back at the rumpus, the investigators had asked him to draw a layout of the apartment. He complied, no problem. They brought him a cup of coffee. They asked him if he wanted anything from the vending machine, their treat. Skittles, please. Sure, great, Skittles. Next question: how many people should they expect? Oh, just two ladies, but he couldn't remember their names. That, too, was no problem. He dumped the bag of Skittles onto Cataroni's desk and ate all the orange ones first, then the greens. When Hart called him a lunatic, K-Lo raised his candy-stained hands in the air, guilty as charged. They all laughed except for Janice, who asked about guns in the apartment. What about dogs? Any dogs? No, no. Great, great. What about M&M's? Hart asked. You eat M&M's like you eat Skittles? That was the last question they asked K-Lo, because they stupidly assumed he'd told them everything worth knowing.

"This is a day care?" Janice said.

"Well," he said, "yeah, technically. But only like during the day."

Rose Marie stepped alone out onto the balcony with the cell phone still wedged against her shoulder. Dressed only in those sweatpants and a PROPERTY OF HOGWARTS hoodie, she seemed poorly prepared for the whirling winds up here, but she didn't start shivering or anything, didn't stomp her feet like K-Lo or tuck her hands under her armpits. Probably she still felt warm from the kitchen. She passed K-Lo a tiny manila envelope, just like the one the DJ had given Janice, except this one bulged with crack rocks, presumably eight of them as per K-Lo's eight-fingered request. Or maybe they were fake crack rocks, made out of baking soda and Anbesol. Didn't matter. Selling fake drugs was a felony all on its own. More to the point for Janice, it would still count as a buy. When K-Lo handed her the envelope, she slipped it into her back pocket, even patting it a couple of times to make sure it hadn't immediately disappeared. Three down, Lieutenant Prondzinski. Only one more to go.

"What you want me to tell you?" Rose Marie was saying into the phone. "He's got that order of protection on you, understand? You come through now, it's the police all over again, and then where we at?"

"How much?" Janice asked her.

"Can I tell you the God's honest truth?" Rose Marie said. She held up three fingers for Janice, one on her left hand, two on her right. "The God's honest truth is that if you was here at four to pick her up like you was supposed to . . . well, I'm just putting that out there is all."

"One twenty," said K-Lo, her interpreter.

Prior to arriving in LeFrak, they'd spent a few minutes coming up with their cover story: despite his whiskey-colored skin, they couldn't pretend to be related because that might come back to bite him in the ass — *You didn't know your fucking cousin was a cop?* — and they couldn't pretend to be lovers, either, because in an improvisational moment he might try to grab at *her* ass, and so they'd decided on coworkers at the Steinway Street Kinkos, where K-Lo really did have a part-time job. Janice felt she knew enough about photocopies to bluff her way through any potential questions — she'd even helped Cataroni scan the serial numbers on tonight's buy money — but it seemed as if all that brainstormed backstory would prove irrelevant, a waste of energy like so much else. Questions? An interrogation? Please: Rose Marie had hardly bothered to look at her. In almost any other buy scenario that would've been fine, preferable really, but for once Janice wanted a dealer to remember her face. She wanted to return

219

to this apartment the following week, without the complications of a CI buffer. A long-term drug case against a day care — a day care! — would guarantee her promotion. "Nursery Nightmare," the *Post*'s headline would say. "Hero Cop Puts Drug-Dealing Nannies to Sleep."

"You got a scale?" she asked.

"A scale?" Rose Marie said, her hand now on the receiver.

"Yeah. A scale. You know, to weigh shit? I'm not trying to get ripped off here."

Before Rose Marie could complain to K-Lo or ask for the envelope back or tell Janice to just *look* at the rocks for fuck's sake or go searching all over the apartment for a small enough scale or really even do anything at all, Janice had already jerked open the sliding-glass door. She crashed through the safety gate toward the little girl's screaming. The Magic Marker had been abandoned. Her father was dragging her toward the door, yanking her off her feet. From somewhere deep down in her skinny chest, the girl howled with an entirely adult panic and rage.

Half a lifetime ago, when Jimmy Gellar was writer's-blocked, he had asked Janice why Gabby Guyana had decided to become Captain Richmond Hill — revenge? crushing guilt? childhood trauma? intergalactic responsibility? — but for Janice there was no one thing that could explain why she herself had joined the police force but instead an almost infinite number of things, a partial list of which might include that she bit her nails, tore up coasters, peeled labels off bottles, guessed in record time the ending of *Murder on the Orient Express,* wanted the benefits of a purposeful life, wanted the benefits of a city job, wanted the automatic salary bumps, had never seriously considered doing anything else, hated bullies, had assumed even before her father had started beating her mother that everyone harbored a dark and secret interior life, had crushed on Encyclopedia Brown as a young girl and Agent Mulder as a teenager, was once called a nigger by two white cops in a patrol car, and, perhaps most important, she always, no matter what, took a definitive side in arguments, especially ones that had nothing to do with her, and in this LeFrak City living room the pickings were easy.

While the neighbor lady hovered in the background, Rose Marie's sister slapped at the man's head. He kept his arm raised, to shield himself from her blows instead of knocking her across the living room as he easily could have. It was the one thing to be said in his defense. His other hand, though, was gripped unforgivably hard around the little girl's elbow.

In a voice she hadn't used for over seventeen months, Janice said, "Hold it."

He did the opposite and let the girl go. A small yellow dandelion pierced his lapel button, something Janice had failed to notice earlier. In the struggle — which had momentarily stopped, the woman no longer slapping at the man's head but tensed to resume at any moment — some of the weaker petals had come loose and lay curled on the carpet. Cold air from the balcony riffled Janice's hair. She stepped farther into the living room. Because she didn't have a badge pinned to her chest, the others didn't actually have to listen to her, but nobody seemed to realize that yet except for the girl. Seeing her chance, with everyone around her collectively paused, she sprinted into the kitchen through the left-open safety gate.

Janice caught up to her easily, but the girl had already grabbed a paring knife off the countertop. A baby carrot went skittering across the tiles. One of them must have accidentally kicked it running in here. Without pausing to consider the consequences, desperate only to escape from her father, the girl — who had already killed one child — plunged the paring knife into the tiny hollow between her chest and her throat. She stumbled forward as if an invisible hand had slapped her viciously between the shoulder blades. An involuntary gurgling opened her mouth. Instantly regretful, hoping to undo the hurt, she reached for the knife to pull it out, but Janice got to it first and kept the blade in the girl's neck as a plug for the wound. The blood loss would've killed her in minutes. Together they sat themselves down on the floor, her head in Janice's lap. An exhaust fan spun loudly. Barely visible against the girl's skin, purple ink cobwebbed her arms. As she kept trying to exhale a breath that wasn't there, Janices filled the kitchen. There was the Janice who barked at Rose Marie to call the police, the Janice who told the sister to fetch towels, the Janice who hoped K-Lo had enough sense to run to the investigators, the Janice who watched the father chewing on the flap of skin at the base of his thumb, the Janice who gripped the knife handle, the Janice who pressed her fingertips beneath the girl's one good eye to trap the tears, and the final Janice, the liar Janice who kept whispering, *You're okay, you're okay, you're okay.*

■ ■ ■ ■

Afterward she went downstairs to sit in the parked Impala's backseat. Her calves ached from walking down all those steps. Crusted in blood, her nails were unchewable. Uncharacteristically for McCarthy and Duckenfield, they both sat with their knees pressed together to give her more room, and Cataroni had twisted himself around in his shotgun seat to look at her. Sergeant Hart's eye contact, however, came exclusively through the rearview. K-Lo, before going home, had told the investigators everything he knew, and now Janice told them the rest: that the paramedics took the girl away with a tracheotomy tube bobbing in her throat, that when the uniforms arrived Janice showed them her fake Janice Singh driver's license, that in all the confusion she'd forgotten to pay Rose Marie for the drugs.

"It's technically not a buy, then," Hart said.

"I know, I'm sorry, it was just so —"

"Don't be sorry," he said quickly. "Nobody's mad at you."

She snapped at the hair tie around her wrist until the little knobby bone there went numb. "Can we just get out of here?" she asked. "I'd just really like to get out of here."

"Yeah, of course," Hart said. He pulled out of the LeFrak parking lot, and when he saw an opening in the traffic he turned onto Junction Boulevard, skipping the express-ways and taking the long route back to Flushing, past 24/7 check-cashing joints and a shop that sold safes. After a few blocks of silence, he said, "So what do you want to do?"

He'd asked the windshield, but she knew he was talking to her. "Go home," she told him. "Take a sleeping pill, take a shower."

"No, I mean what do you want to do with the drugs?" he asked. "We can write it up as a buy . . . if you want. We can put in the paperwork that you paid for the rocks, and just figure out what to do with the cash later. Or? We can all stay late filling out forms explaining why you got the rocks but no buy. Or just get rid of the shit, fuck it, whatever you want, it's up to you."

"I don't care."

"No, no, no," Duckenfield said. "It's got to be your call. Right?"

"It's got to be her call," McCarthy agreed.

She thought of Pablo Rivera, the rumpus's town crier. Despite the investigators' soft tones and apparent goodwill — surely temporary, a possible by-product of the

225

blood dried on her cheeks — Pablo Rivera would have warned that all this might be an integrity test, that one of these men might work undercover for Internal Affairs. Probably not, but she knew too well the pitfalls of insufficient paranoia, what happens when safety gates are left open and dealers sell to strangers. She passed Cataroni the manila envelope and all the buy money.

"Do what you want," she said. "But for me? I don't want to lie on any of my paperwork."

She saw Hart nod at her through the rearview. At the next red light, he poured all eight crack rocks into his Altoids tin. He left the money with Cataroni, who'd return it to the department's considerable coffers. The manila envelope went out the window. She didn't know if she'd passed the test or failed it, but she did know that Hart would write up tonight as an unsuccessful mission. Uncle botched an untouchable buy. The drugs she took away from LeFrak no longer existed. She wished she knew the little girl's name. When asked if she'd survive, one of the paramedics had said she seemed tough.

Saturday morning the *Post* headline read, "Bad News Bear: Fed Bails Out Wall St. Giant." The fat Sunday edition covered a crane collapse that sliced through three buildings, rubbled another, and killed four construction workers in midtown Manhattan. No mention of the little girl, though, thank God, nor did she appear in the *Times, Newsday,* or *Daily News.* Janice was too afraid to call the hospitals. On Monday — "Let the Madness Begin!" said the *Post* — needing a change, something drastic, she asked Fiorella to come with her to a fancy hair salon in Forest Hills. Hector the Magnificent, with only a half day at school, tagged along to raid the lollipop jar. While Fiorella tried to maintain a neutral expression, an Argentinean stylist named Beto got so worked up describing his operatic love life that he accidentally chopped off almost all of Janice's hair. When he spun her around to face the mirror, she cried. She'd wanted drastic, not *drastic.* But to make Beto feel better, she lied and said she'd never once in her life gotten a major haircut without weeping immediately afterward. It didn't work. He started weeping himself. Hector, truly magnificent, said he preferred the shorter hair, as did Fiorella, but when Janice got home her mother hadn't even seemed to notice her arrival, much less that she'd gotten a new pixie cut. Vita was sitting at the kitchen table, completely absorbed, at last shredding her junk mail, not with a proper shredder like a normal paranoiac, but with an X-Acto knife, one strip, one credit card offer at a time. Even more disconcerting, the whiteboard read JIMMY GELLER, misspelled, in her shaky new handwriting.

"Was he here?" Janice said. "Did he come by the house?"

"Was who here?" Vita asked, cutting another line down the page. When she finally looked up, she said, "What did you *do*?"

"Don't even. I hate it." Janice chinpointed to the whiteboard. "What'd he want? You didn't tell him I live here, did you?"

Vita stared at the board for a few long moments before giving up. "I'm not sure."

"Well, did he call or —"

"I don't know! I've got my own stuff going on, okay? I can't be keeping track of your every little thing."

She reached for an envelope promising more affordable auto insurance. It was one thing for her to call the remote control the picture-stick, but yesterday lipstick had become the mouth-painter. Lipstick! You kidding? She had no *use* for affordable auto insurance. With deteriorating motor skills, both literally and figuratively, she'd already donated her car to the Alzheimer's Association. Three piles of junk-mail confetti lay on the table, as if she planned to throw them away in three separate garbage cans scattered throughout the neighborhood. Jimmy's name might as well have been written in invisible ink. And yet, on these otherwise mind-befogged days, there would be moments simultaneously hopeful and heartbreaking when she'd remember it was Mrs. Hua's birthday and pop over next door with a tinful of breakfast bake. Or when, within seconds of Vanna White turning over the first few consonants, Vita would shout out, *Chairman of the board games* or *Beloved family pet peeve!* How do you reconcile that? How can both these Vitas occupy the same body? Janice sat down at the kitchen table to take hold of her mother's lavender-scented hands.

"Is he somebody from work?" Vita asked her. "Did I screw up something important?"

"No, not at all." Janice slid her mother's hands up into her new haircut and held them there, the palms perfectly warm against her scalp. "What do you think?" she said. "Too short?"

"To be honest?"

"No," Janice said.

"I like it better long."

"Like yours."

"Yeah," Vita said. "Exactly. Beautiful like mine."

The next day at work, Sergeant Hart told her she looked like a lesbian. It was, needless to say, a volunteered admission. It shouldn't have surprised her — a month earlier, when Gonz started sporting an investigator-like mustache, Hart had asked, *With a nose like that, why underline it?* and if an uncle ever dared show up to work wearing a tank top, he'd compare their arms to French fries — but, well, Janice had foolishly assumed their post-LeFrak cease-fire might last a little bit longer than a single weekend. You know what happens when you assume, though. He sat on the edge of her desk and asked if she knew what a fool's mate was.

She took a chance: "As in like your wife?"

"Is that supposed to be humorous?" he asked Tevis, who was filling out department softball lineups at the adjoining desk. "Does she think this is standup-comedy time?"

"I think it was more like a defense mechanism," Tevis told him. "Against what is clearly going to be another one of your mean-spirited lectures."

"Actually," Janice said, "I was really just trying to build up a kind of jokey rapport."

Sergeant Hart held his hands over his alleged heart as if touched. "A fool's mate," he explained, "is a thing in chess where you make two moves and all of a sudden the game's over. White brings out a pair of pawns, exposing the king. Then you move a bishop and a queen, and it's checkmate. Sayonara. There you go, the fool's mate, but really you can apply it to any game that's over before it starts. And who's the fool? The loser, right? But let me tell you something: you win like this a couple of times, especially when you're just learning, and it's the only way you want to do it. The *only* way. And no offense, but I've seen this with plenty of female undercovers in my time here. You come in, shake your ass a little on the street, and it's a bunch of quick buys. But then a few months fall off the calendar. People start recognizing that ass. Now you're playing opponents with a little more experience, but guess what? You don't have the moves. You never learned, you never got a feel for that long middle game, where chess, real chess, is gonna be won or lost. Because you didn't have to work in the beginning, you're unwilling to work now."

She said, "That's completely —"

He sock-puppeted his hand, slapped his fingers and thumb together to go *yap, yap, yap, yap, yap, yap, yap, yap.* In the last week alone, Fiorella had tricked two separate teenagers into selling her spliffs that the poor bastards had rolled for themselves. A pair of buys for the 112 Precinct. Six-plus hours of department-approved overtime. Morris made a buy off a dealer who'd stashed his stash up his butthole. For the 103 Precinct, three hours of overtime; for Klondike, four hours of crack jokes. Grimes bought a twist of rocks at the homeless shelter where he used to live. A buy for the 113. Over at Zully's Bubbles Laundromat in Astoria, Puffy bought a dime bag off a moron who'd accidentally washed and dried all his weed. A buy for the 114. According to the rumpus board, James Chan had somehow made three buys for the 108 Precinct, but he kept all the details to himself. Pablo Rivera bought a Xanax off a guy who may or may not have secretly worked for Internal Affairs. Either way, it counted as a buy for the 106. At a Bayside multiplex, while on line for *Horton Hears a Who,* a big-time Eddie Murphy fan sold Eddie Murphy an eight ball. Mark it up for the 111 Precinct. For the 109 Precinct here in Flushing, Richie the Receptionist —

without even having to go outside — bought crack down in the fucking lobby, off a dealer who thought this was an insurance building or something and had only been looking for a warm place to count his cash. Buys across the board, padded paychecks throughout the rumpus for everyone but guess who? Gonz had done nothing for the 115. Tevis had made a buy — thank you, Tevis — but Janice had of course missed his positive signal. Remember that? She'd also jinxed the unjinxable K-Lo, turned down the investigators' subsequent offer to make it right, spent her off time at a so-called beauty salon, and her rumpus hours guzzling soda over a garbage can and insinuating to her superior officer that she considered him a fool. Today's schedule would unfortunately provide her with limited opportunities to redeem herself. She was supposed to be the ghost this afternoon while Tevis would be the one making buys. Attempting to make buys. After Sergeant Hart walked away, she knocked her knuckles against her desk, to get a little magic started for her, for Tevis, for Beto and her mother and everyone really except the drug dealers of Queens.

# Chapter Seven

What do you look for? Men, mostly. Particularly men of a certain age, somewhere between fifteen and twenty-four. Baggy jeans, but not so baggy that whoever's wearing them couldn't run away if chased. A lot of people of color unfortunately. A lot of short people of color for whatever reason. Coats or shirts that hung way down past the waist. An overlong belt that dangled between thighs like some sort of Darwinian advertisement. Sensible shoes. People who looked cold but weren't wearing gloves. Fidgeters and neck-scratchers with candy-caned eyes. High-traffic areas: outside bodegas, a block up from subway exits. The vacant mean-mugs of the chronically bored. Ears without headphone buds. That crocodile-looking motherfucker over there with the beaded eyes and snaggled underbite and arms so short they barely breached his jacket cuffs. To-go coffee cups, especially cups that were never sipped from, without any steam twisting off the rim. The only non-Filipino outside the Philippine National Bank. Two men talking without eye contact, the both of them facing the street. That's what you looked for when you were the uncle, but Janice the ghost was supposed to watch only Tevis — his unbuttoned coat, his uncovered head — as he struck out with the crocodile, the non-Filipino, the two men who'd talk to each other but not to him.

Her hands were full of flyers. *¡Enderece su pelo!* Straighten your hair! *¡Enderece sus dientes!* Straighten your teeth! She threw them all away in a KEEP NEW YORK CLEAN trash can. At the intersection she turned around and saw an old Chinese lady picking recyclables out of the garbage. "When trying to determine if he's being followed, the experienced agent will fold an unimportant piece of paper, leave it atop a rubbish bin, and then glance back after a few strides to see if a tail has taken the bait and reached for the paper," from the *Top Secret Spy Tech Official Training Manual,* a small binder she'd sent away for as a kid and obsessively internalized. Over the course of three Christmases, her father spoiled her with the Spy Tech fingerprint kit, a motion detector, walkie-talkies, a periscope that could peer around corners, a pair of sunglasses with mirrors on the outer edges, and a camera hiding inside a Good & Plenty candy box, everything but the high-quality long-range microphone. In hindsight the microphone's omission seemed deliberate. When she'd exhausted the full line of Spy Tech toys — or at least the line of Spy Tech toys her father was willing to bring into the house — she told anyone who asked that she wanted the Clue Master Detective Edition board game next Christmas. Then felt stupidly surprised and weirdly guilty when she unwrapped six Clue Master Detective Edition board games.

The Nextel said, "Any buys?"

Later the Nextel asked, "How about now?"

Tevis eventually expanded his purview to include men over the age of twenty-five, tall people, white people, tight pants, the Filipinos outside the Philippine National Bank, women and children, and a Mexican guy selling roasted peanuts. Forget about steam escaping or not escaping from coffee cups. If you had ears, Tevis had questions: *You holding? You got twenty? A little help? Hey, can I ask you something real quick? You seen the guy? The guy who's always out here?*

"No," the dealers answered when they

bothered to say anything at all.

It took Tevis two hours to walk one mile down Roosevelt, from Sixtieth Street to Seventy-Ninth, where he ducked into a corner bodega for some cigarettes. Closer to Corona now, the streets were turning increasingly Latin, with the ubiquitous travel agencies beginning to advertise South American vacations only. The curried chicken puffs on Sixty-Fourth Street, the soy garlic Korean fried chicken wings on Seventy-Second, and the flavorless grilled-chicken deli sandwiches on Seventy-Sixth all became chicken mole tamale carts, Argentinean chicken empanada stands, the famous *Pollos a la Brasa Mario* with whole birds roasting in the windows. Jesus Christ, Janice was fucking starving. From across the street she watched Tevis limp out of the bodega, slapping a pack of menthols against his palm, all his tricks going at once, the cigarettes serving as a *pasaporte universal.* A block later, outside a bar called La Escuelita, he found a pair of smokers, one of whom was, no joke, wearing a rainbow flag tied around his neck. Dark papers covered the bar's windows, just like at the rumpus. A blinking neon sign above the door requested PRIDE. The other smoker, the one without the cape, apparently didn't have any matches, so he offered Tevis a monkeyfuck, lighting up his cigarette with the cherry at the end of his own. Please, oh please, Janice thought. Be holding something, anything, a crinkled joint, a tab of Ecstasy turning to dust in your wallet. She wondered if Tevis was flirting, a possibility more likely with his kel on the fritz. A possibility even likelier now as he followed the two guys into the bar.

She wanted to run across the street and sneak in behind him. Sit on a faraway stool and sip a hot toddy . . . but of course she could not. With the possible exception of her father's Long Island monstrosity, there wasn't a place in the world where she'd be more blatantly conspicuous than a Latino gay bar on a weekday afternoon. To get out of the wind, she stepped inside the glass diorama of a sidewalk bus shelter, where she waited with a small crowd of people who all looked exhausted. Their work shifts over, they at least would be going home soon. The Q32 came then left, immediately followed by another that had no one to pick up except Janice, who wasn't allowed to leave. Through the Nextel, Sergeant Hart asked for an update. She told him the uncle had gone into a bar; he told her to keep up the hard work. Her feet were freezing in her boots. She imagined that when she got home — if she got home — she'd flick her pinkie toe and see it snap off, go skipping across the kitchen tiles. For the first time since morning she remembered her dream from the night before, about a bat that flew into the house through a poorly screened bathroom vent. The bus shelter began to slowly refill. Claustrophobia shoved her out onto the street. Another Q32 pulled in to gobble up everyone but her. When Sergeant Hart asked for another update, Janice — cold and crabby, with an image of Tevis drinking from a piña colada — let it spitefully slip that uncle was still in the gay bar. Hart thanked her with genuine gratitude, the happiest she'd ever heard him. The old stoop-backed Chinese lady, the one who'd picked through the trash can earlier, pushed a shopping cart full of bagged recyclables past La Escuelita's front door. Janice was actually only assuming it was the same Chinese lady. Was that racist? Was *she* racist? Was it profiling to pay particular attention to a well-dressed Arab man double-parking a Taurus on the corner? He ran across the street, up the block, and beyond the avenue, where she couldn't see him anymore. Less than a minute later, he came jogging back with both hands in his coat pockets.

She moved without thinking. He already had the car door open, but before he could get behind the wheel she had grabbed his arm. She told him her name was Janice.

"And you must be Mohammad, right?"

"Ayad," he said, somewhere between disappointed and confused.

"Oh. Sorry. I was supposed to meet a Mohammad."

He leaned against the car, folded his arms across his chest. "I can be Mohammad."

"You're Ayad with the pretty wife, right?"

"What?"

See you later. She hurried across the street in the direction he'd come jogging from, toward the traffic signal's blinking orange hand. The expression on his face may have been bewildered or annoyed, worried about his hypothetical wife; Janice didn't know because she didn't bother to turn around and look. Instead, as she went past the avenue, she turned to see if La Escuelita's front door had swung open, afraid she might lose Tevis, afraid he might come out and catch her. She reached into her purse to put the Nextel on silent. Up the block, in a lonely spot away from Roosevelt's foot traffic, a bored-looking Mexican man leaned against the plywood wall of a construction site. He was over six feet tall, over two hundred pounds, with a giant dark birthmark fuzzing his fat cheek.

"You seen Ayad?" she asked him.

He bent forward at the waist to look past her down the block. Paper flyers covered the plywood wall, which was low enough that he could scramble over it if ever necessary. She saw hair- and teeth-straightening offers like the ones she'd thrown away earlier. The psychic with the reasonable rates — DON'T GIVE UP HOPE, SEE MADAM SANDRA — had her sticker beneath a section of the wall that said NO FLYERS in small letters. The guy, Janice. Pay attention to the guy. His bubble jacket extended far enough past his waist to conceal any gun bulges. His arms were big enough to crush the breath from her lungs. All the neighborhood dealers lately seemed to be huge. When he leaned back against the wall, the paper flyers crinkled behind him.

"You know Ayad?" he asked.

"Yeah, sure," she said. "I was supposed to meet him here."

"That a fact?" The guy's lips barely moved when he spoke, as if it pained him to talk to her. "You like literally just missed him."

"You're messing with me."

"Not yet I'm not," he said. "What you

241

thinking you need?"

She opened her purse, careful not to let him see the handgun sitting at the bottom. With a steady hand she passed him a twenty. He held it up to the sun, like an outdoor bank clerk, and then smiled or maybe grimaced, she couldn't tell. Maybe, upset, he was chewing on the insides of his cheeks. She looked behind her to see if Tevis was crossing the intersection — no, thank God — and when she turned back around the guy was spitting a baggie of crack rocks into his palm. They looked real, with a dawnish discoloration around the edges, not that she cared. She shoved the saliva-wet baggie into her pocket, not her purse, which would've been harder to clean.

"So, listen," the guy said. He scratched at his ear, but really he was just trying to cover up his leech of a birthmark. "Are you and Ayad like —"

"Thanks a lot!" she said over her shoulder.

Back on the avenue, a 7 train roared across the el tracks. The pigeons had long ago scattered, but Roosevelt's more sensitive children were just now plugging their ears. She paced outside La Escuelita, its windows too sturdy to rattle, too dark for her to see through. After the train had passed, in the relative quiet it had left behind, she whispered into her Nextel. *I made a buy? Hello? Do you copy? I made a buy.*

Three down, one to go.

She told the investigators that she had maintained her post outside the bar. The whole time. Never left it. The Mexican dude? He had approached *her.* Understand? *He* was the one who'd initiated the sale, practically *forcing* the rocks on her. What was she supposed to do? Say no? Just because she was ghosting? Tell him to fuck off and sell his drugs to someone else: a child, a nun, a recovering addict? After making the buy — outside La Escuelita, mind you — she watched the Mexican wander around the corner, the dude so fat and so slow that she bet the investigators could catch up to him easy. Because Sergeant Hart needed the overtime, he chose to believe her. Detective First Grade Chester Tevis, however, was as always a whole other story. While McCarthy and Duckenfield were head-steering the birthmarked Mexican into a p-van, Tevis met her three blocks south of Roosevelt, at the investigator car, away from any potential witnesses except for Cataroni and Hart in the front seat. She sat on the warm hood and tried to rub the chill out of her arms. She was afraid to look into his face. She stared at his throat instead, his coat buttoned to the top even though he hadn't made any buys. He had been close, though, he told her. He had been just about to make a buy when he got this mother-f'ing call on his Nextel. Cataroni and Hart, with the dashboard heat blasting their faces, could see Tevis standing over her but probably not hear what he was saying.

"Fourteen years I've been doing this," Tevis told her. "Fourteen years and I've *never* had a ghost leave me. Not once."

"You're not listening," she said. "The whole time, I'm telling you, I was outside the —"

"No," he said. "This is to my face now. You're peddling this nonsense to my face, Itwaru."

"You're not listening!"

"*You're* not listening. Tell them whatever," he said, gesturing to the investigators, "but you gotta understand I'm not falling for this, Itwaru. It doesn't work on me. I'm the one who *taught* you how to lie."

Wrong. Her father taught her how to lie — don't hesitate, don't overdetail, don't change stories, because no matter how angry people seem, they really do want to believe you — but she didn't tell Tevis that. "I swear to God," she said. "I never had the bar out of my sight."

"My life's at stake with this shit," he whispered, cursing for the first time in front of her. "I can't . . . I have daughters, understand? I can't be playing this game." He reached into his pocket for the Kangol cap, as if to signal the end of their transaction. "I know your eighteen months is coming up. Just so you don't get in any trouble with that, it should probably be you and not me to ask Prondzinski for a partner switch. She'll give it to you, I'm sure. Tell her . . . I don't know. Tell her whatever you want. You'll think of something, I can guarantee that."

"What is this?" she said and hopped off the Impala's hood. "You're breaking up with me? Over *this*?"

"I can't work with somebody I don't trust," he told her calmly. "Those are the rules. Those are *my* rules. And I don't give out second chances, ever. It's why I'm still alive."

"But I didn't even do anything wrong!"

"Oh man, it's convincing, Itwaru. I gotta congratulate you, I really do. You know what you sound like? You sound just like a drug fiend. Like an actual frickin' drug fiend."

Hart rolled down the Impala's window to hurry them along. It was time to go, time for him to go at least. With the Mexican officially in a p-van headed to the 115 Precinct, McCarthy and Duckenfield needed the Impala to come scoop them up. But — feeling magnanimous, high on the anticipatory pleasures of time-and-a-half — Hart offered to drop the uncles off at their car first. It was over a mile away in Woodside, parked where they always parked it for drug runs, across from the Himalayan Yak, but Tevis said he'd rather walk.

"She'll go with you, though," he told Hart. "Right, Itwaru? You want to get into Investigations anyway, yeah? Before you move on to the commissioner's office?"

"Trouble in paradise?" Hart asked.

Tevis opened a backseat door for her. He wanted to make this a bigger deal than it needed to be? He wanted to disparage her ambition? Dissolve their partnership over a misunderstanding, walk back to the uncle car alone through the cold, well then fine, whatever, go walk back to the uncle car alone through the cold. After she settled herself in the backseat, he clicked the door shut for her, not at all slamming it as she would have. Cataroni turned around to make a sympathetic *yikes* face. She expected

Hart to say something nasty, but the Impala just sped away toward Roosevelt and left Tevis behind. The radio played WFAN sports talk, the investigators' post-buy ritual. The story of the minute: Tiger Woods's sixty-five-million-dollar mansion. Up ahead a young brown woman ran out into the street. She had jumped out from between two parked cars, dressed all in black like a shadow, her ponytail flouncing in the Impala's headlights. To curb his boredom, to teach her a lesson, Hart gunned the engine then braked just short of murder. The woman was frozen; something heavy-sounding shifted in the trunk. Cat25oni ricocheted hard against the dash, but Janice, who had sensed this was coming, had her arms extended, her hands braced against the driver's-side headrest, as if the foot on the brake was her own.

Turn the clocks back six months. Zip across the country. Zip into a new country, into Mexico, where the famous Sierra Madre Mountains green the northwestern coast. It starts here. Actually it starts under the ground, in the rich soil, with seeds sprouting roots, which sprout stalks five feet tall. Imagine a farmer. To better picture him, give him something a little strange, like an eye patch. At night his hands twitch through his dreams. During the day he snips thousands of marijuana buds off hundreds of marijuana plants. Keep it in the family: the buds then go to his sisters, who live in a nearby adobe with outrageous electricity bills and a satellite dish that snatches dubbed American television dramas out of the air. One sister loves *Grey's Anatomy,* the other favors *Lost,* and they have little to talk about as they set their brother's buds in a ten-rack industrial dehydrator. After that, they bunch the buds into bricks, wrap those bricks up in cling wrap, and coat that cling wrap in grease, motor oil, and mustard, a smell not unlike Brother Itwaru's. Up the driveway comes a 1999 Honda Civic, modified, with its battery hidden in the trunk. Under the hood an empty shell of a dummy battery waits for three of the sisters' bricks.

Now you have to find someone ambitious or desperate or both. It never takes long. There's a town not too far away from the adobe — El Rosario maybe? — and in this town there's a nineteen-year-old boy. Let's give him a snazzy name, something that hints at his bravery and eventual suckerdom, something like Jerónimo Chávez Morán. The Sinaloa cartel, or rather someone on behalf of the Sinaloa cartel, pays

Morán five thousand pesos, roughly four hundred and fifty American dollars, to drive the Civic twenty miles north to the Otay Mesa border crossing. He has been instructed to take the far-right customs lane, where a border agent has been instructed to stop the car on behalf of the Department of Homeland Security. The drugs? The drugs are immediately found. The DHS agent calls over his superiors, who attempt an interrogation, but Morán can tell them nothing because he knows nothing. He hasn't even been paid yet. Meanwhile, on the far-left lane of the Otay Mesa border crossing, a tractor-trailer carrying 6.9 metric tons of marijuana enters the United States.

In the backseat of her parents' SUV, a little girl looking out the window tugs an imaginary handle above her head.

The trailer's air horn responds with a satisfyingly noisy *honk-honk*.

Throughout Texas, Arizona, New Mexico, and California, shady mechanics tinker on tricked-out trap cars. In the spirit of Manifest Destiny, we'll send the tractor-trailer into California, into a nondescript warehouse with a nondescript name, less Vandelay Imports than Sunny Brothers Shipping Company. Workers there diversify the 6.9 metric tons of marijuana into a small fleet of vehicles, each one specially equipped with hydraulics that — when the doors are locked, the left-turn signal is blinking, and a switch beneath the dash is engaged — raises the backseat to reveal a secret compartment. Stopping only for gas, beef jerky, energy drinks, and more gas, it takes two guys working in shifts seventy-four hours and a significant amount of bickering to drive one of these cars to the East Coast, to a stash house in the mostly residential neighborhood of Mooreseville, North Carolina.

That was three and a half months ago.

Yesterday, a pair of Queens drug dealers drove up from North Carolina with a marijuana-stuffed suitcase in the trunk of their shitty rental car. Shitty because the passenger's-side window rolled down but not up, as if ghetto touched. Both dealers caught terrible head colds. Professionals, they persevered. When they got home, they sold an ounce of weed to an overweight black kid, Dwayne Jenkins, an ambitious, desperate, American-born nineteen-year-old. Today, on this particular afternoon, you'd find him outside his mother's apartment building, straddling a construction horse over a deep crater in the street. He had a system: he kept on his person a max of three baggies at a time so that if a DT from Narco ever rolled up on him, he could slip the evidence through a hole in his pocket. From there it would drop down his pant leg and into the crater beneath him. The only hitch: whenever he sold his third baggie, he had to hustle back across the street into his lobby, which is to say his mother's lobby, where he kept his stash in her mailbox. It was fifty-seven degrees outside, way warmer than yesterday, and all the jetting back and forth had him sweating above his ass crack. With his teeth and long fingernails and the patience of the severely stoned, he picked at the sleeve seams of his sweatshirt so as to turn it into a more breathable sweat–tank top. It was surprisingly difficult work. He had one sleeve off and was biting at the other when he saw a dude from around the neighborhood, a real sleazebucket named K-Lo, who everyone knew suffered from a dangerous blabber infection. He was of course coming Dwayne's way. K-Lo had brought along with him a slice of hot mess, an Indian chick — dot, not feather — with a twitchy eyelid and chapped lips. Outside of Dwayne's mother and certain bowling-alley waitresses, she was the most exhausted-looking woman he'd ever seen. She walked quickly, though. Behind her, across the street, out in front of his mother's apartment building, more heads showed up, but they definitely weren't customers, or at least they weren't his kind of customers.

"You got twenty?" the girl asked.

"Forgive her," K-Lo said. "She . . . we work together? At the copy center? And she's not exactly the star of customer relations over there. Dwayne, this is Janice. Janice, this is Dwayne. See how that works, Jan?"

"You got twenty?" she asked.

"I do," Dwayne told her. "But it's not so safe right now, know what I mean?"

"No," she said. "I don't know what you mean. Can you hook us up or what?"

"Five minutes ago, no problem. That's what I'm trying to tell you. But now? I can't be doing nothing with police all up in my face."

"What?" she said.

"What?" he said in a girly falsetto meant to mimic her panic. He chin-pointed across the street, where a Chevy Impala sat parked at a fire hydrant. Four antennae rose up out of the trunk, one for every plainclothes in the car. "I mean, are they for real?" Dwayne asked. "Four pissed-off looking white motherfuckers sitting in a tow-away zone? Doing nothing?"

"Unbelievable," she said.

"Believe it," he told her. "I'm gonna have to go, but I'll be back here tomorrow, same spot and everything, if y'all looking to get hooked up again."

"I need it today," she said.

"Well, good luck," he told her. "But you're gonna want to be real careful, just saying. Keep your eyes open, yeah? Where there's some cops there's more cops, and they'll bust you for nothing."

She didn't even thank him. But that was all right: he was the Godfather, Saint Dwayne, protector of dumb bitches the world over. After K-Lo dragged her away, Dwayne pushed the last two of his baggies through the hole in his pants pocket. It'd be a loss of forty dollars, but since they cost him only ten dollars per, it really was only a loss of twenty, the cost of doing business, a small price to pay for peace of mind. Plus, truth be told, he needed to justify his sore asshole. Why straddle this construction horse if he wasn't going to make use of its crater? The baggies dropped down next to one of his sweatshirt sleeves and a bag of Cheetos he'd emptied earlier. He wiped his hands together, problem solved, nothing to worry about. Before crossing the street and walking past that gauntlet of cops, he pulled out his cell to call his connects, the dudes who'd driven back up to Queens from North Carolina.

"Hey, yo," Dwayne said. "You know that Indian chick you was telling me about? Did she have short hair or long?"

It was the day after the Tevis breakup. For this afternoon's shift, Gonz had been ghosting her, not a permanent arrangement, God willing, and not by request, either — she hadn't talked to Prondzinski yet — but because it was his turn in the preestablished rotation to work the 115. As if in apology, the Big Bosses also teamed her up with K-Lo, the superstar CI who'd dragged her to all the neighborhood parks, where somehow they just kept striking out. Hardly any of the dealers were where K-Lo had said they'd be, and when they were, they weren't selling what K-Lo said they'd be selling. *Uncle continues to be hopeless,* Gonz probably said into the Nextel. And when she at last did come close to making a buy, the investigators of course spoiled it by accidentally parking across the street. Yeah right. Accidentally, her ass. Ten minutes later, five blocks south of Roosevelt, off the grid and away from the dealers, she shoved her face close to Hart's through his open driver's-side window. She called bullshit. The investigators made a mistake? Parked on the wrong corner? Hadn't noticed her talking to Dwayne? Bullshit, bullshit, bullshit. Spittle flew out of her mouth. She accused Hart of sabotaging her out of some sausage-club loyalty to Tevis, and she wanted to know what the fuck. Inside the Impala, Cataroni and McCarthy and Duckenfield all gawked with disbelief. Gonz and K-Lo slithered closer behind her, as if to eavesdrop, which was unnecessary since she was shouting. When Hart opened his mouth to respond, his breath punched her with acid reflux.

"Who do you think you are?" he said.

"I —"

"Who do you think you *are*?" he said again, the implication being *I'm a sergeant, your superior, capable of stripping your vacation days, writing you up for insubordination, killing your career with a bad annual review, kicking your thick ass back to patrol. That's me. Who are you?* It was a question she didn't know how to answer. To move her face away from his own, he powered up the window. His door swung open and smashed her knees. He stepped out of the car, unfolding himself to full height, waiting for her to say something, anything, and when she didn't, when she did nothing except pedal backward, he pointed a finger at K-Lo and barked, "You! J-Lo, K-Lo, whatever the fuck . . . you wanna get paid in cash?"

Always prepared, K-Lo said, "Or?"

Hart picked three crack rocks out of his Altoids tin and dropped them one by one into K-Lo's palm. She'd never seen anything like it. K-Lo's face registered zero surprise, though, as if this had happened plenty of times before, but then again maybe not: he kept his body half turned, ready to take off and run in case Hart changed his mind. Gonz, meanwhile, was staring at a plastic bag wrapped around a telephone-pole wire. She probably should've looked away, too, for the purposes of plausible deniability. Paying CIs with drugs — or failing to report an officer who paid CIs with drugs — was not only against departmental regulations but illegal, obviously, potentially punishable with jail time. Hart would keep the cash, K-Lo would sell the rocks for more money than he would've been paid for today's services, and everybody everywhere would win, except Janice, of course. For cues on how to behave she turned to the investigators in the Impala, but she couldn't see them anymore from where she was standing. Bright sun inflamed all their windows.

"Gonz," said Sergeant Hart. "You want a ride back to the uncle car, or what?"

Hopeful, Gonz looked at her — a chance to listen to WFAN sports talk with the investigators! — and she waved him along. Their shift, and by extension his ghosting responsibilities, had ended five minutes earlier. Now at least she could walk back to the uncle car by herself, without him snarking next to her the whole way. *What were you thinking, Itwaru? You on your period or something?* They'd have the drive back to the rumpus for all that. Assuming he waited for her at the uncle car. Assuming he didn't ditch her completely, although not even Gonz was that much of a prick. He'd probably wait for her at one of Woodside's Irish pubs, probably Saints & Sinners, where he'd have enough time for a beer and a couple of shots, lucky him. What was she waiting for? Standing here for? K-Lo had already left: he went east with one hand protectively plunged into his pocket, his fist presumably curled around the rocks. And so she went the other way: back toward Woodside and the uncle car, solo, just like Tevis the day before. As always she moved quickly, even outpacing the Impala for half a block before it left her behind. The Nextel in her purse put the time at exactly 3:40. The nineteenth of March, a Wednesday. She'd never forget it. On Judge Street, between Britton and Vietor Avenues, she paused to watch a little black kid practicing his killers, hitting a handball off the side of an apartment building, down where the bricks met the sidewalk so the ball would dribble back to him, unreturnable. The Latino with the flaming eyeball grabbed her from behind.

Before she recognized him, she recognized the tattoo: a bright blue iris, burst capillaries, flames trailing down his neck, as if the eye had combusted straight out of its socket. She recognized, too, the awkward angle of his jaw, the small white nubbins of his teeth. Acne scars — something she hadn't noticed before, but then again she hadn't been this close before — pocked his cheeks, over which he'd applied a thin layer of flesh-colored foundation. Other than the makeup, he looked exactly the same, his goatee as finely groomed as it was the only other time she'd seen him, two Saturdays ago, on line at the taco cart. Now he had a hold of her elbow. Behind him, as if she were living a daylight nightmare with all her secret monsters collected on one sidewalk, stood Korean Marty, miserably coughing into his armpit. Since last she'd seen him, he'd grown a hard dark walnut of a hematoma above his eyebrow. Marijuana fumes wafted off his big body, but his apparent friend, the Latino, smelled strongly, overwhelmingly, of baby powder.

"Get your fucking hands off me," she said.

"Oh, jeez," he said. With both his hands raised in apology, he leaned slightly backward at the waist without actually stepping away from her. "Sorry, sorry," he said. "I didn't realize I was hurting you. Was I? Come on, was I hurting you?"

Korean Marty pressed two fingers to the base of his throat and in a raspy voice said, "That's her, man."

"You got a haircut," the guy said.

Again: why was she still standing here? She stepped around the little black kid, who like all city kids knew how to mind his own business. He was bouncing life into his handball, getting it warmed up for another practice serve. If she told him to call 911, she knew it would only provoke them. At the end of the block, with her arm clamped over her purse, she turned onto Britton Avenue, which seemed wider, more open. The bright afternoon sun blanched the sky. Deep in her ear she heard the voice of her father, who used to hang his head out her bedroom window to watch her come home from school. Walk calmly, not quickly. If you gotta look back, then take a peek, once, over your shoulder, but don't ever turn around.

She turned around and saw the two of them three paces behind her. The skinny Latino nodded at her, smiling. Her elbow still felt hot where he'd grabbed it. She walked faster, did everything wrong, hunched her shoulders and tightened the struts in her neck. On the opposite side of the street, three teenage girls sat on a stoop, two of them texting, the third staring at Janice with an inexplicably sour expression, as if she held her responsible for something. A block away past Ithaca Street, Janice passed a tall brick building with the penitential air of an elementary school. An hour earlier, she could have sought refuge in a crowd of mothers waiting for their kids to be released. She could have disappeared inside their haze of perfume, their chattering gossip and complaints, but by now that final school bell had already rung.

She reached into her purse for the Nextel. Unsure of the men's proximity, she did not dare ask for backup. Instead she slipped the rubber hair band off her wrist and double-wrapped it around the Nextel's silver transmitter button. Communication could go only one way now, from herself to the ghost.

Gonz couldn't chirp her back, ask her why she was tying up the line, but she didn't need him to chirp her back. She needed him to listen. She hoped the sports talk on the Impala's radio wasn't playing too loudly. The purse hung unzipped off her shoulder. A foot clipped her heel and she stumbled forward before catching herself.

"Careful!" the Latino said.

Without turning around, she said, "You two better stop following me."

"We better," he said.

At the next intersection, she turned off Britton Avenue and onto a long and narrow one-way, Gleane Street, where two- and three-family homes crowded one another. Metal bars protected the windows and air conditioners. Thick trees shaded the sidewalk. To caution drivers, city workers had written SCHOOL X-ING in bright white letters, but to Janice, walking against the nonexistent traffic, it appeared mirrored and upside down. She hoped she was going the right way. She wanted to get onto Roosevelt, but here in Elmhurst, away from the easy crosshatch grid of Jackson Heights, her sense of direction tended to wobble. It seemed familiar, though, this Gleane Street, or at least she thought she'd heard of it before. But where were all the people? A hose seemed to have recently washed down this section of sidewalk, but where was the hoser? Somewhere nearby the 7 train rumbled, the best noise she'd heard all month, for she could assume at least that she was getting closer to Roosevelt and the protection of all its commuters. She couldn't see the avenue or the train yet, but she did see, a full block ahead, a red-and-black flag saying TERRAZA CAFÉ. When she slowed down, the Latino made no effort at all to keep himself from bumping into her.

"Oh, jeez," he said. "I'm sorry. You okay? I didn't hurt you again, did I?"

"I'm going to the Terraza Café," she told them, her mouth turned toward the shoulder with her purse. "My man's waiting for me there, okay?"

"And I bet he's real big. Is he? Do you think he'd maybe want to have a word with us?"

"Now?" Korean Marty said in his hoarse voice. He looked at his watch, a Movado, the schmancy kind without any numbers on the dial. Most likely a Chinatown knockoff. He was squinting at it, as if that hematoma had doubled his vision, or maybe he hadn't yet figured out how to read its dark, empty face. Two fingers once again went to the base of his throat. "I don't know, Pauly. At

*Terraza*? I don't think so."

"Don't be difficult," Pauly said. Probably the Cerebral Pauly she'd heard about at Marty's, the one who'd hidden the kung fu dummy. He said, "We'll dip in real quick is all, get you one of them hot teas for your cold."

"But —" Korean Marty said.

"The kind with the whiskey and lemon," Pauly said. He turned to Janice and told her, "We gotta meet the mans, right? The big muscular mans? I bet he's just pissed off all the time. Is he? Does he, like, talk with his fists? Oh, forget it, don't tell me. I don't want to go in there with any, like . . . you know. You know what I mean."

She walked slowly to give the investigators more time. She even thought about stopping to pick a penny up off the sidewalk, but she decided to step over it instead. The three seconds it would've bought her wasn't worth the possibility of a brain-sloshing kick. Farther down the block a sudden storefront appeared, the Dream Hair Salon, wedged between houses. Its tough women in pink curlers might've harbored her nicely, but she'd already told Gonz where to go. She kept walking. Past empty beach chairs on the sidewalk. Past four blue dumpsters in a dead-end alleyway that separated an apartment building from, at last, the Terraza Café. As was typical for places around here, dark cellophane covered the windows. On the bar's brick front a bright mural depicted a neighborhood landscape of squiggly 7 trains and golden saxophones and a long line of multicolored children holding hands. When she reached the entryway, Pauly and Korean Marty separated so as to position themselves on either side of her. When she tried the door, it was locked.

MIERCOLES said the sign. CLOSED.

Korean Marty's thick arms cinched around her, his hands locked beneath her breasts. When he lifted her up off the sidewalk, she pedaled on air. Nervous, looking for witnesses, Pauly had his head turned toward a sliver of Roosevelt Avenue, where pedestrians on the early side of rush hour walked home along the grid. Not a one of them would be able to see her. Not on this little veinlet of a street, which branched away from Roosevelt at an angle that would keep her obscured. Her shoe had fallen off. With Pauly's head still turned, she kicked the side of his knee. He crumpled to the ground, but that didn't help her with Korean Marty. Not at all. He still had his arms wrapped tightly around her from behind, his struggled breathing wet against her ear.

She snapped her head back, hoping to explode his nose, but instead hit the sharp bone of his chin. A light burst. Dark squiggly flyspecks floated past her eyes. Her feet still couldn't find the ground. He held her out in front of him and they moved quickly backward, together, away from Pauly picking himself up off the sidewalk, away from Terraza's front door. With a groan, Korean Marty turned and by necessity she turned with him and was tossed. She weighed nothing. Beyond the rooftops, the blinking lights of an airplane moved by degrees closer to somewhere. Beyond the plane, a white and tumbling sky.

She bounced off a dumpster and landed in the alleyway, blood filling her mouth. She couldn't tell yet if she'd bitten into her cheek or her tongue. A cold spike of pain deadened her arm. On the other side of the alleyway, atop the adjacent apartment building, blocky graffiti letters spelled out TORCH. She rolled over onto her good arm, onto her stomach, with her face turned toward the rubbery smell of a construction cone. The straps of her purse entangled her wrist, but it didn't seem as if anything had fallen out. She still had her gun. As she was trying to get up off the ground, Pauly kicked her in the shoulder and spun her onto her back. He straddled her, all his weight on her chest. A long-bladed knife materialized in his hand and he cut through her purse straps cleanly, easily, as if they were merely baker's string. He tossed the bag behind him so that she'd understand his disinterest in her money. When she turned away from the knife, she saw Korean Marty pushing a dumpster into the alleyway's mouth.

"Marty thinks you're a cop," Pauly said. "But you're just a snitch, correct? Just a tough-cookie snitch?" He eased the cold knifepoint between her lips until it pressed against her teeth. A small white scar interrupted the goatee beneath his jaw. "Listen," he whispered. "You gotta stop squirming here."

Because the alley terminated in a dead end, Korean Marty, who saw them first, had nowhere to run. Duckenfield and McCarthy pinned him to the dumpster as Hart and Cataroni came running toward Pauly. Before they could reach him, he chucked his knife onto Terraza's rooftop, where a startled crew of pigeons fluttered up into the air. And then he, too, was flying away from her. His arms were outstretched, his twisted face in Cataroni's hands.

She sat up to watch him slam Pauly into the concrete. She didn't yet have the breath with which to speak, but everyone else seemed to be shouting: Korean Marty, receiving kicks in his fat stomach; the investigators, doing the kicking. Two older white women streamed out of the house across the street to ogle and accuse. They looked like sisters, spinster twins, although one dyed her hair brown and the other had left it gray. Above everyone's heads, the dark cloud of pigeons beat its wings toward a safer rooftop.

"You okay?" Sergeant Hart asked her.

He offered a hand, but she stood up on her own. Her elbow throbbed like a heartbeat. Behind a window in the TORCH building a tiny Asian girl peered out at her. Without thinking Janice waved, as she always did when she caught children staring at her, and the girl's face immediately vanished behind a crooked set of window blinds. The investigators were putting cuffs on Pauly and Korean Marty. Janice moved her arm to see if it was broken. She stomped around the alleyway in one shoe to pick up all the things that had spilled out of her purse, which she supposed was now technically her clutch: the Nextel, a compact, her cell phone (broken now), an earring she thought she'd lost, a granola bar, and a tube of red lipstick. Her badge was back at the rumpus, in the top drawer of her desk. Her gun had thankfully remained nestled at the bottom of the bag. Without taking it out, she released the magazine and chamber bullet so she couldn't accidentally kill anyone. She zipped the bag shut and tested its weight, which felt just heavy enough. Was she okay, Hart wanted to know.

It took three pairs of cuffs — one on each wrist, and a third linking them together — to restrain Korean Marty without dislocating his shoulders. He sat on the curb next to Pauly, who also had his hands braceleted behind his back, albeit in only one pair. He looked considerably more comfortable. He had his head thrown back and his legs stretched out into the street, as if he were sunbathing. He was smiling. His eyes were closed.

Duckenfield, who was about to search him, said, "You got any needles in your pockets, you better tell me now."

When Pauly shrugged, Janice swung her handbag by its tattered straps into his face.

"Shit," said Sergeant Hart.

Pauly lay turtled on the sidewalk, either unwilling to get back up or unable to with his hands cuffed. She tried to kick him dead in the dick, but for the second time that afternoon she felt a pair of arms encircle

her from behind. They belonged to
Cataroni, who also had his chin hooked over
her shoulder. He kept asking her to take it
easy. Easy, easy. Take it easy. She spat blood
on Korean Marty, not much — turned out
she'd bitten her cheek, not her tongue —
but enough to mist his pant leg with flecks.
He screamed at her in what must've been
Korean. Probably cast a hex on her of some
sort. Yeah well, get on line. She tried to kick
Korean Marty in the dick as well, but
Cataroni was dragging her into the street,
where the two old ladies stood invoking civil
rights. The Impala still had three of its four
doors open from the roll-up on the alleyway.
Even the engine was still running. Unwilling to lash out at the old ladies, she kicked
a dent into the car's body that she immediately regretted. Honest to God, she'd
only meant to make some noise. Gonz drove
the uncle car slowly past her down the street
without stopping. When Cataroni brought
his mouth back to her ear, to beg her to
relax, she writhed and cursed until at last
he seemed to understand. To protect her
cover, she needed to get herself arrested.

"I'm going to have to restrain her," he told
Hart.

"Fuck you," she said, relieved.

Without raising any objections — that

dent in the Impala would be a paperwork disaster — the investigators watched Cataroni cuff her hands behind her back. He eased her onto the curb next to Pauly, where brown water from the dumpster raced down a canal between sidewalk panels. To keep herself from crying, she tried not to blink.

The problem, which had necessarily gone unspoken among the investigators, was that if charged with felony attempted assault, Korean Marty and Pauly would have to go to court, and if they went to court, they'd have a constitutional right to know the identity of their accuser. The real identity, not the fake one. Janice Itwaru, not Singh, the name on her department-issued bogus driver's license. Local parasites finding out she was a cop would obviously be problematic, but it was equally problematic — tactically, legally, morally — to just cut them loose, an act of leniency so unprecedented that it would've only cast more suspicion on Janice and her relationship to the police.

Cataroni took her purse. He brought it into the Impala under the pretense of dumping its contents onto the backseat, the better to search through them, but really — she assumed, she hoped — he was stashing her baby Glock and bullets on the car floor, next to all the investigators' empty Jamba Juice cups. When he came back out onto the street he had the Janice Singh driver's license pinched between his fingers.

"I know her," he said.

"You know her," Hart said.

"I picked her up a little while ago. Right around here. For solicitation."

"Solicitation?" Hart said.

"Prostitution. What did I say? Solicitation? No, no. Prostitution."

McCarthy, catching on, kicked the treaded bottom of Pauly's boot. "You her pimp or something?"

"I knew I knew her," Cataroni said. He lied easily; if not for his granite chest and freckled nose, he might've made a good uncle. He handed Sergeant Hart the fake license. "I just couldn't place her till I saw the name. I picked her up for prossing maybe two months ago, but you know what? She never showed for her court date. I got the whole rest of that day off."

The investigators left the knife where it lay, on Terraza's rooftop, protected by a perimeter of razor wire. Without a weapon, the overburdened ADA would dilute the charge down to a misdemeanor, and if Pauly and Korean Marty both pled no contest, then they'd most likely receive some jackoff punishment along the lines of anger counseling. But to guarantee — and this was where Cataroni really impressed her — to guarantee that they all avoided court, it would probably be best if the complainant herself was a criminal. Even better, what if she, too, was arrested on the day of the incident, for failing to report to an earlier court date? There wasn't a wrinkle-shirted ADA who'd even touch that one. Not only would Korean Marty and Pauly expect to avoid trial, but an arrest would have the bonus benefit of boosting her cover's credibility throughout the neighborhood. Assuming, of course, she avoided getting kicked back to patrol.

McCarthy was ordering the two old ladies to disperse under penalty of an obstructing government administration summons. Sprinters stuck in the blocks for too long, the other investigators went to work: Duckenfield searched the perps' pockets, where he found their wallets and IDs, and Sergeant Hart called his homies in the Warrants Division, or maybe he only pretended to call his homies in the Warrants Division. Maybe he really called 1-800-Mattress and talked to what must have been a very confused operator. After he hung up, he announced that Ki Soon Paek and Paul Miley Tejada were both clean, sheet-wise, without any records attached to their names, but the chorus girl, Little Miss Rockette Janice Singh, had, as predicted, an open warrant for her arrest.

"For guess what?" Hart said as he returned the phone to its belt cradle. "No one wants to guess? For failure to report to a court-mandated appointment following an arrest for . . . for what? No one? Really? No one wants to guess? For prostitution, ladies and germs, just like our boy called it."

McCarthy, overdoing it, shook Cataroni's hand.

"Ain't that impressive?" Hart said. He stared down at his audience on the curb, as if legitimately waiting for an answer, but Janice couldn't think of anything to say and both Korean Marty and Pauly had withdrawn into their inalienable right to silence. "Well, *I'm* impressed," Hart said. "The kid, he's got a sharp eye. Brain like a trap. Would you believe he's Italian? With the red hair on him? How about this? Would you believe he's not even a detective yet? But his day is coming, let me tell you, and no wonder, am I right? A kid like this? Some people just get it, you know what I'm saying?"

"Congratulations," Pauly said.

"Shut the fuck up," Hart said.

While they all waited for the prisoner

273

transport van to arrive, Cataroni retrieved her fallen shoe from outside Terraza's door. A silver tack had gone through the sole. Maybe today, maybe months ago. Anal, a corrector, truly a detective — if not in rank yet then in temperament — he tried pulling out the tack, but his fingernails, like hers, weren't long enough. Giving up sooner than she would've, he crouched down at the curb and wedged her foot roughly into the shoe, her fairy-tale moment, not at all how she'd imagined it.

# CHAPTER EIGHT

A rainbow forest of scented cardboard trees dangled from the p-van's rearview mirror. With the windows rolled down, the heater was cranked as high as it would go. The two uniformed cops up front were probably chewing multiple sticks of mint-flavored gum, too, and wore thick VapoRub mustaches, but nothing was going to mask the van's more persistent odors of unwashed clothes, unwashed bodies, urine, diarrhea, vomit from too much to drink or too little, and the rank dread sweat of men and women on their way out to jail. In the second-to-last row, Janice breathed with her mouth open. A gash in the seatback in front of her hemorrhaged brown-yellow foam. Normally she would've picked at it, but her hands were still cuffed behind her back. Her shoulders burned. Her elbow had gone numb. She had to pee so badly she worried she'd catch a UTI. At frequent intervals,

Pauly Tejada, who was sitting behind her, leaned forward and took deep-gusto whiffs of her hair.

In the middle of the van, a white crack-head shouted toward the front, "Hey, I got heart pills I need to take, man. I'm serious!" Someone else said, "I got a shit I need to take!" Someone else, not as loud, said, "I think I need to go to a hospital, for real. I got like a subdural hemorrhage from where you motherfuckers busted up my skull piece."

Four hours of this, with the cops up front never once turning around.

When the van finally reached max capacity — Wednesdays were slow days — the uniforms up front disgorged all their passengers into the 115 Precinct. Once inside, the men went one way; the women, another. For the purposes of decorum, each female inmate was ushered separately into a claustrophobically small room by a pair of lady cops, one to conduct the searches, the other to protect the department against sexual harassment accusations. Fingers in latex gloves picked through Janice's hair. She opened her mouth and stuck out her tongue. She allowed a strange pair of hands to cup the underwires of her bra. Needle-nervous, the cop checked her pockets in a cursory way, but lingered along the inseam of her crotch. Outside the room, a barely audible radio played what sounded like classical music, but Janice could hear only cymbal crashes and the occasional whale groan of a tuba. Ordered to strip out of her jeans and underwear, she squatted over the concrete floor so that any potential contraband stashed up her asshole would plop to the ground.

Even with all those precautions, however, someone, somehow, had managed to smuggle into the female holding unit a small pile of cheap paperbacks. Or, more likely, the 115's CO allowed his officers to slip books through the bars. They were all romance novels — all with QUEENSBORO PUBLIC LIBRARY stamped along their tops — and before sitting down she chose the one with the most straightforward title, *Ruthless Magnate and His Virgin Mistress.* Her fingerprinted fingertips left ink smudges on every page.

A white woman dozed in the corner of the cell, waking herself up every time her chin crashed into her chest. Another white woman wept into her hands. Her ear looked cauliflowered, like a wrestler's. A pretty black girl was rubbing circles onto the woman's back to console her; maybe they knew each other, maybe they'd just met. Far more upbeat was the clique of hookers, who all seemed to be legitimately enjoying themselves, as if jail provided a much-needed vacation from their corners and alleyways and mattress-equipped carpet-cleaning vans. Two of the girls pantomimed loading a giant invisible bazooka. With impressive attention to detail, the trigger girl dipped her shoulder under the bazooka's weight while her friend loaded it from behind. Ready to go, fire in the hole, they both fell back from the recoil as an invisible rocket flew across the width of the corridor and landed in the boys' holding cell. Janice would've clapped, but her elbow felt too stiff to move. And in different circumstances, the boys might've played along, scrambling for cover, but with a population six times as large as the female cell, they had neither the room nor the inclination. Bare-chested, over a dozen men lay on the floor with their balled-up T-shirts serving as pillows. The rest sat on benches along the walls. They called out for lawyers, doctors, phone calls, cigarettes, and sandwiches, but were entirely ignored. Janice couldn't see Korean Marty, who may have been obscured by the rules-and-regulations sign posted to the bars, but she did see Pauly. He sat in a primo spot in the middle of the bench, swaddled in a blue wool blanket. He stared across the corridor at her, but she refused to give him the satisfaction of staring back. She kept her head down to her novel, its spine bent backward so he couldn't see the title. Something — his staring, the dust bunnies beneath her own bench, the countless midges floating about — made her skin itchy. With nails barely adequate for the job, she scratched her face, her neck, her arms, the tops of her hands, and she was still scratching, seventy-something pages later, when the handsome magnate, more idiotic than ruthless, spurned the tremendously horny mistress from his bed, and when, in real life, an even handsomer detective arrived outside the female holding unit to tap a pair of handcuffs against the bars.

"Which one of you beautiful angels is Janice Singh?"

"That's me," said the bazooka-loading prostitute. "Where we going?"

For the first time in what felt like a month, Janice, the real Janice, laughed. A uniformed officer opened the cell at the detective's request. A black guy, with cute-nerdy glasses and a soft face of almost movie-star symmetry — Jesus Christ, what had this cheesy magnate done to her? — the detective introduced himself as Geo Hamilton of the Queens Division Warrants Squad. When he saw the enlarged plum on her elbow, he cuffed her from the front, a tactical no-no. She tucked a few stray strands of hair behind her ear, as if to give Pauly across the corridor a better view of her face. Which she most certainly did not want to do. She didn't know why she did it. She worried he'd read too much into the gesture, as she herself was reading too much into it, and she continued to worry about it — of all the things to worry about! — as Detective Hamilton brought her to the cage where she reclaimed her possessions, and then to the book where she was signed into his custody. Together they went through the heavy wooden doors of the 115 Precinct. Down on the corner a beat-up Buick was waiting for her.

"Hi," Tevis said, leaning out the driver's-side window. He wore a black tracksuit made out of some bizarre, heretofore-unknown material: an alien fabric that seemed to turn liquid when he drummed his hand against the door. "Hurry up," he said. Then, when she came closer: "What the heck they do to your face?"

"My face?" she said.

Stooped in front of his side-view mirror, she saw ink streaks along her chin and forehead and everywhere else she'd been scratching. She also saw that Tevis was wearing not a tracksuit, but a garbage bag with holes cut out for his arms and neck. Why not? Drained, confused, feeling increasingly shriveled every moment, half afraid that if tonight's luck continued along its current trajectory she'd slip through the grates of a street gutter and land in an underworld lorded over by sewer gators, she began to totter toward the passenger's-side door, but Detective Hamilton called her back. She was walking away with his handcuffs.

"You don't want to ever get used to wearing these things," he said as he unlocked her.

She collapsed into the passenger seat, rubbing her wrists. She'd never been in Tevis's personal car before and was surprised to see a plastic container of half-eaten takeout salad festering in the footwell. Through the open window he and Hamilton debated whether Hamilton still owed him a favor, or if now Tevis owed him the favor, or if instead all their competing favors had nullified one another, the whole thing seeming less like an actual argument than two boys

281

not knowing how to say good-bye. They settled on a fist bump. As Hamilton was walking back to the precinct house, Tevis reached under the seat, not for a bottle of coconut rum as she'd hoped, but — even better — the baby Glock 9mm that Cataroni must've given him. When she had it back in her hands, she started to cry.

"Aw, criminy," he said, clearly as embarrassed by her crying as she was. He gripped his mangy leopard-print steering-wheel cover, afraid to even look over at her. "Don't . . . don't do that, Itwaru. It's okay. A little hard time's good for the soul."

She wiped away the tears as fast as they came, smearing more ink across her cheeks. She was a mess. To see exactly how much of a mess, she flipped down the sun visor to check its mirror, but there was no mirror, just a bunch of papers that fell into her lap. All the pages were yellow, ripped out of legal pads, notes of some kind that Tevis had written to himself. She didn't read them. She didn't want to read them. She wanted only to stop crying. He took all the pages from her, crumpling them up, and tossed them into the backseat without caring where they landed. For whatever reason, he was apologizing to *her.* She didn't understand why. She didn't understand anything. Four separate winter coats lay across the back-seat. She sucked snot back up into her nose and asked him why he was wearing a garbage bag over his body.

"To lose a little weight," he explained. "Walk a few miles in one of these bad boys and you're gonna start sweating out the pounds, let me tell you."

"I'm not sure that's too healthy," she said.

"I'm not sure you're much of an expert on what's healthy," he said, smiling. He turned over the ignition and the car filled with light and R&B and cranky beeps insisting they buckle their seat belts. "So where we going?" he asked. "I can take you home, or, if you want, I can get you drunk at a bar and then take you home. Doesn't matter to me one way or the other."

"My car's back at the rumpus," she said.

"Forget it. Whatever we end up doing, I'm driving you home. And I'll just pick you up tomorrow before work, okay? Or if you got errands to run or whatever, I'll come by first thing in the morning, whatever you want, just let me know."

"Are we partners again, Tevis?" she asked.

"No, but we're still friends, right?" He flicked on the turn indicator. "So where are we going?"

Worried she might start crying again, she

felt the heat crawl up her face. Friends but not partners: how mature, how completely ridiculous. When she kept her own grudge books, she wrote every name in permanent marker. Maybe that was her problem. She didn't let go. The radio played a song she didn't recognize, but like all R&B it was about a heart-scorched whiner who's finally had enough. She turned the dial through static before giving up and hitting the power button. "Home," she told him.

"Not a bar first?"

"Just home, please," she said. "But thank you. Seriously. For everything."

The car's headlights eased out of the parking spot and caused the dark street up ahead to tremble. "Hey," he told her. "Put on your seat belt."

They stopped before they'd ever really gotten started, at a 24/7 gas station a few blocks away. She was reminded of a quickly aborted Itwaru-girls-only road trip to Jones Beach, back when Brother filled the garage with his "hobby cars" and Vita had to always find parking on the street. The day of the trip Vita pulled out of a too-good-to-be-true spot in front of the house, only to immediately reverse right back into it. Change of plans: they took buses out to Rockaway, Janice and Judith eating their salami sandwiches and runny peaches between transfers. Tevis, though, just needed some gas. And maybe some provisions. So as not to freak out the potentially armed gas-station attendant, he peeled off his garbage bag. White piping climbed up the legs of his pajama pants. Sweat sopped his lucky shirt, the one with the Looney Tunes characters in gangsta poses. He wanted to know if she needed anything. Coffee? One of those celebrity magazines? She needed nothing, she told him, but he apparently didn't believe her. He came out of the gas station with two Marino Italian ices, the kind with the little wooden-oar spoons pressed flat to their tops.

"Cherry or watermelon?" he asked.

"Cherry."

"You sure?"

"Watermelon."

"Oh, good." he said. "Because cherry's sorta my favorite."

Back on the road to Richmond Hill, he turned the heat all the way up and asked her to hold his Italian ice against the vents. It was around one thirty in the morning. Only a few gloomy taillights ruddled the parkway, but he still drove as cautiously as he always did: both hands on the wheel at four and eight o'clock, like a bus driver, so that in the event of an accident the airbag wouldn't break his thumbs. Before changing lanes, he turned on his blinker, checked his rearview, his side-view, and his blind spot, which was unnecessary because as far as she could tell he didn't have any blind spots.

"Give it back," he said, reaching for his Italian ice. "You don't want to melt it *too* much. You're really just sorta trying to thaw it around the edges a little. I mean, you can attack right away, but if I'm gonna spoil my diet, I'm gonna want to do it correct, yeah? So what you want to do . . . look at this guy. Hey, buddy, nice signal there. . . . So what you want to do is, well, take the lid off obviously. Give that a good lick. But here's where the real innovation comes in. Because we got the edges nice and soft, we use the spoon to like flip the ice over in its cup, so we can start at the bottom with all the sugar crystals and thick syrupy goodness, but you gotta be real careful when you're . . . oh, son of a biscuit."

The ice, in the process of being flipped over, capsized out of its paper cup and slid down the front of his T-shirt.

"Frick my frickin' life," he said. "That's gonna stain. That is just totally gonna stain."

"You want mine?" she asked. She had no

intention of eating it, had only been pressing it against her elbow. "Watermelon? Your second favorite?"

"I'd probably spill it," he moaned. Real quick he took his eyes off the road to scowl at the streak of red down his shirt. Even Bugs and Taz looked annoyed, but the gangsta versions of Bugs and Taz always looked annoyed. "What do you think?" he asked. "Is it gonna stain?"

Her household chores included vacuuming, corralling water glasses, doing the dishes, which amounted to putting dirty dishes in the dishwasher, occasionally inserting that sticky blue pod thing along the inside of the toilet bowl, and double-checking the locks and gas burners before bed every night, but stains? She knew nothing about stains. But you know who did?

Vita ran down the back porch steps toward the Buick. It was past two in the morning, an hour when she should've been sleeping naked in bed, and yet here she was, wide-eyed in blue scrubs with the pink drawstring knotted at her waist. She'd probably kicked off the sheets at midnight. Stared out the window for an hour. Eventually getting dressed in the expectation of having to answer the never-used front door for a pair of uniformed cops who'd avoid eye contact and mumble hollow condolences and split open the earth beneath her bunion-plagued feet.

"I'm fine," Janice said, already out of the car and rushing toward her. "Everything's fine."

"I kept calling!"

"My phone broke."

"Then borrow somebody's!" Vita said. She cupped her hands around Janice's cheeks. "What happened to your face? Where's your car?"

"It's a long story."

"I love long stories," Tevis said as he stepped, smiling, out of the car. "Savita, I'm telling you, this whole thing is one hundred percent my fault. I took her out to this classified operation where —"

"Don't," Janice said, because she'd lie to anyone on this planet except her mother. "I'm sorry," she told her. "I should've found a way to call."

Not that Vita would have ever held him responsible anyway. Normally a gigantic black guy lumbering down a dark alleyway would've dried the spit from Vita's mouth — actually, full disclosure, despite or perhaps because of her marriage to Brother Itwaru, normally a black guy *period* would've dried the spit from her mouth — but ever since she'd met Tevis over a year ago, she had rightly or wrongly credited him with the daily miracle of her daughter returning home alive every night. For him Vita only ever had hugs, cheek kisses, flirty ballbusting, and leftovers. She walked over and pressed a hand over his heart.

"Are you okay?" she asked.

"I'm not sure."

"It's Italian ice," Janice said.

Tevis tugged on the hem of his shirt, gently, to avoid stretching out the neck or accentuating his man-boobs. "You think it'll stain?" he asked Vita. "I'd hate to have to get rid of it."

"Fancy shirt like that, I don't blame you," she said. "Come on, I'm sure I can scrub it out." Without waiting for his false protests, she climbed back up the porch steps, her round tush pendulous in the blue scrubs. "You better park that piece-of-shit car of yours in the garage, though," she told him. "If you leave it blocking that alley, my lunatic neighbors will slash all your tires."

He did as he was told. Then — without having to be told — he walked backward into the kitchen, to freeze any ghosts who might've attempted to follow him inside. An unnecessary precaution. Any potential ghosts would've been too busy trying on the new boots Vita had picked up from Goodwill. Still, though, the gesture brightened her face and more than justified the plate of leftover fried chicken she'd already put in the microwave for him.

"You like curry green beans?" she asked.

"I love curry green beans."

Asked to fetch some rubbing alcohol for his cherry stain, Janice trudged up to the second-floor bathroom, where she sat on the edge of the tub with her head between her knees in the emergency crash-landing position. When she closed her eyes she saw Terraza's front door. So she tried not to close her eyes. She stared up at the ceiling fan vents, as if waiting for the bat from her nightmare to come flying out. In the dream she'd thwacked it with the wooden end of a plunger, both her and the bat naked, silent, fighting for their lives. Blood had risen to its fuzzy back slowly, like a developing Polaroid. Its dream back. Its dream blood. With an exfoliating bar of organic chamomile soap — thank you, Judith — she washed the ink smudges off her hands and face. She filled a tumbler with New York City tap water and drank it all down before the billowy clouds could turn transparent. She couldn't believe how thirsty she was.

She couldn't believe how badly she wanted to share her bed with someone tonight, with Puffy or Cataroni or old Jimmy Gellar or Detective Hamilton, a lightly snoring body to fortify the edge of the mattress between herself and the door. Pathetic? With her tongue having almost been cut out of her mouth, she granted herself full permission to be as pathetic as she wanted for the next twenty-four hours. She found the rubbing alcohol in the medicine cabinet, next to a prescription bottle of her mother's antianxieties, which Janice felt tempted to take but couldn't because the Big Bosses randomly drug-tested her. She wanted a drink, a real drink, but there wasn't any booze in the house.

On her way back down the stairs, she half hoped, half dreaded that she would catch her mother making out with Tevis, but instead found them on entirely opposite ends of the kitchen. Like a veteran bachelor, he stood shirtless over the garbage can eating a leg of fried chicken. Dark hair coiled his belly. His eyes brimmed with the manic glee of a diet-breaker who knew he'd be back here again tomorrow, probably right on time for breakfast. Maybe then he'd get his curry green beans, which apparently her mother had forgotten to serve him. She'd forgotten to wait for the rubbing alcohol, too. Marooned on the other side of the kitchen island, she poured hot water from the electric kettle into the sink, where his shirt lay taut and rubber-banded across a salad bowl. Her face was disappearing behind a veil of thick steam.

The next day, after Tevis brought Janice to work, but before she actually walked out into the rumpus, Richie the Receptionist told her two things. One: he had taken her advice and invited both his girlfriend and her lesbian roommate over for dinner tomorrow night at his place, where he intended to cook penne alla vodka with a whole lotta vodka. Janice wasn't so sure that was her advice exactly, but okay, good luck. The second thing Richie told her was that, excluding present company of course, Narcotics seemed almost exclusively to hire small-minded, mean-spirited buffoons who loved nothing better than when their victims got riled, and so it was probably in her best interest if she went with the flow, rolled with the punches, and just sorta tried to play along.

"Play along with what?" she said.

A present lay waiting for her on her desk. At least it looked like a present: a white cardboard box wrapped up in green ribbon. On the drive over here, she had told Tevis that she was dreading having to explain the eggplant on her elbow, but obviously the story had already circulated, no doubt exaggerated, too, its details juiced up on the performance-enhancing devices of cell phone and Nextel. The entire rumpus seemed to stare at her as she came in, everyone except for Puffy, who was over at One Police Plaza finally getting sworn in as a detective. Fiorella sat with one leg crossed over the other and her foot bobbing nervously. Under her desk, where only Janice could see, she tamped down the air with her hands, as if to say, *Be cool, take it easy.* Poker-faced, Janice untied the green ribbon. Inside the box, atop tissue paper, a note — written in a surprisingly elegant, seemingly feminine hand — said *For the girl who has everything,* except *everything* had been crossed out, replaced by *blown her cover.* That she had in fact maintained her cover seemed like a technicality not worth arguing. Beneath the tissue paper, she found a long black burka, headscarf included.

"Who do I thank?" she asked.

Nobody gave her an answer, not that she'd expected one. Back when she worked patrol, a rookie cop got shot at while off duty by some maniac who emptied an entire clip at him but missed every time. The next day his supposed friends papered his locker with pictures of slow-mo bullets zipping past Neo from *The Matrix.* No one asked him if he was all right, because the question would've implied that he might not be all right, that one day *they* might not be all right. Still, though. A papered-over locker was one thing, a burka another.

She carried it into the bathroom — the one in the rumpus, not the one on the third floor where she took her secret poops — and came back out a ghost, her sheet black instead of the more traditional white. Gonz of course wolf-whistled. Under her gaze, visible only through the small viewfinder of her headscarf, his oily smile widened in anticipation of her reaction. She wouldn't give him one. Nor would she do a little twirl for the investigators, as Sergeant Hart was requesting. Give her a burka and she'd wear it, but that's all. Let them worry about what she was thinking. Let them invent the expression she wore behind her mask.

That expression, by the way, was a determined one. She made a list of corners to visit the next time she went out to make buys. She finished her photocopied chapters of *Sway: The Art of Gentle Persuasion.*

"Persuasion's efficacy," Dr. Rearsman writes, "increases tenfold when the active participant moves beyond objective observation into a more empathic engagement with the Other's subjectivity." Janice put a penciled checkmark in the margin. Slowly, deprived of a reaction to satiate them, the men in the rumpus turned away from her, bored, as per the burka-makers' intent. In a last-gasp effort to rile her, however, Sergeant Hart bought her a BLT sandwich, which sat untouched in her out tray. She wanted to call her sister to let her know that the hair-tie idea had pretty much saved her life, but Janice's phone was still broken and she didn't know Judith's number by heart. Although she probably wouldn't have gotten ahold of her anyway. *Hey, it's Judith, you must've missed me. . . .* She went online to research assisted-living facilities for the inevitable. She googled "Jimmy Gellar." No romantic intent here, just simple curiosity. He had, after all, tried to contact her first, either by phone or at the house, possibly to pass along the name of a drug dealer he wanted to point her toward, or maybe the old black guy who snapped her picture outside the meth clinic was Scotch-taping flyers of her overwrought face to telephone poles, or maybe, whatever, shut up, it didn't matter. As per last night's bathroom treaty, for the next fifteen or so hours she had permission to do any sort of pathetic shit she wanted, including but not limited to looking for her eighth-grade crush on the Internet. Google came back at her with twenty million irrelevant hits. On the White Pages site, as she dragged the mouse across its DUNDER-MIFFLIN pad, she looked for "James Gellar," "J. Gellar," and just "Gellar." She tried a Facebook search, but as a nonmember could click through only the first few results. Of course she could have easily found him on DECS or one of the other intradepartmental databases, could've pulled his driver's license even and looked up his address, but that would've carried her far outside the bell curve of ordinary human craziness, and so instead she created a temporary Facebook profile under the harmless pseudonym "Gabby Guyana." She maybe found him. She couldn't be sure — the name said "Jim Gellar," but the personal info came up as private and the profile picture was of a horse — but she sent a friend request anyway. Her very first. While she waited for him to get back to her, she liked both the *Harriet the Spy* and Alzheimer's Association pages. She made an official request for her sister's friendship, debated searching for Fiorella's and Puffy's pseudonymous profiles but ultimately decided against it so as to keep some segment of her life separate from the NYPD, and spent a shamefully long time flipping through the public photo albums of two cunts who in the ninth grade tossed Janice's brand-new Jansport book bag onto the roof of the 4 Aces Car Dealership on Atlantic Avenue. For long pockets of time she forgot she was even wearing the burka at all, remembering only when she tried to bite her nails, or when the fabric caught itself under the wheels of her chair, or when Detective Puffy Okazaki surprised everyone by showing up at the rumpus to water the potted philodendron on his desk.

"What did I miss?" he asked, picking up her sleeve with two fingers as if the fabric were radioactive.

"Nuthin'," she said.

He dragged her away from the public computers and over to her desk. Apparently no one had called to tell him about her alleyway incident, or if they did call, they didn't get through. He'd kept his phone off all week, afraid to hear a lieutenant on a voice mail telling him the Big Bosses had changed their minds and he was to report back to patrol, effective immediately.

"You wouldn't get a call," Tevis explained. "If you got new orders, they'd come in through the —"

Puffy said, "Can somebody please just tell me why Janice is in a goddamned burka? That is Janice in there, right?"

The other uncles deferred to her. It was her story; she got to tell it. "You go first," she said. "The whole promotion ceremony. Start to finish. Don't leave anything out."

"It was fine," he said. When she kept staring at him through her headscarf's viewfinder, he said, "It was nice."

Janice, who expected her own promotion — knuckles rapping desk — would be the climax of her entire life, said, "It was *nice*?"

He lay down across her desk. What'd she want him to tell her? It was fine. It was nice. It is what it is. Whereas other detectives received a grand coronation of flashing photo bulbs, uncles got rinky-dinked with a secret reception in a tiny office, behind a closed door. Due to space limitations, they were supposed to invite only one guest, usually a long-suffering spouse, but Puffy said he'd brought along an entire entourage — sisters, brothers, parents, stepparents, high school principal, even a priest — as if he were collecting potential witnesses to testify on his behalf in case the department ever tried to short him on his detective-grade paychecks. When the ceremony ended, he skipped the usual congratulatory family dinner and drove here instead, to surround himself with people who appreciated exactly what it meant to alchemize a silver shield into gold. And to water that philodendron.

"Your turn," he said. "Why you in a burka?"

She insisted on holding his badge while she told her story. The shield's surprising lightness must have distracted her; she opened with finding the burka on her desk, then had to loop back to the alleyway, then had to loop even further back to Marty's apartment, then had to jump forward to the taco-cart line. Insignificant details, like the kung fu dummy, she described in relentless detail, but she forgot about Gonz driving by in the uncle car. Puffy, as befitted his new detective status, poked holes in her story. Why wasn't she working with Tevis? She looked over at him before answering: because the rotation had paired her with Gonz for the day. All right, but how come the investigators put her in the p-van when they could've easily held her outside Terraza under the pretense of waiting for somebody from Warrants? Because, well, she didn't know why they didn't do that. They didn't think of it? They weren't as practiced at lying as Detective Puffy Okazaki?

"Gimme my shield back," he said. That the Big Bosses had stupidly switched out her everyday partner and that the investigators had failed to make the very best decision didn't seem to surprise him too much. They were the Big Bosses and investigators. He expected them to bungle their jobs. They were outside *la familia de los tíos.* But Gonz? "I still don't understand why he'd leave," Puffy said. "He was the *ghost.*"

Over at the next desk, an eavesdropping Tevis nodded with enthusiasm.

She said, "I *told* Gonz he could go. Well, actually, I sorta like waved him along."

"That's not your decision to make," Puffy said, still lying on his back. "That's not *Gonz's* decision to make. Man, I wouldn't be surprised if he was the one who sent the investigators to the kid's corner in the first place. Just to screw you over."

"Not even Gonz would do that," she said, surprised she was defending him.

Puffy made her tell the story all over again, from the beginning, and this second turn through she felt strangely distant from the Janice who got tossed into the alleyway, as if her current burka-wearing self really were a ghost. Or a superhero without any resemblance to their puny alter ego. By the time she'd finished, Puffy had sat up in his agitation and eaten her BLT without seeming to realize it. He rolled off her empty folders and went over to Gonz's far cleaner desk.

"Stand up," Puffy said.

"What for?" Gonz asked.

"Just stand up, all right?"

Gonz had his feet up and was reading *The Sporting News*'s twenty-four-page baseball preview pullout, which he had actually pulled out, as if he felt compelled to follow orders, just not Puffy's orders. "What for?" Gonz said again.

"I wanna see who's taller."

"I'm taller."

"I wanna see."

"That's ridiculous. Just because you get promoted doesn't make you suddenly any taller."

"Jesus Christ," Puffy said. "Are you gonna stand up or not?"

"What *for*?"

And so Gonz was still sitting when Puffy punched him in the head. Clearly he'd hoped to stand him up to knock him down, sucker-jab him right in the chin: what her Academy instructor had called the bigger man's knockout button. But when Gonz refused to rise, Puffy had to settle for an awkward downward blow. He was a liar, not a fighter. Gonz was both. Like a ram, he had protected himself in plenty of time, tucked his jaw to his chest, and Puffy ended up drilling the top of his skull, the very worst place to hit someone. She couldn't hear it from where she was sitting, but she saw in Puffy's face that his knuckles had shattered.

"Now look at what you've done," Tevis told her.

Gonz was already out of his chair and pinning the howling Puffy against the buy board. His bad back smeared the numbers. The board itself crashed to the floor. With reaction times dulled by alcohol and neglect, the uncles reached Gonz only after he'd driven his arm into Puffy's throat. Big Bosses staggered out of their private offices like moles into the light. Prondzinski had one of her precious paper clips in her hands, absently untwisting it as if she intended to pierce someone through the heart. Investigators craned their necks. They pressed their phones against their chests, their oblivious callers jabbering into wrinkled ties. A baby-faced confidential informant, brought into the rumpus for a debriefing, climbed onto his rolling chair for a better view. Everyone, it seemed, was standing, except for Inspector Nielsen, who was presumably sleeping off a migraine under his desk, and Janice, who felt too stunned to rise.

"That nigga bought me a soda one time!" said the chair-surfing CI.

Nobody asked him which one he was talking about, Puffy or Gonz (odds went to Puffy), but Sergeant Hart did tell him to sit the fuck down.

Uncles pulled Puffy toward the stairwell. They kept telling him to calm down, but of course he couldn't calm down with all their hands on him, of course he only became further envenomed, pushing them away one by one. His delegation thinned as he neared the stairwell until it was just him and Fiorella, an experienced tantrum-manager. She didn't touch him. She didn't tell him what to do. According to the text she later sent, she drove him to the Emergency Department at Flushing Hospital, only twenty minutes away, where a nurse put his broken hand in a cast. He'd be off active duty for months. After that, when it came time for his disciplinary hearing, Tevis speculated that Puffy would cry temporary insanity. Mental breakdown as a result of too many job stressors. Or something like that. The Big Bosses would have to transfer

303

him to the rubber-gun squad, a departmental purgatory where he'd sit in a cramped room listening to wiretaps, doing his crosswords, and drawing a detective-grade salary.

"That's genius," Pablo Rivera said. As they did after every disaster, the uncles had convened around Tevis, some of them sitting in chairs, others balanced on desk edges. "He staged the whole thing," Pablo Rivera said. "It was a con game from the start! He knows IA's coming to get us and found a way to leave without losing any of his benefits!"

"If that's true," Eddie Murphy said, "it was a fabulous performance."

Morris the therapist said, "Or maybe he really did have a mental breakdown."

"Or maybe," Pablo Rivera said, reconsidering, "he was working undercover for Internal Affairs, sent here to spy on us, and this was how he extracted himself."

"Isn't it obvious?" James Chan asked, surprising everyone by speaking aloud. A war vet, a former paratrooper, he stared off into the distance, toward the wild saffron sunsets of Afghanistan. "He fought for the only reason there is: to prove his love."

"What's that supposed to mean?" Janice asked.

The uncles turned to her with obvious disapproval, annoyed that she'd disavow a crush they all knew existed, annoyed her witchy Caribbean enchantments had gotten Puffy banished from their work lives. "I didn't ask him to hit anybody," she said, unsure if she was arguing with them or herself. "I can fight my own fights."

"The ones worth fighting for," James Chan told her sadly, "always say exactly the same thing."

"Oh, how fucking deep," Gonz said. He was on his way past them toward Captain Morse's office, most likely resisting the urge to rub his sore head. "You want to know what I think?" he asked. "I think you're all a bunch of immature faggots with nothing better to do than run your immature faggot mouths."

Via speakerphone Richie the Receptionist thanked him for the pep talk. But it didn't have the same zeal with which Puffy delivered the line. *Used* to deliver the line. Spines curved, the other uncles moped back to their desks.

At the end of her shift, she skipped the communal happy hour at A.R.'s Tavern and drove to a random dive bar closer to home, with buffer stools between the lonely patrons and almost nonexistent lighting. She'd never been there before. She didn't even know the name of the place, just that its windows were thickly dark. She ordered a Guinness with a Jameson chaser. Or a Jameson with a Guinness chaser. However you want to call it. A framed photo of Mr. Met's encephalitic head stared at her from the wall. Video screens played the keno numbers. She'd left the headscarf in her car but was still wearing the rest of the burka, which somehow did not discourage a balloon-bellied Guyanese man from offering to buy her a drink. She let him. He wore too much hair gel and body spray, which is to say he wore hair gel and body spray, and when talking he had a bizarre habit of rubbing a pinkie across his left eyebrow, but — silver lining — his Adam's apple protruded like an arrowhead, which for some reason she'd always found attractive.

She bought the second round: more Guinness, more Jameson. The fourth round was a kickback round and so she was still on the hook for the fifth. Eventually, boringly, he asked her about the burka. She told him she was an actress, which was sort of the truth but didn't actually answer his question. He told her he was a fourth-year law school student at Columbia, which wasn't the truth — she felt fairly certain law schools lasted only three years — but she didn't call him out on it. She even let him buy another round, no beer this time, just the whiskey. When his screaming wife showed up in a parka over sweatpants, Janice closed out her tab.

Careful now. Because she knew most drunk-driving accidents occur within a couple of miles of home, she drove with her car seat slid all the way up and both hands on the wheel. At this late hour there were only a few other drivers on the road, but still . . . she must remain vigilant. The radio stayed off. She didn't talk and drive, or text and drive, but she couldn't have anyway because she still didn't have a phone. A pothole clattered her teeth, a reminder to slow down, that the road was disappearing too rapidly beneath her car. As she turned off Atlantic Avenue onto a more safely deserted side street, she checked her rear-view and side-view mirrors, Tevis-style, perhaps lingering a little too long in the world behind her. When she looked back out the windshield, something twisted and screaked. Too close, the airbag broke her nose. Maybe broke her nose. Blood gurgled in her throat. The turn signal kept clicking. Already deflated, smelling like clothes-dryer exhaust, the airbag lay pathetically across her lap. She'd hit a parked car, it seemed, a red Subaru hatchback, sideswiped it before crashing into a telephone pole. She needed a do-over machine. Outside the windshield, the purple night canted left.

"Shit," she said, suddenly sober.

She stepped out of the car and was almost roadkilled by a pearl-white Mustang zipping past her, its driver going forty, forty-five down this residential street. A sticker in its back window said ALL AMERICAN CAR CLUB. Another sticker beneath it said THE UNIVERSITY OF DELAWARE. Without stopping, the Mustang raced through a red light; high above the intersection, a camera flashed, catching his license plate, his face, and maybe even Janice in the background, pinned to her car with a hand against her chest. She could get fired. If patrol officers had caught her driving drunk, she could tin them, tell them she worked Narcotics, and they'd probably let her go — maybe even follow her home to make sure she made it — but not if she'd caused an accident, not with all this damage. On her own car, nothing terrible: a busted headlamp, a dented fender. Per usual she'd given out worse than she took. The Subaru's front and back doors had crumpled inward. Its broken glass pebbled the street, reminding her of the glass outside the Laundromat on the night Caspars and Barnes were executed, a memory that didn't even belong to her. The side mirror hung dangling from where she'd knocked it off. Or maybe re-knocked it off. Red duct tape was wrapped around the mirror's base, as if applied after some previous accident, the owner taking the trouble to buy a color that matched his paint job. He probably lived right here on this block. Maybe in one of the apartments that still had its lights on. When she heard what sounded like a window sliding up along its grooves, she hurried back into her car. Her first bit of luck all day: the engine turned over on her first try, praise the Almighty. She kept to the speed limit all the way home.

# Chapter Nine

Fuck my life. She woke up the next morning needing water, coffee, huevos rancheros with lots of Sriracha, a teeth-scrubbing, a tongue-scrubbing, a hot shower, an alibi, a mechanic, and more sleep, but the first thing she did was go to the window. No squad cars sat parked outside her house. Not yet at least. The woman reflected back at her in the glass looked destroyed. Dark bruises mottled the bags beneath her eyes. Blood crusted her nostrils, but the nose itself felt merely stuffy, not broken. She went into the bathroom to cover up the bruising with bronze-colored concealer and must've done a pretty good job of it, too, because when she came into the kitchen her mother didn't seem to notice anything unusual, other than that Janice was awake and sentient at seven-something in the morning.

"What's going on?" Vita said. She sat at

the kitchen table amid her never-shrinking stacks of unopened mail, her eyes peeking over an early-edition copy of the *Post*. "Escape!" said the back headline. "Duke Survives Scare." Behind her, soap bubbles gushed out of the dishwasher. Like an oil stain, they rainbowed the light, oozed across the floor mat and tiles. "You hungry?" she said. "You want me to make you some breakfast?"

"Did you put the wrong kind of soap in the dishwasher?"

"Shit," Vita said.

She knelt on the tiles to mop up the water with what was nearest at hand: her copy of the *Post*. A newsprint photo of Senator Obama disintegrated beneath soapsuds. The front and back covers fell apart. She seemed frantic, unable to pull out sections of the paper fast enough, too mind-muddled to stop the problem at its source. Janice turned off the dishwasher.

"Maybe we should go out for breakfast," Vita said from the floor, looking up at her like a child.

"I wish I could, but I got some errands to run before work."

"Errands?" she asked with a mother's instinct for entirely justified suspicion. "What kind of errands?"

311

"Like buying you flowers. A huge bouquet to show you how much I love you."

"Yeah right."

"Yeah right, what's your favorite flower?" Janice asked, hopeful she'd remember the answer was lilies.

Kneeling in a mess she'd have to clean up all on her own, with little bubbles clinging to her ankles and fingers, Vita offered only the standard good-bye: "Be good," she said. "Don't forget to call if you get overtime."

Janice took side streets into the Cypress Hills neighborhood of Brooklyn, only ten minutes from home. With her headlamp busted, she wanted to get off the road as quickly as possible and so she turned into the first auto-body repair shop she saw. The little sign on the door redundantly said WELCOME! OPEN! The big sign in the parking lot said WOMEN FRIENDLY, which she didn't know whether to find offensive. She expected a dark garage, manned by mechanics in overalls, but instead walked into a temperature-controlled waiting room with a coffee bar and leather couches and a young black guy, her age, with more grease in his hair than under his fingernails.

"I gotta get my car fixed."

"Well, you have certainly come to the right

place," he said from behind his counter. He had a nervous tic of some sort that caused his eyes to blink rapidly. "Have you used us before? Are you already in the system?"

"The system?" she said, and was handed a paper questionnaire asking for her name and address and phone numbers, work and private. The make and model of her car. Her license plate and credit numbers. Her insurance info. An accident report (if applicable) made out by the New York City Police Department. She said, "Do I still have to fill all this out if I pay in cash?"

"What do you mean?"

"What do you mean, what do I mean? If I pay in cash, do I have to fill all this out?"

"Uh," he said. "I guess . . . I don't know? I guess it'd depend on the sort of repairs you were looking for?"

She told him she needed a new headlamp, a new fender, and a new airbag, but said nothing about the accident. She told him she was also thinking about different tires and maybe a color change. In response he blinked his eyes, as if snapping mental photographs.

"You can talk to my boss," he said. "If you want. But I think once the airbag's been deployed, we have to make an official report to the —"

"Thanks for all your help."

"Hey, are you all right?" he called after her as she went through the door. "You want a cup of coffee or something? It's free!"

She drove one-handed back to Queens, repeatedly punching the stupid roof of her stupid car. When her knuckles began to hurt, she banged the back of her stupid head against the stupid headrest. It was early still. The Subaru's owner may not have left for work yet, but if he had, he hated her now without knowing her. Don't worry, pal: she hated herself even more. To find somebody skilled and sleazy enough to fix her car without draining her bank account or requiring an accident report, she drove from the Jackie Robinson Parkway to the more congested Van Wyck, then went farther east on Roosevelt than she ever did on foot for work, past Shea Stadium, past orange construction cranes erecting the platinum-blond trophy wife of the Mets' future stadium, Citi Field, a half-completed brick-and-steel husk of a ballpark with enormous gray scaffolding bags hanging off the rotunda walls like scabs on a wound. She turned onto Willets Point Boulevard, a valley of ashes and auto repair shops, the sky there grayer than anywhere else in the borough. Semitruck trailers, stripped of their wheels, sank into the mud along the sides of the road. Graffiti covered the shops' security gates, which were raised only a few feet off the ground so mechanics could scuttle in and out beneath them while keeping the garages' inner workings concealed. Exclusively male, each one of them in jeans and a hooded sweatshirt, they peered under hoods and pulled gravid garbage bags out of trunks. She had never driven herself here before, but she knew from countless backseat trips where to go, where to turn, when to slow down for workers running out into the dirt road with paint buckets and sandblasters, when to roll up her window to avoid the errant seat-soaking spray of an industrial hose. Throw a dead cat and you'd hit a shady mechanic; throw a dead cat with money in its mouth and her father would catch it.

It had been double-digit years since her last visit — with Judith, knocking golf balls up and down the artificial putting surface in their father's office — but the shop looked exactly the same, except on the roof two American flags snapped at attention instead of just the one, the second likely added to reinforce Brother's patriotism after men who looked vaguely like him knocked down the Twin Towers. She parked out in front, beneath an awning that said BROTHER AUTO PARTS SALES. For reasons she never thought to question until now, the phone number listed on the sign had its area code in quotation marks. They were probably cheaper than full-on parentheses, she realized, and the realization — the power it gave her over her miserly father — made stepping out of the car just a little bit easier.

She found him at the back of the shop, surrounded by bulky tool chests and motor-oil smells, with a golf putter held behind his neck as if to stretch out his shoulder muscles. He annoyingly wore the blue-and-orange tracksuit Judith had given him for his birthday. A sweaty Latino, one of Brother's many shifty employees, was trying to explain the housing magnet issue in a re-manufactured windshield-wiper relay. Whatever *that* meant. Janice couldn't really follow what he was saying, nor could her father, who didn't even seem to be trying. He kept nodding along without actually listening. His obvious disinterest, his heavy wristwatch, the putter across his shoulders, and the bulging stomach beneath his track-suit were all meant to indicate to anyone who passed through here that Brother Itwaru was a super-important Big Boss.

"My God," he said when he saw her. A little flustered maybe, he blindly passed the putter over to his assistant. "What are you doing here? Is everything all right? Is Mom okay?"

Never your mother, never your mom, only ever Mom, as in where's Mom, don't tell Mom, let's make Mom some breakfast, let's put salt in Mom's sugar dish, lookit what I bought Mom, you think she'll like it, you better because I bought you girls the same thing. To her face she was always Babe.

"I need a favor," Janice said.

The Latino kept his head down as he walked away. A mechanic in the valley of ashes, where shop owners occasionally burned their garbage and favors were understood to be of a criminal nature, he knew enough to leave them alone. He crab-walked under the security gate, taking the putter with him, perhaps to practice his stroke in anticipation of himself one day becoming the Man.

"A favor," Brother said. "From your dear old dad, huh? Well, isn't that interesting."

"Are you gonna rake me over the coals on this, or are you gonna help me out?"

"This is how you ask for favors?"

"This is how you help people?" she said, but her voice — bouncing back to her off

317

the titanium rims along the wall — sounded childishly bitter. She took a three-second breath to help her start over. "I can pay you," she told him. "Whatever's fair, I'll pay. I'm not trying to get anything off you for free."

"You're an exhausting human being," he said. "You know what your sister told me? When you stormed out of the house on my birthday?"

"Is this your fifty-first birthday we're talking about?"

"She told me that if I wanted you back in my life — and obviously I want you back in my life — then I needed to win you over with tough love. 'Man up,' she told me. 'No more groveling.' "

"I don't remember any groveling."

Now it was his turn to take a deep breath. To impress upon her that he did not have all day to waste on a prodigal daughter — credit his new Judith-inspired toughness — he looked down at his watch, a faceless Movado like the one Korean Marty had worn, except her father's was almost certainly real, almost certainly having fallen off some unlucky gambler's wrist.

"I was in an accident," she told him. "And I was hoping you could take a look at my car. Please."

"Are you all right?"

"I'm fine."

He must've been thinking especially hard about something because his tongue filled the pouch of his lower lip. "Was anyone hurt?" he asked.

"No one."

"Are you sure?"

It must have been her haircut. The haircut he hadn't even commented on yet. It must've made her look like somebody else, a ruthless, toothless scumbag who hurts people then lies about it, so you have to ask her twice. Afraid of the mounting pressure behind her eyes, she addressed herself to all the doorless cars stacked behind him like books. Never mind, she said. She apologized for coming down here, and before he had a chance to respond she walked away, under the security gate and onto the dirt road, where two men walked past her carrying a pane of clear glass. The air felt charged for a rainstorm. Her father's putter lay abandoned on the ground. She stepped over it and so did he, coming out after her, not to beg any sort of pardon but to inspect firsthand her car and its damage. In a kind, pacifying tone he told her this particular Ford Focus model had notoriously touchy air bags, too easily engaged. He slapped at the headlamp's dangling eye with an expert's bold gruffness. He asked if the engine had been making any funny noises since the accident, which out there in the road he called the incident.

"What do you mean?" she said.

"What do you mean, what do I mean? Has it been making any funny noises?"

"Like what?"

"Like whoopee cushions and joy buzzers," he said, annoyed, or maybe just pretending to be annoyed. "Go get behind the wheel so I can take a look. And stop being such a poop stain."

While he tinkered under the hood, she revved the engine in park, a gearshift away from running him over. On her sixteenth birthday, eager to better prepare for the police academy, she had begged him to teach her how to drive, not in this hunk-of-shit Ford, but in the Brown Beauty, his 1971 Pontiac LeMans, a hardtop four-door sedan with beautiful whitewall tires, the same car Popeye Doyle commandeers at the end of *The French Connection.* Brother lasted one instructional trip around the block. A little more patient, her mother took her out for two lessons — two! — before finally sending her to the Alamo Driving School's Mohammed Ahmed, a chatty instructor whose foot continually hovered over the shotgun brake, a teacher not unlike Tevis in that regard.

"Switch," her father said, and so they switched. He took her seat while she stood outside the car looking in. He kept his cowlicked head turned away from her, the better to hear the *vroom* of his foot on the gas. "I think you got lucky," he told her. "I think you're just gonna need a little bodywork."

"How much would it cost for a new paint job? Maybe new tires?"

"How about a different license plate?"

"Just so we're clear?" she said. "Nobody got hurt."

"Then you're doubly lucky. Were you drunk?" When she didn't answer, he folded up the air bag and tried stuffing it back into the steering wheel, but it only spilled back out across his stomach. "You need to be careful," he said. "You're genetically . . . what's the word? Predisposed. Maybe socialized, too. At a young age. I don't know."

"When should I pick up the car?"

"I'll call the house."

"Call my cell," she said, a little too quickly. She needed to buy a new one, but she imagined she could retain her old number. Whatever it took to keep him from resuming contact with Vita. "It'll just be easier to get ahold of me that way," she said. "What with work and —"

"Sure, sure, I'll get the number off Judith," he said, as in: *Oh, you thought this would be a secret? Oh, you didn't know I talk to your sister every night? That she's number two on my speed dial, after voice mail but before Barbara, before my AA sponsor, before all my great Great Neck neighbors, my alleged jogging buddies, this shop right here with its 718 area code?* He smiled and said, "So how's Mom?"

Mom? Mom was banned for life from the Starbucks on Queens Boulevard because she'd gone behind the counter to scream at a barista, although she says she went behind the counter only to look at the bulk tea prices, and started screaming at the barista only after the barista had screamed at her for crossing an apparently sacrosanct border that was poorly designated in the first place and open to debate. This morning she filled the dishwasher with soap instead of detergent. The green beans, the rubbing alcohol, the picture-stick, the mouth-painter, Jimmy Gellar's name on the whiteboard: she'd forgotten them all. She said she didn't send you that photo of me in uniform, but maybe she did and can't remember, or maybe she's started lying. A formerly anal bookkeeper, she can no longer be trusted to pay the monthly bills. She has dementia, *that's* how Mom's doing, but to answer your question the way she would want it to be answered?

"She met someone," Janice improvised. "A little while ago. She just seems sorta . . . I don't know. Just sorta smitten, I guess."

"Really?"

"You sound surprised."

He attempted what he probably considered was an innocent looking shrug. Obviously uninterested in continuing this conversation, he picked her purse up off the passenger seat and passed it to her through the open window. "You need a ride wherever you're going?" he asked.

"No thanks," she said. Because she was an idiot, because she was hungover and had dementia stalking her DNA, she hadn't entirely realized that when she left here, she would necessarily be leaving without her car. She looked up. Dormant raindrops grizzled the clouds. She said, "I was actually looking forward to the walk."

You couldn't call her ungrateful, she did thank him for the offer. Closer to work than to home, she walked to the Willets Point train station, where she caught a 7 local to the end of the line. She expected to step off the el and into a rainstorm, but here in

Flushing, only one stop away, the sun was brightly shining. Chinese sidewalk merchants encouraged her to buy their ox bones and toy helicopters and miniature leather Bibles. If only drug dealers were as friendly. Somehow, at the nearby Flushing Mall, she got bamboozled into an iPhone, which came with Internet access and downloadable apps and an extended memory voice-memo program in case she ever needed to dictate her autobiography. After taxes and the sucker warranty it cost almost seven hundred dollars, but at least she got to keep her old number. Jesus Christ, though. In penance she ate lunch at a frighteningly inexpensive dim sum restaurant, which didn't provide English menus but did display Queens's most depressed catfish floating in a tank of green water. Janice tapped an apologetic finger against the glass. She thought about calling her mother on the new phone but didn't want to find out that the police had come by the house. Hours early for her shift, she took the Q65 to the rumpus, not realizing until she walked through Richie's reception area — once again blame the hangover, the hungry dementia — that she'd left all her keys dangling in the car ignition, not to mention a burka in the backseat.

"Ah, shit."

"Is it that obvious?" Richie responded. "You can see it in my face? I tell you, Itwaru, you called it. With the penne alla vodka? I get a big magnum bottle of the stuff. What I don't put in the sauce, we're using for shots, and this is in addition to the red wine. Then the roommate? She opens up another bottle of vodka. The sauce, it probably came out terrible, you could strip paint with it, but it don't matter to us because at this point? We're hammered. All three of us. Okay, so now what? I go, hey, who wants to lie down? Anyone feel like lying down? Next thing you know, the three of us are in my bed, the girlfriend from Payroll, the lesbian roommate, and me in the middle, jumping out of my skin. Now you got me this far, kid. You told me, 'Alcohol.' If I wanted to make it happen, 'Alcohol.' But what came next, how to truly seal the deal, that was always gonna be on me, right? So I go, 'Hey, is anyone sort of hot? Should we maybe get a little more comfortable?' The girls, they're just giggling like they don't really know what I'm talking about. Actually, though? I *am* sorta hot. I don't know if it was all the steam from the pasta, and the alcohol, of course, that played a part. I always get flush from red wine.

Especially if it's South American. Anyway, long story short, the girls start making out with each other. Right there in the bed, with me lying in the middle. Fact. Then they start touching each other, like for real, heavy duty, but I'll spare you all the details because I don't *know* all the details. I've already passed out. The only reason I know any of this at all is because when I finally wake up in the morning, the roommate's vamoosed, but the Payroll girlfriend's still there. Sobbing. She says she is quote unquote sexually confused now. Is that incredible? So now I'm suddenly single, I've got a hangover feels like an elephant literally took a dump on my face, and don't get me started on all the leftover pasta in my fridge that's got me sick just thinking about it. Story of my life. But the whole reason I'm telling you all this? Other than that it's nice to get off my chest and I'd figured you'd want to know, but the whole reason really is that I wanted to thank you for at least getting me halfway there with the drunk girls in the bed and all that. Things didn't turn out the way we hoped, but that's my fault, not yours. Seriously. And if you ever need a favor? Consider it done. Guaranteed. That's an official IOU."

"Oh, that's okay," she said, unsure if he

was messing with her. "I really don't think I should take credit for any of that."

"Itwaru?" he said. "I'd be upset if you didn't."

The main takeaway from Richie's story: there weren't any dark-suited Internal Affairs investigators waiting for her in the rumpus; otherwise he probably would've led with that. Actually, there weren't many people in the rumpus at all. She'd never seen it so empty. Half the uncles were out making buys; the other half, like her, still had hours to waste before they'd have to show up for work. Desks were occupied only by investigators. She was alone in the forest to see the tree fall. Without any uncles around, the investigators didn't mix martinis or parade cigarette girls, as she might have imagined, but instead filled out forms responding to the endless call-ins — my building's superintendent smokes weed, my rival drug dealer sells drugs — that clogged the department's already sluggish arteries. Janice meanwhile had nothing to do. To please Tevis, she could've asked Prondzinski for that partner change, but she didn't want to bother the lieutenant now in case IA showed up later, plus she worried Prondzinski might have unfairly held her responsible for the Puffy/Gonz fiasco, plus of course she was still hoping to get Tevis to forgive her. Nothing's easy. Because insurance concerns forbade her from even pretending to do work before her shift started — what if she got a paper cut? — she signed into her new Facebook account, not on a rumpus computer like a cavewoman but with her twenty-first-century smartphone. Jimmy Gellar's name was waiting for her in the message box.

03/20, 3:34 PM
Dear Miss (Mrs?) Guyana,
Wow! So nice to hear from you! How long has this been your FB name?
    More important — how did you manage to escape from Ned Shu's diabolical death trap? What was it again? A cage of starving tigers? A vat of hot oil? Or can you not talk about it? Is this line secure?
    Should we meet up in person?

Today, 2:28 PM
hahahaha. nice to hear from you too. especially after the craziness from last time . . .
hey did you happen to talk to

328

3:03 PM
I did! I went by your house to
see if your parents still lived
there which sounds way creepier
than it really was but I just
wanted to drop my number off
and apologize for my
boneheaded move outside the
clinic. I'm seriously incredibly
sorry about that (the
boneheadedness) and felt awful
for forever but if it makes you
feel any better I'm being
punished for it RIGHT NOW
because the guy on the computer
next to mine is literally watching
porn. In the library!
   Speaking of rude you've
ignored my let's meet up
suggestion. You also ignored my
super clever miss/mrs question.
Is that because I should be
calling you Detective Guyana?
My bad!

   3:08 PM
   no not Detective yet but i should
   be finding out about that any day

now. (i literally just knocked my knuckles against my desk.) and no r in my Ms. either. how about you? whatve you been up to these last hundred years?

3:16 PM
hello?

3:16 PM
you still there?

3:21 PM
Sorry, sorry. Had to switch computers before my computer got ejaculated on.

3:22 PM
yuck

3:23 PM
Tell me about it.

3:27 PM
What I've been up to these last hundred years: no r in my ms. either (wait, that makes no sense) but I am currently getting my associate's degree from LaGuardia Community College.

The dream is to go on and get licensed in alcohol and drug counseling, maybe get a master's in art therapy or something . . . I figure it'll be like when Mike Seaver on Growing Pains becomes a substitute teacher and he knows whenever someone's about to throw a spitball because he's done it all before. Anyway that's the plan. We'll see how it goes. I'd love to hear your thoughts on those final Growing Pains seasons (the Dicaprio years) but I'm running out of computer time here. We could try meeting up in person but that would be (ahem) the third time I suggested it and I don't want to come across as somebody who can't take a hint.☺

> 3:29 PM
> no hints at all. i've just got a ton of stuff going on at work right now and it's hard for me to find the time to do anything

3:30 PM
Well, I don't mean we have to

meet up this very second! I'm
not crazy! How about tonight?
Or Saturday?

> 3:32 PM
> you think i get weekends off like
> a normal human being? fri and
> sat = work nights = the nonlife
> of a cop

3:33 PM
Well I can't do Sunday (sad for
you) because my niece is getting
Christened and I'm an awesome
uncle but I do have Monday
free. What do you say? Hurry up
and let me know because the
librarian is upset I've exceeded
my time limit. And I find her
very scary.

> 3:35 PM
> i do have mondays off actually

3:35 PM
Great!

> 3:36 PM
> maybe we can meet up for a cup
> of coffee

3:39 PM
hello?

4:03 PM
New computer! Scary librarian
off my back!

4:06 PM
Coffee is super boring, but you
know what isn't boring? Coney
Island! When's the last time you
been? The rides won't be
running this early but it's
actually nicer that way and the
weather's supposed to be really
great on Monday. (I just
checked.) What do you think? We
could do the boardwalk and eat
hot dogs. And shoot the freak if
it's open.

4:07 PM
what the hell is shoot the freak?
is it even legal?

4:09 PM
Shoot the freak is exactly what it
sounds like and totally legal but
probably shouldn't be. If you
don't like hot dogs there's a

really great pizza place near
there. Or we could do hot dogs
AND pizza. Are you in? Memory
lane? Pick you up at 2 for a
super fun day?

> 4:17 PM
> it would be really nice to catch
> up but i can't be out too late, is
> that alright? i gotta work the next
> morning

4:18 PM
Awesome! No problem! Where
should I pick you up?

> 4:21 PM
> i'll be over at my mom's all day
> monday so just come thru over
> there i guess

4:24 PM
Great, great, great! Really
looking forward to it . . . Coney
Island can get a little dicey
though so make sure you bring
your domino mask, Gabby
Guyana. Just sayin.

4:29 PM
domino masks sounds like a
superhero thing. you must have
me mixed up with somebody
else . . . just sayin.

She thought she must've had herself
mixed up with somebody else: a fourteen-
year-old schoolgirl with elaborately layered
pushdown socks and multicolored jelly
bracelets. That embarrassed, embarrassing
eighth-grader shared Janice's rumpus desk
with many other Janices, all of them fighting for armrest space. She hadn't felt this
crowded with selves since the LeFrak disaster. There was, for example, the rabbinical
Janice who scrutinized Jimmy Gellar's
Facebook responses with a Talmudic attention to detail. Why didn't he have any
classes on a Monday afternoon? Did his less
than subtle probing into her marital status
indicate less than platonic motivations, and
if so should she have clarified that she
intended to pay for her own pizza and hot
dog(s)? A more present, embodied self —
reluctantly engaged in actual, more serious
problems — mistook every rumpus shadow
for an IA investigator. When Tevis showed
up for work, a groveling Janice asked him to
extend the deadline on their partnership

dissolution. Because she'd be the uncle tomorrow and he'd only be the ghost, he acquiesced to a couple of more days, so long as she promised not to enter any apartment buildings. Done. Still groveling, she thanked him with chicken parm subs from Benateri's. Suddenly suffering — cheap dim sum *and* chicken parms? — she peed diarrhea up in her secret third-floor handicapped bathroom. Add to those Janices the nail-biter, the hair-tie-snapper, the crackhead Janice Singh and the superhero Captain Richmond Hill and her alias Gabby Guyana and finally the latest Janice, the newly forgetful Janice, her mother's daughter, whose shift had ended before she remembered to call for a cab.

Tevis spotted her on his way out of the parking lot. She stood shivering with her hands retracted up her coat sleeves, her back to a pretty yellow house abutting the Narco building, a house where if the inhabitants ever smoked weed they had better first cram towels under the doors. Tevis drove a couple of car lengths past her before backing up. He was either curious or concerned or both. His window rolled down. He asked her what the heck she was doing.

"Waiting for a cab."

"Where's your car?"

She heard R&B out of his speakers but couldn't really see him sitting in the dark of his Buick. She went over to him. She leaned her face through the open window, as she'd done to Sergeant Hart two days earlier, another accidental echo she hadn't asked for or known how to interpret. The little care tag stuck up out of the back of Tevis's T-shirt. To her surprise he'd apparently joined her mother on the short list of people Janice was unwilling to lie to.

"I hit a parked car and telephone pole last night," she said. "Then fled the scene because I was drunk."

The passenger's-side door unlocked for her. Because Tevis was the most conscientious human being she'd ever met, he made her call the cab company back and cancel her order. After she got off the phone, she expected him to immediately launch his interrogation, or at least tell her an instructive anecdote, but he seemed content to just stare at the road. She would've had more questions to answer in a taxi. Where we going? What do you want to take, College Point Boulevard or the Grand Central Parkway? Tevis, without asking, without a fare to pad, headed straight toward the Van Wyck. They drove in silence almost all the way home, through a post-mortgage-crisis Queens stuck in developmental limbo with unmanned cranes on either side of the expressway. Public-housing skeletons waited for stimulus money to finish their windows and doors. Up in the sky, planes beat a path out of JFK.

"Shit," she said, by far her most commonly expressed sentiment of the month.

She put the probability of her mother remembering at roughly 33 percent. And even if she did remember, there was only like a 51 percent chance her feelings would be hurt, for an overall potential disappointment score of . . . something or other. She could've figured out the exact number on her fancy new cell phone, but it didn't matter. She said she'd do it, so she had to do it. Plus, *Sway: The Art of Gentle Persuasion* suggested that you can get people to trust you — and she of course wanted Tevis to trust her again — by asking for a supersmall favor, one that can't be politely turned down, and afterward the antagonist will convince himself that he can't dislike you *that* much, otherwise he never would've done the favor in the first place. . . . Never mind that Tevis was already doing her a favor by driving her home two out of the last three nights.

"What's the matter?" he said.

"I'm sorry, but can we make a stop real quick? I promised my mother I'd get her some flowers."

"Are you kidding?" he said. "There's nothing I'd rather do."

They pulled into the alleyway with a gas-station bouquet of droopy carnations that cost more than they should have. Because it was dark out, after midnight, he insisted on waiting in the car until she could get herself into the house. Even though she was a grown-up. Even though she had a gun in her purse. But, of course, no keys. She rang the bell, thankful to have these carnations to hand over — sorry to pull you out of bed, swarm your chest with panic, make you scamper down the stairs fully convinced that I've been killed — but Vita opened the door right away, completely awake, in a lovely black-and-white dress with jade earrings brushing the tops of her naked shoulders.

"My baby girl," she said.

Tevis stepped out of the car with what appeared to be an automatic reflex. He fiddled with his belt, his pinkie finger discreetly checking to make sure his fly was all the way up. Forget small favors. Forget chicken parm subs. Janice had her irresistible mother. As he climbed the back steps, Vita turned to him, perhaps to position herself more flatteringly under the porch's golden light, and when she did she gave Janice a clear view into the kitchen, where her father sipped tea at the cluttered table. A white moth flew into the house through the open door. Her father raised his mug in Janice's direction, as if to toast her good health and fortunes.

"You look stunning," she heard Tevis say. Brother leaned forward, suddenly interested, but from where he was sitting he could see only Tevis's hands, Tevis's black hands, stealing the flowers from Janice so he could give them to Vita himself.

"So what's the big occasion?" Tevis asked her.

Brother had already left his chair. He came over to lean against the doorjamb, one foot on the porch, one foot still in the kitchen, as if reluctant to step entirely out of the house, as if worried he might not make it back in again. His shoes and socks were off. He'd missed a loop on his Movado wristwatch and she wished she could remember if it was like that earlier. "I think you're the occasion," he told Tevis. "She got all dressed up because she knew you was coming. And with flowers! The big charmer!"

"I'm sorry," Tevis told Vita. "I didn't realize you had company."

"Oh, that's not company," she said. "That's the degenerate ex-husband. Degenerate ex-husband, I'd like you to meet Detective Chester Tevis."

"A cop!" Brother said. "How perfect! Brother Itwaru, Detective Chester Tevis. So very nice to finally meet you."

Their hands met in the middle for a quick shake. Not at all the tarsal-crunching macho pump-athon that Janice had expected. But why should she have? They were all adults here, right? Even her. Even though — sleep deprived, half delirious — when she'd first seen her father inexplicably sitting at the kitchen table, part of her had wondered if she'd somehow stumbled up to the threshold of 1999, if the refrigerator was back to being covered in photographs instead of magnets and the microwave had a turn dial, the telephone a curly cord, if Judith was up in the attic bedroom IM-ing her boyfriends on a Y2K-prone computer.

"Brother?" Tevis said. "Is that your real name?"

"One of them," he said. "How long it take you to grow a beard like that?"

She didn't hear Tevis's response. She was

watching the moth flutter back out of the house. It flew toward the porch light, a typical moth, singeing a wing on the bulb before careening down the alleyway. The men, typical men, hadn't seemed to notice it, but Vita did, or at least appeared to. She hugged the bouquet to her chest, aware that ghosts took many forms.

"I'm cold," she announced. "Chester, would you like to come in? I got some leftover pepper pot I can reheat."

"You do?" Brother said.

"I really shouldn't impose," Tevis said.

"You should do what you want," she told him. "Or? You know what? You should do what I want. And I want you to come inside and eat some of this pepper pot."

She brushed past Brother into the kitchen. She went in forward, not backward, a mistake inviting all the neighborhood's malevolence to go streaming in after her. Like, for instance, her degenerate ex-husband. He hung a conspiratorial arm across Tevis's shoulders, pushed his wicked mouth close to Tevis's ear. "Next time?" he said. "If you really want to get her going? Splurge a little and buy lilies."

Janice slumped down at the kitchen table. There were four chairs, room for everybody in theory, but two were already occupied by the pagoda stacks of voided checks, credit-card offers, and presidential campaign letters. Vita stood over at the counter, chopping half inches off her flowers' stems, while the boys simultaneously, to their apparent embarrassment, reached for the only other available chair.

"Oh, sorry," Tevis said. "Were you sitting here?"

"Not at all," Brother said.

"You weren't sitting here?" Tevis asked, pointing to the empty tea mug on the table.

"No, I was, but please go ahead."

"No, no, no," Tevis said. He pulled out the chair for him. "Here. Take it."

"I'm fine. Really. I've been sitting all day."

"No, no, no!"

"It's fine!"

And so they both ended up standing, awkwardly, with their thumbs hooked into their waistbands. Fine by Janice: she kicked off her shoes and propped her feet on the empty chair. Out on the porch she had spent so much energy trying to read everyone's reactions that she almost forgot to have one of her own.

"What are you doing here?" she asked.

"Saw I had your house keys," Brother told her. "Figured I oughtta drop them off. Save you a little hassle."

"Let himself right in, too," Vita said.

His arms spread out wide. "And we been catching up ever since."

A policeman for seventeen years, accustomed to keeping his shoes on no matter what, Tevis swung his gaze from Brother's hairy toes to Janice's stocking feet. He said, "Should I take my boots off, or . . ."

"You don't usually?" Brother said. "It's called being polite."

"Don't listen to him," Vita said as her fancy German knife sliced through another carnation stem. "You wanna leave your shoes on, leave your shoes on. However you're comfortable. If you got your gun on you, you wanna shoot him, go ahead."

Brother was the only one who laughed, probably because he was the only one who thought it was a joke. From a wooden bowl beneath the window, where the Itwarus kept — for reasons mysterious to even them — spare buttons and dead batteries, he pulled out Janice's jangling house keys. He threw them at her and she caught them easily, just as she used to catch the clementines he tossed, the remote controls and tissue boxes, everything really except for the bottle he whipped into the wall behind Jimmy Gellar's head. DO NOT DUPLICATE said the back-door key, but she imagined her father could've finagled his way around that without a problem.

"What time did you get here?" she asked him.

"Don't know," he said.

"You don't know?"

"Sorry, Officer. I don't remember. That sorta thing happens when you get older." He turned to Vita, whose shoulders had tightened over the cutting board. "Matter of fact, I'd say that happens to everybody. Right, Janny Bananny? Why I bet you couldn't even tell us what you were up to last night."

"Does Barbara know you're here?" Janice asked.

"Oh yeah, she knows," he said. "I don't keep no secrets from Barbara."

Vita cried out in pain. The fancy knife, flung away from her, clattered into the sink. At first Janice thought she was annoyed, or maybe her feelings were hurt, but then the blood arced across the cutting board. Janice was the first to reach her. On instinct, without thinking, she slipped her mother's finger into her mouth. Then the boys crowded in with all their bullish concern: what happened, are you okay, does it hurt, let me see, run it under cold water, wrap it up in kitchen towels and hold it high above your heart. Janice staggered backward, feeling claustrophobic, swallowing blood. She dropped to the floor on her hands and knees. Despite all her emergency training, she couldn't get her heart to slow down. The kitchen tiles gleamed brighter than they ever had. The smell of soap bubbles lingered. She crawled past Tevis's boots and Brother's feet to the baseboard beneath the dishwasher, where she at last found her mother's severed fingertip. Its manicured nail was painted pink, its skin uniquely whorled. When she stood up, too fast, making herself dizzy, Vita thrust her hand out at her and blood more black than red splattered Janice's chest.

Another knife, she thought. There were just too many of them in the world. Her father got ice. And a kitchen towel, which he knew to look for under the sink. Tevis, as he'd done earlier with the flowers, stole the fingertip out of Janice's hands. Everyone was moving, scrambling. Everyone was in everyone else's way. Janice retreated to the kitchen table to sit down and massage her temples. A rooster-shaped sugar bowl fell off the kitchen counter and shattered. It starts small with a fingertip, but next week maybe Vita forgets to wear an oven mitt and scorches her palm grabbing a cast-iron frying pan. After that, a broken bone stumbling down the stairs, her body coming apart in pieces like a vacant house. Outside on the porch someone was banging on the door. Somebody was hollering. The knob turned and the door flew open and raging in the entryway stood Mr. Hua, their lunatic neighbor. *Motherfucking car,* he said. *Blocking the motherfucking alley!* Completely insanely he was punching his own hip. He wore black waiter pants and a white shirt spotted with grease from the Chinese restaurant he owned in Bayside, next to a police precinct actually, where he most likely hocked secret loogies into the wonton. *Motherfucking car,* he said again. *Inconsiderate people! No one can get fucking in or out of the alleyway!* He seemed ready to take another step into the house when he noticed the gun pointed at his chest.

"Jeez Christ," he said. "It's okay, no problem, no problem."

Janice sat with her elbows on the table and her baby Glock in both hands. She told him to leave. She hadn't pointed her gun at anyone in over a year, not since she'd worked Housing in Queensbridge, but unlike all those other times she rested her finger outside the trigger guard. Still, though. As Tevis would surely have told her, you shouldn't point a gun at someone you have no intention of killing. For Mr. Hua, the barrel's quarter-inch diameter must've looked like the world's largest, hungriest mouth. To her shame, his pant leg darkened with urine. She laid the gun flat against the table with its barrel pointing toward the nearest wall, away from everybody, and he at last did as she'd asked: left the house, walking backward through the entryway, even pulling the door shut behind him. From the safety of the alleyway, he called her a crazy bitch psycho.

"Jeez Christ," Brother said in a Charlie Chan accent, but once again he was the only one to laugh.

The checkered kitchen towel wrapped around Vita's hand had thickened with blood. There wasn't any time to ask Janice what she'd been thinking pointing a gun at a man she'd known since childhood, but there was, however, a dispute as to who should have the privilege of driving Vita to the hospital. Her fingertip sat atop ice cubes in a plastic sandwich baggie, ready to go. She wanted to call a cab, Janice an ambulance, both getting overruled on the grounds of unnecessary expense. Tevis promised to break all the traffic laws getting her there, but Brother promised the same, plus he said they wouldn't have to wait once they arrived because he knew the Jamaica Hospital night guy, by which he probably meant a janitor.

"Let's go," Vita told him.

"You sure?" Tevis said. "I really don't mind taking you."

"Yeah, but I'd feel too guilty," she said. She reached behind his neck with her good hand to tuck the tag back into his T-shirt. "It's very sweet of you to offer," she said, "but if I'm going to inconvenience somebody, I'd rather it be family."

"Ex-family," Janice said.

Brother made an exaggerated ouch face meant to demonstrate that her attempt to sting him had failed; meanwhile, she knew he wouldn't have made the face at all — eyes scrunched, lips pursed — unless she'd actually stung him.

"It's really not an inconvenience," Tevis said.

"Of course it is," Vita told him. "That doesn't even make sense."

Apparently she didn't think it made any sense for Janice to accompany them either. For what? To sit in a hard metal chair for three hours, go into her buy day of work tomorrow with a possible nosocomial infection? You kidding? That would only make

Vita more anxious. On general principle alone, she wouldn't *allow* Janice to come with.

"Be good," Vita said on her way out the door.

"Yeah," Brother said. "Be good."

After they left, Tevis at last took a seat next to her at the kitchen table. He eyed the baby Glock, as if tempted to put it back into her purse, or maybe even take it home with him before she put a bullet in somebody or swallowed one herself.

"So," he said.

"So."

"That's your dad, huh? Has he been coming around a lot lately? Is that why you've been acting like a butthole?"

"Like a crazy bitch psycho, you mean?"

She'd driven drunk. She hit and ran. She was a criminal, and so was Marty who trained a pregnant pit bull to guard his stash, and so were his pals Korean Marty, who threw her into an alleyway, and Cerebral Pauly, who tried to cut out her tongue, and so was the black guy who sold heroin to her outside the meth clinic and the white DJ who sold her coke and the Mexican who sold her crack rocks from his mouth, and so too was Prondzinski, who threatened to demote her if she failed to reach her quota, and so was Sergeant Hart, who paid off CIs with drugs, and so were the banks, and the baseball player who lied to Congress, the governor who slept with hookers, and so was Sean Bell, who got shot, or maybe the four cops who shot him were the criminals, or maybe none of them were criminals, it was just one of those things. Maybe she had rabies. Maybe her ghost bat was actually a real bat that had punctured her neck with its frothy fangs. Maybe a ghost had hexed her. She had, after all, made one guy piss himself and had piss dumped into her lap. She watched a little girl stab herself in the throat. Judith wasn't talking to her. Her mother smoked weed, attacked her when she came home, and was quickly disappearing. Her partner ate fried chicken over the garbage can with his shirt off a day after breaking up with her. She missed positive signals, abandoned uncles, wore a burka, got arrested, flirted with a married man, and cut off all her hair. Investigators yelled at her to make buys, then parked so close to the set that she couldn't make a buy. Her elbow was still bruised. Her nails were still a mess. This upcoming Monday she had what might have been construed as a date: to shoot freaks with a recovering drug addict, the creator of her alter ego. One of her alter egos. Maybe a recovering drug addict. She was going to get booted back to patrol. She spent seven hundred dollars on a cell phone. Her favorite *Rubí* character fell off a balcony and crashed through a glass coffee table. Her rumpus crush broke his hand on her rumpus enemy's head. She pointed a gun at Mr. Hua! She worked with crack-heads, alcoholics, exercise junkies, professional liars, a movie star, a paper-clip-hoarder, an ex-paratrooper, a woman who wore rubber Joker masks, and an inspector who hid all day under his desk, so yeah, fine, guilty, she was a crazy bitch psycho, but how could she not be?

"It's been a tough couple of weeks," she told Tevis.

The back door flew open again. Not Mr. Hua this time, in the entryway with a shotgun and a vengeful curl to his lip, but her father, out of breath, as if this supposed marathoner had exhausted himself climbing the porch's four steps.

"My car," Tevis said, understanding before she did.

"I can't get around it," Brother panted. "I tried. Couple different ways, but I'll take your side mirror off if I get any closer."

"You parked in the *garage*?" Janice asked.

"What?" he said. "Were you using it?"

Tevis told her he'd see her tomorrow at the rumpus. In other words, find your way there on your own. For the first time in their relationship, he bent down to kiss her on the cheek before leaving. He and her father walked out together through the back door. Left behind, afraid to sit still, she picked all the sugar bowl shards off the floor, vacuuming the bits she couldn't see, along with the sugar itself, then wiped blood off the countertop and finished chopping the remaining flower stems. Without any proper vases in the house, she pulled pint glasses down from the cupboards. She arranged the flowers in threes and fours, never twos, because she didn't want Vita to think they stood in for her and Brother, the carnations' pairing a sign from the universe that she should reunite with her ex-husband. This was less Janice being crazy than it was Janice inhabiting the particular craziness of her mother. Upstairs in Vita's bedroom, she placed a single flower on Vita's nightstand, next to a book on mindful meditation and, God help her, two more lipstick-stained water glasses. She felt too tired to wash them. The porch and kitchen lights were both waiting for Vita to come home. To get an update, an expected time of arrival, Janice called her mother's cell, half expecting it to ring somewhere in the bedroom, but it went directly to voice mail, a cheek-puckering taste of her own medicine. She stripped out of her pants and bloodied blouse. Under her mother's covers, clutching a down pillow that smelled powerfully of henna, Janice fell asleep the only way she knew how, by pretending to be dead.

She woke up a full ten hours later with Vita snoring beside her and the carnation in full bloom. Some asshole downstairs kept ringing the doorbell. At the far end of the hall her alarm clock was honking. Somehow, after ten hours of sleep, she still felt exhausted. She had to pee, too, but first she threw on one of Vita's short silk robes and clambered down the stairs to the front door, where through the peephole she saw the fish-bowled faces of two uniformed police officers.

"Who is it?" she asked ridiculously.

"Janice Itwaru?"

*No,* she wanted to say. *I'm Janice Itwaru.*

Procedure dictated the patrols should have identified themselves as police right away, but maybe they saw her eye darkening the peephole and had assumed she could figure it out for herself. They were both men, both white, one a little tanner than the other. To

flaunt his curly hair, the fairer-skinned officer kept his cap clipped to his belt, against
regulations. Her name tumbled out of his
mouth again. She was told to open the door,
but humidity and obsolescence had kept the
wood swollen in the frame. Already apologizing, on the defensive, she asked them to
meet her on the back porch.

A stoic, uniformed Janice — pinned behind the glass of a mantelpiece picture
frame — watched a skimpier, more frantic
Janice race through the living room. She
was fucked. Maybe. If it was just a single
eyewitness who'd stepped forward, someone
who'd seen — *thought* he'd seen — her hit-
and-run the hatchback, then she could
probably lie her way toward reasonable
doubt and possibly retain her job, or at least
avoid jail time. But if that Atlantic Avenue
traffic cam had snapped a picture of her
license plate . . . it wasn't even worth thinking about. Eager to appear as if she was
eager to cooperate, she had the back door
open and was standing on the porch when
she heard a loud thump, followed by some
cursing. The fair-skinned cop came around
the corner massaging the top of his capless
head. He looked furious, ready to kill
someone, or at the least chop down that
alien fruit tree, but his partner could not

have seemed happier. But then he did get happier, his smile widening when he saw Janice standing on the porch with her mother's short robe wrapped tight around her body.

"What is that?" he said. "Silk?"

"You boys want some coffee?" she asked.

They followed her into the kitchen, where she noticed for the first time all the black ants crawling across the floor. Dozens, maybe a hundred of them. They did not march forward in a single line behind a foreman dancing out orders but instead swarmed like looters for the sugar she'd apparently done a poor job of vacuuming. Disgust tightened the cords in the fair-skinned cop's neck. Never mind that the rest of the kitchen was clean, minus all the junk piled on chairs. Never mind that fresh flowers covered the table, albeit in water glasses. She hoped that back when she'd worked patrol, going in and out of project apartments, she'd managed to hide her repugnance a little bit better than he did, but she knew she probably hadn't. She threw a bloody dishrag over the ants, her face smoldering with embarrassment for both her past and present selves.

"What the hell is all that *noise*?" he asked.

"My alarm clock."

The cop who liked her robe said, "We've had plenty of coffee already, Mrs. Itwaru, but thank you for asking."

"Miss," she corrected, because every bit counted.

The other cop rested his hand on the butt of his holstered gun, in a probable attempt to intimidate her. "Miss Itwaru," he said, "do you have any weapons on the premises?"

She told them she didn't understand. They told her in response that a criminal complaint had been made against her for assaulting a Mr. — and here the fair-skinned cop had to consult his steno pad — a Mr. Jianheng Hua with a deadly weapon, which was a felony by the way, and what did she have to say about it? The relief vaulted out of her on a single sob. Her ass dropped down into the nearest, paperless chair. She rubbed sleep boogers from her eyes, explaining to the cops her own side of the story: that Hua had trespassed onto her property, into her house, which was a misdemeanor by the way, and so she pointed a gun at him and politely asked him to leave.

"You got a permit for the gun?" the fair-skinned cop asked.

"I'm on the job."

"You're a *cop*?" he said, tripped up by her

brown skin, vagina, and address, which was in the actual city where she actually worked, meaning she shat where she ate instead of living out on Long Island like a normal PO. "Why didn't you say anything?"

"I didn't know why you were here," she said, which after all was the truth.

"Where you work out of?"

"Queens Narcotics," she said and watched their eyebrows go up. "I'm an uncle."

She'd somehow never said it out loud before: I'm an uncle!

"Dang, you out of the bag already?" the tan one said. "How old are you?"

"You can't ask a girl how old she is," said the other cop, her defender now. He leaned against the counter, visibly relaxed, because hey, listen, even the cleanest kitchens can get ants sometimes, right? "What's it like working undercover?" he asked. "Pretty crazy?"

"Pretty crazy," she said.

Upstairs the alarm clock stopped honking.

"Internal Affairs is probably the worst part of it," she said, and both cops nodded, eager to agree. "It's like they got a hard-on for uncles. I'm serious. Since the Sean Bell thing? They just looking to cut us down. Any excuse." Did she really need to keep going here? Did they really not get it yet? She plucked a droopy petal off a carnation and rolled it between her fingertips. "I'm saying, just you watch," she told the patrols. "A guy makes some bullshit criminal complaint? Doesn't matter he comes into *my* house first. IA will just turn it all around and make it seem like —"

"Oh," the tan cop said. "Come on, no, don't worry about it." He looked to his partner for confirmation. "Right?"

"Please," he said. "This is some paperwork we done already lost."

After they left, she went to get the vacuum cleaner and found her mother sitting on the staircase. She wore a thin T-shirt and underwear without her robe to go over them. Her knees were pressed together, her feet splayed apart like a pigeon's, the veins along her hands as thick as licorice. Through the underwear's sheer fabric, Janice could see the dark sponge of her pubic hair. Nothing made sense. This young woman, who had always seemed even younger, looked suddenly old, as if overnight she'd turned old, old all over her body except for a pair of terrified eyes that would have belonged more rightfully in the face of a child. She gnawed, as Janice would have gnawed, on her finger's bandage and gauze.

"Don't do that," Janice said.

"Don't tell me what to do," Vita said savagely. "I heard voices. *Men's* voices."

"The police," Janice said. "About last night. Mr. Hua. It's nothing, I took care of it." As she spoke, the spirit of her mother's panic shot through her like a chill. She gripped her own elbows to keep herself from trembling. "You hungry? You want me to make you something to eat?"

"What happened to my finger?" Vita wailed.

"Oh, Mom," Janice said and went up the stairs to hold on to her.

# CHAPTER TEN

For young Mikey Sharpe, a natural taxono-
mist and lover of lists, there was only one
sport: handball, and of that one sport there
were only two subsets worth considering:
Chinese handball and American handball,
in that order, from best to not-quite-as-best.
His classification system did not include the
so-called team handball nonsense played at
the Olympics indoors with goalies and
referees. Or the beach version, which Mikey
couldn't even wrap his head around. Or any
of the other naked emperors cluttering
handball's Wikipedia page. Handball, real
handball, was played outside, without goalies, away from sand, against a wall with an
actual — and this should be obvious but
apparently wasn't — handball, of which
again there were only two preferred types:
the light blue Sky Bounce and the heavier
pink Spaldeen. They both smelled like summer and kicked up nicely, but the Sky

Bounces were a little easier for him to find. A stationery store on Roosevelt Avenue sold them for a dollar apiece.

Between American handball and Chinese handball, American was by far the more popular, especially down at the Seventy-Eighth and Ninety-Fifth Street parks, where the older boys wore fingerless gloves over their palms. With American you had to smash the ball into the wall. With Chinese, the ball got bounced into the wall. Rule-wise it was the only difference, but that one difference led to five distinct yet interrelated advantages, in ascending order of importance: Chinese handball did not require gloves, which were more expensive than he could afford on his allowance; it privileged touch over force and angles over aggression; with longer points, more people could play at a time; with more people playing, there was a whole lot less running; and, as in baseball, its slower pace led to a super-hilario insider language of killers, Hindus, egg rolls, babying, watermelons, wormburners, and cobble smashers.

Mikey's specialty was the killer, a soft-touch shot that kissed the base of the wall before dribbling back, unreturnable. Unbeatable, he dominated the I.S. 145 handball court from the beginning of recess to

362

the loud-ass bell calling every eighth-grader inside. Actually? Technically? He dominated *one* of the I.S. 145 handball courts. The playground had a single, freestanding wall: on one side, the side grafittied with a fire-spitting dragon, kids played American style, which Mikey thought unfair because dragons were Chinese; the other side of the wall, his side of the wall, was a pop-art mural of rainbow figures dancing and hugging. Totally lame. He recognized the style from a Keith Haring exhibit, one of the many so-called cultural events his mother dragged him to in an attempt to discourage him from sports and/or turn him gay. Some, though, were not entirely terrible and his top five from best to fifth best were: an exhibit of Richard Avedon photographs, an exhibit of Calder mobiles, the musical *Ragtime,* the musical *Joseph and the Amazing Technicolor Dreamcoat,* and a swing-dance class they took together outside Lincoln Center but had to stop after only ten minutes because he ran out of breath.

Next September he'll enter the ninth grade at Newtown High, where his older brother, Chris, was the star athlete. And where the PE department had an actual handball team with an opportunity to win actual trophies like the ones with plastic baseball and basketball players on Chris's side of their shared bedroom. There was a problem, though, and it was a sucky one. Newton's PE department, and the Public Schools Athletic League as a whole, played handball American-style only.

In their bedroom, getting dressed before dinner one night, Chris told him he just needed to build up his lung capacity, that's all. Mikey asked him what a pothead knew about lung capacity. Their mother was frying sausage and peppers in the kitchen, too far away to have possibly overheard, but Chris still punched him so hard in the arm that Mikey's fingertips deadened. Mikey couldn't believe it. Unique among older brothers, Chris had never really hit him before. Afterward, while Mikey cried like a loser, Chris put his arms around him, apologizing into the swirled hair atop Mikey's head, telling him that he could do anything he put his mind to. Seriously, anything. Mikey just needed to take things one step at a time, to not get ahead of himself. For instance? When Chris was scared of the baseball, he started fielding grounders on his knees after batting practice. See, one thing at a time. Fast-forward a year and he was Newtown's starting shortstop. He used to have a mad-weak crossover, so he began playing pickup games left-handed, which was probably what he was doing right now over at the Seventy-Eighth Street courts, fighting against the dark on this mega-cold Saturday.

And Mikey on this mega-cold Saturday? He was playing American handball by himself against the apartment building's brick exterior. And Mikey's inhaler? Upstairs on his bedroom dresser. One thing at a time. To keep his lungs fresh, he stopped all his rallies after six shots. Yesterday he'd gone up to five; tomorrow he hoped to do seven. Here we go: with some gangster topspin he sliced the ball for an ill killer, bringing a touch of the Chinese style to this American game.

The Sky Bounce squirted away from him.

A few feet away it ended up trapped under the high-heeled boot of a woman who must've been watching him this whole time. He'd seen her before, he thought. Earlier in the week maybe, with two dudes on an afternoon much warmer than this one. She looked a little grimier than he remembered. She wore baggy jeans, an orange thug cap, and a gray sweatshirt too small for her, but was still totally pervable. His top-five girls were black girls, obviously, followed by Indians because they all seemed to have nice skin and big ta-tas, then Latinas, Russian girls, and finally Asians, mostly because of Tiffany Chen's bouncing ponytail, which he sometimes followed half a block behind on the way to school. This lady right here appeared part black, part Indian, a perfect combo. She reminded him of a favorite porno video with brown boobies smushed up against a shower-stall door, an image that came easily to mind during his own afternoon bathroom sessions. He looked away from the woman, embarrassed, as if she somehow knew all the things he'd been thinking about, all the guilty things he'd ever done.

"You practicing your killers?" she asked him.

He couldn't believe it. "You play?"

She bounced the ball to him, but because he was Mikey Sharpe, loser extraordinaire, he fumbled it and had to go chasing after it. There were whole games, like Suicide and Asses-Up, where now he'd have to face the wall so she could peg him.

"How old are you?" she said.

"Sixteen," he lied.

"Sixteen," she said, more to herself than to him. "I've seen you around, right? You're the neighborhood Romeo? The Heartbreak Kid around here?"

He tried to think of how his brother might answer that. The neighborhood Romeo? A million years ago Cindy Friedman apparently had a crush on Mikey, but she moved to New Jersey before he could do anything about it. At a birthday party last February he went into a closet with Tiffany Chen for seven minutes of quick pecks — well, more like two minutes of quick pecks — without any tongue even, and she hadn't spoken to him since and he had no idea why. Him? The Heartbreak Kid?

"Not really," he said.

"Exactly what a player would say," she told him. "How many girlfriends you got?"

He shrugged.

"Too many to count?" she asked.

He didn't know what to tell her. He didn't think his brother would even know what to tell her. She terrified Mikey, and he didn't want her to leave, both at the same time. He threw the ball up high in the air and caught it one-handed, to show her his earlier fumbling had been a fluke.

"You live around here?" he asked her for lack of anything better to say.

"Next thing you're gonna hit me up for my number," she said, smiling, pulling out her cell phone like maybe this whole thing might really happen. But nope. She must've just been checking the time, or seeing if she'd gotten a text, because the phone went right back into her pocket. "You know I've been out here all day?" she asked him. "Up and down all these streets. For *hours*. I even had a pigeon shit on my shoulder, you believe that?"

Sure, he believed it. The five worst New York City animals: roaches, pigeons, squirrels, subway rats, and silverfish. He couldn't see it, though, this shit on her shoulder, but then again it was getting late, getting dark out. With the sun setting, his Sky Bounce was beginning to look more indigo than baby blue.

"You're really sixteen?" she asked.

"Of course," he said, unable to keep himself from shrugging again.

"Let me ask you a question. You got your ear to the ground, right? Outside all day? Practicing your killers, hollering at the pretty girls. Where I gotta go to cop some weed around here, huh? Not a lot. Just enough to get a little joint going, you know what I'm talking about? A little party like. I been hitting up people all day, Romeo, and you're pretty much my last hope."

A tiny camera kept him under surveillance as he rode up in his elevator. Padded blankets hung on the walls, protection from possible scuff marks and dings. All week he'd taken the stairs, pausing at every landing to re-up his breath, but he didn't have time for that now. He worried the lady would leave if he didn't get in and out of his apartment fast enough. Part of him, the loser part of him, hoped she was already gone.

The apartment door slammed behind him, startling his mother, who should've known better. She sat at the kitchen table with her fabric scissors and tomato pincushion and foot-pedal Singer, making her rainbow-fish quilt for yet another one of the expectant mamas in the building. He waved at her. Since morning, every twenty minutes or so, he'd pit-stopped into the apartment for snacks, bathroom breaks, inhaler hits, and glasses of the powdered Gatorade she had to make by the gallon. There was nothing at all for her to be suspicious about, except perhaps that for the first time in his life he closed his bedroom door softly behind him. A chair went under the knob. The search for his brother's stash took only seconds, Mikey finding it exactly where he expected to find it: in a VHS clamshell case that on the outside said DAZZLING DUNKS AND BASKETBALL BLOOPERS, but on the inside contained pictures torn out of nudie magazines, a pocketknife, their father's dog tags, and a little plastic baggie of weed, stems, and seeds. He removed only one bud, not knowing if it would be enough to get a little joint going. He hoped so. If his brother happened to notice any of his weed missing — unlikely, but if he did — Mikey felt prepared to make a full denial and he would be believed, he knew it, because like every criminal in their mother's mystery shows, he was the least likely suspect. The bud radiated heat in his fist as he walked out of the bedroom. With a strained attempt at innocence and the handball bulging his back pocket, he crept past his mother, who asked him to please not let the door slam, but by the time he'd heard her it was already too late.

He must've taken longer than he'd thought — invisible movers had filled up the elevator with furniture — but the lady was still waiting for him outside the building, on the sidewalk where he'd left her. The loser Mikey felt a little disappointed. And you know what? There must've been a loser part of her, too, because she seemed almost disappointed herself, smiling without pleasure or warmth, as if she'd hoped he wouldn't have come back. Or maybe he was imagining things, overthinking things. Only after slipping the bud into her palm did he realize he should've put it in a baggie first.

"It's really good shit," he said, by way of an apology.

She nodded, still looking disappointed. The bud seemed preposterously small in her hand, unfit for the littlest of little joints, but when two burly white men came out of the building carrying a futon, she shoved that weed deep into her pocket. Her hat came off, her hair shorter than he'd expected. She tried to give him a twenty-dollar bill, but he waved her away.

"It's on the house," he told her.

"Don't be silly."

"No, seriously."

"No, seriously," she said back at him, a little scary now. "You have to take it."

"I don't even have any change."

She patted the pocket where she'd put the weed. "It's really good shit," she reminded him. "It's worth at least twenty bucks."

Well, all right, fine, but only because he already had a list brewing of what he could do with the money: since the weed was technically his brother's, he could sneak the twenty into Chris's sock drawer (yeah right); or Mikey could hoard it himself for a future occasion; or take Tiffany Chen to see

*Meet the Browns* at the Jackson Triplex; or, most tantalizing, order off eBay a pair of padded Owen 922 handball gloves, which cost exactly $19.95 including shipping. He had money, he had options. After the woman walked away, he whacked the ball off the ground and into the bricks, forgetting for a moment that he was supposed to be playing American.

Four down. None to go. Now what?

Later that night, from behind her regal desk, Lieutenant Prondzinski said, "I shouldn't even be telling you this. It's not . . . it's not the proper way, but I thought you'd want to know sooner rather than later. So you could prepare yourself. Get that anxious brain of yours in the right headspace. It's not proper maybe, to pass news like this directly, and so early, but I figured I owed you as much after your tenure here in Narcotics. Your entirely admirable tenure, I should add. Next week, not this week upcoming, but the following week, the start of next month, you are to report right here for work, do you understand?"

Not at first. For an entirely absurd moment Janice thought right here meant *right* here, as in this office, as in she was getting leap-frogged to lieutenant, but when that entirely absurd moment passed she was able to understand that right here meant the rumpus, as in not patrol, as in she will officially last the magic eighteen months with Narcotics, she's made it, mission accomplished. And so again: now what?

"Thank you," she said.

"The gears tend to grind slowly, so I'm thinking it'll probably be a few more weeks before you can get sworn in at Police Plaza. But your pay bump will be postdated from the first of April, that I can guarantee. And rest assured, this isn't an April Fool's gag, ha-ha!"

"Ha-ha," Janice said.

"All joking aside? I'm proud of you. I hope that doesn't sound condescending. I don't mean to talk down to you, Itwaru, but I am legitimately proud of the work you have done here. I'm serious. You are an asset to this department. But now that you're going to be a detective, three buys a month just isn't going to cut it anymore. It just isn't going to get the job done. As a detective, you're expected to make better numbers than that, okay? Not from me. I understand how hard it is to bring in three in a month. I get that, Itwaru. But these expectations are coming from up high, understand? The bar has been raised. And I, for one? I am completely confident you're going to rise to this new and exciting challenge."

"I made four buys this month," Janice told her.

Prondzinski looked down at the mess of file folders on her desk without actually opening any of them. "Is that what the buy board says?"

"I don't know. Maybe it hasn't gone up yet?"

"Well, whatever. Three buys, four buys, you're gonna have to do better from now on."

"I'm a little confused," Janice said. To keep herself from sliding out of the rigged chair, she gripped the sides of her seat, her fingers feeling only wood, no scratched-in initials or wads of gum. "You told me I had to make four buys. You *said* that. You said I wouldn't get promoted otherwise. But now you're telling me you thought I had *three*? And I was gonna get the shield anyway?"

Prondzinski shook her head vigorously. "What you're talking about sounds like a quota system, and we don't do that here. You're getting promoted, Itwaru, because of the exceptional promise you've dem-onstrated these past eighteen months. And also? To be real for a second?" Behind her, a shadow play of rain drifted across her paper-covered window. "With this Sean Bell fiasco, with the new hiring standards, with your boy Puffy gone, with recruitment dropping across the department, how the fuck would I find a warm body to replace your ass, even if I'd wanted to? Now, if there are no further questions . . ."

Back at her own desk, in her own seat, Janice battled claustrophobia with small sips of air as the uncles surrounded her. Four buys! In a month! With a week to spare! She was a natural, she was a gangster, she made them all look bad, seriously, don't do that, stop making us all look bad. Fiorella, more excited than anyone, wanted to celebrate at A.R.'s Tavern. Tevis said he'd come for a drink. Klondike and Morris looked up from their *Post*s — the headline, honest to God, read "Why Sad Women Want Sex" — to offer to buy the first round. At the promise of free booze, Grimes slid jeans on over his pajama pants. Eddie Murphy couldn't go because he was in a California recording studio doing voiceover work for the next *Shrek,* and Gonz couldn't go, either, because he wasn't invited, although he reassured them he wouldn't have gone anyway because he had to take a trip to pound town

— his words — with the chubby white girl from Jackson Heights. Pablo Rivera kept asking Janice if Prondzinski had mentioned Internal Affairs at all. James Chan of course said nothing, but everyone assumed he'd come to A.R.'s because he always went to A.R.'s. Five miles away, Mikey Sharpe sat in the 115 Precinct's Youth Office handcuffed to a metal bar as he awaited an overnight transfer to the juvenile detention center in Jamaica. Richie the Receptionist promised she wouldn't have to pay for a single drink, but she bowed out with the excuse that she'd already called a cab to take her home. The uncles accused her of ditching them for the third night in a row, of acting all uppity now that she was making detective. She said she felt sick.

Late Monday morning, Internal Affairs woke her up with a phone call. She pulled off her sleep mask. The number on her phone had come in as unlisted, but she answered anyway, hopeful it was her sister. Instead it was a Caribbean-sounding woman requesting Janice's presence for an informational meeting that afternoon at Internal Affairs' Manhattan offices. Whether the information at this informational meeting would be for Janice's benefit or theirs, the woman didn't say. But she did give her the address: 315 Hudson. Third floor. Bring your ID and badge. If Janice was coming from home — because they of course knew where she lived — the woman suggested the Van Wyck Expressway. Or, if Janice preferred public transit — was that irony winking there through the woman's maddeningly chipper tone, as if she understood perfectly Janice's problematic car situation? — the E train to Spring Street, although, fair warning, that would probably take twice as long.

"Can you tell me what this is about?"

She was already out of bed, pacing the carpet, a finger wedged into her free ear. Her father's beat-up *I Ching* almost tripped her. On the other end of the line, long Caribbean fingernails clicked at a computer keyboard. If the woman had been calling from the rumpus or any other precinct, Janice would have heard papers rustling, but Internal Affairs employed more technologically sophisticated methods.

"I'm afraid," the woman said, sounding completely unafraid, "that any questions and concerns will have to be brought directly to your case officer at this afternoon's informational meeting. Would three thirty work for you?"

"Do I have a choice?"

"I'm sorry, I don't understand the question."

Janice had her hand on the bedroom's doorknob, ready to go running out of the house. "Do I *have* to go to the meeting? Is it mandatory?"

More typing, which Janice understood now had nothing to do with her or her situation but was instead just the woman multitasking, trying to catch up on her backlog of other numbers to call, other dumb cops IA had caught in their vise. "Again," the woman said, trying to get her off the phone, "you'll have to address that with your assigned case officer at the meeting."

"I have to go to a meeting to find out if I have to go to a meeting?"

"Until further notice we strongly advise that you keep this entirely confidential, for your own benefit more than anything."

Janice hung up on her. She wished she had a landline to slam into a cradle, not this flimsy plastic cell phone with its pathetic tiny cancel button. Her arm hairs stiffened, a prelude to diarrhea, but before she could get to the toilet, her mother banged on the bedroom door asking if she wanted train tracks: a soft-boiled egg with sliced toast. No! It was an overzealous no, a child's no, and it made Janice feel even worse, but if her mother saw her now, she'd press her fingertips beneath Janice's eyes and tell her she had nothing to worry about, she hadn't done anything wrong, she couldn't have done anything wrong, offering unequivocal forgiveness without even knowing the charges because it was Vita's job to offer unequivocal forgiveness, and Janice would then puddle and evaporate and miss her informational meeting.

"You okay in there?" Vita asked, with her bandaged hand surely hovering over the other end of the doorknob.

"I'm fine!"

When Janice finally did get downstairs, she vacuumed all the rugs, its motor plenty loud enough to prohibit conversation. She could've called Tevis for help, or Fiorella, or her union rep, or she could've dusted her mother's crystal dolphin collection. She dusted her mother's crystal dolphin collection. In the living room Martha Stewart was showing Vita how to deseed a pomegranate. In the kitchen Janice threw away her unasked-for portion of eggs and toast, certain she wouldn't be able to keep it down. She changed the refrigerator's lightbulb. To resuscitate the carnation petals, she chopped another inch off every stem. Because her mother was never going to do it properly, she cleaned the table and its chairs of *all* their receipts, junk mail, outdated newspapers, and credit card offers, which she ripped in half without opening, but before tossing the supermarket circulars she forced herself to examine the photos of missing children above the address label, their faces age-progressed to the current moment. Those poor parents, those poor mailmen. Upstairs she took such a long, hot shower that afterward she couldn't find herself in the mirror. It was only one o'clock in the afternoon. IA had not called her back. Perhaps they expected — perhaps they knew — she'd arrive promptly for her meeting even though she'd hung up on them. Maybe they were used to that. She got under the covers and tried to pretend she was dead, but her eyes stayed stubbornly open, just like on a real corpse, and she was still awake an hour later when Jimmy Gellar rang the doorbell.

"Jan!" her mother hollered up the stairs. "There's a mister here to see you!"

For the first time since dementia had struck there were four perfectly decluttered chairs available in the kitchen, but both Jimmy and Vita seemed too nervous to sit.

They beamed at her as she came down the stairs, as if she was wearing a long silk gown with room on the shoulder strap for a corsage, instead of these frumpy shorts and pit-stained tee. Vita looked especially pleased. She must've thought it all made sense now: Janice's morning moodiness, the neurotic cleaning, her lack of appetite, the ridiculous amount of time spent stowed away in the bathroom. A boy! Of course! And a polite boy, too, one who'd already removed his shoes and set them neatly by the back door.

"You got a haircut," he said. "It looks great."

He wore a clean white button-down tucked into brown corduroys, with a short cable-knit cardigan, all of it totally nerdy and grown-up, his transformation from Jimmy to James complete, except around his waist, where he had — she smiled to see it — a nylon belt with a brass Superman buckle. Also suddenly around his waist: Vita's arm as she corralled him into one of the chairs. The sole benefit of her mother's illness seemed to be the loss of every white-cloaked neuron afraid of black people.

"Can I get you something to eat?" she asked now that she had him trapped in a chair. "While Jan puts on something a little nicer, maybe? I picked up the most beautiful roast beef from the Italian market."

"Actually I'm going to need a rain check," Janice told him. "I'm really sorry, but I just got called into work last minute. To do this thing."

"You don't have work today," Vita said. "Go on upstairs and get changed."

"That's what I'm saying, I got called in. Last minute."

"I understand," Jimmy said, not understanding at all, probably assuming she was just brushing him off; she couldn't even tell the truth persuasively anymore. He stood out of his chair. "Why don't you just hit me up on Facebook when you're —"

"Don't be silly!" Vita said, pushing him back into the chair. "Just call them back," she told Janice. "Tell them you had plans already. They'll understand if you explain the situation."

"I'm really sorry," Janice told him. "Maybe next week? If you're free?"

"Is it your period?" Vita asked. "Because I'm sure I've got a pill around here somewhere."

*"Mom!"*

Jimmy stood up again.

"You don't ever go out!" Vita cried. "If you made more of a social effort now and again, maybe you'd be able to —"

"Hey, Jimmy," Janice said. "Can we try talking about this upstairs, please?"

"Great idea," Vita told them both. "I'll get started on those sandwiches."

Unlike old times, they did not hold hands on the walk up the stairs, but once inside her room they did retreat to their usual positions: Janice cross-legged on the rumpled bedspread, Jimmy at the old wooden desk, half turned in the chair to face her. Through his eyes she saw her room as embarrassingly unchanged, a life-size diorama exhibit in the Janice Itwaru Museum of Standing Still. The same carpet, the same window blinds, the same girl in shorts and a T-shirt, the same Teddy Ruse-ah-velt quote tacked to the wall. Take a Polaroid of this room now in 2008 and line it up next to a Polaroid from 1997, and you can play the Photo Hunt game, just like on the Megatouch screens at A.R.'s Tavern. Spot the differences: a gun safe, an iPhone charger, bras of a larger cup size hanging off the doorknob, the Ruse-uh-velt poster-board a few inches to the left to cover up the dent in the wall.

"I could do next Sunday," Jimmy said. "If that works for you."

She might be in jail next Sunday. She

pulled a goose-down pillow into her lap, the sharp end of a tiny feather poking up through its seams. She of course plucked it out, but another feather came right up into the seams to take its place. She plucked that one out, too. She should keep going until there wasn't any pillow left so she'd have an excuse to buy something new for this amber trap of a bedroom. Her meeting started in less than ninety minutes. Her father had long ago taught her that the harder she worked now, the easier things would be later on. He also taught her how to snake quarters out of a pay phone, how to find pennies on the street, not to listen to music on the walk home, not to look over your shoulder more than once, that the biggest guest star was almost always the killer, that pigeon shit led to good luck, and Jimmy Gellar was bad. With the sharp end of the feather she scratched at a spot on her arm that wasn't even itchy.

"You got a car?" she asked.

"I do," he said. "I mean, today I do." Without any goose feathers in front of him, he dragged a hand across her desk, as if looking for a pencil, something to futz with, but there wasn't anything there for him to hold on to. A much cleaner desk since he'd last been here: another hundred points for the Photo Hunt game. "I borrowed my brother's Volvo," he told her. "For our big date that got canceled."

"Date?" she said. "I thought we were just —"

"You're ignoring my dig about you canceling on me."

She went to tuck her hair behind her ears, but it was still too short to stay back there. "Are you guilt-tripping me?" she asked.

"A little. Don't you think you deserve it?"

"Rarely," she said, "but I think that might be my problem."

"Well, you're lucky you only got one."

On the way into Manhattan, between bites of his roast beef, he said, "Nah, not really. That was a time in my life where I wasn't really finishing much of anything except blunts. But it's funny, you know? Since running into you again? I've been giving it a stupid amount of thought. Do you remember where we left off? We had to get her into a death trap? So I'm thinking we set the final scene on Halloween. Earlier that day, Ned Shu is campaigning for Queens borough president, saying the current president, his opponent, is responsible for the recent spike in crime. And while he's saying all this, a ninja pops out of nowhere and runs a kitana sword through Shu's shoulder. He survives, but Gabby Guyana, who was working security for the press conference — cops do that, right? — she shoots the ninja dead.

"Later that night, she's undercover, dressed up like this defenseless woman in Richmond Hill, when two more ninjas pop out of nowhere. But you don't mess with Captain Richmond Hill, right? She ghetto-touches their nunchucks. One of the ninjas gets wrapped up in barbed wire. The other she hangs upside down from a lamppost. When she searches the ninja's pockets, she finds these grainy black-and-white surveillance photos of Ned Shu going in and out of his campaign office. She assumes another attack on his life is like moments away, so she rushes over to his office to warn him. Here we can have a funny little scene of her riding the 7 train. Holding the pole or whatever. And when she gets to Shu's office, she sits down in a chair across from his desk and tells him everything she knows.

"But see, what she doesn't know is that Shu's been behind all this from the start. He's a crime boss, ordering extra robberies and stuff to discredit the current borough president. He planned his own assassination attempt. He sent the ninjas after her and put the photos in their pockets, knowing she'd come over to warn him, and when she did she'd sit down in his chair and trigger a pressure-activated device synced to a bunch of TNT beneath his desk. The desk, that's the death trap. And the bomb will explode if she stands back up.

"It's sort of ripped off from *Lethal Weapon 2*. The toilet scene? But there are no new ideas, so whatever. I'm thinking I could use some really cool Chris Ware–like arrows and caption boxes to direct the reader's eye from the chair to the desk, maybe even the bomb's wire could serve as panel borders, I don't know. Like I said, I've been giving this a stupid amount of thought.

"So because Shu's the villain he has to explain his whole plan obviously, and he tells her that a similar explosive device is about to derail a 7 train, probably killing a bunch of trick-or-treaters in the process. I haven't really figured out all the wrinkles on that one yet, to tell you the truth. But there's gotta be some sort of ticking clock, otherwise she'd just be able to sit there till morning.

"Okay, so he's about to walk out of the room. He's on his way to where the train's gonna crash, right? So he can like pull some maimed kids out of the wreckage for the photo op? But before he leaves, she says, 'How do you know I won't just stand up now and kill us both?'

"And he goes, 'You may be an A-rab, but you don't seem like the suicide-bombing type.'

"Final panel. Her teeth are clenched. Her eyes narrowed behind the domino mask. She says, 'I'm Guyanese, you son of a bitch.'

"And that's all I got. 'To be continued in next month's thrilling issue of *Captain Richmond Hill.*' So what do you think? I'm open to feedback as long as it's glowing."

Because Internal Affairs' Caribbean Richie the Receptionist equivalent couldn't abandon her front desk, she asked a heavyset white guy waddling out of the commode to please deposit Officer Itwaru in the nearest informational meeting room. It was set up exactly as Janice had expected: a gray table, gray chairs, gray walls, and a security camera rolling in the corner above the gray door. An hour early for her meeting, her interview, her interrogation, whatever the fuck they wanted to call it, she assumed she'd have to wait here alone for at least that long, plus the requisite extra fifteen minutes of sweating-out time, but almost immediately after the heavyset white guy left the room another heavyset white guy came breezing in. He looked too young for the gray in his hair, too wide for his suit. He looked, actually, like a former football player, with paperwork folders and a three-ring binder and a laptop all tucked under one arm as if he needed the other to shed tacklers. He wouldn't stop smiling. In a thick Lawn Guyland accent — its origin farther east than Great Neck, more like Syosset or even Montauk — he introduced himself as Lieutenant John Lenox, but go ahead and call him Johno. His hand, when she shook it, felt calloused from weight lifting.

"What do you want?" she asked.

"Your help!" He set his things in a neat pile on the table and sat in the chair across from hers. "I know it's a pain to be calling you in like this. And I wouldn't even be asking for your help if, well, it's ironic actually. The feds? Homeland Security? A little while back, they opened a money-laundering investigation on this joint in Queens. To make sure there are no other claims on the place, they punch the address into DECS and what do they see? They see we've been running our own investigation there for a while now. Of course that doesn't stop *them*. It's full steam ahead as far as they're concerned. We're talking about cash money, and the feds aren't going to let a little NYPD investigation get in the way of their cash money, you follow? But then what happens? They run into a bit of a confuzzlement. On *their* end of the investigation. Something they can't sort out on their own. So they go, 'Hey, no problem! Let's get that dumb fuck Johno at IA to do our jobs for us!' Interdepartment cooperation, right? Osama bin Laden with his dick in my ass all the way from Timbuktu, pardon my French. But the problem, the problem on my end, is that for the life of me I can't untangle this little confuzzlement either. So now I've got to reach out for your help. Because it was a Narcotics investigation. On our end, I'm saying. And maybe, the way this thing's going, you'll have to reach out for someone else's help, and they'll have to reach out for someone else's help, all the way down the line, but I really don't think so. I really think you're our guy on this because the joint, the establishment, it's the Pure Magic Dance Hall. On Roosevelt Avenue? You been there, correct?"

On the ear end of a never-ending monologue for what seemed like the last three weeks, she had at first assumed the question was rhetorical. "I'm not sure," she said finally, trying not to move in her seat.

"Really?" He made a show of searching through his paperwork folders for something. "Because I'm pretty positive I've got a file here saying you made a buy at the joint just a couple weeks ago."

"I make a lot of buys."

"Oh I bet!" He pulled out the sheet of paper he'd pretended he hadn't been able to find. "See, right here. March twelfth. Two weeks ago. Not even." He began to read off the page: " 'Undercover . . .' That's you, your name's down at the bottom here . . . 'Undercover purchased a fifteen-milligram pill of the controlled substance OxyContin from the bathroom attendant, Latina, mid-forties, dark hair, brown eyes, five foot three, approximately a hundred and sixty pounds.' "

He pushed the report toward her, its front side streaked with gray from God knows how many photocopyings. Worried her hands might start trembling, she didn't reach for it but instead read it right there off the table, hunched forward in her chair and sitting on her fingers. What'd she remember? All the perfumes. The lady saying everything was pay-what-you-will, like at the Natural History Museum. When Janice finished reading, she looked up to see Lieutenant Lenox still smiling. He filed her report back into his folder.

"Do I need my union rep here, Johno?"

"How's the coffee in Narcotics? Is it terrible? It's terrible here, let me tell you, but I got one of those French presses. It's pretty decent. Gotta lock it up in my desk so no one steals it, but that's life in Internal Affairs." His chair legs scraped across the floor as he stood up. "I'm going to make a pot, you want some? I'll put it in a clean mug and everything."

"No, thank you."

"See, that's how deep you undercovers go! Turning down a cup of coffee? It's amazing! It's like you're not even cops anymore. How about a soda? A bottle of malt liquor? Ha-ha, just kidding. But seriously, we got Sprite, Coke, Diet Coke . . ."

She pulled her hands out from under her thighs. "Listen, I really don't mean to be rude —"

"Uh-oh," he said.

"But I sort of have to leave pretty quick here. It's my day off, you know. And if this is going to take all afternoon, maybe I could just come back another time or —"

"How about this?" he said. He opened the laptop and turned it toward her. Somewhere inside its thin casing a fan blade started whirring. On-screen a black-and-white video waited for his pointer finger to press play. When he came around to her side of the table, she could smell the aftershave on him, even though gunpowder stubble still darkened his cheeks. It was typical of a certain class of investigator: putting on aftershave without actually shaving, deodorant applied under shirts, suit jackets sprayed with Febreze. He probably hadn't gone home in days, the kind of detective she hoped to one day become. "I'm going to get some refreshments," he said. "In the meantime? While you're just sitting here? Take a look at this video. It's security footage from the club. The night you were there, the twelfth. And the camera, it was directly above the booth where the DJ sold your partner Detective Tevis . . . let's see if I can remember this exactly . . . three-point-five grams of powdered cocaine. In a small manila envelope. That sound about right?"

Flushed with heat, she unzipped her jacket and hung it on the back of her chair. She crossed her legs at the knees, as if to make herself smaller, more invisible, while Lenox loomed behind her, presumably still grinning. The happy former football player who got to call his own plays.

"Now the problem," he said, "is not the

quality of the footage. It's actually pretty excellent for once. The problem is that I don't know what this Detective Tevis looks like. Not like you do. So what would be great is if you could just watch this video, you follow? And hit pause as soon as Tevis shows up to make his cocaine buy."

He patted her on the shoulder before leaving. The chair she was sitting in was stupidly uncomfortable, but at least it didn't keep scooting her forward like the one in Prondzinski's office. At least there was that. She hit play on the video, which as promised was of an impressively high quality. No audio, though, not that anything would've been heard over the house music's hard bass. Positioned — hidden? — behind the DJ booth, the camera clearly showed the white kid from behind, with enough light and definition for her to see a record wobbling on his turntable. Apparently money launderers spared little expense when it came to internal surveillance. Or maybe the camera belonged to the government. Maybe they had another one outside the club's bathrooms where Janice had given Tevis the coke. Lieutenant Lenox, or some Internal Affairs IT guy, had cued up the video so that she saw herself come on-screen fairly quickly, after only a couple of minutes. The

Janice on the laptop wore that stupidly shimmering shirt. A black-and-white face, unmistakably her own, leaned into the DJ booth to say something. She didn't know if lipreading was admissible in court. She didn't know if, when Lenox returned, she should ask for a lawyer or if outside involvement would only make this more official than it necessarily had to be. More real, even. What had seemed at the time to last only an instant took forever on tape. A hand with raggedy fingernails swapped forty dollars for a little manila envelope of reasonably priced cocaine. For him, it would've been a criminal sale of a controlled substance, a class B felony. For her, she didn't know.

She minimized the video player. Digital file folders covered the computer desktop with incomprehensible labels of seemingly random letters and numbers. She found one, though, with a *Q* and an *I,* maybe for *Queens* and *Itwaru.* She could've clicked it open, or she could've gone through any of Lenox's actual folders piled on the table, but she knew she was under surveillance. Get with it, Janice. You have always been under surveillance. She closed the laptop and pushed it away from her. She had a better idea, or at least better than flipping through folders looking for her name: she could turn on the iPhone's voice-memo app so she'd have her own digital record of whatever happened next. She reached into her purse, but Lenox — who this whole time had probably been watching her watch herself — was hurrying back into the room, as if afraid she might try to contact Tevis, or worse: her union rep.

"I know you told me you were all right," he said, "but I brought you some coffee anyway. Just in case." He'd also brought a bag of popcorn for their movie date. Again he carried everything in one hand: the creamer packets, the sugar packets, and the two mugs, all in his calloused palm, with a corner of the popcorn bag pinched between his fingers. He dragged his chair over to her side of the table. The popcorn went between them and he opened the bag as if it were a book so they could both reach in at the same time. Steam carried buttery smells toward the ceiling. When he noticed — or rather when he pretended to first notice the closed laptop — he said, "You found him? It's done?"

She didn't bother looking at him. Dark burn marks dotted the inside of the bag, but the kernels themselves looked perfectly popped. He grabbed himself a fistful, yet ate them only one at a time.

"Let me ask you this," he said. "Did you see yourself? The pretty lady buying drugs?"

"You thought that was me?"

He shook his head. "Wrong question. Will a grand jury think it was you?"

She had never taken illegal drugs, not once in her life, but she imagined that when a trip went bad it felt something like this. To slow things down, to try to seem cooler than she actually felt, she poured some creamer into her coffee. She had nothing to stir it with, though. Lenox's mug displayed the IA logo, its stern westward-facing eagle, but her own mug had dialogue balloons superimposed over an inky-black backdrop. DO YOU KNOW HOW I FIND YOU IN THE DARK? it asked. OOH BABY, said a smaller balloon. KEEP GOING, LIKE THAT. DON'T STOP, DON'T STOP.

"The first time I watched the video," he said, "I thought maybe Detective Tevis had made his buy off the DJ when the kid was on break or something. Not in the booth, you follow? Off camera. But then you watch the whole thing and you see the kid *never* leaves the booth. Doesn't even start packing up his records until the place is already closed, barbacks or whatnot putting the joint's chairs up on tables. And by that time,

you and Detective Tevis had signed your-
selves back into the Narco logbook. All the
way back in Flushing. Weird, right? So then
I'm wondering, well, maybe they got their
paperwork switched up. You bought off the
DJ. He bought off the bathroom attendant.
And you just accidentally put the wrong
names on the wrong reports, which is bad,
don't get me wrong, but it's maybe not
criminally wrong."

She watched his fat, wet mouth chew up
another popcorn kernel.

"But I'm a dumb fuck," he told her. "I
forgot the bathroom attendant was a lady.
In the ladies' room, obviously. Unless I've
been mistaken this whole time, and Detective Chester Tevis is actually a woman. Is
that the story here? Because that would
clear a lot of this up."

"Is he going to be in trouble?"

"What about Janice Itwaru?" he asked. "Is
she going to go to prison? Because right
now? What it looks like? It looks like a falsi-
fied buy report. Misdemeanor perjury is
what it looks like. And we're not even talking yet about what you did with the DJ's
drugs."

"I'm not a dirty cop," she told him.

"Glad to hear it. Because that's the alternative theory. You've gotten yourself jammed

up here, but you are for the most part an honorable cop, so honorable — the theory goes — that you're willing to help open up an investigation into your boy, Sergeant Hart."

"Hart?" she said. "That's what this is all about? You're gunning after Hart?"

He shrugged. He sat facing her in a power position, leaned way back in the chair with his hands laced behind his head. Of course he wanted Hart. The man was guilty of excessive force, harassment, quota pressures, possession, paying off CIs with drugs, conspiracy to embezzle funds from the department, building a deck without a permit, possible flaking, possible steroid injections, criminal misconduct, and that snazzy catch-all: actions detrimental to the integrity of the police force. How much of all that Lenox was aware of, she had no idea. But he surely knew Hart made eighty-five K a year, with imminent pension benefits that would pay him half that annually for the rest of his fit and trim life.

"We'd need you to wear a wire," Lenox said. "Do a little acting. Nothing you're not used to."

Her first sip of coffee tasted terribly tepid. She considered spilling it onto the laptop, but copies of that video were surely backed up on servers, easily downloadable and waiting on a subpoena. "I don't know," she said. It was the most honest thing she could've told him. "What you're asking, you're asking me to be a rat. I don't know. That's not something I'm used to. Not at all." She rubbed her face, her hands smelling like her sister's chamomile. "I need some time to think about it."

He reopened the laptop, which had apparently kept playing the security footage this whole time. When he pulled up the video player, though, Janice was no longer in the frame. The DJ was still spinning his records and the dancers in the distance were still bouncing, but without any audio they all seemed weirdly staged, stiff somehow, as if they were extras on a film set. So as not to smear it with butter, Lenox tapped his knuckles against the screen.

"Here was the time for thinking," he said. "But you didn't. There was no thinking. So now you're in a spot where if you don't want to pitch in, help us get an actual bad guy, you're going to be suspended. As in right now you're going to be suspended." He sucked at his gums, perhaps to loosen a stuck popcorn hull. "And if you talk to Tevis?" he said. "If, God help you, you talk to Sergeant Hart about this, well, now you're impeding an investigation. And then what happens? We show up at that house of yours in Richmond Hill. Put the cuffs on you. Scare the bejeezus out of your mother and —"

"Okay," she said. "I get it, I get it. But I'm going to need you to take Tevis off the hook, too. The both of us. For any and all wrongdoing."

Lenox's smile returned. "You're not exactly in a position, Officer Itwaru, to be calling the shots here."

"Well, I'm calling that one," she said. "So what's it gonna be?"

# CHAPTER ELEVEN

When she came into the rumpus early Tuesday morning, her first shift back at work since leaving Internal Affairs, Tevis asked her if she'd had a nice weekend. She tilted her head back, unsure of what he knew. Did he know that in her purse she carried a gift from IA? A super-fancy digital recorder, smaller than a cigarette lighter, with a voice-activated microphone that had automatically turned on as soon as he started talking? According to her new best friends at Internal Affairs, he did not know about any of that. He knew nothing. He knew nothing and will continue to know nothing, you follow? They hadn't gone to Tevis, she imagined, because they figured he would've turned down any deal they tried to offer him. Not only that, he would've tipped off Hart and squashed the investigation before it could even get started. With a stoic grace, he would've

402

submitted to a punishment of dead-end desk jobs for the rest of his career. Janice, on the other hand. Janice, they could trust to act the rat. Really, though, a comparison between them wasn't fair at all. Tevis had only three years left before he could cash in his pension. Three years. Go ahead and bury him. Even in the most dead-end of dead-end desk jobs, he couldn't run out of oxygen before the end of three years. Janice had three years *on* the job, seventeen to go. You couldn't compare their situations at all. The question then became, if Tevis found himself in her position, would he jam up Sergeant Hart? Probably not. Probably Tevis would quit the department before backstabbing a fellow cop. Unless of course that fellow cop was truly doing the dirty. *That* was the question then. If Hart had flaked someone, planting drugs on an innocent person, she'd no doubt feel a moral obligation to jam him up. But if, like James Chan, he had jiggered the vending machine to dispense free soda cans, she wouldn't. For that matter she shouldn't. So where does paying a CI off with drugs fall in the spectrum of obligatory action? Should she even care that K-Lo volunteered to walk away with crack instead of cash? Should IA? Well, yes, IA should certainly care, but it was their *job* to police the police. Not hers. But then again, hadn't she sworn an oath, an oath she actually took seriously and still remembered verbatim, to faithfully discharge her duties as a police officer in the New York City Police Department to the best of her ability, so help her God? And — she could hear her sister's condescending voice now — wasn't it the Narcotics Division's responsibility to *subtract* the amount of drugs from the street, not add to it? Okay, fair enough, but Hart hadn't exactly flown down to Colombia to strip and alkalize any coca leaves. Not at all. Instead, without personally profiting or otherwise receiving any monetary compensation, he had given drugs that Janice had bought off the street back to the street. It was a zero-sum transaction, as any cigar-chomping banker could've told you. Plus, investigators had to fill out a heap of paperwork for every orphaned quantity of drugs, and another heap for compensating a CI through the official channels, so really, by allowing those two problems to dissolve each other, Hart had freed up the man-hours to subtract even more drugs off the street. That kind of big-picture thinking could be extended to ask the more utilitarian question, was the world a better place with Sergeant Hart or

Officer Itwaru working for the NYPD? Because that was the choice here. One or the other, and to her the answer seemed obvious. Unfortunately, only a psychopath, or maybe a sociopath — Janice had never been able to figure out the difference — would use that sort of math to justify ruining someone else's career. She should ask her father what he'd do and just do the opposite. She should call K-Lo. Because what if he had sold the drugs to some honor-roll student who would've one day grown up to cure AIDS but had OD'd instead? But that of course was entirely speculative, and perhaps it didn't matter what K-Lo did with the drugs, perhaps it mattered only that Hart had hoped to avoid some paperwork, which hardly seems like a crime worth prosecuting. The question *then* became, was this a crime so undeserving of prosecution that she was willing to lose her job over it, to effectively render meaningless the last three years of her life, and to enter a historically bad job market without a college degree? Should mitigating economic factors bear any weight on her decision? Was it irresponsible of her *not* to consider them? What about her mother eventually needing twenty-four-hour nursing care? What about Tevis's pension? His alimony payments?

Should she even consider the near certainty that if the positions were reversed, Hart wouldn't hesitate to fuck her over? Or the near impossibility that IA would be able to keep her cooperation a secret? That for the rest of her career she'd be under suspicion, which in the hermetic universe of the NYPD amounted to factual certainty? That a verminous stench would cling to her wherever she went in the department? But was her fear of others' disapproval so strong that she'd forsake her *own* hopes for the future: to do substantive police work in an elite unit like Homicide or Counter-terrorism? Was that fear not childish, not cowardice? Wouldn't ratting out Hart, therefore, be the adult, brave thing to do? But wouldn't it be braver, more adult, to accept sole responsibility for her mistake? The question then became, shouldn't she just man up? Accept IA's outrageous punishment — seventeen years of desk work, potential expulsion from the police force, potential (although unlikely) jail time — shouldn't she shoulder all that without dragging anyone else into the muck with her? But *could* she accept that punishment without dragging anyone else down into the muck? Because, again, what about her mother? And Tevis? But shouldn't he at least have a say in whatever sacrifice she made on his behalf? Or would that invalidate the very nature of sacrifice, i.e., that it is a voluntary, independent decision? Was that even accurate? Better question: what sort of woman, dressed in a ritual toga, balanced on the lip of a volcano, and what sort of idiot woman wouldn't grab the nearest douchebag sergeant by his overtight Polo shirt and toss him into the lava instead? There! There you go, unappeasable Earth Spirit, Zule, Waponi Woo God, what have you — *there's* your fucking sacrifice. But no, no, that wasn't the answer, either. That wasn't even the question. The question now was — was what? Forget the moral imperative, the utilitarian argument. The question now was, did she have a nice weekend?

With IA's digital recorder silently running in her purse, she said, "It was fine. How about you?"

The ex-wife hadn't let him see his kids, he told her. When he'd rung the bell on Saturday morning to pick them up for his weekend visit, no one had come to the door. Plastic-bagged newspapers covered the welcome mat, an invitation to every B&E man in the neighborhood. He rattled the doorknocker, admittedly a little harder than he should've, and it came off in his hand.

He flung it into the neighbor's yard. Then he threw the newspapers off the porch, and then some potted plants, and then a loose brick, and then the welcome mat itself, and then when he thought he'd run out of things to throw, here comes the ex-wife. Stomping down the hallway in a towel to curse him out like in the bad old days. Asking him if he was drunk. Asking him who was going to clean up this mess, as if it weren't *already* a mess with stacks of unread newspapers piled in front of the door. She told him the girls were at a sleepover and that she'd left him a voice mail to that effect, which was absolute balderdash, but she did later send him a text saying, NOT SURE I CAN HAVE YOU AROUND THE GIRLS WITH UR TEMPER ISSUES, in all caps just like that. Give him a break. Sunday he spent alone in his apartment drinking whiskey and listening to a boxed set of Bill Withers CDs. Monday he baked and devoured a coconut cream pie.

Janice, who to her shame couldn't even remember his daughters' names, said, "Oh, Tevis, I'm so sorry."

"What for?" he asked. "It's not like it's your fault."

Her head turned to watch Sergeant Hart swish and rattle past her on his way toward the bathroom. She didn't follow him. Obviously. But when he returned to his desk, she didn't approach him there, either, because she doubted she could get him to say anything incriminating with all those other investigators from all those other precincts sitting nearby. What she needed to do was get him alone, or at least relatively alone. She maybe had a chance when he went to the copy room, but she thought she'd look too suspicious standing there inexplicably holding her purse up to his mouth. Right? No, not right. She of course knew she was just being a total wuss. After another hour of sitting still, she hid up in her secret third-floor bathroom, where she sat on the toilet and turned the digital recorder over in her hands. So far she'd only managed to record Tevis humming "Ain't No Sunshine." Come on, Janice! Come on! Let's try this again, and remember: you do this for a living; the only difference now is that the microphone actually works.

Back down in the rumpus, she followed Hart into the kitchenette. Even there, though, she couldn't get him alone. Gonz was sitting at the high top with the day's *Post* spread out in front of him. "Shoot or Die" said the headline. "Bell Cop Tells: Why I Had to Fire 31 Bullets." His desk — the cop's, Michael Oliver's — remained empty over on the far side of the rumpus, but every narco uncle and investigator had already talked the topic into the ground months ago, and Gonz seemed far more interested in the sports section. His head popped up, though, when he heard Hart come into the kitchen.

"Hey, how are ya, Sarge? You see the game last night?"

"Nope."

"No?" Gonz asked. "Isles–Pens? It was a barn burner."

"Still didn't see it," Hart said.

Poor Gonz, she almost felt sorry for him. She must've looked almost sorry for him, too, because he was mean-mugging her now, stink-eyeing her. She set her purse down on the high top. For something to munch on, an excuse to be in here at all, she reached for a huge plastic tub of pretzel rods while over on the other end of the kitchen Hart reached for an even bigger plastic tub of muscle powder, collectively purchased by the 115 investigators.

"What's that, Sarge? The MET-Rx?"

Rather than answer Gonz directly, Hart showed him the label, which guaranteed an "xtreme blast" and reassured potential users with a promise of hard-core laboratory testing. Red and yellow lightning bolts, or maybe veins, exploded across the background.

"That stuff makes me all bloated," Gonz said.

"That's the point."

"Oh yeah, I know, but it makes me all mushy."

"When the amino acids hydrate themselves, they're going to draw in water and increase volume. That is their purpose, Gonz. To turn them into muscle fibers, you have to actually work out."

"Yeah, I know."

"What is it?" Janice asked. "Steroids?"

"Why?" Hart said. "You trying to build up some muscle mass?"

"Aren't you worried it'll shrink your dick?" Gonz asked her.

Grimes puttered into the kitchenette, barefoot and yawning, in his white pajamas and droopy sleeping cap. His eyes were half closed. He found a dirty mug in the sink, gave it a quick rinse, and shook the water droplets out onto the floor. Like the pretzel rods, fancy single-serving French vanilla creamers had materialized in the kitchen somewhere around November, shortly after Richie had taken over reception duties. Grimes poured nine of those creamers, *nine* — Janice counted — into his mug, which he then put in the microwave for exactly twenty-one seconds.

When his eyes widened enough to notice everyone looking at him, he said, "What time is it?"

According to the clock on the microwave, it was eleven seconds, ten seconds . . . After the ding, he took his mug and puttered out of the kitchenette, back toward his thin mattress in the cot room.

"We sure do work with a bunch of assholes, huh, Sarge?" Gonz asked.

"Don't be such a grump," Hart told him.

Later that afternoon, Puffy surprised everyone by showing up at the rumpus. He said he'd come by only to clear out his desk. Nothing to get excited about. With his undercover career over, or at least on hold, he'd shaved the beard off his face, his bare cheeks plumper than she would've imagined, as if maybe he'd been eating better since leaving Narcotics — less junk food, fewer taco carts — or maybe, without any buy stressors chewing up his insides, he'd filled out to his more natural weight. A blue cast, thick as bark, spread down his forearm to his fingertips. Only five days had passed since the uncles had last seen him, but they all swarmed around him, everyone but

Gonz of course, and Fiorella, whose son was off from school on spring break. James Chan, flitting over Puffy's shoulder, looked particularly happy to have him back.

"So where you been?" Morris said.

"Are you serious?" Klondike asked him. "Do you not remember? The big fight? Sticking up for Itwaru's honor?"

"Now, hold on," Janice said.

"No, yeah, I remember," Morris said. "Jesus, you kidding? I'm asking where he's been *since*."

"Medical leave," Puffy told them. He held up his cast, the cotton webbing around his thumb already pearl gray with dirt. "Next week I'm taking a psych eval, which I'm pretty sure I'll fail. And after that, I'm guessing I'll end up in a Viper room, listening to wiretaps all day."

Pablo Rivera said, "You better be careful. I heard IA keeps secret cameras in them rooms to make sure you don't fall asleep."

"I'm not going to be there very long," Puffy said. "My plan is to put in a request for one of those ergonomic chairs? On account of my back?"

"They'll *never* give you one," Tevis said.

"Exactly. I'll put in a couple more written requests, leave a paper trail, and when nothing shows up I'll sue the department for disability. I pretty much got it all figured out."

The other uncles nodded, smiling their big smiles, pleased and impressed, but a little resentful, too, a little disappointed in him, as if he were a combat soldier who'd shot off his own toe. Or maybe it was just Janice who felt all those things. She sat in his chair as he cleaned out his desk. Richie brought over a big black garbage bag so he could take home the things he wanted to keep: his clock radio, Ping-Pong balls, crossword puzzle dictionary, teakettle, Andrew Wyeth print, and the potted philodendron plant that to the uncles' collective embarrassment had died without anyone noticing. He assured them he could revive it. He gave Richie a postage meter that for some reason had been stashed in one of Puffy's drawers. Grimes got a pair of electric socks. No one wanted Puffy's autographed picture of Tiny Tim the ukulele player, but okay, no problem: he stuffed it into the black garbage bag. His flask, waffle iron, and knockoff colognes purchased from the old Korean lady at A.R.'s Tavern: into the bag. He kept his EpiPens, too, because apparently Puffy was called Puffy because he was allergic to peanuts. Who knew? When he found a Sharpie in a bottom drawer, he asked everyone to sign his cast. He put a pair of wading boots in James Chan's arms. He even went over to Gonz to try to give him a silver candlestick, but Gonz handed it back to him without a word. Later the uncles wondered if Puffy had wanted only to get Gonz's fingerprints on a weapon-like object. Either way, it went into the bag. So did his photo albums. His Nerf basketball net. His books: *How to Win Friends and Influence People, Mind over Back Pain,* and *Rip Off: A Guide to Crimes of Deception,* a manual her father could have written. Klondike and Morris each wanted Puffy's dominoes, so he gave his set to both of them and told them to share. Yeah right. He gave Tevis his CB radio so he'd always have someone to tell stories to. The mood was turning sentimental. With his desk almost halfway cleaned out, he bequeathed the pipe and deerstalker hat to Janice, who was of course next in line to make detective.

"I can't," she said.

"What's the matter? You haven't made your four buys yet?" He took the deerstalker from her and put it on her head. "Don't worry so much, Jan. You're a lock — it's in the bag."

She wished he meant this bag, this big black garbage bag, that he had a detective

415

shield down there for her, or a doctor's note excusing her from participating in activities related to Internal Affairs. She stuck the pipe in her mouth. Her signature on his cast looked pathetically small. She wanted to ask him if he'd punched Gonz for her or to get himself out of Narcotics, but she didn't know which answer she'd rather hear. Probably neither. Before she could even thank him for the bequest, Lieutenant Prondzinski came over to tell him he had to leave.

"I'm just cleaning out my desk," he said.

"Believe me, I can see that," she told him. "But you're not allowed to be on the premises while off duty. It's an insurance issue."

He could've pointed out that Grimes, by living here, was off duty and on the premises for at least two-thirds of every day, but instead, no rat, Puffy honorably kept the dispute focused on himself: "So when can I come by and get the rest of my stuff then?"

"Well," Prondzinski said, "if you were reinstated in Narcotics? And you happened to be on duty at the time, then you would absolutely be allowed on the premises, no problem."

"So only if I was still working here," Puffy said.

"And on duty."

"But if I was still working here —"

"And on duty," Prondzinski added.

"Right," Puffy said. "But if I was still working here and on duty, why would I need to clean out my desk?"

"It is what it is," Prondzinski replied.

All the uncles — minus Gonz, minus Fiorella — followed Puffy to the stairwell. Richie, now that he had a working postage meter, promised to ship the rest of his stuff through the mail. Catch you later, Puffy! Because of the cast, no one could shake his hand, so they took turns patting his arm and squeezing his shoulder. Keep in touch! The uncles lost sight of him when he went into the stairwell, which seemed to swallow him into its darkness, but they continued to hear his giant black garbage bag thumping every step on the way down. Janice wished she'd gone in for a hug. She imagined he would walk out of the lobby and into a claustrophobic Viper room, a five-by-seven closet full of stultifying surveillance tapes. Eight-hour days, five days a week, headphones piping background chatter directly into his brain. It was crazy. Crazy-making. When she pulled the Sherlock Holmes pipe out of her mouth, she saw that she'd left deep bite marks in the stem.

Over the next few hours, Hart made almost

a dozen trips to the bathroom. Maybe to snort coke bumps off his Altoids tin. More likely to drain some of the water he drank by the gallon. She wouldn't know. She went the rest of her shift without going near him.

Back at home, before going to sleep, or rather before attempting to go to sleep, she left a voice mail on Lieutenant Lenox's work phone saying that she had failed to collect anything good. As the Spy Tech manual would've suggested — if it had included a chapter on intradepartmental communication — she chose only vague words for her message and did not refer to Sergeant Hart either by name or by rank. She said she hoped to deliver better results before the end of the workweek. But what she *really* hoped for? She didn't know. She didn't know what to do, didn't know what she even wanted to do.

As an afterthought, before hanging up the phone, she added, "By the way, this is Janice Itwaru."

# Chapter Twelve

Early the next day, too early, hours before she needed to get out of bed, a pack of sports-talk hyenas raided her kitchen. Her eyes snapped open into darkness, always a panic-struck starter to her day. She tore off the sleep mask. Her legs kicked away sheets. At a volume she did not think possible, the tiny kitchen radio blared an argument, literally a screaming argument, over how long it takes to go to the bathroom at Yankee Stadium. She recognized the hyenas' voices from occasional drives with the 115 investigators, but when she hurried down the stairs in what used to be her mother's robe, she saw not Sergeant Hart, as her nightmare logic had expected, but Brother Itwaru, alone at the kitchen table and reading the *Post.* Hillary Clinton's lies about facing down a Bosnian sniper had kicked Sean Bell's shooter off the front page. On the back, the Yankees' Alex Rodriguez denied steroid allegations. As if in solidarity, Brother wore a black-and-white pin-striped tracksuit, probably a Father's Day present from his number one daughter. Not that he rooted for the Yankees, or was even a baseball fan. Too close to cricket, he always said. The most boring game on earth. Scattered across the kitchen table was a small heap of Wednesday's mail, which he'd surely picked through already, just as he'd surely cranked the radio's volume to get her out of bed. He put down the paper to ask her if she had remembered any of her dreams.

She rubbed at her eyes, but nope: he was still there. Afraid her mother might be cooking him French toast or possibly coming up out of the basement with a basket of his laundry, Janice poked her head into the kitchen.

"Mom went to church," he said, anticipating her. "Because I'm the Antichrist, I guess? I offered to drive her, but she said she wanted to . . ." He turned two of his fingers into legs and walked them across the table over another heap of junk mail and bills. "There's no talking to her sometimes, you know?"

"Church?" she said. With apparent seriousness, one of the hyenas was claiming it took five innings to return to his seat after leaving for the bathroom, minimum, five innings *minimum.* She turned off the radio. "And you decided to — what?" she asked. "Just stick around?"

"Oh, I came to drop off your car. The one that I fixed for you. And repainted. Free of charge. You remember what I'm talking about?"

"Thank you."

"Well, I hope you like hot pink."

He was kidding. He'd fixed it, sure, but he'd repainted it black, the cheapest color, or rather he had someone who owed him a favor repaint it black because his own autobody shop didn't handle that kind of detailing. She thought it nicely suited her new status as a villain. Rather than block the alleyway and risk stopping Mr. Hua's heart, Brother had parked on the street, in an impressively tight spot between SUVs. He ran his hand along her new front bumper with genuine pride. The temperature had pushed up into the fifties, warm for a March morning, but still too chilly for her robe. As she hugged herself against the cold, her father pointed out all the bodywork. He'd put in a new air bag, he said, and replaced the oil, coolant, sparkplugs, and transmission fluids. But all this of course came pork-barreled with a hitch, albeit only a minor one: she'd have to drop him back off at Willets Point. Actually? Since he couldn't sit in a passenger seat without continually pressing a phantom brake pedal, she'd have to come with while he drove himself back to work.

"Let me go change," she said.

"But I like you just the way you are!" he told her, because despite everything he remained a dad, incapable of ever resisting a stupid dad joke.

When she came back outside in jeans and a hooded sweatshirt, he was still trying to extricate himself from that parking spot, putting that new front bumper of hers to work. She got in next to him. Three years she'd been making payments on this car, a graduation present to herself after making it through the Academy, but never before had she sat in its passenger seat. At least not that she could remember. She had of course sat up front next to her father in plenty of other cars to plenty of other places: school dances, bat mitzvahs, the Crown Fried Chicken on Archer Avenue. To afternoon dives where sympathetic bartenders let her play with the soda-fountain gun. Around Richmond Hill on cool-out trips whenever Vita locked herself in the bathroom. Once, when Janice was ten, maybe eleven, he took her to Long Island, to a white lady's house with a front yard full of pebbles. While Brother and this woman she'd later know as Barbara supposedly looked under cars in the humongous garage, Janice watched *Inspector Gadget* on the humongous television, certain something was wrong without knowing exactly what. At the commercial breaks she'd wander into the kitchen and throw away expensive-looking cutlery. Later, on the drive back to Queens, he purchased her silence through incrimination, by taking her to the big R-rated movie that summer, *Die Hard with a Vengeance,* which her mother had forbidden her to see. She fell asleep before the end, not that it mattered. She had broken the rules just by going. He didn't ask her not to tell Mom; he hadn't even needed to take her to the movies in the first place. Daddy's little girl and a junior spy, she could be counted on to hoard all his secrets.

Back then, like now, he drove with an unbuckled seat belt. Back then, though, the cars didn't seem to mind, unlike this one, its dashboard dinging at him with a shrill insistence, stubborn but not half as stubborn as her father. It gave up after only a block, defeated.

"So how you been?" he said into the silence.

"Fine. The usual."

"And work? Everything's good over there?"

"Sure," she said.

She tried turning on the radio, willing to listen to even those yapping hyenas, but Brother's mechanical tinkering had apparently activated its antitheft microchip, an intended deterrent to petty boosters like Henry Vega. If only. To override the chip, she needed to enter her secret security code, which she of course did not know.

"Mom tells me you went to bed kinda early last night," he said. He looked over at her. "She told me a lot of the time, though, you'll hit up the bars before coming home. Like an after-work thing? A stress reducer? How many nights a week you think that is?"

"You're kidding, right?" She tried laughing. "Is there a point to this brand-new curiosity of yours?" she asked. "Because it's sorta coming out of nowhere for me."

He fluttered his lips to show her she was exhausting him. Without checking blind spots or even signaling, he turned onto the Van Wyck, which would take them on a straight shot to Willets Point. A ten-minute drive. Maybe fifteen, the way he was soft-footing the gas. For perhaps the first time in his driving life, he did not rush over into the express lane but stayed put on the right-hand side of the expressway, barely above the speed limit.

"It's a poison," he told her. "Alcohol, I mean. Everyone knows that, of course, that it's a poison. But what happens is once you start drinking enough of it, *you* become poisonous. I definitely was. When I was drinking? I was toxic, poisoning Mom – "

"You were beating the shit out of Mom."

"Yup," he said. "Poisoning her. Poisoning you girls. Bouncing off walls, couldn't even walk straight. And maybe I'm the last person in the world you want to talk to about all this, I get that, but you gotta reach out to someone because it only gets harder. I'm telling you, Janny. It's an awful thing, an *awful* thing, having to run away from everyone you love just so you don't end up poisoning them to death."

Her martyr father. All the sacrifices he'd made on the uphill road to his Great Neck mansion. Questions she could've asked him: Did he miss birthdays sixteen through twenty-four because he thought he might poison her? With his presence? His voice on the other line, his signature in a card? Did he think he would've poisoned her if he'd shown up to her high school commencement ceremony like Georgia Hawley's father, who'd clapped enthusiastically in the back row, eventually reuniting with Georgia's mom, eventually having a reconciliation baby Georgia couldn't even visit in the hospital because the nurses assumed she was too old to be a sibling? Would Brother have poisoned anyone if he'd sat unseen in cavernous Madison Square Garden for Janice's Academy graduation? Or maybe he had. She could've asked him that, too: Were you there? All this time? A benevolent ghost raising the tiny hairs along the back of my neck? "You don't have to worry about me," she told him.

"I can't help it," he said. "It's my job."

"I appreciate what you're doing here. With this whole — what would you even call it? Like an intervention? But I'm fine. Really. I'm okay."

"Really?" he said.

"Really."

He reached across the console to put his hand on her knee. She let him. On the other side of the window, construction barrels dotted the shoulder for miles. Drivers drifted out of her side-view mirror to pass Brother on the left. The speedometer sputtered into the early forties. When the car itself began to curve toward an off-ramp, miles away from the Willets Point exit, she realized he'd stayed in the slowpoke lane not to extend their time together, or at least not only to extend their time together, but so he could merge more easily onto Queens Boulevard. He headed west, in the opposite direction from where he worked.

She squeezed the hand on her knee. "What are you doing?"

"Calling bullshit," he said. "You're fine? Don't worry? Jesus Christ, pumpkin. Who do you think taught you how to lie?"

Always prepared, probably having looked it up ahead of time, he drove her to the only AA meeting in Queens with a Wednesday meeting at that particular hour: the Woodside Catholic Charities Diocese, located in a block-long brick building around the corner from Roosevelt Avenue. An older obese white man with tennis balls on the bottom of his walker went shuffling up the steps to the main entrance, followed by a young black guy carrying a blue duffel bag and wearing a Huxtable sweater. MENTAL HEALTH CLINIC said a sign out in front. Her father backed the car into a metered spot. With a practiced flourish he slipped her NYPD parking plaque from behind the sun

427

visor and flung it onto the dash. He had to be kidding, although of course she knew he wasn't. He probably hadn't paid for parking all week. The smile he turned toward her was falsely apologetic, entirely infuriating.

"This is one of the twelve steps?" she asked him. "Drag your daughter to a meeting?"

"The twelfth," he said. "Carry the message to other alcoholics."

He came around to the other side of the car to open the door for her, but she wouldn't get out. She looked past him, at the dilated black pupil of a security camera above the building entrance. The weirdest thing: her legs were shaking and she didn't know why. She had a couple of hours before she needed to show up at work; an insurance risk, she had another couple of hours before she even *could* show up at work. Her father's knees cracked as he squatted in front of her.

"I'm not going to force you to do this," he said.

"You can't."

"That's right." He tilted his head toward the building. "It ain't really how it works, anyway. The company line is if you don't want to go, don't go. But I think it would be good for you. Seriously, Janny, I don't see what you got to lose."

"I work around here," she told him. "I probably got half the people in there locked up."

"It's not NA," he said defensively. Still squatting, a heavy man on old haunches, he gripped the door to keep himself from dropping into her lap. "Well, actually," he said, "we do get a *few* drug addicts every now and again. But that could work out perfect for you, right? With your cover, I mean. To boost your street cred?"

She explained that her street cred gets irrevocably shattered every time she makes a buy. Forget about her street cred. Her *cover* gets irrevocably shattered every time she makes a buy. She explained that when dealers get cuffed, they're told they're under arrest for selling to an undercover cop.

"But the guy can't necessarily know that it was you, right?"

"They usually figure it out when the cops show up right after I leave."

"But that's so stupid! Why wouldn't they wait?"

"It is what it is," she said, the line popping out of her for the first time, and her eyes widened with embarrassment.

"Understood," Brother said, not really understanding. He looked at his Movado's numberless face. "You don't gotta wait for me," he told her. "I'll just take a cab when it's over. But if you change your mind, the meeting's in room four, you can't miss it." With a hand on his back he stood up, groaning. "And feel free to keep that parking plaque," he said. "I made plenty of copies."

Having squatted for too long, he hobbled up the steps to the main entrance with less mobility than that morbidly obese white guy. She crawled over the console into the driver's seat. Terraza Café, she knew from experience, didn't open until four, but the nearby Ready Penny had started serving drinks hours ago. Not that she would've gone there or anything. It was just a thought, a cloud passing through. She punched possible PINs into the radio until the screen locked up on her. Vita right now was probably praying for Janice's soul. Maybe even kneeling in a confessional booth on her behalf, but for what? A petite white girl with short blond hair climbed the steps into the building. Janice pulled her sweatshirt's hoodie over her head. She tightened the drawstrings as much as she could, but when she looked in the rearview she still saw too much of her face. Enough to get recognized. Her head slumped. Her stupid legs wouldn't stop shaking. She rolled her eyes, reached into the backseat for the burka.

For once, movies and TV had gotten it pretty much right, probably because a depressingly high number of those screenwriters attended daily meetings. She'd expected gray walls, stark lighting, metal chairs arranged in a circle, a banquet table with coffee and cookies, and everyone to be staring at her as she came into the room. She got tan walls, stark lighting, metal chairs arranged in rows, a card table with percolating coffee but no cookies, and everyone staring at her as she came into the room. The burka was supposed to disguise her, not make a mockery of the meeting, but the young black Huxtable, who'd been reading aloud from a leather-bound book, stopped in the middle of a sentence, and the old obese white man looked as if he'd just caught a sudden whiff of shit. The only one smiling was her father. He was also the only other person in the room. She hadn't expected him to recognize her so quickly, but maybe he hadn't. Maybe he just appreciated the idea of an alcoholic devout Muslim trying to take it one day at a time. Before she could escape, he hurried over to pour her some coffee. Up at the front of the room, to an audience of three now, Young

Huxtable resumed reading.

"I saved you a seat," her father whispered.

They sat in the middle, surrounded by a dozen empty chairs. The petite blonde she'd seen enter the building earlier wasn't an alcoholic apparently, or maybe she was and had just gotten lost in this enormous labyrinth. Maybe she was in the bathroom knocking back a shot of vodka and would walk flustered through that open door any moment now. Janice hoped so. She wanted another woman in the room, but really she would've taken just about anyone. The more people, the less likely she'd have to speak, the very idea of which terrified her for reasons she didn't want to think about. Hello, my name is Janice and I'm an alcoholic? It seemed impossible. So far, though, as Young Huxtable continued to read aloud, the Woodside chapter of Alcoholics Anonymous seemed like — knock on wood — a nonparticipatory lecture, like church or high school civics, or even a bar late at night with a single blowhard holding forth while everyone else pretended to listen. Her unwashed breath cooked the inside of the headscarf. She leaned forward in her seat and tried to pay attention, for no other reason than to shut off her logorrheic brain. With his more frequent pausing and the way he now stammered through words, Young Huxtable appeared to have gone off book, but he still stared straight ahead at its pages as if afraid to make eye contact. Her father once again put a hand on her knee, this time to quell her jiggling legs. Huxtable was saying something about free will. About the culture's misguided obsession with personal agency, headier stuff than she would've imagined. Protected by metal bars, a clock ticked loudly on the far wall. If meetings lasted an hour — and from TV, she thought they did — then there were only fifty-four minutes to go.

Two Latinos walked in side by side, as if they'd just been holding hands, the both of them dressed for a different season in fitted T-shirts and shorts. The same rigmarole all over again: Huxtable went momentarily quiet, the old obese man sneered, although perhaps he'd never stopped sneering, perhaps his face was just like that, and her father stood up to pour the guys some coffee. Brother Itwaru running for mayor wherever he went. The next latecomer, however, beat him to the pot. A Latina in nurse scrubs and with a long braid of ponytail snaked over her shoulder, she helped herself to a cup while Brother was still making his way down the row of chairs.

He looked defeated, then annoyed when she took the pot around the room to top off everyone's cups. Janice gave her a big smile, unseen behind the headscarf. Young Huxtable meanwhile had given way to the white guy, who told a rambling story about living under a car, the logistics of which Janice found hard to follow and even harder to believe. Another heavy white guy, although thinner than the first, came into the room reeking of alcohol. He took a front-row seat as if in penance. The nurse brought him a cup of coffee, but because he had his face in his hands she left it for him on the floor, where it seemed statistically inevitable that he'd kick it over. When the first white guy finished his monologue, the second white guy started his own. Out of the rotation, Janice thought. And thank God. Because this was Queens, where start times were considered approximations, more bodies filed in late: a stylish young Asian woman in designer sunglasses, looking lost, as if she'd come to the wrong room; a bespectacled, baldheaded, vaguely Indian-looking Latino whom Janice immediately recognized as K-Lo.

He sat in the last row, in a corner chair where he could see everyone at once. She doubted he was an alcoholic, recovering or otherwise. More likely he attended meetings — AA, NA, Gamblers Anonymous, Overeaters Anonymous, Sex Addicts Anonymous — all over the borough for the access to others' secrets. He had one leg crossed over the other and his foot bobbing with excitement. When the nurse, who'd brewed a new pot, brought him a coffee he nodded his thanks but stashed the cup under his seat without taking a sip.

Her father was standing. The second white guy had finished sputtering, it seemed, and Brother wanted to get his own confession in before somebody else tried speaking out of turn. Like K-Lo, he seemed less nervous than eager. He gripped the seatback of the empty chair in front of him and introduced himself by name, as an alcoholic, the only one in the room to have done so, but everyone still knew the next line.

"Hi, Brother," they all said, even Janice.

"The fifth time I hit rock bottom, I woke up to the police banging on the front door of my house. Bang, bang, bang, like how they do. I roll over in bed, okay? To tell my wife to go downstairs and sort it out, but she's not there. The police, they want to know what happened last night. I say, 'What do you mean, what happened?' And I'm very scared, right? I've got my two daughters watching TV in the room. And the police are telling us my wife's at the hospital. With everything above the shoulders okay but her body they tell me is done. Like beat to hell. I go, 'When? How'd this happen?' Turns out I'm how it happened. And I believe them, right? I don't remember but I believe it. If Savita says so. If that's what she says . . . The cops are having to take me to jail now, but I'm asking about the kids, what happens to the kids, six and eight years old? The cops, they're trying to help me out. They go, 'Do the girls have grandparents they can stay at for a while? Any family friends, neighbors you can trust?' I say we got none of that. Both sides of our family's back at home and it's not like I'm the best-liked guy in the neighborhood these days. So it's off to lockup for me, Child Protective Services for the girls. When my wife finds out, she goes buck wild. Runs out of the hospital. She's the one that bails me out of jail even, but I still can't go home, so I check into a motel. The Kew Motor Inn? Not too far from here? I've got a nice little view of an alleyway outside my window and there's a liquor store across the street where if you want anything, you gotta talk to the guy through bulletproof glass. I'm living in the motel room less than two hours when I tie the bedsheets to the headboard and jump out the window. I don't want to hang myself in the shower, scare the maid half to death, but I figure they can cut me down in the alleyway — no one's got to see anything too gruesome. But I'm too heavy. From all the drinking, I guess. Go figure. The headboard snaps, comes flying out the window with me. Now the cops are waking up my wife. 'What happened last night? Your husband's in the hospital with a concussion and two broken legs.' That's the rock-bottom number-five story. I made a promise to myself and my family that I'd never touch another drink after that. After lucky rock-bottom number thirteen, I move out of the house for good. I was working the program by then and I'd write my daughters these long ten-page letters I find out never really got into their hands. Because their mother, I guess. She tore them up maybe and I don't blame her, I really don't. It's a good thing she did that, I think. I was a poison, you know? I was a poison that had to be flushed out of everybody's system. But what I wanna know now: am I *still* poisonous? If I tell my youngest about those letters, am I doing it to be selfish? More for me than for her? Not like she's gonna jump into my arms over a couple letters, believe me. She's not like that. She's got . . . she's got a hard bark on her. But see, I *want* to tell her, I want to be a part of her life somehow. I just worry that because I want those things, I should do the opposite. For her sake. As God is my witness, I'm not sure I know how *not* to hurt people, you know? So what am I supposed to do? I don't know. I really don't. I haven't had a drink in eight years, including today. And with that, I think I'll pass. Thanks very much for listening."

Except for the drunken white guy, with his own problems to noodle over, and her father, who was easing himself back into his chair, everyone in the room turned to look at her, as if they knew, as if they'd somehow ID'd her as the youngest daughter. But no, come on, don't be so paranoid: it was her turn, that's all. They were only waiting for her story.

"Do I have to speak?"

"What'd she say?" asked the obese white man. "I can't hear what she's saying."

"You don't have to do anything you don't want to," the nurse said, a preposterous lie. "It's entirely up to you."

"Then I think I'll pass."

"Great!" the nurse said as she stood up. "So there's this guy at work driving me crazy . . ."

When the meeting finally did end, everyone circled — even the drunken white guy — to hold hands and recite the "Our Father." She had her own father on one hand, squeezing tight; K-Lo on the other, his palms grossly sweaty. Like her, he had abstained when his turn to speak had come around, probably one of the few times in his life he'd passed on an opportunity to run his mouth. *And forgive us our trespasses,* they said. About her father's speech, she wondered only if Judith knew about the letters, and if so for how long. Janice couldn't really give it any more consideration than that, because she at last had a plan coalescing and needed to concentrate. Afraid K-Lo might recognize her eyes, she stared at the floor.

"Amen," said the AAers. And then, arms raised, they shouted, "Keep coming back! It works if you work it!"

The circle broke apart, but people still hung around the room to fold up chairs and kill the coffeepot. Young Huxtable hawked religious literature out of his duffel bag. The nurse was telling the drunk guy about an evening meeting over in Astoria. To delay returning to the outside world with its neon-lit bar signs, some of the other members had formed a new circle — a smaller, chattier circle — everybody sipping on coffee except for K-Lo, which made her nervous because he always knew things others didn't, like maybe he'd seen Young Huxtable cleaning out the pot one time with toilet water. Or maybe Mrs. Lo insisted he drink only decaf. Janice went to go fold chairs in the back of the room, where she knew her father would follow. She felt his hand on her arm, gently turning her around. The fluorescents' stark lighting tinseled his teary eyes.

He said, "I hope you don't think I'm trying to make it seem like Mom was the bad guy, because that's completely not what —"

She shushed him. She didn't tell him — she shouldn't need to tell him — that she would never consider her mother the bad guy. She couldn't. No one could. Not if you'd met her. Not if you'd ever seen her, behind a scrim of steam as she poured hot water onto a T-shirt, or sitting big-eyed on the stairs with the tattered end of a bandage between her teeth. Bad guys didn't look like that. They looked like Korean Marty and Cerebral Pauly. They had the giant sloping forehead of a Ned Shu or an Ed Shu or ex-governor Eliot Spitzer, or they had Commissioner Ray Kelly's preposterously punchable jaw. Bad guys were married guys who flirted with tipsy women in bars. They had evil cackles and miscolored eyes. White cats on their armrests. They sold drugs. They hit and ran. Hit and retreated cowardly to Viper rooms. They busted through back doors uninvited, wore droopy dandelions in their lapels, and tossed little girls' book bags onto the roof of the 4 Aces Car Dealership on Atlantic Avenue. They asked their Yankee teammates to inject their ass cheeks full of steroids. They sat behind big desks like Lieutenant Prondzinski. They slept under bigger desks like Inspector Nielsen. They looked like Sergeant Hart. They looked like Gonz. They looked exactly like Gonz. They mocked *Rubí* like Gonz, avoided A.R.'s Tavern like Gonz, called people pussies and faggots, abandoned their ghost posts, sucked up to investigators, sneered, strutted, snarled, and were despised like Gonz. You want to know what a bad guy looks like? That's what a bad guy looks like.

She told her father, "I need a favor. The guy in the glasses, the one who came in last . . . don't look. After I leave, I need you to go over to him and say, 'Hey, how was that crack Sergeant Hart gave you?' And then walk away. Take a cab back to work and don't let him follow you, all right?"

"What?"

But she was already walking away herself. She knew he'd do it. She also knew an anxious K-Lo, worried about the potential loss of his CI gigs, would call Hart later tonight, probably sooner. That's why she needed to get out of here straightaway. She had a three-point plan now — sit still long enough, clenching your jaw, and something's bound to occur to you — but this part here with K-Lo was only the first bullet. Send him to Hart, who'd want to know what the guy at the meeting had looked like, how he acted. And K-Lo would say, *I don't know. Overweight? Sorta sad? Told a story about blacking out, beating on his wife, and didn't seem to get in too much trouble over it,* and Hart would say, *A cop, no doubt about it, probably Internal Affairs.* Janice knew exactly how he'd think. She knew the catastrophic film festival in his brain would project a silhouetted image of the IA building in Manhattan. Shit, what didn't she know? How the movie ended, for one, but she had a few guesses. If Internal Affairs jammed up Hart, he'd assume she was the snitch and so he'd snitch on her, not to IA, but to all his department-wide cronies and goons, who'd block every promotion she ever came up for, if they didn't kill her first, sending her into a drug bust without backup, Serpico-style. Even the uncles would shun her, unless she could cast a more convincing villain to play her part. On her way out of the room, when she heard Young Huxtable's mini-groan, she knew without having to turn around that the drunk white guy had finally kicked his coffee cup across the floor. She ran, the burka's dark material billowing around her legs.

She needed to find a bad guy. That was the second bullet. Or rather, she needed to *fabricate* a bad guy. Make a preexisting bad guy seem even badder. Because K-Lo might spot her if she hung around the building, she drove six blocks away, to a corner pay phone on Roosevelt Avenue, but apparently a frustrated juicehead had recently ripped out the armored cord. Imagine the news he must've received. Janice got back in the car, where she tore off her swampy burka. She sped to a pay phone she knew still worked, her pay phone, outside the Corona bodega with the music-making carousel-for-one taxicab. No one was riding it. No Korean Marty across the street, either, or any pigeons perched beneath the el. No snow left on the sidewalks. While the inevitable 7 train shrieked overhead, she found fifty cents at the bottom of her purse. She didn't think Gonz's Pure Magic fuck buddy was originally from Long Island, but the accent out there was the whitest one Janice could approximate, and so before dialing she practiced saying, *It'd be horrible if I spilled coffee on my new Prada bag. It'd be the worst if chocolate melted in my drawers.* Outrageously competent, Richie the Receptionist answered before the first ring had finished ringing.

"Queens Narcotics," he said.

She kept her back to the pay phone so no one across the street could sneak up on her. "Can I talk to Gonz?" she asked, pronouncing it *tawk*. "Raymond Gonzalez?"

"I'm sorry," Richie said, "but I can't transfer you unless you know the extension."

"Oh," she said, as if surprised. "Well, can you give him a message, please?"

"I can't confirm that anyone by that name even works here."

"Can you tell him I'm sorry?" The pay phone shell's sticker continued to offer fortune-telling services — DON'T GIVE UP HOPE! — at reasonable rates. She said, "I've been trying to get ahold of him on his cell, but . . . can you tell him I was just feeling so pissed off, you know? Like literally crazy. Sir? Hello? Can I ask you a question?"

"Yeah, of course," he said, probably with his pen poised above a pad of paper, determined to get every detail correct before broadcasting the story throughout the rumpus. At the top of that pad: the number that had come across his caller ID. "Go ahead," he told her.

"If you make a complaint on a cop? Like an official complaint? And it isn't entirely true . . . is that like against the law? Can you go to jail for something like that?"

*Click,* said the receiver. She might've chosen that same moment to hang up on Richie herself, but Korean Marty — who'd come out of the bodega with an open bag of cheese puffs — did it for her, slipped a hand behind her neck to depress the little flap. As usual, he wore his beloved white leather jacket and looked worse than the last time she'd seen him. The hematoma above his eye had faded a bit, but now deep purple scratch marks grooved his cheeks, where some poor woman must've raked him open. A dial tone whined in Janice's ear. He pulled his hand back to lick orange cheese dust off his fingers.

"Who that you was talking to?" he asked.

"*El hombre? Siempa de la tango* or some shit?"

She kept the phone in her hand in case she needed to bust up his nose. Her car, her personal car, with her personal license plate, sat parked in a tow-away zone ten feet behind him, with an NYPD plaque faceup on the dash. She said, "You owe me fifty cents."

"For what?"

"For the phone call you just cost me, you fucking moron."

"You're real cool, you know it?" He angled his hip toward her, an invitation to reach into his pocket for the change if she wanted it that bad. "Matter of fact," he said, "we was just talking about how cool you are."

"Who's that? You and your rapist buddies?"

"See, but what we can't figure out is if you're a cop? Or one of the snitches on their payroll? I'm thinking cop, personally, the way them DTs beat up on us with like a vengeance."

Bells chimed above the bodega's door as a young, tough-looking Chinese woman came out onto the sidewalk. She had half her head razored bald and a plastic squeeze bottle of lemon-lime Gatorade. The dial tone gave way to an apologetic robot operator asking

446

Janice for more money. The Chinese woman ripped off the bottle's plastic seal with her teeth. She drank while she walked, her head tipped back, and Janice, thirsty now herself, wanted to chase after her — take me with you, so long as we don't pass any alleyways — but Korean Marty used the distraction to slide himself in front of her. Back her up against the pay phone. If she tried to get past him, she'd clip her shoulder against his, initiating the kind of contact he was surely dying to finish.

He said, "How much they get paid, them snitches? On average like?"

"I wouldn't have a clue."

"I'm serious," he said. Cheese dust ringed his mouth. "All the people I know? I could help you clean up the whole neighborhood practically."

By which he meant he could help her clean up his competition. "What about Marty?" she asked. "Would you set him up?"

Another overhead 7 train gave him some time to think it over. He closed up one eye, the hematoma eye, perhaps a tic of his when concentrating especially hard, like her father with his lower lip. After the train passed, Korean Marty said he really didn't know if he could set up the other Marty, and ridiculously she admired his hesitation, his reluctant sense of loyalty.

"I guess it would depend," he continued. "Maybe. I don't so much mind standing out here all day, but I'm a little tired of him putting his hands on me, know what I mean?"

Did she know what he meant? Of all the people to ask her this? Oh my God, never mind, forget about that teensy moment of admiration tingling the corners of her mouth. She wanted to bust up his nose after all, but instead she handed him the phone and explained that she had a number he could call if he was really serious about becoming an informant. Then she turned around and dialed it. Even with her back to him, she felt only partly afraid that he'd punch her in the kidney or put her up in a headlock. They were on Roosevelt Avenue, with all its potential witnesses going to work, coming home from work, buying cheap electronics or tacos. Plus the number she dialed was a short one, with only three digits. When she turned back around, he put the phone tentatively to his ear. Strands of his greasy, bowl-cut hair spilled over the receiver. As soon as the 911 operator came on, asking for his emergency, Janice slipped away, left him standing there holding the phone.

He hung it up in its cradle without saying a word. He wanted to talk to an *hombre,* not a dispatcher. He wanted to talk to someone like Hart. Rather than risk Korean Marty spotting her parking plaque — or worse, her license plate, which was registered to her address — she decided to leave her car behind in Corona. She'd come back for it later. She'd gone the last few days without it anyhow. She walked east down Roosevelt, past the bodega, past the musical taxicab, past a scrawny Mexican murmuring, *social, social, social* for counterfeit SSN cards, all the way to the Ninety-First Street el stop. She'd take the 7 to Flushing, then a bus to the rumpus. On her way up the el steps, she did not peek over her shoulder to see if Korean Marty was following. She didn't have to this time. She heard him munching his cheese puffs two steps behind her.

She kept climbing. If she had showed her badge to the baldheaded MTA guy in his glass MTA booth, she would've gained free admittance through the emergency door, but instead she vaulted the turnstile for the first time in her life, tucked her legs, and hit the ground walking. Korean Marty did the same. There were no patrol cops to ticket them. The baldheaded MTA guy wasn't paid enough to care. On the Queens side of the tracks, Janice walked to the end of the platform but kept away from the edge. Sharpie horns bedeviled a skinny Latino in a poster for HIV prevention. Korean Marty, whose job required constant standing, dropped into a bench seat behind her.

With the last 7 passing through just a couple of minutes earlier, there were only a few other passengers waiting with them on the platform. Had she been looking up from the street, she could've watched the pigeons to gauge the next train's arrival; here, above the tracks, she relied on twitchy air currents and ground rumbles. As far as she could tell, Korean Marty had not moved since sitting down. She reached into her purse to turn on her phone's voice-memo app. IA's recorder, she assumed, would run on its own. Somewhere in her purse she also had a makeup compact that she could've taken out to keep an eye on Korean Marty behind her, a Spy Tech–approved surveillance method. She could've done a million things. Two million things. When a 7 train finally did come squealing into the station, she could've stepped on at the last second, like in *The French Connection,* or stepped off at the last second to wave at him from the platform as the train skyjacked him away.

But she didn't. She got on the train and stayed there, holding on to a pole as he sat in a nearby seat, all the way to Main Street, Flushing, the end of the line. Before standing up to follow her off, he threw his empty cheese-puff bag on the floor.

"You're just gonna leave that there?" she asked.

He said, "People get paid to pick that shit up."

Down on the street, dark gypsy cabs circled the station while a miserable traffic cop mimed directions to keep them moving. She could've gone to him for help. More alternate universes: she could've hailed one of the taxis. Told the cabbie to step on it, drive the wrong way down a one-way, make a sudden U-turn, pull over abruptly around a blind corner. She could've lost Korean Marty with ease in the raucous Flushing Mall, gone into a dressing room wearing this burka and come back out in her jeans and hoodie. Instead? Instead she led him to the bus stop. And when the Q65 arrived, and when he didn't have a MetroCard or exact change for the fare, she flashed her badge at the driver to get them both on.

"Wow," he said, sitting down in a seat reserved for the handicapped. "That's a real badge, man? For real? You're really a cop?"

"Do you even know why you're following me?"

Happy to have an answer for her, he smiled. "I was told to!"

"Well, you're doing a great job."

"That's really nice of you to say."


Twenty minutes later she let him push the yellow tape strip to call for their stop. She wanted to believe that had she arrived for work alone, Richie would've immediately hit her up with the latest Gonz gossip — have you heard, have you heard? — but as it was, given the nature of his gatekeeping responsibilities, he had to keep quiet and glare at the interloper, Korean Marty, who hung back to read the words on the rumpus's pebbled glass door. QUEENS NARCOTICS. He looked like he couldn't believe it. His hand was inches away from the letters, as if he were afraid to touch them. After signing in at the front desk, she dragged him out into the rumpus by the sleeve of his leather jacket. It was half past three. Every on-duty uncle was in the lounge watching the *Rubí* replacement, *Amigas y Rivales,* except for Gonz, who sat at his desk with a work phone cradled against his ear and a cell phone in front of him. She doubted he even would've recognized Korean Marty, but the investigators surely would. She pushed him into the chair reserved for visitors, off to the side of Hart's desk. The 115 boys were all there: Cataroni next to Hart, across from the indistinguishable Irishers, McCarthy and Duckenfield.

"Remember this ugly face?" she asked them. She put a hand on Korean Marty's shoulder, its metal zipper still cold from outside. "He wants to sign up as a confidential informant."

"Now hold on," Korean Marty said.

Hart blew his nose into an ancient handkerchief that had seemingly never been washed. "What's next?" he asked, his eyes cast toward the ceiling.

Janice pulled Internal Affairs' voice-activated recorder out of her purse. "See this?" she asked Korean Marty. "This little bad boy? This has got you clear as crystal, my friend, saying you'd help us set up your pal Marty."

"I said I'd think about it!"

"Well, we can play the tape for Marty, see how he interprets all your soul-searching."

"My what?"

"What are you doing?" Hart asked her. His usually rancid breath smelled like a eucalyptus cough drop. "This isn't even your job. We recruit CIs, not you."

"I'm thinking about a career change," she said. Part three of her three-point plan: she tossed him IA's recorder. "Nice, huh? It's running right now, you can't even hear it. I'm telling you, Sarge: one hundred percent, top-of-the-line equipment. You don't even have to push any buttons to turn it on. Now ask me where I got it."

Because if they left the rumpus they'd have to sign themselves out, because the Queens Narcotics Division by its very nature teemed with big-eared busybodies, because Grimes was probably sleeping on a cot in the only other relatively private area, she brought Sergeant Hart up to her secret third-floor bathroom to tell him the whole story. Sort of the whole story. She made sure to lock the door behind them. Downstairs, the investigators grilled Korean Marty. Up here, she sat on the edge of the sink without putting her full weight on it, composed, or pretending to be composed, the purse in her lap, while Hart stalked the few square feet of bathroom tiles available to him. Swishing and rattling. The recorder in his hands looked as small as a wafer.

"When did you meet with them?" he asked.

"Yesterday."

"*Yesterday?* And you're just telling me now?"

Quietly, to keep her voice from echoing, she said, "What? I was supposed to call you? I wasn't sure they hadn't tapped your phones already."

He began rubbing the top of his head. Shorter, heavier breaths came sputtering out of his nose. He couldn't think all this through fast enough, but surely now the catastrophic film projector was flickering on with images of his wife in yoga pants, Thomasina's Haverford tuition bill, a possible trial, foreclosure, a voided pension. Sick with the flu, or rather convinced he was sick with the flu, he untucked his white Polo shirt to ruffle the hem, to work up a little cool air for himself. Before his legs could buckle, he sat down on the toilet seat.

"You know what they asked me?" she said. "They asked me if I'd seen the Altoids tin where you keep your drugs. They know it's a fucking *Altoids* tin, Sarge. I said I'd never seen anything like that, but all they did was smile. They want me to record you paying off CIs again with drugs. They know about the crack you gave Kevin Loquaio *last week,* Sarge."

His big hand covered the recorder's microphone. "This thing is on right now?" he whispered.

She gestured for him to stand, and when he did she took the recorder from him and dropped it down the toilet. Water splashed disgustingly onto her shoes. Clean water, but still. She flushed the toilet, afraid the recorder might gurgle back up at them, but it was small and light enough that it disappeared in one go. See you later. See you never.

"I'll tell Internal Affairs I lost it," she said. What she'd actually lost was Korean Marty saying he'd think about setting up Marty, but so what, he was never part of the plan anyway, just a bonus, a happy accident, and she figured the investigators could break Korean Marty down on their own without resorting to an audio tape. From her own experience getting interrogated she knew now to set the clock ticking. "We don't have a lot of time here, Sarge. What other questions you got?"

"Jesus Christ," he said. "Jesus H. fucking Christ." Without seeming to realize it, he had sat himself back down on the toilet seat. He tore off some toilet paper to rehonk his nose. "What the hell is going on here, Itwaru?"

"That's not a real question," she told him.

"Okay," he said. "Right. Okay. The drugs. What'd you tell them about the drugs."

"What drugs?"

"What *drugs*?" he asked. "The rocks, Itwaru. The rocks I gave K-Lo, what the hell are we talking about here?"

And there it was.

"I said I didn't know anything about it, but I'd see what I could turn up." She stood over him, as Lenox had stood over her. "I mean, *someone's* telling IA what's going on here."

"Cataroni?" he muttered.

"Not a chance," she said, thinking of the way Cataroni had safeguarded her cover outside the alleyway. Thinking that Gonz's gossip must not have yet blazed through the rumpus, that it was perhaps still just a spark eating up oxygen along the reception area. "You kidding? Cataroni? The guy idolizes you." In a dreamy, distant tone, as if she really couldn't remember, she said, "Who else was there last week?"

He looked up at her with new interest. "Why'd they go to you?" he asked. "You see what I'm saying? Why weren't they worried you'd come right to me and tell me all this?"

She hadn't thought of that. Blame it on the bottomless cup of AA coffee, the nurse who kept refilling it, the eggs Janice hadn't eaten, her hollowed-out stomach. A sticky, clammy film clung to her unwashed teeth. She said, "I guess they just trusted me."

"IA? They just trusted you? That's awfully weird, Itwaru, because it's their *job* not to trust us."

To her surprise, she didn't feel any temptation to start biting her nails or flicking the hair tie off her wrist. She didn't need to. This was her job, this was what she did. "I haven't been entirely honest with you," she told him. "Last year," she said, making it up as the words left her, "I contacted my union rep about possibly filing a complaint against you. For bullying."

"You've got to be shitting me."

"I never really followed through on it or anything, but I guess it got passed onto IA, and so they figured I'd try to help them out. I'm sorry. It was a year ago. *Over* a year ago. I didn't so much understand the culture around here yet."

"Seriously, when have I ever bullied you?"

The doorknob jiggled as someone tried to get into the bathroom.

"One sec!" they both called out, then looked at each other, embarrassed.

She reached behind him to reflush the toilet. By now IA's digital device was floating beneath the city, where it would record only sewer sounds, but she couldn't have whoever was standing in the hall hear what she had to say next.

"We'll record a new tape," she told Hart, whispering. "One that makes it seem like you never did anything wrong. Okay? The whole thing, it'll be scripted." Certain he wouldn't completely trust her until she pressed her advantage, she said, even quieter now, "But if I do this, I'm gonna need you to bring me over into Investigations. Like right away, none of this eighteen more months of waiting around for things to happen. Cash in a favor with Prondzinski, however you do it, but I am *done* with this uncle shit, you understand?"

That last part was the most sincere thing she'd said all day. In response he made no response, instead dumping the contents of his Altoids tin down into the toilet. The crack rocks, the mints, they looked roughly the same. Once the tank had refilled with water, he sent everything irretrievably down the drain. Afterward, surged with relief or hostility, or gratitude, or nervousness, surged with *something* — his neck was turning a splotchy red — he stepped closer to her and nodded his agreement to all her terms and conditions. Even without him opening his mouth, she could smell weak traces of eucalyptus. He turned to leave, the back of his pants spotted with toilet-seat pee dribbles, and she wondered why he couldn't feel them, or if he could but just didn't care. She turned around real quick to check her reflection in the mirror.

Who else but a ghost would know about her secret private bathroom? On the other side of the door, Tevis was hugely grinning, clearly delighted to have caught a twosome in the unisex, but his smile warped into something more strained when he saw who they were: Hart tucking in his shirt as he walked out, Janice looking guilty behind him. What must he have thought of all that flushing? A used condom's stubborn reluctance to go down the drain? Into his armpit, he had wedged a copy of the *Post* for the shit he'd planned to take. Hillary Clinton was presumably still in trouble for telling lies. Duke basketball was still alive. Tevis let Hart hurry past him, but he reached out and caught Janice by her wrist. Once again — a carpeted hallway, the rubber soles of his boots — a bolt of static electricity forked from his body into hers. Already halfway to the third-floor stairwell, Hart paused to turn around, reluctant to leave behind a co-conspirator.

"Give us a sec," Tevis told him, and on

460

another day, in a sturdier mood, Hart might have resisted on general principle, but for once he simply did as he was asked and retreated down the stairs. The instant they were alone, Tevis said, "Do you know what you're doing?"

"I'm not sure how to even begin with a question like that."

"He has a wife, you know that, right? And a daughter? Not much younger than you? I mean, I would've thought of all people, you'd —"

She put her hands on his shoulders, no spark this time, and went up onto her tiptoes to kiss him on the cheek. He smelled mildewy, probably from an overused, underwashed towel hanging on a nail in his bathroom. Her mother would have taken such tender care of him. Later, back at Janice's desk, for both her benefit and their own, the other uncles will describe betrayal-by-betrayal today's episode of *Amigas y Rivales,* which apparently was just starting to gain momentum. Right now, though, Tevis's beard prickled Janice. He was a good man, the best one she knew. She should've told him that. She should've told him that when she grew up, she wanted to be half as good as he was. His cheek on her lips had felt dry and weirdly cold, somehow bloodless. A third-floor office worker, a young white guy with an older man's beer gut, went around them into the bathroom, not seeming to care who they were or what they were doing here. Her shift started soon, if it hadn't already. She knew she would see Tevis again, back at his desk in a few minutes, for plenty more days, if not weeks, if not months after this one, but she also knew that she was saying good-bye here, that she couldn't continue to taint him as a friend, partner, protégé, or surrogate daughter. She came back down onto her heels. As she walked away, she reached into her purse, dug under her badge and gun to turn off the phone's voice recorder.

■ ■ ■ ■

# FIVE MONTHS
## LATER

■ ■ ■ ■

# CHAPTER THIRTEEN

From the backseat of an Impala outside Marty's apartment building, Detective Federico Cataroni said he wanted to be the ram. Detective Mark Duckenfield turned around to say no way. Not a chance. He had always been the ram and he would continue to always be the ram. Okay? Got it? Safe to assume Conor McCarthy *also* wanted to be the ram, but as the 115's new sergeant, he had to be the last one through the door on no-knock raids. Correction: the 115's *relatively* new sergeant. Almost half a year had passed since Internal Affairs had put Hart on modified assignment in the Queensbridge projects, where he sat in a basement watching live-feed security footage, Monday through Friday, from nine a.m. to five p.m., forty hours of weekly reality TV. Even there, in that basement torture chamber, he probably still had more legroom than Detective Itwaru in this

Impala's backseat.

Don't think about it. Don't think about your calves. Don't think about your knees. Don't think about your belt cutting into your stomach. Alone among the investigators, she had no interest in being the ram, not that the others would have even let her. The ram was the guy — and it was always a guy — who on no-knock raids swung the actual battering ram, an all-steel cylinder two and a half feet long and more than thirty-five pounds. It required a low center of gravity and stupidly strong arms.

"I'm just saying, how come I never get to do it?" Cataroni asked.

"I keep telling you," Duckenfield said. "*Historical precedent.* What about that don't you understand?"

While they continued to argue, Detective Itwaru filled out paperwork. By hand, in ink, even though she'd have to type it all up back at the rumpus. But better to get a head start at least, to try to keep pace with the endless gush of mostly bogus Narco complaints stuffing the folders on her desk. Got a neighbor you don't like? Call 911 and say he deals weed. Patrol will go out to take a look, but because they can't really do anything, they send the complaint back to the dispatcher, who sends it on to One

466

Police Plaza, which sends it on to the Narcotics Division investigators, who have to physically eyeball the location before closing that file just to reopen the next one. A stack of manila folders sat in her lap. The Impala's dashboard vents were lousy with air conditioning, dialed up way too high. It was hot out but not that hot; she was cold but didn't complain. On the seat between her and Cataroni a plastic bag of banana peels rotted. Apparently the potassium kept the boys' stomachs from cramping after weight lifting. She wouldn't know. In a car all day, or at a desk, without the daily anxiety of going undercover, she'd gained seven pounds since joining Investigations. She hadn't read the *Post* cover to cover in all that time, either, not even on her days off, especially not on her days off, when she refused to *look* at type print, but driving to work this morning she'd heard the Mets had won last night, 5–4, to extend their first-place lead in the division. After the September collapses of the previous seasons, it really looked like this might be their year. More magical thinking: soon, maybe within the next few months, she'd snag a transfer out of Investigations and into Special Victims, the next rung on her ladder.

"Here we go," said Sergeant McCarthy.

Korean Marty and Gonz were rounding the corner toward the apartment building. They both knew the Impala was there, but didn't look in its direction. The plan: they were to go up into the apartment, make the final buy in the NYPD's case against Martin Nils Snyder, come back outside, prop the lobby entrance open, verify Marty was indeed alone and unarmed, and give the investigators the go-ahead to knock down his mezuzah-protected door. Simple. Old friends, on their fifth assignment together, Korean Marty and Gonz chatted all the way to the building's entrance, Gonz probably thrilled to have someone in this world left who'd talk to him. With his kel-mic broken, she couldn't hear what he was saying, nor could she see Tevis, the ghost, who might've been hiding behind that idling van or inside the bodega or the hair salon or the Laundromat or the Peruvian *picantería* or maybe even inside the apartment building already, anywhere really but inside this car next to her. Cataroni passed her a plastic container of dry granola and Grape-Nuts. She passed it back to him without sampling.

When Marty buzzed open the lobby door, she texted Jimmy Gellar, whom she paid a Brother-subsidized ten dollars an hour to sit on the couch with her mother and watch the Game Show Network. EVERYTHING OK? she wrote. PROB GOING TO BE HOME LATE. Once they got Marty to the 115 Precinct, they'd spend hours pressing him to give up his connect, whom they'd eventually use as bait to catch the guy above him, then the guy above that guy, then the guy above that other guy. A yellow taxi drove past her window. A sound like wind howled through her head. She opened one of the folders in her lap, a narco complaint on an address five blocks away, near the Thirty-Seventh Avenue Starbucks that had finally opened. *I'm observing a regular amount of foot traffic for the area,* she wrote. *Based on the available firsthand evidence I see no reason to keep the complaint open.* She reached for another folder, on a Jackson Heights garden co-op where she imagined all the residents were white. *I'm observing two teenage Caucasian males lingering near the building doorway but after twenty minutes I have observed no hand-to-hands or other suspicious behavior to indicate this is a narcotics hot spot. Based on the available firsthand evidence I see no reason to keep the complaint open.* Already her wrist had cramped up, with hours of typing still waiting for her. On her drive to work this morning, before she heard the Mets score, she saw an ad for

LaGuardia Community College on the side of a bus. TOO BUSY? it said. GOOD. It was worth remembering: in these times, in this city, she at least had a job. A pudgy black kid, who may have had a job of his own, pedaled out of the Laundromat on a wobbly blue bicycle. If still an uncle, she would've stepped in front of him, grabbed ahold of his handlebars. Dealers frequently used kids as couriers because they could ride through projects and on sidewalks without patrol officers stopping them. Ass in air, elbows out, he turned the corner heading south, but she transported him a mile away in the opposite direction, over to a single-family house, an alleged narco hub near Northern Boulevard. The block's resident grouch had probably smelled pot smoke coming out of their windows one time, or had maybe tired of their outdoor cat climbing up his bird feeder. *I'm observing a little kid on a bike in front of the location but no apparent drug activity. Based on the available firsthand evidence . . .* Was Tevis in that Peruvian *picantería* right now sipping on a pisco sour? Did Gonz's feet reach the floor from Marty's wicker Papasan chair? Outside the bodega, a bearded homeless man — she squinted to make sure it wasn't Tevis — tried to beg some change or cigs or

470

both off a pretty Latina with a baby in her arms. Detective Itwaru couldn't find a use for the woman or the child, but she did send the homeless guy to a pool hall near the Brooklyn-Queens Expressway. *I'm observing a transient near the entrance, but on the sidewalk I see no visible drug paraphernalia,* by which she meant needles, blunt guts, or sandwich baggies with their corners twisted off. *Based on the available firsthand evidence . . .* She closed that folder and opened a new one. *I'm observing,* she wrote without knowing what to say next. A complaint lay waiting for her in every file beneath this one. The scenes changed at random, just as they did for uncles, but here in Investigations she always had to be the same person.

"Here we go," Sergeant McCarthy said again.

Together Korean Marty and Gonz came walking out of the apartment building. Not talking this time. A few minutes later, Tevis's voice came over the Nextel to report that the target was indeed alone in his apartment, unarmed but with four pit bulls.

Detective Itwaru got out of the car first and stretched her creaky body. She heard Cataroni radioing the van — not the p-van, but the idling white van across the street, where Lieutenant Prondzinski and Captain

471

Morse sat with eight other investigators and all the equipment they'd need to raid Marty's apartment. The TAC plan back at the rumpus had already assigned everyone roles. Duckenfield rams the door, Cataroni goes in first behind a crazy-heavy bulletproof body shield, followed by another strongman behind another bulletproof shield. They were the fury, the cue to Marty's sphincter to release the shit into his drawers. Two other investigators would cuff him, two more would search his house, and two more would stand outside, below his window in case he tried to run down the fire escape. Obviously Morse and Prondzinski would remain in the van. Detective Itwaru and another newbie investigator were on animal control. She hefted a fire extinguisher out of the van. Three of the four pit bulls were still puppies, she assumed, and a high-powered blast of ammonium phosphate should chill them the fuck out. Her animal-control partner — a baby-faced white guy with a perpetual perspiration mustache — would then swoop in to apply the nooses. That was the plan. On paper, at least. First things first, the uncle was supposed to prop open the lobby door on his way out, which he had of course forgotten to do.

"That fucking asshole!" said Sergeant Mc-Carthy.

"That *stupid* fucking asshole!" said Detective Duckenfield, happy to have another reason to hate Gonz, but even happier for the excuse to break some more shit. He rolled cricks from his neck. His knees bent down into the power lifter's position. With a quick exhale of breath, he hit the door above the lock then dropped the ram real quick before its momentum could toss him into the lobby. Half a dozen floor tiles shattered. "It's called expertise," he said, flexing his biceps. "It's called historical motherfucking precedent."

If everything went right, the building's superintendent would send a bill to Martin N. Snyder, c/o the New York State Department of Corrections.

The investigators rode up in the elevator. All of them together: nine men, one woman, four nooses, two body shields, a battering ram, a fire extinguisher, a signed no-knock warrant, and ten raid jackets with POLICE in bright letters across the front. "That's gotta be some cockroach," said a nervous, claustrophobic Detective Itwaru, quoting *Ghostbusters,* but no one seemed to get it. Cataroni's blue eyes goggled at her from behind the skinny viewfinder of his body shield. She knew that any one of her former uncle colleagues would've immediately answered back with, "Bite your head off, man." Bill Murray, guys? Ever heard of him? She was chewing on the insides of her cheeks. Full of adrenaline, at last allowing the raid's anticipation to rush through her, she'd given herself an ill-timed case of the giggles.

Off the elevator, the investigators crept down the hall. It was early afternoon. Most people were at work, or at least should've been at work, but some had stayed behind to cook what smelled like curry and watch what sounded like courtroom shows. A television in one apartment and a television in another were apparently tuned to the same station, with a slight delay between them. This, too, Detective Itwaru found inexplicably hilarious. The investigators kept creeping. When they reached Marty's door, a middle-aged white woman came out of the apartment across the hall. She wore a granny housecoat, as if she intended only to go down into the lobby to collect her mail, but she froze at the sight of all those black jackets and body shields. She ran back into her apartment. Detective Itwaru thought she'd gone to hide, but the woman returned a moment later, holding a horizontally

474

positioned smartphone, its small crystal light glowing red like a dragon's eye. Her finger manipulated what appeared to be a zoom button. Detective Itwaru imagined getting shot in the head, her mother falling down stairs, a dog's gnashing teeth, Jimmy Gellar with a heroin needle in his arm, the little black girl from LeFrak with the paring knife bobbing in her throat, whatever horrible thing she could think of to keep these giggles from jumping out of her. Her shoulders were shaking. Briefly she considered biting the fire extinguisher's hose.

"Return to your residence," Sergeant McCarthy whispered.

"You are on *my* property," the woman said, staring at them through her camera phone. "And I am within my rights to film civil servants on my property. And to post it online if I so please."

"You are obstructing government administration," McCarthy hissed.

"I know my rights!"

Whereas Hart would have tossed the woman down the stairs, McCarthy instead threw up his arms, defeated. "Hit the fucking door already!" he yelled at Duckenfield.

"This one?" Duckenfield asked, pointing to Marty's.

"Oh my God," Cataroni mumbled. "This is totally why I should be the ram."

A hurried Duckenfield rolled his neck, flexed his knees, and started his swing, all at the same time, which happened to be the very worst time, for Marty was opening his door to investigate the hullabaloo out in his hallway. Without anything to stop it, the battering ram rocketed Duckenfield into the apartment. His two hundred and fifty-something pounds, plus the ram's thirty-five, caught Marty center mass in the chest. Cataroni, unable to see clearly through the shield's viewfinder, rushed in and tripped over their bodies. The other strongman with the other shield vaulted in after him. The pit bulls started barking, their voices echoing as if already kenneled. Two investigators went to cuff a purpled Marty on the welcome mat, followed by two more investigators to search the apartment, followed by the nervous newbie investigator with the perspiration mustache and wire nooses. Behind them all, safe at the rear, Detective Itwaru ran in laughing.

# ABOUT THE AUTHOR

**Matt Burgess** is the author of the novel *Dogfight, A Love Story.* A graduate of Dartmouth College and the University of Minnesota's MFA program, he grew up in Jackson Heights, Queens.

The employees of Thorndike Press hope you have enjoyed this Large Print book. All our Thorndike, Wheeler, and Kennebec Large Print titles are designed for easy reading, and all our books are made to last. Other Thorndike Press Large Print books are available at your library, through selected bookstores, or directly from us.

For information about titles, please call:
(800) 223-1244

or visit our Web site at:
http://gale.cengage.com/thorndike

To share your comments, please write:
Publisher
Thorndike Press
10 Water St., Suite 310
Waterville, ME 04901